# The

# Girl

## at the

# End

## of the

# World

# The

# Girl

## at the

# End

## of the

# World

## Volume I

Collected
by
Adele Wearing

www.foxspirit.co.uk

The Girl at the End of the World Vol 1 collected by Adele Wearing

Cover Art by Dave Johnson
conversion by handebooks.co.uk

ISBN:

978-1-909348-53-0 mobi

978-1-909348-54-7 epub

978-1-909348-55-4 paperback

A Fox Spirit Original
Fox Spirit Books
www.foxspirit.co.uk
adele@foxspirit.co.uk

*For Vincent Holland-Keen, Alasdair Stuart and Steve Savile*
*who were there when my world cracked open and never left me*
*alone in the dark. Thank you.*

# Contents

## Part 1

## Part 2

# Part 3

# Part 1

*"Apocalypse is a frame of mind." [Nicodemus] said then. "A belief. A surrender to inevitability. It is a despair for the future. It is the death of hope."*

Jim Butcher,
*Death Masks*

# Antichristine

## James Bennett

### 1.

Faith is the new girl. She shuffles into Mr Jaworski's science class and stands at the front before all the desks and the sea of eyes. She stands under the wooden cross and the clock, next to the teacher's desk. Already the other kids are judging her. Already they're laughing. They don't like her stripy stockings. They don't like her black dress or her hair that looks attacked by crows. The stockings, dress and hair mean she is different and therefore weird. *Weird* isn't *good* in the 8th Grade. Faith is the new girl and will never be like them.

'This is Faith, the new girl,' Mr Jaworski says. He goes to pat her shoulder, thinks better of it. 'I trust you will all make her welcome. Faith, please say hello.'

Faith doesn't say hello. Some girls sat up front snigger. One of them, a skinny blonde in a pink tee shirt and non-existent skirt, pops some bubble gum and says, 'She's the new girl? I thought she was here for dissection.'

Everybody laughs.

Mr Jaworski doesn't laugh.

Faith doesn't laugh.

Mr Jaworski says, 'Christine Collins, the class comedian. One more peep out of you and it's detention."

'Yes, sir. Sorry sir.' The girl, Christine, doesn't look sorry. She crosses her supermodel legs. A smile hangs under her nose job. A lot of money went into her teeth. They're too white. Too perfect. Almost as perfect as the hate that Faith feels looking at her. Looking at her and imagining her head bursting into flames, her hair crisping, her eyes melting, her smile becoming a sealed line of dripping, liquefied skin.

Christine Collins implied she was a frog. A dead frog. Wars have started for less.

11

It's OK. Faith doesn't need the girl to like her. She doesn't need any of them to like her. This is her fifth school in as many years and she knows the drill by now. She takes a breath. Gets it over with. Why waste time?

'Baaaaa!' she says in a loud voice. 'Baaaaa!'

She stares at Christine Collins and the other sheep as she takes her lunchbox out of her bag, pops the lid and brings out the cockroach she's been keeping in there. The fat, bristly monster she found behind the fridge at home. She stares at Christine as she shoves the insect into her mouth, crunches and chews it before the whole class, then grins. The bug's legs stick out, wriggling, between her silver braces.

Faith is the new girl. She will never be like them.

2.

When you're thirteen, the world is always ending.

Faith would have begged her dad not to drop her off at the gates in his old pick-up truck. The school is just another pointless building in a pointless town in a pointless state in pointless America. In a pointless world. Universe, etc. Her dad keeps moving, chasing jobs. Or running from something. Faith isn't sure. She would have begged her dad not to drop her off at the gates if he wasn't made of stone.

3.

'We won't have any of that in our school,' Mrs Morgan says, a permed mountain sat behind her desk. Her dark dress and white hair make her look like a killer whale. 'We won't have any smoking, swearing, spitting, vandalism, hair pulling, skipping class, food fights,' she takes a breath, scrunching Faith's resume, her official report, between her chubby hands, 'and we especially won't have *bugs*. What on earth were you thinking?'

Faith didn't say, 'I was thinking of Christine's head on fire.'

Faith hears herself say, 'They laughed at me. Christine Collins -'

'Is a straight A student and head cheerleader for the Bulls. You'd do well to get along with her.'

Faith doesn't say, 'I want to blow her brains out with my daddy's shotgun. Watch the smoking mess slide down the wall at the back of the class.'

Faith says, 'Yes, Mrs Morgan.'

'We were all young once, Miss Borden. We were all new at some point. Try not to make a nuisance of yourself.'

Faith says, 'Yes, Mrs Morgan.'

Faith doesn't say, 'Fat fucking bitch.'

4.

All told, it's a cunt of a day.

5.

That night, she eats chicken soup with her dad in the old wooden house that looks sorry for itself on a street vomited straight out of the 'Hick Street' manual and watches some TV. She doesn't tell him about her day and her dad doesn't ask. He drinks beer and communicates in belches. Punctuates with farts. Men toss a ball around on the flickering screen. Faith consoles herself that a hundred years from now, all of them will be dead. She goes upstairs to do her homework, but only manages to doodle in the margins of her essay. Next to the question about Mr Darcy, she writes:

*DIE CHRISTINE DIE*

Those teeth. Too white. Too perfect. Too *non-incinerated*.

Then Faith feels guilty and pulls out the shoebox under her bed. In the shoebox are some bits of her mother's jewellery. She saved them before her dad could sell them after the funeral. In the shoebox are some dead bugs. She forgot to feed them. A cigarette. A lighter. A hairpin, which she puts in her pocket for later. In the shoebox are three of her daddy's razors. She wants to use them, but she knows he'll see. Instead, she lightly caresses the edge of one blade and then licks the tip of her finger. Licks the thin line of blood. It tastes like Monday.

She says her prayers. Her curses.

Later, her daddy comes upstairs and tucks her in. He doesn't always do this, only when he's drunk. Faith would have told him to stop, that she's too old for this now. Faith would have begged him if he wasn't made of stone.

## 6.

Thursday and the world is still ending.

Armed with bag, Bible, pens and lunchbox, Faith sits in the back of the class and survives History, Geography, Maths, English and Religious Studies. No one talks to her. She talks to no one. Now and again, she looks up and watches Christine. Tall, blonde, beautiful Christine. Christine who exudes perfume and apparently oxygen for boys, who seem to surround her in a constant ring, hanging on her every sigh, her every hair flick and crossed leg. Faith imagines taking a chainsaw to those legs, the blood spraying from the severed arteries and splattering her face as the girl wriggles and screams in her daddy's garage. Then she finishes her paper on the Book of John. The class breaks for lunch and Faith sits alone in the canteen. She eats stale sandwiches. Who knows what's in them? Baloney? Dead rats? Someone flicks peas at the back of her head and Faith ignores it. Just when she thinks she's survived Thursday, the apocalypse happens.

Gym class.

'Holy shit,' the girls say in the locker room, after tossing a pointless ball around for a pointless hour in the pointless sports hall. 'Holy shit, you're wearing boy's underpants.'

The laughter sounds louder here, echoing off the lockers and the cold blue walls.

Faith doesn't say, 'My dad bought them from Walmart in the sale.'

Faith says, 'Leave me alone, you plastic whores.'

The girls grab her crow-pecked hair and push her in the shower. It hurts. Their hands are cruel and the water is cold.

Faith doesn't say, 'My dad, he doesn't care about these things.' (She has her mother to thank for the braces.)

Faith just swears and struggles and screams.

When they back off – a teacher is coming – she stands in the cubicle and turns off the tap. She sees that Christine Collins hangs back, watching. Christine hasn't touched her and her eyes look very bright. Faith imagines what her eyes would look like on the end of a hairpin, just poked out quickly at a prayer meet, dropped into the tithe bowl. Doomed to watch the rest of them dancing.

'Fucking freak,' the girls say. 'Lesbian. Weirdo. Pig.'

Faith pisses herself. She does it right there and on purpose. Urine soaks the front of her Y-Fronts. Urine trickles down her left leg and swirls down the plughole, a yellow statement of defiance.

Christine and the girls have no words for this, but they point, mewl and pull faces.

7.

Thirteen is not a lucky number. Mr Rogers told them that this was because at the Last Supper, there were thirteen people sitting around the table, including Jesus, who got crucified, and Judas, who hung himself from a tree. Mr Rogers told the class the special word that means fear of the number thirteen: *triskaidekaphobia.*

Faith is thirteen. All of the above.

It's relevant to her, because Faith thinks maybe, probably, her Last Supper isn't that far away. It comforts her, a little, to know that the end of the world depends entirely on her.

The gym teacher, Miss Howard, doesn't even look at her. She doesn't even shout. Instead, she hisses. A snake.

'Clean yourself up, you disgusting brat.'

Thus Thursday ended.

Amen.

## 8.

The weekend passes in a blink and for the next week Faith doesn't exist. As far as the class and the school and the world etc. are concerned, Faith doesn't exist. Not many people know how ghosts feel. Faith could tell them. She could tell them that ghosts are real and most of them are living. She sits in the arctic winds at the back of the class and survives, a shadow, a ninja, with her secret. Nobody asks her about it.

Faith is the new girl. And she'll never be like them.

She watches Christine Collins through hooded eyes. Christine texting on her mobile phone under her desk during the monthly exam. Christine isn't cheating; she's too clever for that. Straight A clever. No shit. Christine is texting Warren Gray, who has asked her out to see the new *Superman* film on Friday after school. Faith knows this because how could she not? The boys tease and the girls giggle and it's the subject on everyone's lips. They twitter like birds and laugh like hyenas. The school ark. Christine sits and blushes and preens and texts on her mobile phone. Faith doesn't have a mobile phone. She doesn't have a date either. Boys smell kind of funny to her.

Faith imagines Christine trying to type with broken fingers, each one crushed, firmly and quickly, with the hammer from her daddy's toolbox. Or maybe Faith would use the pliers and peel off her fingernails, one by one. Not the fake ones with the painted dolphins, but the real ones underneath. Peel them down to the skin. As Christine whispers behind her hand to the girl sat next to her, passing on some (no doubt amorous) message from Warren Gray, Faith sits and imagines that.

Her dad sometimes drops her off in the old pickup truck and when he remembers, he picks her up. He drives her back home to the old wooden house that looks sorry for itself. That week, he only comes and tucks her in once. Her daddy, the stone. It's still the apocalypse, but on a minor scale.

## 9.

On Thursday, Faith sits up at the back of the gym where it's dark and cool and no one can see her if they were looking. Would they see her anyway? She's invisible by now. Her special talent. A superpower. She watches the Holy Rollers. She watches Christine Collins bounce and jump and roll and spin, practising her cheerleading. Pompoms ruffle. Beiber blares from the boombox. He whines about love and babies and hey girls and things Faith either hasn't heard or doesn't give a fuck about. The other girls bounce and jump and roll and spin and pause for occasional high fives, but Faith is only looking at Christine. Only has eyes for Christine. Christine of the golden hair. Christine with the centrefold legs. Christine who could so easily fall and break her neck.

## 10.

It's an obsession, right? Faith knows it's an obsession.

It hasn't happened before, not like this, and the obsession snowballs. She dreams that it's Christine tucking her in and she rubs herself so hard between her legs that she layers bruises on bruises. Then the guilt comes again, a sly, suck up friend, and the razorblades sing in the shoebox under her bed, singing, singing, singing.

Christine lives in her head now. A worm chewing her heart. Faith has got to do something about it.

Her daddy doesn't wake up in time for school and it's suddenly Friday. The amount of empty beer cans on the living room floor tell her that daddy isn't going to work today and bruised or not, aching or not, she has to make her own way to Hell. When Faith looks at the kitchen clock and rushes her grits and hurries out into the rainy street, she's already late for school. The weather undoes the attack of the crows and turns her dress into a trash bag. Black, wet strands are hanging in her face and she almost doesn't see the cat, lying there at the side of the road. The thing mewls like the girls in the locker room. There are tyre tracks in its fur. Faith does the noble thing. The right thing. The little crack sounds like a change in the nature of things. In the universe, etc. It sounds like a decision. A choice.

Faith walks through the puddles with oil slick hair, her bag bumping heavily against her thigh.

Nobody notices that she's late for class.

Faith doesn't say, 'Fuck you. I could have been dead.'

Faith doesn't say, 'My dad kept me up late last night.'

Faith mumbles 'Sorry' and sits down.

Nobody notices. Nobody cares.

At some point, the world will end.

## 11.

They notice and care after Geography when Christine Collins opens her locker in the hall and the dead cat falls out. Intestines slop down the front of her top and splatter her non-existent skirt. Blood dribbles on her supermodel legs. Christine screams like a cheap horror movie and then crumples to the floor and cries. Faith knows that she screams and cries because she's watching from the end of the corridor, smiling with the hairpin stuck between her teeth. She knew it would come in handy. School padlocks are not hard to pick.

Faith watches the other boys and girls gather around Christine. Teachers arrive, flapping and squawking. Paper towels rustle from the bathroom. A swarm of locusts, perhaps. Mr Jaworski leans in to pat Christine's shoulder, thinks better of it. The killer whale barks commands. The gym teacher, Miss Howard, looks like she's going to puke.

It's a glorious moment. A perfect moment. The moment doesn't last.

Faith isn't a ghost anymore. She's the subject on everyone's lips.

Nobody questions who did it. Faith lets the teachers take her to the office, stand around her in a circle and shout. They tell her how disgusting she is. They tell her she owes Christine an apology. They tell her they're calling her dad.

Faith doesn't say, 'I didn't do it.'

She doesn't say, 'It wasn't me.'

Faith says, 'Burn in Hell, you motherfuckers. I hope you all die in a car crash.'

Naturally, they send her home.

## 12.

It's Friday afternoon and Christine Collins is still going on her date. She's still going downtown to meet Warren Gray and watch the new *Superman* movie. Faith thinks this says all you need to know about Christine Collins.

Faith doesn't do what the sheep tell her. Last place she is going to go is home. Her dad hasn't gone to work and is probably on his second crate by now, too drunk to answer the phone. Maybe they'll send him a letter. He's received letters like that before, so the surprise element is kind of old. Like the underpants, like the stale sandwiches, her daddy doesn't really care about those things. There is always another pointless town down the road. Always another pointless school. It isn't the end of the world.

Or at least not part of it.

Christine Collins, the Whore of Babylon, is. Faith says to herself it doesn't matter what happens now. It doesn't matter what I do. I'm a dead frog and tonight, I'm eating my Last Supper.

She hangs around the chapel until Christine comes down the steps, freshly showered and wearing a pale green summer dress that she probably bought just for the occasion. The makeup on her face is five years too old for her. She looks more like a model without it. It's still raining and the dress is out of place. It's the kind of day for tears, for floods, tornados and Judgement. It isn't a day for romance.

Faith follows Christine Collins. She's invisible and doesn't keep to the trees. She follows her past the cemetery where the dead lie waiting. She follows her past the church with the sign warning passersby about the Lake of Fire. She follows her past the backed up traffic, car horns blaring like Trumpets of Doom. She follows Christine all the way downtown and into the Bottomless Pit, otherwise known as the Mall.

In the Mall, she loses sight of Christine Collins. Christine Collins has either gone up in the Rapture or Warren Gray has whisked her off somewhere in the crowd. You have to watch boys. You can't trust them. They smell funny and they like to tuck you in.

The queue outside the movie theatre isn't that long, but Faith can't see the Whore or her Tempter, Beelzebub Warren Gray. Jesus looks down on her from a billboard, except he's wearing a red cape and tights. The movie theatre isn't letting kids in yet, so they couldn't have gone inside.

Faith does a circuit of the escalators. She sees the maintenance door propped open. A mop is keeping the gap. Faith goes to the gap and peers in. Then she sees Christine Collins and oh my God oh my Lord she sees Warren Gray with his spiky red hair and his leather jacket and his jeans bunched around his ankles. One of his hands is around the Beast, the great horned Dragon of the Abyss. His other is around Christine's neck. Warren Gray is sweating and grunting. He is trying to attack Christine with the Beast. Christine is wriggling and squealing. Her green summer dress is Eden torn. She doesn't want the Beast to bite her.

The revelation stuns Faith. She doesn't know what to do.

She wanted to break Christine's nose job. She wanted to break the Whore.

Now it seems she is only the Woman. Maybe only a girl.

Faith doesn't say, 'You asked for this.'

Faith doesn't say, 'Ha ha.'

Faith is a ghost and a ninja and holy. In that moment, she is actually holy.

Faith says, 'Get your fucking claws off her, you creep.'

Beelzebub turns. The Beast turns in her direction, glaring at her with its terrible eye.

Beelzebub growls, but all Faith has to do is open the door. Just a little. Just a crack. Beelzebub lets go of Christine and lets her slide down the wall. Beelzebub pulls his jeans up. He feints a dart in Faith's direction, but then just spits. Spits at her feet.

'You fucking faith school girls,' he says. 'Bible bashing sluts.'

Then he turns and is off and is gone, a Dragon returning to Hades.

13.

If there is a prophecy (there isn't one), then all of it would have come true.

Faith doesn't believe in fate. Thirteen isn't lucky for some, whatever people might think. Thirteen isn't lucky for Faith or for the girl on the floor.

She helps Christine up. Christine stops crying. Oddly, she strokes Faith's hair.

'I know,' Christine says. 'I hate it too.'

Faith doesn't say, 'You can't trust boys. You can't trust them because they smell funny and they like to tuck you in.'

Faith doesn't say, 'My daddy likes to tuck me in. He tucks me in so tight at night. Around my shoulders at least.'

Somewhere a trumpet is sounding. It's probably the Mall speakers. Probably Justin Bieber.

Faith says, 'Now you have to help me.'

Christine Collins smiles a white smile and says, 'How?'

Faith says, 'You have to say I was with you all day. You have to say we saw *Superman*.'

Christine Collins doesn't ask why. It's a new Heaven and a new Earth and somehow, she just knows. Standing there, they are both new girls and whether the town, the world or the universe cares, Faith and Christine are new girls and they will never be like them.

Christine comes home with her anyway.

Later, they watch the flames lick up around the old wooden house that feels sorry for itself. Hand in hand in the garden, they watch Armageddon unfold.

# Coming Back

## Tracy Fahey

My world ended precisely two months ago. I awoke from a coma to find myself gone.

I'm in a strange bright room and someone is shouting at me. I strain to move my head. There is a hard plastic mask fastened to my face like a hideous carapace. I claw at it weakly, bones like water, eventually managing to knock it aside. My hand falls, exhausted. Something is wrong. I squint. My arms are splayed, like Christ crucified, with one, two three, *four* tubes poking out. *What's happened?* I try to croak, but my mouth is ashen, cracked with thirst. Intense weariness smothers me, utter and boneless. A doctor stands at the foot of my bed. She is rude, squat and froglike. She barks at me 'You stupid girl! Didn't you know you were sick?' Possible words muddle together, and stick in my dry mouth. I can only look at her, stupidly. My brain blunders inside my skull like a moth in a darkened room.

I am in a waking sleep; I see people pass by my bed. Their faces blear and swim as my eyes slip closed. When I open them, I see a blonde nurse, her hair a halo under the fluorescent tube. I know I must look terrible, a tangle of machines and untidy flesh. I try to joke, but the words jumble and slur. She looks at me. I see her brisk kindness in her eyes. She takes my wrist. I clutch her hand. It is warm and solid. I fall into sleep again, down the dark tunnel. Coming back I see the angry doctor making notes on her clipboard. I open my mouth to tell her I'm sorry, but I'm gone again.

Words keep penetrating. 'Coma' – I have been in a coma, they say, over and over again. I don't remember. I know I have been away. I am sick they tell me. Very sick. I have undiagnosed Type 1 diabetes. There is a lot of information about blood sugar. They show me insulin pens. It is too much. There is nothing in my head except a fuzzy blackness. I gaze down. I am wearing unfamiliar pyjamas. I have no idea how I got them, or who put them on me. I don't want to know what happened to my slack, lifeless body in the emergency room. It was not me. Like a large, strange baby, I lie in bed; my waxwork-self fed, sponged, injected. Drugged up, half-waking, I live in a perpetual swoon. I am a ghost in the machines. I sleep at an angle, arms outstretched, tubes pushing nutrients into the soft marshmallow of my arms.

All over the small ICU, worlds end, softly, one after another. The man beside me keeps coughing. I can't sleep. He coughs on and on, his breath tearing at his throat between bouts. I am almost hysterical with rage - *Stop!* I yell inside my head. I roll my head hard from side to side in anger, one of the few movements I can make. But he doesn't stop. The wet, tearing sound goes on and on. Behind the curtain I hear more and more murmuring. The door of the ward opens, closes, and then opens again. In the morning the noise has stopped. The curtain between our beds is still drawn, but the visitors have gone. 'I'm sorry' says the blonde nurse gently, as she rearranges my sheets. 'He passed away in the night. I am quiet. A small, mean, part of me enjoys the new silence. Otherwise I feel nothing.

Emotions have drained out of me, like urine down the catheter that lies warm against my leg. (I have no idea how or when they attached it, my brain flails away from the very idea. The thought of having it removed makes me shrink into the sheets around me. I am afraid of more pain.) All I want to do is lie in bed and doze off, again and again. The only thing that rouses me is the sight of a needle. Then I cry and beg, drawing my arms as close to me as I can with the tubes knitted into my skin. The tender crook of my left elbow flowers with appalling roses of red, black, yellow, blue, a horrid clustering of repeated punctures, fingerprints, incisions, invasions.

People come in to visit. I find it hard to remember them. I am *too tired*, the nurses fuss, too tired for visitors. There is a sister, and a father. They both have dark hair and seem familiar, yet not, all at the same time. They stand like statues, sadly looking down at me. Sometimes one of them will cry. They bring me things, fruit, water, books. For the first time in my life, I can't read. I look at the pages and the words crawl around each other. I know I was away and the world ended. That is all. My stomach tells the tale of my journey back, livid with injections, a map of reddened and bruised flesh.

Sometimes I wake and there is a man by my bed. He arrives at night, but never by the main ward door. From time to time I will see a golden spill of light fall from behind the nurses' desk on the furrowed linoleum of the floor. He steps out into the dim, hushed light of the ICU. Often he will walk up and down, looking at the four beds in the ward. I don't know what his name is; in my head he is the Visitor. He only sits beside my bed. I don't mind. He sits quietly, large dark eyes fixed on my face. At first, he says nothing, just looks. There are no questions, no tears and no needles. It is strangely relaxing. He doesn't wear a white coat, or a nurse's uniform, just a nondescript brown suede cardigan. This makes me like him more. One night he lifts a lock of my hair up to examine it. 'You could change it, you know'. They are the first words I have ever heard him speak.

'Why?' I am intrigued.

He looks at me coolly. 'Because you're not the same any-more.' He is the first person to say it. I stroke my hair and nod. 'People like you, who become so severely ill, often find it difficult to remember things. Don't try; it's a good kind of amnesia, death amnesia.' I like that phrase, sounding it silently in my head. He nods at me. 'You're not the first to go away. But you're one of the first to come back here. You have to change now.'

'Why?' It seems to be the only question I can ask.

'Your old world is over. Forget about it. If you want to fight, to keep going, stop trying to remember.' There is a low groan from one of the other beds. He looks over his shoulder, then back at me. 'You know what I mean, don't you.'

'Yes'. I think I do. I close my eyes. When I open them, he is gone.

That is our longest conversation. He comes back again, but only at night, only when the ward is quiet. He offers me advice – 'Stop trying to remember. It can't help you now', sometimes even praise – 'You look stronger', but he refuses to answer my questions, even the one that plagues me, *who am I?*

Now I can walk. I can pretend. From time to time I smile at people when I realise it is appropriate to do so. I arrange my face in a listening attitude when they speak. I hold myself together tightly. If I unravel, I am afraid someone will find me out. I am hollow.

The worst bit is when they move me to one of the main wards. Everyone tells me this is a good thing. It feels like leaving the only home the new me knows. I shrink from the strange smells and noises of my new environment. There is still a wall of greaseproof paper between me and myself, both transparent and opaque. I can remember a misty before-time, I can remember the ambulance, the repeated questions, opening my mouth to tell them my name, but the words going the wrong way, falling down the back of my throat. Then nothing. 'Tell the man I'm going,' I say to the nurse. She is properly confused. 'Who?' *The Visitor* I think, but can't say. Hesitantly I say 'The man who comes at night.' I sound like a child. Her face clears, 'Oh, you mean Pat, the night nurse? Not a bother, of course I will.' I keep quiet. It is not Pat. Pat likes to read tabloid newspapers and drink tea, and even, sometimes, to sleep behind the nurses' station when everything is quiet. The other man does none of these things. The nurse pauses, raises a finger in the air – 'Wait!' She disappears behind her desk, and then returns with a large, shabby black handbag. I look behind her. The wall behind the station runs smoothly, with no surface deviation. The door out of the ward simply isn't there. I shake my head, confused. My eyes keep doing this, playing tricks on me. Some days my vision doubles, blurs. Some days I see moving specks out of the corners of my eyes. 'Here, it's yours.' The nurse holds out the bag. 'Thanks' I mumble and drop it on my trolley. I push the heavy trolley slowly ahead of me to my new bed, placing my unsure legs one after the other, all the way down the corridor. I don't look back.

In this ward, I am no longer special, no longer tended by the calm, antiseptic nurses of the ICU. The nurses here are rushed, hardy, terrifying. 'How do you do this again?' asks a nurse, casually squirting excess insulin from the needle as she reads the instructions on the cardboard box. She pinches a fold of my stomach and injects me with a quick stab. I whimper slightly. 'Now don't be like that' she chides. 'Sure, look at the wee size of that needle. It won't hurt you.' She is maybe five years younger than me, but she has the brisk, bossy tone of a much older woman. The mint green paint on the walls is chipped and stained. For most of the day I pretend to be asleep, only waking to eat or stare at the ceiling. I feel well enough to be bored. I want to see my Visitor. He is the only person who talks to me like an adult. But he doesn't visit me in this ward. Maybe it is because there is no demarcation between day and night here. I am in a room with two old ladies with severe respiratory problems. They smell of old clothes and, disturbingly, of urine. 'We don't sleep,' one of them gargles at me, almost proud. Nor do they. Night after night, they sit up like giant squatting birds, watching old movies, the staccato gunfire of westerns or the mawkish syrup of Hollywood violins providing a soundtrack as they breathe noisily behind their grim respirators. I take to wandering the green-lit corridors, scratchy-eyed and exhausted. 'Where are you going?' they caw in unison as I slip past them.

Homesickness gathers thick in my throat, like throttled tears. I want to go back, but I don't know where back is. The handbag reveals some clues, I search it carefully, laying out all my possessions on the bed, and then shaking the bag gently to make sure nothing has lodged in the crevices. There is a paperback horror novel, The Dead Zone, as well as a Kindle. *I liked to read*, I think, wistfully. There is a tattered notebook filled with scribbling I find difficult to read. Most pages are covered with plans about work – dates of meetings, endless to-do lists. I can dimly remember the large red-brick building I work in and the smell of waxed tiles in the corridor on Monday mornings. Faces of colleagues pass through my head when I see their names. The problem is no longer that I cannot remember; it is that I feel nothing when I do. This scares me slightly. Some of the scrawled entries are diary-like scraps. I read until my eyes blur, but I don't understand them. I discover that I like Japanese food – *really? Isn't that mostly raw fish?* I also seem to watch a lot of horror movies, something that I cannot believe I will ever do, or want to do again. My smartphone is an even better source of information. I've charged it up and keep its settings switched to silent, as I watch the number of missed calls mount up, steadily, day after day. Messages continue to buzz through, concerned, sympathetic, and then filled with a kind of frustration. 'Please text back. You know I'm worried about you.' I don't really know who they are. No-one is as worried about me as I am. I don't reply. I am more interested in the photos I find on it. I look at the photographs of my careless self, face cracked in a great smile, hair blowing in the wind, surrounded by an endless pageant of buildings, landscapes, people. Sitting in the hard hospital bed, I cannot remember what it was like to feel so enthusiastic. There is even a video of me making a message for a friend. It *looks* like me. It *speaks* like me. It *moves* like me. I feel a wave of despair at the impassable walls between myself and myself. *If you want to fight, to keep going, stop trying to remember.*

I try, I really do. No-one told me coming back would be such a long journey. The weeks on the ward tick by. The harsh sound of the ventilators and the tinny TV keep me awake at night. I am desperate to escape. *If you want to fight, to keep going, stop trying to remember.* So I fight. I fake it. I take my sister's hand when she comes in, and call her by name. It's easy, she's told me it so many times before. I tell my father I feel much better. Both of them live at the other end of the country – I know that if I reassure them, they will stop visiting. I show the nurses how well I can I inject myself. Under it all, I cannot feel anything. I cannot let myself feel anything or I will feel everything. The tears, anger, humiliation, fear are brimming inside me. One false move and it will all overspill, tumultuous. Better to move through the days, slow and deliberate, measuring, injecting, waiting. I am a metronome. Four punctures a day. Four measurements. Four readings. Four injections. Four sets of numbers. Good numbers are five, six, seven. Bad numbers are any others, an infinite universe of possible numbers. The blood ritual hurts. My fingertips bruise, the pads of the third and fourth finger on my left hand are pocked with hard punctures. Needle after needle. Each measurement is a worry or a sweet relief, a small wedge of time that leads to the next one. Every needle prick is a reminder of difference, my new, abnormal body that must be controlled like a science experiment. This afterlife is no wraith. It is leaden, monotonous. Even the fear is cyclical. It is a new, careful world. *If you want to fight, to keep going, stop trying to remember.* I stay alive. I don't do anything else that requires effort. I measure my energy like a miser, hoarding it, doling out just enough energy to walk through each day. No more. Sometimes even lying in bed I can feel the energy drain out of me, like water from a tap. In my head, I am forever marked 'fragile'. I handle myself with care.

One night I drift into the Emergency waiting room. I can hear voices, urgent, calling.

'Can you wake up?'

'It's very important you stay awake! Come on, good girl'

'Did you have a fight with your boyfriend?'

'Don't cry' Their voices rise.

'Stay awake!' I am rooted to the spot, a fascinated eaves-dropper on someone else's dark moments. *Tell me more.* I sit on the cold plastic chair in my mystery pyjamas and wait intently for the story to unravel. There is a dull, repetitive sobbing and more cries of 'Good girl! Stay awake now!' Then there is silence, the urgent bleeping of a loud machine and the sound of a door closing. I feel a strange sense of disloca-tion – *Was that me?* Echoes stir within me; they flutter and almost, but not quite, become memories. I am haunted by that most terrible of ghosts, my own shadow-double.

I start to walk back down the corridor, then pause. I see a man in the distance. He is wearing a brown jacket – or car-digan? I scrunch up my eyes against the cold green light. Yes. He looks like he is the right height. My heart is beating fast. Heedless of my energy, of the slippery floor, I run around the corner, then pause, baffled. The long corridor stretches before me, empty but for a trolley bed, stripped bare apart from a lone pillow.

Even the nurses comment on my health now. 'You look lovely and rosy,' says the bossy one approvingly. 'We'll have you home any day now.' The thought is exciting and alarming, in equal quantities. I know where I live. I've seen the address written down in my own looping handwriting. I am good. I am obedient. I plot my escape, like a prisoner on the World War II movies that play on the ward TV, night after night. I am still faking it, but more and more successfully every day. Now I know the hospital, and all its crevices. I prowl the corridors. I've even found a place to sleep, a tiny visitor's lounge on the floor above me. I lie there, on the lumpy sofa, savouring the far-off buzz of noise, the slip-slop of sensible nurse shoes passing, intersecting, moving off into the distance. Sometimes I hear the urgent *wargh-wargh-wargh* of the ambulance outside, the brakes, the shouts of the paramedics. I roll myself up in the prickly woollen blanket and snatch a few hours sleep.

It is on one of those nights he finds me. I wake up, and there he is, serene as ever, darkly outlined against the yellow glass of the internal window to the corridor. I sit up, excited.

'You're almost ready to go.' His voice sounds kind.

'Yes'. I hug my knees to my chin. 'Any day now, they say.'

I see the outline of his head nodding.

'Just remember to keep looking ahead. Keep facing the future. Don't look back. If you can see it, it can see you.'

I am confused. 'What can see me?'

'Nothing you can remember. 'He touches my hand. His hand is cool and smooth. I feel the worn butter-soft texture of his cardigan sleeve. 'When one world ends, another can begin.'


And now I'm home, or in the house the old me used to live in. In spite of my Visitor's advice, I can't stop thinking about myself, my old self. *Who was I? Where did I go? Did I dream?* I walk around the house and examine all things I've loved, clothes, books, paintings, looking for clues, a way back in. *Who was I?* I don't have to work now. I'm on sick leave from work. My old thoughts are gone. When I sit and think, there's a curious nothingness that almost feels like peace. Instead I look, intensely, at details around me, a glinting, frail cobweb, a smudge on a window pane, a piece of thread coiled on the floor. Life is very beautiful and very strange. Sometimes I stir and realise evening has melted into night; the room has become so dim I need to switch on the large lamp. The yellow glow chases the shadows back to the edge of the room.

Home is not a place I am comfortable in. I move jerkily through the unfamiliar territory of my former life. The walls that surround me cannot protect me from my own treacherous body. I still sleep in jagged patches, waking, confused, alarmed at the silence, no respirators, no footsteps, no trolley trundling by. I'm still walking at night, but on a larger scale. I walk alone in the darkness, my feet tracing circles around my old ways. I walk the same paths, down my street, past the lit windows. I consult my notebook with its lists. Here is where I went out for my last birthday. Here is where I worked. I stop at each monument to myself. Nothing. I look at the houses – such a thin shell that separates inside from outside, light from darkness. The walls keep everything outside. I am not afraid of anything outside. Sometimes I think I see him on the dark streets, my Visitor, but it is always someone else, some boy, some man, some woman. I miss his calm air. I even miss his brown cardigan.

Mostly I miss his advice. I try to remember it, and to forget what came before. I delete the photos from my phone. They make me feel inferior, like a bad photocopy of myself. Then I delete the numbers. I get my hair cut short, and dyed a defiant, platinum blonde. My face gains colour. I wear red lipstick. I am cold and careful. I test, measure, inject. My doctor says I am a perfect patient. 'Gold star standard,' he smiles, pleased, as he checks my numbers. Under my calmness, I am angered by his praise. This is not a feat. This is a fight. My new body must win, every time.

The only thing I have in common with the old me is that I still read a lot. My tastes are morbid. At first I Google 'diabetes' and eavesdrop on forums. Most of them are based in the US, and are full of sad little misspelt tales of amputations and complications; there are too many former patients resting with Jesus for my liking. Instead I switch to reading endless articles about people in comas. I am especially fond of miracle recoveries. People who hear things. People who see white lights, deceased family members, even themselves, spread and helpless, far below in hospital beds. For me, in the darkness there had been only darkness. The only light was the buzzing fluorescent tube in the ward ceiling when I came back. But still I read on, avidly. Somewhere in this morass of articles I will find what I am looking for.

Sometimes I just sit and look out of the window. In spite of my Visitor's advice I slip back sometimes and wonder - *where was I?* In my body, I know; I know that I was somewhere and only part of me returned.

Sometimes I let myself remember what I saw in the soft darkness. It was nothing I should be afraid of. It was only her after all, my old self, that I lost that night. In the night I can sometimes hear her wandering around inside this new body that lies heavy as a slug on my bones. She is lost, forlorn, forever my dark echo.

*If you want to fight, to keep going, stop trying to remember.*

So I face forward. I fight. I keep going. When one world ends, another begins.

# The Borrowed Man

## James S. Dorr

What is a man? To a ghoul a good meal, perhaps, in time. In the Tombs, a client.

But, to a woman…

Her name was Melantha and she was a rich woman of the New City, one of that new breed that claims independence. That is, she was one that was not in great haste concerning marriage, content in its stead to spend her own money. But she was more, also: One trained as a scientist — and, as some rumoured, as a Necromancer as well. This latter I do not know.

Some said she went alone into the Old City for this last learning. She went alone where most people do not go, or, if they must, go in closely guarded groups, in that its ruins are a refuge of ghoul-kind. Of ghouls I do know much — but that is not my story.

Rather, my story is of Melantha, and what she did after she came to the Tombs.

I took her here, you see, I, too, a resident of the New City, a corpse-train master who plied the Causeway across the great river that separates these lands, bringing the dead to rest. I, a haggler, an over-seer whose job as well was to bargain for grave-sites, for stones and outlooks as might be pleasant not just for the corpse itself, but also those it had loved — those who loved it back sufficiently to pilgrimage here themselves in turn, bearing new grave-gifts, every fifth yearing for its death's-reminiscences. Sometimes more often. I was one who thus, sometimes, conveyed the living as well as those less-lively through the grim gate to these marble-walled tomb-lands. And, once their business was brought to completion as well as my own, disposing as favorably as I might of this, whatever my new dead cargo was, I generally took back these living as well.

But not Melantha who called me aside then. 'I will not go back,' she said.

'What?' I answered. 'My lady, you must. Whichever it was you came to visit, however great your grief, the night is almost ended. Soon the day-sun will rise in the east, back over New City where we must flee, hastily, to escape the poisons of its actinic rays. Its heat and its brightness — at least we must chador ourselves, even now, in our thickest garments. See — to the east — that glow? The glow of false dawn?'

'Yes. I see it,' she said.

'Then you know that we must hurry,' I told her. 'We must quickly mount the lead corpse-cart, now empty. The others are waiting, the drivers and pullers. The guards of the other carts, waiting as well, for us to start.'

Melantha shook her head, pushing her hood back, crimson-gold hair cascading about her shoulders and arms. Catching the torch-glint. 'Then start them without us,' she said. 'I have bribed the gate-guard for shelter, a place to wait out the day. Tomorrow night I have work for us both to do.'

She smiled at me then, her scarlet lips pursing. She shook off her chador, letting the near-transparent silks beneath scarcely conceal bare flesh, soft-curved and white-skinned, her delicate waist and smooth, rounded hips, her breasts and her shoulders. She looked up and kissed me — lightly, on the cheek. Then reached down once more to finger at her belt, drawing forth a small bag.

Letting its contents chink!

'And,' she said, still smiling, but now with a tone of business to her voice, 'I can reward you.'

Thus it was, you see, we in our stations — hers high, mine low — that that would be my reward alone. Brass or, at most, gold coins. Though others in the Tombs, high-stationed in their ways, might hope for other things.

Yet, in the Tombs, they are strange in their customs.

Unlike we, they do things not for money, at least not alone

— and at least on occasion. Or even for pleasure, but sometimes for love only. Or, on other times, curiosity. So I have seen myself!

So I have noted, I who on one occasion was asked right out by Melantha what my name was.

I answered: 'I have none. You know that my lady, that it is the custom that we corpse-train masters be not so burdened. That we be called only after our corpse trains, the sectors of the New City where they are gathered, their number of carts, their times of departure. For surely that is all our clientele need to know…'

Melantha smiled. She often smiled these nights, now that she had found, in the Tombs, an unused tunnel near to the north wall — the Tombs' most ancient part, save for the crested hill of its centre — for us to stay in.

'Even the dead of your clientele?' she asked.

'Especially the dead ones, my lady. For why should they, of all, wish to know more than this: That they will go safely on this last journey — their fleshly forms, that is — protected from ghoul-kind, those that would despoil them. That they will have grave-goods…'

'I see,' Melantha said. 'And yet I might give them more — parts of them, anyway.'

I shrugged, saying nothing. It was not proper for me to question, a poor man to ask knowledge of a rich lady.

Only to answer.

'I have,' she continued, 'been working myself, even during the heat of the day now that we have shelter, strong, cool marble slabs both above and surrounding us. While you have roamed abroad at night to procure us food and drink, I have explored the Tombs itself and talked to its curators, its keepers of records, of who — and what — have been where. Who moved, who still at rest. Histories of most, at least, who have been brought here.'

'Of who have been buried here, yes,' I said. 'I too talk to curators — or at least, talking to others, I hear gossip.'

'Yes,' she said, still smiling. It was that smile, I think, that had we been closer-born in the New City, nearer each other in wealth and rank — instead of, as it was, she born of wealth and I to near-poverty — might at that moment have caused me to love her. To not just lust for her charm, as many even here in the Tombs seemed to, but truly to wish for her, for those things she wished. For her to share one's bed, to be sure, but soul to soul — secrets. Other things sharing, too. Yet, as I say, there was distance between us.

And I, no more than a corpse-train master still, listened as she spoke on:

'Yes,' she repeated, 'I know you hear gossip. It is what you corpse-train masters do, is it not? Thus to know who has died, who might need transport. Which families are rich enough. Which perhaps, not so rich, but still so filled with care for their decedents that they might yet find money, beg, perhaps, of their neighbors the grave-gifts, the bribes for the corpse-tenders, grave-diggers, all the rest. It is a lucrative trade, is it not, this over-seeing...'

'And, yet, with expenses...'

She nodded. 'And yet, yes, with expenses too, so that the money made is not much, but that is not my point. Rather, one gains a wealth of knowledge. A better ability to sift out histories, to know what is true of a corpse and what not true. What solidly based on fact and what mere rumour. And that is your talent.'

I waited. 'Yes?' I said.

'That is what I would now have you use for me. Come,' she said. She led me down the tunnel we slept in, apart, on bare pallets, veering right to the one we sat inside when we ate our dinners — those times we ate indoors when, outside, there might be caustic storms raging, acid rains scouring down — then to another where she kept her clothing, her chador and day-masks when she was not wearing them, extra silk tunics and kirtles and even gowns, kept there in readiness for such festivals as the Tombs-folk will sometimes celebrate. Through all these she led me, and then to another where she stored her jewellery, that which she did not wish to wear at the moment, and other things of hers, her brushes, cosmetics, which I was not to touch; then through another which I saw she had furnished as if it were some extra, private bed chamber, but not spare and Spartan as that which we kept to with its separate, narrow mats, but filled with cushions and softness and luxury — and at that I wondered; and finally to one more, a final branch-tunnel which I had been told not to enter alone. And indeed, up to now, had not even known for sure of its location.

I entered this with her, I holding the lantern, and inside I saw: A table. An ancient book. Glassware and tubing — a vast profusion of strangely-shaped vessels. Another table of a sort I recognized, long and narrow and metal-sided, one that was used by the Tombs' embalmers. A couch and a lamp filled with glowing fungus, set as if for study, and more scrolls and parchments. And shelves at the chamber's sides.

Shelves that were filled with bones.

'Yes,' she said. She must have seen me look startled. 'My bones,' she said. 'That is, bones which I have procured. Bones from the Tombs here, bought from the curators — some they did not wish to sell me at first, but I paid richly for them.' Now she smiled again, gesturing to yet more rolled up scrolls.

'These,' she said, 'describe their provenances — where my bones have come from. Who were their first owners. For instance' — she held up a grinning skull as she spoke — 'this is reputed to have held a poet's brain. While this' — she held a leg bone in her hand now, white and encrusted — 'was said to have been in the thigh of an athlete. And so, too, these others' — she gestured now to the shelves, then at the scrolls again — 'those shoulder blades there once belonged to a soldier and carried his epaulettes, back when they had wars, while these fingers once belonged to a sculptor, and those to a man who was gentle with animals, while this rib cage held the heart of a wealthy man. You can see, can you not, what I am aiming at? This foot, the foot of a skillful dancer, those ribs there of a man reputed to have possessed courage. This lower leg bone one of one who walked gracefully, these hips a man's who had had many children — so say the records — these vertebrae, mixed, of men, some strong, some well-looking, all men of firm will who knew what their desires were. Who knew, perhaps, what I want.

'This leg, a lover's…'

I interrupted. 'But what do you want of me?'

Laughing, she went on: 'To read the scrolls with me, to use your instinct to tell me which ones are true, which of these bones have the best "reputations," ones which can stand scrutiny. Which of them are, perhaps, exaggerated. To help me choose from them.' She sat now on the couch, leaving me still standing, looking down on her. I saw the sheen of sweat on her shoulders — from more than just the heat of outside now — the deep-glowing shadow between her breasts. She looking up at me.

'To help me, afterwards…'

She hesitated now.

'Yes?' I prompted.

'To help me then, afterwards — to cross the Causeway back to the New City, to re-form your corpse train, to hear your gossip of who is dying, of what kind of men they are. Who are their families…'

She gestured once more to the bones that surrounded us.

'Yes?' I said again.

She smiled, once more, that smile. 'And then bring them to me. The corpses, that is, or, rather, the parts of them that you will choose for me. The organs. The fresh flesh. The fat. The muscles. That which will best fit with these.'


Oh, I remonstrated. I tried to dissuade her — yet could I do otherwise than what she asked when she had thus smiled at me? She knew her power, my susceptibility. I suspect that of other men also, that is, she had tried them. And so I would, too, do whatever she asked me. Despite my misgivings.

Because you see, the scrolls contained much wisdom, some perhaps overlooked by Melantha in her haste, but to me worth a harkening. A lore of souls in their multiple aspects as well as the flesh that once may have housed them, of wills and destinies, l'ange and z'etoile, of voice and psyche — the parts that add up to make each its own being, its essence as it were — and, yet of others that may have been lacking, in some piece or other, or in death dissipated at varying rates just as flesh, too, gives over to putrefaction first its soft, inner parts, then perhaps muscles, while skin, drying, possibly still remains for all time, outlasting even bone.

Thus it came back, always, to not just animus — the outward motion which, sometimes, we think is life — but to that deep within. Or, if not there, its lack.

But, as I say, that was not Melantha, my patroness's concern. Rather, as she wished, I simply helped her choose, leaving for other times my ruminations. My thoughts of these deeper things. Outwardly, rather, I scurried here and there, checking a fact of a scroll with a curator who might have other scrolls. Seeking descendants to verify legends, to confirm or contradict family myths. To augment family histories.

One such I sought out on the tomb-wall itself, during the daytime — he one of the day-watch who, chadored and sun-hatted, flitted from shade to shade, squinting through day's glare for telltale ghoul-lights, for movings in shadows to warn the next night-guard of. So as I say, chadored too, sweating beneath the sun as if, myself, to become some sort of animate mummy, I spoke with this youth of his grandam's grandsire, or of one who was reputed to be such.

And others, too, I sought, learning from one a snippet of story, another a grain of truth. Then, the next day's coursing, beneath our marbled roof, attaching each story to yet another bone.

Until, at last, Melantha was finished — finished at least with that, her first choosing. 'I shall, you see,' she said, 'borrow a man this way. From this, a bone that held rippling muscles, from that a heart to love. From this, broad shoulders — as you can see lying there even without flesh — and from that, firm buttocks. And those, legs and arms to hold, to clamp about me when I would be so clamped. To othertimes walk with me, othertimes dance with me. Othertimes hold me simply for holding's sake. Yet always — well, you see. You understand me, that we must now flesh these bones.'

I shook my head. 'I understand, yes. And yet still you speak just of flesh. Just of an outward form, a statue as it were, that you might sculpt of meat — one you might animate, even, if what one hears of you is true, of your past education, though even then making of fresh corpses zombies is one thing entirely, while making a man out of bones is another.

But still, in your speaking, you have not said one thing about what will be within, that of its soul-parts…'

Sitting, she smiled at me, spreading her thighs slightly. Cutting me off thus: 'It is not a soul I seek.'


It was not. No. Outwardly she sought a perfect man, but, inwardly — what of that?

But, as before, it was not for me to ask. Nodding, instead, again I did that which she beseeched of me. Even if she had not paid me with brass and gold, how could I have done anything otherwise? How, when each morning I smelled her perfumes in our north-wall tomb's closeness, her attars of river-flowers mixed with her own body's sheen? When in the mid-night I saw her beneath the moon, her sweat-plastered silken gown clinging against her limbs, sliding reluctantly, scraping against her flesh as she moved under it.

Her soft skin peeping through.

When she turned toward me, the thin, sheer cloth of her bodice gaped open, yet tight as well, straining against that which swelled beneath — how, then, could I resist? How, if she paid me too — in brass and gold coins?

As I have mentioned.

Thus I served her, also, in this new phase of her plan, that which took me back into the New City while she remained here. As she had asked, I reassembled my erstwhile corpse train, but in a new way now. A more select clientele. I sent my guards out, my pullers and drivers, my brakemen and callers, to first collect rumours of not just the richest, but especially the best beloved — and, thus, the best lovers — of those freshly deceased. In fact, we eschewed wealth if handsome-ness overrode, when we could not have both, that or firm muscles, or fine features, strong buttocks, stiff legs — other parts stiff as well — straight arms or broad shoulders. Parts to drape on bones already chosen. We made our selections, of multiple carcasses, all of them men's of course — which raised some eyebrows, but we ignored such murmurings then as before, for what can one do that does not cause rumours?

And sometimes, indeed, poorness overcame richness among our selections for the simple reason that one can then bargain to better advantage with those that survived this corpse, to take perhaps just part — possibly also to dig up relatives of a particularly promising strain, a mummified heart, perhaps, part of a brain that cooked hard in its skullcase and so as well, was preserved.

That of a poet, perhaps? Melantha already had a skull waiting that would just fit it. The toes of one graceful in pirouetting — or rather their flesh-casings, their skin, nails, and tendons — again the bones waited. Again, to fit perfectly.

At one such expedition's end I returned to Melantha's work-chamber, not simply handing her my sack at tomb's-door but actually laying its contents out for her, and saw how she had progressed. One leg complete, another muscled, but not yet completely skinned — I saw thus, how she built this construct from toe-parts upward, neither neglecting that which lay between these legs — keeping the flesh fresh with oils and embalming fluids even as spring outside ripened to summer. And with other things as well, more than just ointments, but secrets learned, perhaps, if rumours spoke true, from those of the Old City who defied nature. Or else with advanced science: She did not care which she used.

Quietly she showed me, first leading me through her cushioned boudoir — her inner bed-chamber — to that room adjoining how she had fit parts to thighs, selecting only the best I had brought her. How she had built higher, moulding the torso, the bottom-most parts of it, spreading the legs now, now pressing them side-to-side. Pressing her own body, naked, on top of it.

Blushing, she told me: 'It is not just its own bones that this flesh must fit. Thus, like a shoe, or a new silken garment, I must try it on me.'

Then, smiling, she pointed to its still bare ribcage: 'The heart, I think, not too large. Not so large that it might have tendings to wander — but not too small either. The liver, a sound one. The lungs — these should be virile. I want the chest to heave noticeably when it sighs. And, then, the casing, muscled, of course. But not so much that it must exercise always, lest such things turn to flab, and thus neglect my wants.'

I nodded. I understood.

I took the list that she had prepared for me, of parts for the torso, the chest, the back-muscles. The shoulders and arms would be yet another trip, as would the head and brain. The neck supporting these, muscles and tendons, yet not so thick that the head could not turn quickly, surprising one, perhaps, with a sudden kiss. And thus the lips as well — these on that final trip — not too thick, not too thin.

As with those lower parts, she tested these herself. 'These, too, must fit, you see.' She blushing slightly, not so much on her face as underneath, her alabaster skin showing the pinkness as if from some great heat that grew inside her.

And me, her assistant, charmed by just one glance of hers, unable to resist.

And, yet, misgiving.


Thus it was. Thus it will be in legend, as long as the Tombs endure. The unveiling:

She called it her l'amoureux complet — her perfect man.

And another phase began, this one involving my building apparatus from plans she had drawn up. A trough for water, salted as from the air yet purified as well, large enough to immerse her still lifeless assemblage within its depths. Wires and capacitors, condensers, rheostats — great kites to draw wires forth, seeking the lightning. She explained it to me: 'Animal magnetism,' she said. 'It's akin to an electric current, such as makes lights in the New City shine, but we aren't in New City. Thus we seek the lightning.'

I shrugged. It was not for me to know such things, yet she continued on.

'There is a science,' she said, 'called induction. That is, if a current is placed by a bar of iron, by this the bar will become a magnet. So, too, with animals — and so too with a man — that if a current is passed not through, but around one's body, it too will induce a magnetism or, in this case, life itself. Or so the theory says.'

'Then you would be the first to do this?' I asked. I was beyond my bounds, I knew, and yet she had started this conversation. 'To make, as it were, an artificial soul?'

'As you put it, yes,' she answered.

'Yet still not a real soul…'

She laughed when I said this. She could have had me whipped: Such was her wealth and the power that came with wealth. Such was the magnitude of my doubting. But instead she laughed.

'The behavior alone of a "real" soul will do for me. Just that which gives it life, but that part real enough. And, yes, I am the first. The Necromancers of Old City care not for even that much when they, sometimes, deign to animate corpses. In my case, though, I would have at least some part of soul. Its will — its volition. How could it love me if it did not desire. Yet other parts, its z'etoile — its "star of destiny" — what need has it of that? Is it not I who will provide it sufficient purpose?'

Once more the pale curve of her shoulders grown pink with the heat within them, those parts that swelled below, she turned and smiled at me:

'And, as I've said before, it is not its soul I seek…'

Thus it was, as the Moon of Lovers gave way to the sultriness of the Ratcatchers' Moon, that there was a summer storm. Lightning flashed over both the New and Old Cities and over the Tombs as well. And thus, as we cowered within our tunnels beneath the ground, we having made all the preparations by then that we could, we heard a sudden crash!

'That is not thunder,' I said. I cowered back farther.

'No it is not,' she said.

She pressed around me, pushing me behind her. Running, she coursed through our tunnel-quarters, through the sectors where I was allowed to roam, into her private rooms — letting me follow her — through her as yet unslept-in bedchamber, its veils and its cushions, hearing more crashings behind her workroom door.

She flung it open.

And, he smiling uncertainly, standing before her, she smiling back, she made her acquaintance with her 'borrowed' lover.

That first night and day Melantha did no more than lie beside it in her private bedchamber, her flesh pressed against his, but doing no more than that. 'It is too soon,' she said. 'First it must make itself used to being here, living and breathing, its parts all together. To being here with me. Later I shall show it — make it acquainted with those that have helped me, beginning, of course, with you.

'Later, I shall love it.'

Yet there was more than that: She taught it how to walk. Later, how to speak. She brought it naked one night to the surface, to show it as she had said, letting it promenade in the square, its arm stiffly held on hers, beneath the great pyramid of the Tombs' centre.

Later she bought it clothes, teaching it how to dress. Later she taught it how to remove its clothes, and the best ways of taking hers off as well.

Until at last, she took it above again, this at the full of the Moon of Goldsmelters, having it carry cushions and pillows, and, laying them out in the pyramid square, in front of us all she displayed her triumph. She showed us its muscles. Its skin, as white as hers. Its tousled hair, as blond as an Adonis's. Its strong yet graceful legs. Its hands' adeptness as, now, it disrobed itself, helping her undress too, as, god and goddess-like, they fit flesh into flesh, tongue into mouth, arms and legs intertwined.

Thus, with us all looking on, she let it love her.


Melantha was happy now. How could she not be? She had built a man-form of rippling muscles and firm, hard flesh, yet gentle as well in a way most men were not. She had had it love her, respecting her every wish, smiling when she smiled — and even when she did not — speaking with honeyed words. Dancing when she wished it to dance with her at celebrations and, even if, as I maintained, not wholly souled, feeling the music — at least enough to dance.

That is the thing I saw, I who still doubted. I saw a certain mechanical quality still in its motions, as if in some part a machine, not a man at all.

Yet others scoffed at this: 'A making-love machine then, is

that what you say?' one would ask, laughing. 'Isn't that what she wants?'

And then another would answer, 'Of course it is. Is that not what every woman wants really? That and, of course, jewellery.'

'Jewellery she buys herself. That is one problem — this man she has borrowed from parts has no money — but she can afford it.'

'And we give her jewellery too. She has her ways, you know. Still she retains these: The charm of her smile. The laughing of her eyes, all the more now with joy, now that she has that.'

'It is not the same!' I said. But was it truly not. Had I sensed something which others could not detect, not living near her as I did still, sleeping alone but still in that tunnel where she once slept too, albeit separately, on her own sleeping mat, not as she did now in her secret chamber, cloth-lined and soft-pillowed in heated pas-des-deux rivaling the blazing of even the day-sun, as day followed night and others were sleeping? As remnants of perfumes still wafted in tunnel halls.

And yet… I heard her laugh too, of course, distantly. Snug in her chamber, her built-lover with her. And yet it seemed to me less as the months progressed on, as the Goldsmelters' Moon gave way to the Moon of Hungers — not that she had any that now, at least, were not instantly sated — then that of Fulfillment. Then Darkness and Land's Starving, Death Moon and Crow Moon — these the moons of winter — then that of First Budding. Then Wilting and Tempests — the moons of late spring as the year circled around to the new Moon of Lovers.

And yet others still scoffed: 'She laughs less, you say? But she has no time for that. In fact, I hear tell, that behind the chamber where she uses him, she has another room filled with spare parts so that, when she wears one down, she just takes a new one…'

'Yet it is true,' another said, 'that we see her less. And, when we do… well, when is the last time that one of us offered her gifts, or jewellery…'

When indeed, one might ask. That I had not noticed, I

having not gold enough to buy jewellery — and, hence, not to give it — but it is a woman's charm that she may gain such things. That she is so supplied, even without asking, if not with jewellery then showered with flowers and other small presents to set off her beauty, for that is the way of things.

But she did go out, she and her borrowed man, soulless — or stunted-souled — as he might be, for her magic did not give that. Yet, as I say, they walked abroad by nights. Cuddling, as lovers do, yet greeting friends also, friends she had easily made in the past.

But, as I saw now, it was he who made new friends.


So it was as the Lovers' Moon waxed and waned, giving way now to the Moon of Ratcatchers — coming full circle, the year on its journey, the hot day-sun rising yet redder, yet larger perhaps than the year before, but still a sameness — that I warned Melantha.

'He borrows more from you,' I said, 'than his body parts. More than the skill you used in his construction. He takes now for himself what you could not give.'

She shook her head, frowning, she who a single year prior to now would have laughed. She who would have mocked me — and yet, behind her, I saw the shadow of her borrowed lover smile.

Smiling with her smile.

'You have a tic, lady,' I said, 'of your right eye. A squint in your left one, when once they both sparkled. The eyes are said, you know, to be a window — '

'Silence!' She cut me off. Rightly, I should say, for I, a poor man, to speak so to one of wealth, one who could buy him, or pay to have him killed, overstepped much my bounds. For if a man as I should speak at all, it must be only in praise of such women's beauty.


And yet — her eyes...


And yet, thus, I was silent. It was my place, you understand, that I must be silent, that I must not say also that her borrowed lover's eyes glittered as hers once had — a thing she might notice but put it down to his looking at her, you see. That is a natural thing. And, yet, to not notice…

I had my answer then. Women, you see, put cosmetics on by feel, those of Melantha's high station at any rate, for why should they waste time doing it otherwise? From long years' practice they know where such things go. And when they have lovers — well, lovers will praise them, and their ears are tuned to the slightest nuances. A praise of a lip's fullness brings out more red powder. Deftly the brush strokes, thus. Praise an eye's depth and you'll see slender fingers reach into the kohl-pot, knowing by long use just how to apply it.

And praise parts below these — well, praise with your hands, perhaps, not even using words — she will know what you mean. Once again, though she could, not having any need to look to see herself.

So it would have been as well with Melantha — and so I knew what to do.

That night, as soon as the sun had gone down, I sought out a man I knew, one who was an artisan in the Tombs. I asked a favor. I plied him with brass coins, both brass and gold coins, all that I had left of those that Melantha had given me before. These for his labor as well as his goods, you see.

Then, on another night shortly after, when I ascertained that Melantha and her borrowed love would be gone until nearly the morning, I had my friend come with me into her secret room.

Here, as I had thought, we found no mirrors. For why should she need them, she who had her lover? She who had, she thought, a happiness so great she scarcely would miss them.

Who did not know this love had ruined her beauty.

Except that my friend and I tore down her tapestries, lining her room's walls with looking-glass instead, so she would see her eyes. When she entered, her borrowed man slinking behind her as she reached to brighten her chamber's lamp, thus to look back at him, first she would see her self.

See it as I saw it — empty and, yes, marred.

And…

I did not think that far. It is not for such as I to think much, it is not our duty. I, a corpse-train master, am skilled in hauling dead, that is my talent. I am knowledgeable in bargaining, both with the bereft for money enough to start, then with the Tombs-keepers to gain the best site, the best stone, the best vault, the most deeply-dug grave — all for the one I brought, this the deceased who I represented. I know how to listen, to gossip and hear gossip. To spread my own stories when, say, the reputation of one I have brought should require it.

But in knowing women… well, one hears such gossip too, even of wealthy ones, but one still does not know. One knows not what souls will do.

It was one evening, two evenings, three evenings after their return that morning — three daytimes and nighttimes without a sound uttered forth from that room's closed door — before Melantha re-emerged from her room, once again smiling. A mocking, yet sad smile. Her eyes again flashing, but now with a trace of the glimmer of tears as well.

Once again beautiful.

I do not know these things. Beauty, that is, I can see as readily as any other, but what others said, that perhaps her beauty was just a trace more mature now, and hence held more deepness, I cannot say for sure. All that I know is this: When I entered, at her behest, the chamber that she had left, within I found arrayed on her bed's cushions, as if she had lain on them all those three long days, the parts of a dead man. I found the legs, that between, still in their order, the one stiff, the two flat, but spread apart somewhat. Above was the torso, but flattened itself as well, as if she had fallen on it repeatedly. The two arms were scattered wide, as if they had been flung off thus from one last embrace, while the head, its mouth open, lay gaping at the ceiling above it, itself mirrored also — that more we had done, my friend and I, so that whoever lay below could see their lovemaking.

And, from that silent head, both eyes were missing.

But I do not know these things, not the whys of them. Only what waited behind.

Melantha kissed me, as she had once before, one time, on

the cheek. And, as before, she gave me money. And one more thing also — a thing of more value.

'You have served me well,' she said. 'Not as I would have wished, not in its ending, but that is my fault, not yours. You brought me things, faithfully, each time I asked you — and some times when I did not — and for that reason I give you this as your name: You shall be called Carter.'

With that she left the Tombs, while I, with my new name, elected to stay behind. I, my own master. Eventually I became a gate-guard — I, Carter, a haggler, as it were, from the other side when the corpse trains now delivered their cargoes. It is a skill I possessed.

As for the other — the borrowed man — Melantha's l'amoureux complet — we eventually gathered the parts and burned them, uncharacteristically for the Tombs where we practice earth-burial, but what else could one do? There was no soul to require more from us, or, if there were, whose soul? Whose name would it be that we carved on the gravestone? Or all names? Or any name?

What was left of that, we strewed in the river — again not our custom. But again, what else could we do?

There is honour in both these paths also, of water and flame, even if not our way.

While, as for Melantha, as has been already told she returned to the New City, some saying she became a lover of women. Others say that she finally accepted a man, one at least of great wealth, if not of perfection. But all that is known for sure is this: That when the time came at last for her to be placed on the corpse-cart, to make one more journey back into the Tombs, the offerings, the jewels, the coins that came with her were for one grave only.

# Change of Address

## R. B. Harkess

I needed the door frame to stop myself falling down when I saw who had come calling. Luckily I was already holding it so he didn't see. My expression must have let me down though, judging by the self-satisfied grin that crawled over his face.

I say 'his'. Of course, it wasn't his. His features were super-imposed over the face of the poor bastard he had possessed, but it was close enough. 'How did you find me?' I said, trying to keep my voice level and my eyes focused only on the bridge of his nose.

'Aint'tcha more interested in 'why', Sweetie-pie?' Again, the voice wasn't his but the inflections were. The Texan drawl sounded so wrong. The last time I had spoken to him he had been a nasal New Yorker. 'Wha doncha invite me in, Gill, and we can talk.' He ran his hand over a part of the door-frame and snorted. 'The charm is so weak I could-'

'Why don't you piss off?' I replied. My guts churned, and I felt bile in my throat. My voice was too loud and too high. So many things must have gone wrong for him to be standing there.

He frowned, and his eyes became cold and hard. 'There's a diner outside of town, right before the interstate. You have a real good reason to be there before the hour is up, bitch.'

He turned and walked to the stairwell. I waited until he turned out of sight before I closed the door. It took three deep and shuddering breaths before I could trust my legs, and even then my knees felt like jello. I walked across to the other side of the room and twitched the lace curtain aside. He was crossing the street, heading towards what looked like a budget hire car. As he opened the driver's door he turned and looked right at me, and I saw the smile again before the curtain fell back to hide my face. The beat-up Chrysler drove off and I cursed myself for being so obvious.

The clock on the kitchenette wall said twenty minutes past. Past what didn't matter. When he said 'hour is up', that meant when the minute hand hit twelve. Simon Corvid had found me.

There was no time to shower, so I settled for a liberal spray of deodorant and dragged my brush through my hair a few times. Glancing into the mirror, I winced at how thin my face looked, then decided sorting my makeup would have to wait too – I had some basics in my bag and maybe I could fix myself up later. I changed my clothes, swapping my sweats for a baggy tee and a pair of jeans, and fumbled into my boots before grabbing my bag and heading out the door.

I got to the diner at ten minutes to the hour. It had taken three tries to get the key in the ignition, and I had stalled twice before I calmed myself down enough to drive. I parked, switched off the engine and froze. Whatever Corvid wanted wouldn't be good. I rubbed my hands across my face and dragged in a deep breath. My heart wasn't racing, but each beat felt like someone had kicked me in the chest. Eventually I shoved the door open and climbed out.

Corvid sat… No, Corvid *lounged* in a booth at the back of the diner. The rest of the place was empty apart from the waitress. She seemed almost as wide as she was tall and her uniform was spotted with greasy stains that looked like they'd been there a while. A stale smell of fried food hung in the air, and most of the benches had duct-tape scabs. Corvid grinned easily and waved at the two cups on the table in front of him.

'Made it just in time, sweetie-pie. The coffee should still be warm. Take a seat.' I hesitated, still standing in the doorway. His face went flat, the smile vanishing like it had never been there. 'Sit.'

It wasn't an invitation. I walked slowly across to the booth and perched right on the edge of the seat. I'm not sure why I bothered. I wouldn't be able to run. Not from him. 'How?' I said, struggling to keep my voice level and trying not to look into his eyes.

'By asking the right people the right question. And giving them the right incentive. Kind of like the conversation we're having now.'

My eyes met his, hoping that he wasn't asking what I thought. 'Corvid, I don't do that shit any more. That was part of the deal. If I go back on it, they'll nail me to the wall.'

'If they find out. You know I look after my people, sweetie-pie. One way or the other.'

'Not going to happen.'

Corvid's smile got a little wider, and I flinched as he reached inside his jacket. He barked a laugh and shook his head as he threw a seven by five inch manila envelope onto the table. 'Take a look,' he said, then glanced over at the waitress and snapped his fingers for more coffee.

I opened the envelope, pointed it downward, and gently squeezed the sides. Two photographs slid face down onto the table. Something dark and cold made a lump under my breastbone and I couldn't move for a moment. I made myself reach out to flip them over.

On the left was a grainy shot of my mother, taken through a long lens. The other was my kid sister, hanging with a group of wild-looking girls. The shadow of the waitress fell over the table and I flipped the photos over again. She slopped burnt coffee into the mugs and shuffled back to the counter.

'How?' I said again, and even to me my voice sounded flat and beaten.

'The guy in the witness program office was most cooperative.' Having leant forward to drink his coffee, Corvid now slouched back in his seat. 'Well, after we kidnapped his daughter anyway. We offered her back to him after we marketed her around for a couple of months. She was kind of losing her novelty value, anyway. I heard the rehab was working. Sort of.'

I didn't react. It was the way Corvid worked. The threat was implied. My sister was only fourteen.

The deal the authorities had cut for me was that I went away. They would do the same for my mom and my kid sister. They could be on the other side of the country, or two towns over – I would never know. Meanwhile, I stayed where they told me to, moved when they told me to, and they sent me an envelope of cash every two weeks so I never needed to work or have a bank account. So long as Corvid didn't have me, they were happy. This was going to piss them off, whether I co-operated or not.

'So what do you want?'

Corvid looked annoyed. I'd stated the obvious. There was only one thing he needed me for: a new Portal. When I ran away he had three of them, so either he had burned them out trying to take too much through, or someone had got careless and let the hosts die.

'They'll know,' I said. 'They'll come after me.'

'How? You're the only Underkin in this world. If you hadn't lost your nerve and gone running to them they wouldn't have a clue even now. They had no concept of what was going on until you shot your damned mouth off. They still only have the barest idea.'

He had a point. I was a hybrid, a bastard joining of a human girl and an Angel. Not a heavenly angel; an Angel in Underland. It's a place behind ours, beside ours. A poor copy that runs on something we would call magic and has been stealing technology from us for centuries. I should be impossible. Underkin can't bear to touch a human, but somehow one of them managed to rape my mom.

Most people can't even find Underland, and Underkin can't travel here, to the Real. I can live in both worlds, and I can open Portals between them.

'Where? And when?'

Corvid reached into his jacket again and pushed a square piece of card across the table, face down. I reached out to take it, but he kept his index finger on top. 'Tomorrow night. Ten. No later.' He slid out from the booth and walked off. Seconds later I heard the café door slam shut, then a car spitting gravel. I lifted the card.

I already knew the address. It was one of his warehouses just outside Seattle. I raised my cup and finished the cold coffee. I twitched when the cash register drawer clashed open, and turned to look at the waitress. 'Girl-' she started, her voice a slow drawl.

I frowned and snapped 'What?'

'You want my advice, you don't go anywhere near that man. In fact, you run right the other way from anything he wants you to do. You listen to me, now. I got the sight, and he is *bad*.'

I looked at her, paying closer attention this time. She was from the South, or her family were, and age-yellowed eyes stared steadily out from a face that looked like it was made of old leather. Her lips were pressed firmly together and she scowled disapprovingly at me. I reached into my pocket to pay the check, but she shook her head. I nodded, put everything back into the envelope and left the booth. When I got to the door I turned back and, just very slightly, relaxed the walls I kept around my 'abilities'. The woman's eyes went wide and she took a step back as her hands flew up like startled birds to cover her mouth. Looked like she was right about having the sight.

The warehouse unit was just as run down as I remembered. Weeds struggled up along the margins of the concrete road while news-sheets and grocery bags fluttered against the chain-link fence. Fast-food cartons and plastic cups rolled across the empty car park like eco-hostile tumbleweed. Four floodlights cast green-tinged cones of light across the front of the single storey building, three over the big roller door, the other lighting up the smaller door to the right.

I stopped on the road, early by an hour, and tried to decide if I should go in now or drive off and come back later. I didn't want to spend any more time with Corvid than I had to. The small door opened. Corvid stepped out, glared at the car then summoned me with an irritated jerk of his head.

He left the door open. From outside, the glare made the threshold into a well of darkness. I stepped through, feeling as though I was stepping off the edge of a cliff, and waited for my eyes to adjust. On my right was a flight of metal stairs, leading to the offices above. I stepped past them. What Corvid wanted me to do would take way more space than an office. I looked further along the corridor, saw a pale outline at the far end and started walking.

It could have been a workshop, once. Vague outlines on the floor hinted at the ghosts of machinery. Most of the overheads were off, leaving a pool of light along one edge.

It shone on the Frame like a spotlight, and the two people standing either side of it looked like assistants in a trashy magic trick. Corvid stood just outside the light, hiding something in the shadows.

The Frame was just that; a metal square a little over eight feet each side, made out of something dark and sturdy. Manacles were connected to each corner by chains, and the inside edge of each beam looked serrated. On either side stood one of the Dispossessed, one male the other female. 'Choose,' said Corvid, waving a dismissive hand.

They were both naked, and equally unremarkable. The woman was overweight, but short; the man was her morphic opposite. Neither ideal, but both looked eager and expectant, like acolytes waiting to serve. I couldn't get out of my head that they had been people once. Maybe someone's partner or parent. They said that once someone was infected with Morph spawn there was no way back, but I stood there, looking at them, wondering if that was just a convenient truth.

'*Choose.*' There was an edge to his voice. Something angry, but uncertain, as though more was at stake for him here than just making money. Something personal. I looked back at the mismatched pair bracketing the Frame, and my mind stalled.

'Choose, or I'll choose for you.' Corvid moved in the gloom, reached out for something, and another light flickered on. Its cold light was weak and green, as though shining through seawater, but it was enough to show the chair: basic metal frame with moulded plastic seat, and girl strapped to it with duct-tape. She was slumped, unconscious or drugged, and a cloth bag covered her head.

I knew it was Kate, even though I couldn't see her face. I felt my shoulders droop. I should have guessed Corvid wouldn't rely on threats alone, and I knew he would use her to make me do what he needed. I pushed the anger down, denying it for now at least. Anger wouldn't help me. *Clarity* would help me. *Thinking* would help me. I turned back to the Frame and pointed to the woman. 'Her.'

The man's face flickered into a mask of disappointment, but the woman looked exultant as she took up her position inside the Frame, arms already raised above her head and eagerly spreading her legs like she was taking part in some ugly fetish scene. Without being asked, the man loosely fastened the manacles around her wrists and ankles, then took up a position a pace to the left of the Frame. The woman looked straight at me, mouth slightly open, eyes wide with expectation. Her tongue darted sensuously across her lips and I could feel her willing me to take the next step.

I reached out with my mind and woke the Frame.

The woman made no sound as the manacles tightened around her wrists and ankles, nor as the chains began to retract into the Frame's corners, lifting her into the exact centre. The serrated edges rippled and fidgeted, impatient, and I could hear the woman panting. Her companion stepped closer and placed his hand on the nearest upright. He winced briefly when he made contact, then his face flattened back to impassive neutrality.

Starting from the top, barbed needles fired out from the serrations, clockwise around the Frame. Each made a snap like a Christmas cracker, and was so fast it was almost a buzz. They sank, deep but bloodless, into the woman's flesh, dragging dark threads behind them. In the time it took her to emit a single, shuddering moan she looked like she was caught in a web.

Part of me wanted to turn away, but my eyes were locked on those of the woman. They were wide and glistening, and shone with a horrible expectation. I felt a vibration, so low that my chest rumbled and resonated, and so high my teeth ached. A pulse of energy, invisible but for a ripple left in the air, surged down the wires connecting the woman to the Frame and onwards, into her body. She gasped air back into her lungs and began to glow with a light that blurred her outline. The wires sprang taught with a dissonant twang: and then they began to pull.

The woman's body stretched outward towards the edges of the frame. She should have been screaming, and the barbs should have ripped free from her flesh, but instead her eyes were looking elsewhere, somewhere *beyond* the warehouse, and her expression was one of rapture. No sound passed her lips, except for her sharp, ecstatic panting.

The glow faded; the wires stopped moving. The man standing at the side of the Frame had been replaced by a small pile of dust and bone fragments. The woman was now a pale brown canvas stretched across the Frame. Only her head, hands and feet had survived the process, and I could see a small pouch below her head, that pulsed and hinted of viscera.

I sense Corvid standing next to me. 'Your turn,' he said, but I didn't look at him. I couldn't tear my eyes away from the woman's face, wondering what it was she saw.

All this has been the Frame, not me. It does this shit on its own. It's automatic. You put somebody inside, poke it awake, and it works on them. Opening the Portal is my job. My skill. My curse.

'Where do you want it?' I asked, but I already had an idea. The Underland clusters around our own world. Seattle was no different. Just like Corvid in the real world, the Angels in Underland had their own network of places the same as this. 'Kalek Sum's place? The old warehouse?'

Corvid nodded. 'Kalek is most eager to resume our old trading ventures.'

I kept my mouth shut. I pictured the place in my head, exterior first. An old redbrick place that looked like a sweat shop, but with odd, diamond-shaped windows. Overhead a sky the same colour as mustard gas, static and featureless and leeching the color from everything until your eyes got used to it. Heavy wooden doors.

My mind drifted forward, through the doors and across the cobbled courtyard behind. Into the warehouse itself, across the packed-earth floor, through another door and into a store room. It wasn't big, maybe ten paces wide by the same deep, and ten feet tall. The floor, again packed-earth, looked exceptionally smooth and well-trodden.

Keeping the image in my mind, I opened my eyes and looked into the face of the canvas. She still stared into the distance, so I clapped my hands as hard as I could. She glanced at me, but that was enough. I locked her eyes to mine. For the first time I saw something other than ecstasy in them: a tint of fear. I forced the image from my mind to hers, driving it in with the energy and the will to open the conduit between this place and Underland.

Something black smudged the canvas where the woman's belly-button should have been. Her distended skin quivered and her eyes rolled back in their sockets as the smudge spread outwards, forming a ring.

The ring widened, showing a room with a hard packed dirt floor and a door about ten paces away. The black circle almost reached the edge of the canvas, then rippled gently back and forth until it stabilised. The Portal was formed.

'Very nice,' said Corvid, pushing on my shoulder. 'After you.'

It made sense. If I was on the other side with him, I couldn't try to make a break for it – with or without my sister. I took two steps forward and felt the almost forgotten tingle of transfer. I breathed in, tasting and scenting the familiar musk of Underland, stumbling as I adjusted to the different way gravity pulled. Corvid pushed me again and I walked over to the door. He shoved me sideways just before we got there, then gave three solid thumps on the door and drew back a bolt. I heard a similar bolt being drawn on the other side and the door creaked open, outwards into the hallway.

*My* Corvid, the puppet, bowed and, as he stood, a narrow blade appeared through his back. His body stiffened, then started to crumple as the blade was withdrawn. Inhuman hands with leathery blue skin grasped at Corvid as he fell and dragged him away.

The *real* Corvid stepped into the room, dressed in his trademark, unimaginative black. His cloak was thrown dramatically over his right shoulder, and his right hand held the rapier that so recently murdered the puppet he had sent after me.

Next to him stood Kalek Sum: a petty prince of the Angels, virtual ruler of Underland beneath Seattle. He chuckled softly, and laid a friendly hand on Corvid's shoulder.

'My dear man, you really should take better care of your puppets. They can be used more than once, you know, and there are distinct advantages to being able to be in two places at the same time.' The Angel's voice was gritty, and sounded like it was coming from an old AM radio.

Corvid was starting to look more like his masters than the human he once was. Both wore starched shirts and high collars, with waistcoats and long jackets. Tall hats sat on their heads, and spats protected their boots from the mud.

Kalek looked through the Portal. 'Yes, I do believe I remember this particular room, Corvid. When can we expect the others? I'd really like to start the new imports as soon as possible.'

'Others?' I snapped, then bit my tongue for not waiting until I heard what it was they were going to be shipping. Corvid turned to look at me and gave me a grin loaded with pure malice before turning back to Kalek.

'You said *one*,' I snapped. A split second later the bloody tip of his sword was pressed against my throat. I wanted to swallow, but if I had the blade would have sliced into me. I tried to take a step back but he followed me, keeping the blade against my throat.

'You will open as many Portals as the Sum requires, bitch.'

The Angel reached forward and put a hand on Corvid's shoulder, pulling his sword arm back. I prayed his grip didn't slip. 'She can hardly open them with a hole in her throat, Corvid. Perhaps there is something we can do to focus her mind on the task?'

Corvid relaxed and let the tip drop a few inches. Glaring into my eyes, he pulled a kerchief from his pocket and wiped the blade clean. 'Of course, my lord. Perhaps, as a 'good behaviour' bond, you could offer the sister some-' he paused, moistened his lips and a slight grin twisted the corners of his mouth. '- appropriate accommodation?'

Kalek Sum gave out a dry, barking laugh. 'Capital idea. Capital! Bring her through right away.'

*Shit.* I should have known Corvid was playing me for an idiot. Once he had Kate hidden away by Kalek, I would never find her. He would keep moving her from building to building. Corvid poked me gently with the sword then motioned at the Portal. 'Back on the other side, girl. When you are ready, my lord, we'll send the sister through.'

Kalek nodded. I was running out of time and options. Corvid would cream me in a fight, and he had a blade. My magic wouldn't help; it didn't do combat, just managing Portals. I hesitated in front of the threshold back to the Real, and Corvid shoved at the small of my back. I stumbled through, and spun around to curse at him. He was just stepping through, one foot in Underland, the other heading for the floor in the Real. Without wondering if I could actually do it, I grabbed hold of the Portal with my mind and tried to change the location of the other end.

I don't know why I thought of it. I'd never tried it before. Corvid stopped in mid stride, his foot stamping awkwardly to the floor as his balance changed. He looked at me, his eyes widening as his mouth set in a firm line and he started to swing his sword at me. I took a quick step back and the tip swept past, barely an inch from my belly. Muscles rippled along Corvid's jaw and he appeared to lean forward. He was still coming through the Portal, but he was struggling, like he was wading through treacle.

I closed my eyes, took a deep breath, and twisted the Portal even harder. There was a clatter on the ground and a high-pitched keening from above. A sharp pain stabbed the bridge of my nose and my eyes flickered open. Had Corvid got through? Had he hit me with the sword?

The weapon was on the floor, the Portal's face was whining, and something hot and wet was running over my lips. I explored with my tongue and tasted blood. A nosebleed? I never got nosebleeds. I felt the Portal trying to slip back into place and pushed harder. More pain shot through my forehead. I couldn't keep this up forever, but it was stalemate. If I tried to reach the sword, Corvid would grab me.

I pushed everything I had into the Portal. If this didn't work, Corvid would kill my sister and make me watch, then he might even kill me. The pain in my forehead grew, spreading back to fill my whole skull. Corvid started to scream threats at me, but I wasn't listening. Something tore inside my head, and I sank to my knees.

A wave of heat washed over me, and the Portal's face screamed. It was a nerve-scraping noise, loaded with terror and pain. I forced my eyes open. The Portal had moved, but not to anywhere in Underland. The sky was a coruscating, tortured red, and the landscape nothing but barren rocks rippling in a heat haze. What my curse told me made no sense; the Portal wasn't connected to anywhere. It was right here, just not *now*. Somehow, it was looking into the future.

Corvid was shouting at me again, demanding to know what was going on, twisting from side to side as he tried to see behind himself. I had to look twice to be sure, but he was definitely moving. Slowly, he was sinking backward into the Portal, and there was nothing he could do to stop it.

For a moment I thought about reaching out to take his hand, relaxing my mind and pulling him back through to the Real. Something about the other side of the Portal disgusted me, repelled me, and I wasn't sure Corvid deserved whatever was going to happen to him.

'Bitch,' Corvid yelled. 'Get me out of here. I'm going to pull her eyes out and make you eat them. I'm going to cut her to pieces and make you watch.' His hands were twisted into claws and they reached out to me, and I could hear his terror.

I withdrew my half-extended hand and his swearing rose to a scream. Whatever was pulling him through was working faster. Only his hands and arms were in the Real now. His face was a vivid scarlet, and I could no longer hear his cries.

The last of Corvid was pulled through the Portal. The skin of his hands turned red as well. Was he burning, or was it just a trick of the light? Then I saw his clothes smoulder. He seemed to be pulling at something wrapped around his body, something I couldn't see. Then he was dragged away, pulled from the Portal and thrown through the air, receded from me faster and faster until he vanished.

I got to my feet, wobbling like a newborn foal. My head was splitting and the heat blasting through from the other side brought me out in a fierce sweat. There was something wrong about that place. I had no idea how I'd connected to it, but the link had to be broken. I tried to pull my mind from the Portal, to shut it down, but I was dragged back by something that seared me, that somehow let me know it would be coming for me next. I had to get it closed. I stumbled and my foot kicked the sword. It skittered across the floor, towards the Portal.

I picked it up, my free hand raised to my eyes to ward off the heat, almost falling over as I bent forward. The rapier was about three feet long, less than an inch wide. Could I slice the canvas? But the canvas wasn't there anymore; only the threshold to the Portal. The woman's head still screamed, scrambling my thoughts. I stepped as close as I dared, reached up, and drove the sword into the screaming face.

It slid under the chin, up through the roof of the mouth and into the brain. The screaming stopped and the sudden silence made my ears ring. I stepped back, seared by the heat from the Portal, leaving the sword in the head. It waggled twice as the head tried to move, while blood trickled down the blade and dripped over the pommel. It sizzled and stank on the floor..

The woman's eyes looked down at me, and for a split second before they rolled back into her head, I could have sworn the possession was gone. The canvas started to crackle, crisping in the center. A hole formed, spreading outward and burning like paper held over a candle flame. Before it reached the edge, the canvas exploded in a shower of sparks and burning wafers of crisped skin.

I got thrown backwards, landing on my backside and just missed cracking the back of my head on the floor. I thought about getting up, but it seemed an awful lot of effort. I could hear my sister, struggling against the duct-tape holding her to the chair. She howled through her gag, but she sounded pissed, not scared. She could wait. At least it seemed the nosebleed had stopped.

I lay back on the floor. I just needed a couple of minutes to get my head together. I had a lot of explaining to do, and I probably needed to start packing. Time for a change of address.

# Skin

## James Oswald

It's not a journey you take lightly. Not even today with modern cars, two lane roads covered with actual tarmac, satellite navigation. We didn't have any of those things when I was small, or so it seemed to me. Back then it was an adventure all in itself just getting to the lighthouse.

First there was the drive, leaving home in the middle of the night. Pulled sleepy from a warm bed and bundled into a car packed high with suitcases; bags filled with bedding; food enough for a fortnight. I remember the smell more than anything: the mildewed canvas of the tent, stored damp since the last trip; the sharp tang of methylated spirits for the camping stove, leaking from the glass bottle and soaking into the boot carpet; the exotic fruit and powdered sugar of the travel sweets in their round metal tin with its lid so tight my seven year old fingers couldn't hope to open it and steal one of the precious jewels within.

Mum and dad never spoke in the car. I remember that. I can't remember if there was a radio, but if there was it was never turned on. My only memory is of the engine's throb, the roar of the tyres on the road and the endless miles of scenery rushing past just too quickly to really take in. I could never read in the car; that only made me feel sick. So I had to make up stories in my head to keep me entertained. I was good at making up stories, back then.

The only breaks were for picnics. Breakfast, lunch and tea. Maybe we stopped to fill up with petrol, or maybe the car just drove on wishes. I don't remember that, only the miles and the road and the noisy silence, the pirates and princesses of my imagination. We would drive late into the night, and I would drift from sleep to awake and back to sleep again, the dreams and my stories merging so perfectly I would forget who I was.

There was a little guest house, tucked away in the back streets of some coal-black town where the accents were thick and foreign to my young ears. We always arrived late and left early. I slept in a tiny little attic room, surrounded by the unfamiliar aroma of linen and the noises of a different world.

The second day of the journey echoed the first, only the blurred scenery changing as the car inched slowly across the map. First the road would turn from two lanes to one, tiny triangular signs marking the passing places we never needed to use. Tufts of grass poked up through the tarmac in the middle of the road, and then it wasn't tarmac any more but loose gravel, potholes, twists and turns descending with the evening sun to the tiny little harbour.

In older times even than then, the village might have been filled with families. Doughty women waiting for their men folk to come home from the sea, children growing wild and hard like the rocky coastline they played on. I only knew it as a place of old men, their faces as dry as the fish that hung from frames by the shore, lined like the crags and crevices in the cliffs above the pebbly beach.

There was always a pause here, a chance to get some life back into legs turned stiff by two days sitting in the car. Mum would supervise while dad unloaded everything, carried it down the small stone steps to the jetty and loaded it onto the boat. I never thought to ask who the boat belonged to. It was just there. Days are always long up here in the summer, but even so the light would be fading to that soft ethereal gloaming as we finally boarded, mum and dad and I, and puttered out of the harbour, across the sound to the island.

He'd meet us on the jetty at the other end as if somehow he knew we were coming. The lighthouse keeper always had a pipe between his teeth, and a beard in which little birds could happily nest. He had one of those heavy cloth caps so beloved of seamen that pushed his gnarled and wrinkled ears out like confused turn signals. I never saw him go bareheaded outside, but as soon as he stepped in, the hat would come off to reveal a perfectly bald pate, spotted with brown, the skin so shiny I imagined all his hair had simply lost purchase and slipped around to his chin. He greeted my mother like they were old friends, my father with a curt nod. Me, he'd grab into a great big bear hug, the bristles of his beard rough against my skin. I remembered he smelled of rolling tobacco, rum and the sea. But mostly the sea.

'You're so like your mother,' he'd say every time. Even though I didn't believe it was true. His voice was the rumble of water in the caves, deep and booming and salty. Every time I heard it a little shiver went through me. I knew there would be stories of sailors falling off the edge of the world, of sea monsters dragging ships down to the depths, of pirates stealing Spanish gold and burying it on remote islands like this one, just waiting to be discovered.

I guess we spent two weeks there each summer. To me it felt like a lifetime, every time. The island wasn't big; even as a youngster I could walk all the way around it in a couple of hours. But it was my own little kingdom, stuck out at the end of the world. My refuge from the coiled tension between my parents that I never really understood. Not until I was much older. Not until today.

Back then, with just a few scraggly sheep as my subjects, I ruled a world of my own, battled imaginary foes, led heroic rescues into the depths of the dark forests, otherwise known as the half dozen scraggly bushes fighting to survive in a fold in the land that sheltered them from the ever present wind. I ranged from dawn to dusk without supervision, staying well away from the tent pitched on the narrow strip of sheep-mown grass above the dunes and the sandy beach, returning to the lighthouse keeper's cottage for food and stories.

'You'll have heard of the Selkies, no?' It was one of his favourite tales, and I never grew tired of it.

'Proud sea-folk they were. Seal people who could shed their skins and become something like human for a while. Sometimes a fisherman would catch a Selkie woman in his nets. Sometimes she would take on human form and he would bring her home. As long as he had her Selkie skin, the fisherman would have her heart. She might bear him children, rough and wild as the ocean. She might love him, after a fashion. But should she ever get her real skin back, then she would abandon them all, return to the sea and her own kind.'

A pause then, to be sure he had my full and rapt attention. Perhaps he would have puffed on his pipe, taken a slug of rum before continuing.

'But the water folk are much like us, mind. Some would say they once were us, before the flood took them. They have their families and their feuds, their honour and their shame. And so it was that a young Selkie man fell in love with a young Selkie woman, and she in love with him. Their passion was as the storms that dash ships against the rocks and drag sailors to the bottom of the sea. But it was a forbidden love, for their families had been at war since before Saint Columba crossed the sea to drive the snakes from the land of the giants. Before the painted men came out of the pine forests. Before the ice melted and drowned the land the Selkies had ruled in ancient times.'

Now he had me, the seven year old me. I loved his stories no matter how often he told them.

'Like young lovers throughout history, these two didn't care for the foolishness of their fathers. Nothing was more important than that they should be together, and nothing could ever break them apart.

'Except, of course, their families finding out.

'They banished him to the world above, stripped him of his skin and sent him to live a human life. That was harsh punishment for one such as he, but it was nothing compared to what they did to her. They locked her away in the darkest depths, kept hidden even from her own kind, as if her shame was too great to be admitted. Some say she lies there still, and when the sea is calm you can hear her plaintive crying in the echoes of the gulls.'

I always asked the lighthouse keeper what became of them, these poor, tragic lovers. Surely they were reunited in the end, and all lived happily ever after? He would never say; just rumpled my hair with a weathered hand, shooed me out for wasting his time.

Dad spent his days fishing. That was his thing. He'd take the boat that had brought us here, load it with rods, a net, some lunch, then head out around the rocks. I guess he'd been coming to the place long before I was born. Long before he met mum even. He seemed to know where to go to get the best catch. Fish was our supper every night, cooked on an open fire in front of the tent. Smelling of wood smoke, char and burning oil. Tasting of nothing I've ever tasted anywhere else.

Mum spent her days sitting in front of the tent. Or, just occasionally, on a rock that jutted out of the sandy beach above the high tide mark. I would swim every day, playing with the seals in the bay until my toes and fingers turned wrinkly as prunes, but mum never so much as touched the water. My younger self barely gave it a second thought. Grownups did what grownups did. There was no point trying to work out why. My older self saw the sadness in her eyes as she gazed across the water. My older self knew words like depression, even if I didn't really understand what they meant. Not then. Not like now.

Leaving the island was always a wrench. I learned to associate it with going back to school and all the pain that brought. The journey home, to our drab little terrace in the soot-stained red brick city was like having the life slowly sucked out of me. Mum felt it too, I could tell. Despite her wistfulness, there was something about the island that energised her, gave her just enough strength to struggle on for one more year. But as the land grew around us, pushing us further and further from the sea, her shoulders would sag, her skin take on its normal grey pallor. By the time we reached home all the magic of the holiday had leached away, leaving only half-remembered stories and the sound of the sea booming in the caves.

Mum died when I was thirteen. The biggest surprise is that it didn't come as a surprise. I thought dad would be more devastated than he was, but then I thought I would too. We muddled on, though, and it didn't take long at all for the mum-shaped hole to become just another part of the furniture. I guess I was too busy finding out about sex and relationships, getting into all the wrong music and spending what little money I had on ridiculous clothes. Dad didn't like my choice of friends; I didn't even notice that he had none.

I thought perhaps that year we wouldn't go to the island,

but the day came around and I was woken before dawn by a knock at my bedroom door. The car was packed already, dad anxious to get on the road. I went to climb into the back seat, same as I had always done, but he shook his head and nodded to the front.

'You have to be grown up now,' was all he said. Not another word until we reached the little guest house, and even then just enough to explain to the landlady that my mother had died. I thought for a moment I was going to have to share with him, but in the end I was shown up to the little attic room again.

On the island, the lighthouse keeper greeted me with his usual rough embrace, gave my father even less of a nod than usual then looked to the little boat, empty save for our luggage. Back to me, the words echoing from years past. He opened his mouth to speak, then closed it again. I could see a light in his eyes go out, his shoulders slump a little as he turned and silently headed back into the cottage.

That was the year the magic left the place. Maybe it was never really there, just the product of a child's imagination. I tried to treat it like I had before, but my childish delight at the solitude was soon swept away by the swirling mess of adolescence. It didn't help that the lighthouse keeper hid himself away; no more stories of sea captains, pirates and Selkies. Dad just did his own thing, although he seemed to have an intensity about him more focused than normal. The fish he caught tasted dull. Like old cardboard left to bloat in the sea.

I slept late, curled in my sleeping bag and listening to the shrieking of gulls, the quiet contemplative munching of sheep, the endless wash of waves on the shore. I wandered the cliff tops, increasingly bored, bitter and angry until one day I found myself at the rock where my mother had maintained her silent vigil the year before, and the year before that, and ever further to a time I couldn't remember. A time I'd never known. I was about to climb onto it, nothing better to do, but a hand on my shoulder stopped me.

'That's not a place for you, lassie. Not yet.'

I turned, looked into the sad eyes of the lighthouse keeper, shrugged in that arrogant, ungrateful way all teenagers have, and flounced off back to my tent.

We left the island the next morning. We'd only been there a week. It was to be the last time I'd see it.

Pete was the first one, but by no means the last. I thought I loved him, and he swore he loved me. Boys lie though. They'll do anything, say anything to get what they want. And once they've got it? Well, that's any respect you might have had gone. Not that I had much, not from others, not from myself. I was the odd kid, easy to pick on. Then I was the rebellious teenager doing everything I was told not to. Looking back it's sad, really. I thought I was being different, but really I was just following the herd.

So yes, Pete fucked me. Took away that special thing we're all supposed to cherish. I don't remember anything pleasurable about the experience, just pain fugged by the cheap cider I'd been drinking. Then the next thing I knew I was throwing up in a bin at the bus stop. So much for romance.

It didn't get much better after that. Dad never had much control over me anyway, and he changed after mum died. He didn't go to pieces; there was no rending of hair, no dressing in black. But he stopped caring. About himself, about the house. He stopped washing the car; that weekend ritual that had been such a regular part of life. The way I saw it, he stopped caring about me, too, although every so often I'd catch him looking at me with an odd, unreadable look in his eyes. I'd remember the lighthouse keeper then, his familiar litany - 'You're so like your mother.' It made me shiver every time.

That might be why I dyed my hair, wore the make-up, had the piercings and the tatts. Anything to stop me looking like her, to stop him looking at me that way. It didn't work. Nothing could erase her stain. In time I came to resent her for leaving us the way she had, for making me in her image, for everything that ever went wrong in my life. There were plenty of reasons to hate her.

Dad only tried it on once. I was twenty-one. Back for a few days from college. God only knows how I managed to make it through the education system that far, the way I played up.

But I struggled through the exams, took on the debt, threw myself into the life of a student. Living away from the little terrace house was a freedom I'd not felt since those childhood days on the island.

And then I came home.

Looking back, it was probably the beginning of the dementia. He wasn't drunk; dad hardly ever drank at all. He talked more than I ever remembered, asked me about my course, my friends. When I said I was turning in for the night, he hugged me maybe a little too tight. Kissed me maybe a little too affectionately for a father kissing his grown-up daughter.

Then he came to my room at midnight. I could see from the glow of the streetlights outside that he wasn't wearing any clothes. He spoke soft words, quiet so that I couldn't make out their meaning. Or maybe they were in a language I didn't know. I was paralysed, couldn't understand what was happening, couldn't believe what was happening as he climbed into my bed, on top of me. Hard and wrong and somewhere else entirely in his head.

Perhaps something held him back in the end, some small vestige of sense. Perhaps I just got my shit together enough to throw him off, scramble out from under the covers. I'd barely unpacked, so it didn't take long to get everything together and leave. My last memory of my father alive was his puzzled face looking up from my bed, his voice pleading with words I didn't recognise.

I never spoke to him again.

Life shits on you if you give it a chance, and I've given it plenty. Dad died a week ago, ten years after what I could only ever bring myself to call the incident. He wandered out into the path of a bus early one morning, dressed in his pyjamas. According to the police report, the neighbours said he'd become increasingly erratic in his behaviour. It wasn't spoken out loud, but the implication was clear that someone ought to have been keeping an eye on him. Someone ought to have been looking after him as his mind slowly dissolved away.

Someone.

Me.

I've not exactly made a good use of my life, can't really say

I wouldn't have been better off staying at home, becoming a carer. But if that was the case, I'd probably have smothered dad with a pillow years ago, and made this difficult journey not long after.

And it has been difficult, almost impossible. I don't think I ever knew the name of the island, or the little harbour on the mainland where we took the boat. I only knew that it was the end of the world, as far from home as you could get. And somewhere in my memory the knowledge that home was the furthest point you could go from the sea without coming closer the other way. Strange how I'd never really thought of that until faced with the lifeless, empty rooms, the council letter giving notice to clear the property crumpled in my hand. There was a rented flat in another town a life away, a dead-end job that sucked the soul out of me. I could have gone back there, picked up where I'd left off. I might have lasted another year, might have lasted another ten. But right then all I could think of was the island, the lighthouse and the cold, final embrace of the sea.

Dredging my childhood memories, I recall the bleak industrial town where we used to stop for the night, mum and dad and me. I know where it is now, and that gives me direction. I don't stay there; couldn't have found the guest house if I'd had a week to search for it. A couple of chemical friends to keep me going, I just drive on through the night, oncoming headlights like sparkly jewels in my fractured sight. North and west towards the sea. Towards the end.

Perhaps it's some kind of homing instinct. Or maybe I paid more attention to those long childhood journeys than I realised. Whatever the reason, as I cover the miles far more swiftly than my dad ever did, I start to recognise the road, the hills, the passing place signs and the little tufts of grass forcing their way up through the tarmac. Soon, far too soon surely, I am steering the car past deserted, ruined cottages, down to the tiny harbour and its old stone jetty.

There's no-one about. It doesn't look like anyone has been here in a lifetime. Just the boat tied up, waiting for me. For a moment I worry that I might have to row across the sound, but the engine splutters into life at the turn of the rusty key. I feel no guilt in taking it; this was just as it was meant to be.

The sun is low across the water as I round the point and see the lighthouse. From afar, nothing has changed, but closer in the cottage looks as ruined and dilapidated as those in the village I've just left. There's no sign of the lighthouse keeper, no doubt he died an age ago. The lighthouse itself still stands proud, freshly painted in gleaming white that reflects the orange and red of the setting sun. Empty, all automated now, controlled from some distant office, far from the threat of storms, of being dashed on the rocks and dragged down under the waves.

There's no one to meet me at the jetty, so I run the boat up onto the beach. As I kill the engine, the familiar sounds envelop me, familiar smells transport me back to a different, easier time. I feel myself calming as the cares of a life badly lived fall away one by one. My decision was made a long time ago, but bounded by the land there was always the chance I might change my mind. Here with the gloaming sky stretched over me like a blanket, the gentle rush of waves on sand, the screaming gulls and soft, contented munching of sheep, I know that I can go through with this, that it is the right thing to do.

But first I will revisit old haunts.

The sun casts shadows far longer than the gnarled and twisted trees of the enchanted forest are tall. They 've not grown since last I was here, but I have, and now the playground of my childhood is little more than a wide thicket of shrubs. Nothing to rescue here save the carcass of a sheep, its curling horn caught in the branches. I imagine its struggle, trapped there for days, the initial panic slowly ebbing away to a dull resignation. Hunger and thirst would have weakened it until it finally slipped into sleep and then on down and down. I envy it that last release.

Time has shortened the towering cliffs, narrowed the caves where I once played. The whole world has shrunk, and this island more than most. It's true what they say; you can never go back. I had thought to delay the inevitable until the sun had fully set, but its orange eye hasn't yet dropped beneath the distant horizon as my feet find their way across the rocky outcrops and crunch onto the sandy beach. Above me, the lighthouse keeps its dark vigil, the cottage beside it empty and dead. And there in front of me, the place I knew I would come at the end. The rock where my mother used to sit and stare out to sea.

I know its shape like I know the shape of my hands, but something is different about it now. A few dozen paces on from it, the boat sits high on the sand, beached by the outgoing tide. I'm sure I glanced at the rock when I arrived, saw nothing unusual in the scenery except the emptiness of the lighthouse keeper's cottage. And yet now there is something draped upon the stone. A cape of some kind, grey and shiny in the dying light. It wasn't there before, I am sure. Someone, or something, has put it there while I walked around the island. I reach out, pick it up, marvelling at how light it feels, like it is just the memory of something, not the thing itself. Running the soft material through my fingers, I remember the stories the lighthouse keeper told. I can still hear his gruff voice, feel the cadence of the words.

Without realising it, I find I've climbed onto the rock, draped the cape around my shoulders for warmth against the lazy wind. It feels right in a way I've not felt for far too long. I haven't thought about mum in many a year now. Not properly. For perhaps the first time ever I realise that we didn't come to the island every year for dad, but for her. She needed this place, needed the sea even though she could never return to it.

'You're ready, little princess. You can go home.' The lighthouse keeper's voice is in my head. I know he's not there. Know he was never really there. It doesn't matter anymore.

The sun has gone now, stars fighting to make themselves seen in a sky fiery with the snaking aurora. The sea is calm, a mirror on another world. One where my life hasn't been a spiral of bad decisions and worse luck. One where I rule over all I survey. The sheep and the gulls, the cliffs and the caves, the enchanted forest of stunted, gnarly trees. All around the bay, seal heads poke from the surface, moon-eyes twinkling as they stare at me. Are these my people? Better than any I've met on land.

It's an easy jump down from the stone. I kick off my boots, strip off my socks and feel the sand between my toes. One last glance at the lighthouse, dark and lifeless. One last memory of the world of men.

I pull my mother's skin tight around my shoulders and walk slowly into the water.

# The Ending Plague

## Andrew Reid

The best thing about being an outcast was that you never fell behind on the gossip. Three years ago, they had driven Janna out of the village, and yet since then she hadn't seen a single day of peace from them. For one thing, they missed her herb-lore. Her mother had passed it on to her and then passed on herself, long before she could explain the reasons why it was important to keep the knowledge a secret. Some things just could not be abided, no matter how useful they were to ordinary life. The wandering priests called that an abomination, and there was no room in Heaven for error. Still, when the mob had gathered to cast her out, they were careful not to be too rough about it. She'd even found her things neatly packed and waiting for her at the old shack in the forest. The roof was thatched new as well, as though laid in apology for all the rotten vegetables they'd thrown at her.

It was Valle that kept her from leaving them. They'd taken him from her at first, putting an iron chain round his neck and pulling it tight enough to make him wheeze in terror. He'd never worn a chain in his life, and when they dragged him away, every slobbering, friendly inch of him shaking with fear, she went cold to their nonsense.

The next morning, Valle was scratching at her doorstep, a sheepish-looking blacksmith in tow. They'd had to do it, he said, for the sake of appearances, and dropped a bag of butcher's scraps onto the ground. Valle forgave him, jumping in circles and nuzzling the man's hands, and in that instant Janna did as well.

There weren't many days after that that didn't see at least one villager at her door, offering something to trade in exchange for help with their problems. The gossip came as a perk, nervous voices talking to fill the silence as Janna did her work. The days that they didn't come were gifts, time that she could use to wander the forest with Valle, always looking for plants and fungi to fill up stocks that always seemed far thinner than they should be. Her mother had never been hit in the head with half a rotten cabbage, but then she hadn't seen one tenth of the business - or payment - that Janna did.

It was only when three days passed with no callers that Janna grew suspicious. Two had been a blessing, giving her a whole day to spend sitting on a chair in the sunshine, whittling a stick down to nothing and tormenting Valle with the shavings.

On the third, though, she found herself sitting watching the door, waiting for someone to knock. It felt stupid to do it, to sit idle when she could be doing something else with her time, and yet Janna couldn't find the will to get up and go out. *Someone has to be coming*, she thought. *If I leave now, I'll miss them.* Valle lay at her feet, held in place by the weight of her mood. She could see him working his back legs, desperate to go and piss. He caught her looking, and lowered his head as if scolded. He looked miserable.

Janna got out of her chair, and he was up in an instant, once round the chair and back, bumping her in the thigh as he bounded over to scratch at the inside of the door. She reached for her cloak and, after a moment's hesitation, her gathering basket.

'We'll take the path towards the village,' she said. Valle huffed in reply and pawed the door again. 'No-one will miss us if we go that way.'

It was a bright spring day outside. The sunlight dappled on the forest floor, lifting the last of the morning's mist. For all its beauty, there was something in the air that made her nerves sing on edge. Valle felt it too, and after finishing his business on the walls of the shack - she forgave him that, just this once - he stayed so close to her that she thought he might knock her over as they walked. There was no birdsong, and nothing moved in the undergrowth. Save for Valle and herself, the forest was silent.

They were almost halfway to the village before they found the body. Valle spotted it first, of course, and Janna felt his hackles rising against her fingertips as he halted. She had never seen him so nervous, and his fear was infectious. She felt the tremor in her fingers spill up the length of her arm, spreading cold through her chest as she saw the body lying face-down in the brush ahead.

Janna looked around, but there was no-one else to be seen. Silence and stillness surrounded them. Valle growled again, but it had a different pitch to it. He knew that she had seen the body, and he wanted to know what to do. *I wish I knew*, Janna thought. She stroked his back to try and calm him, and brought her other hand round to touch his face.

'Shhh, Valle. Shhh.' A touch made him sit, and she looked into his eyes. 'Stay here,' she said. 'Stay.'

Janna crept forward, and then felt stupid for doing it, as though she expected the corpse to jump up and run at her. She almost straightened, but thought better of it in the end. She'd learned that the hard way after her mother passed. You went carefully, or not at all.

Closer, and she could see that it was Karel from the village. Karel was a stonemason, but aside from the odd millstone he tended to do more woodwork than anything else. Even face-down, Janna could tell it was him. He was the right size and build, and there was the bald patch on the top of his head that always got burnt crimson by the sun because he was too vain to accept its existence and wear a hat. All that, and she could see his left hand. He'd taken the tip of his middle finger off with a chisel. It wasn't an uncommon accident, but he'd managed to chip the bone so badly that Janna was forced to take it off at the knuckle, leaving him with a stump.

There was nothing she could do to help him now, though. What skin she could see was moon-white and swollen, like something you'd find on turning over a half-rotten log. Janna shuffled closer, crouching now, and as she ducked to look at his face she could see something black had crusted around his mouth and nose. His fingertips - the ones he still had - were blue at the nails. Janna sat back for a moment, confused, and it took her a long moment to work out what was bothering her.

There were no flies. The body was untouched. Carrion

didn't last for long in the wild, and yet nothing had come to feed off of him.

Valle huffed next to Janna's shoulder, and she jumped in fright.

'Don't do that!' He moved forward, lowering his head to sniff at Karel's body, and Janna put her hand out to keep him back. 'No. Don't sniff.' She was certain he wouldn't touch the body, but she was loathe to even let him get close. She put her hand on his muzzle, their signal for quiet, and stood listening to the stillness of the forest for a long minute. 'We need to go into the village,' she said.

Janna stepped round Karel's body and started down the path, but stopped when she realised that Valle hadn't followed. He was standing on the far side of Karel, and when she clicked her fingers, calling him to heel, he just lowered his head, looking down at the man. Janna sighed. The last thing she wanted was to walk back to the shack for a shovel, but Valle had pricked her conscience.

'Fine,' she said. 'We'll bury him, and then go to the village.'

She buried Karel just off the path, digging a shallow pit alongside where he lay and levering him into it. In the end it felt worse than just leaving him, but Janna trusted her instincts. Whatever had killed him was still there in his flesh. The carrion-eaters could sense it, even if she couldn't, and although Karel deserved a proper grave she didn't fancy joining him in it. A dead man's dignity wasn't worth the risk.

With every step she took towards the village, the more Janna wanted to turn back. And yet, as afraid as she was, she couldn't bring herself to do it. She reached the forest's edge and found the fields beyond untended. Along the road, more bodies; mostly men from the village. Jon. Burchard. Andreas. All young, fit men. All of them fallen on the road to her shack. They were coming to find me, she thought. Burchard lay at the end of a long trail, drag marks mixed with coughed-up blood. He had stumbled and fallen a fair distance from the tree-line and dragged himself the rest of the way. He'd always been a stubborn bastard. Sheer will had carried him further than flesh alone could manage. It hadn't been enough. Valle trembled at every corpse they passed, and with each stop it took longer to coax back into motion. Janna understood his reluctance. Nothing good lay ahead.

The village was deserted. No-one came out to greet her, or even to throw vegetables. No smoke rose from the chimneys. The buildings seemed to huddle together in silence, a pool of forbidding stillness that made Janna's steps falter. It was like coming to a clearing in the forest and finding a bear-trap set in the undergrowth. It was Valle's turn to urge her on, and he nudged at her hand. She stroked his head, glad of the company, and continued on.

Janna knocked at the first house she came to. With no answer, she tried the latch, which lifted easily. The door swung open, presenting a darkened room and air that felt hot and tight, like a wall against her face. 'Sit, Valle. Stay.' She pressed his back as she said it, reinforcing the command, and went inside.

She didn't need more light to see what had happened. The whole family - a woman and her husband, two girls no older than five apiece - all curled together in bed. The girls had died first, but the parents had been too sick to move them. They'd held onto their bodies and died in their turn, each with a cloth pressed to their mouths to keep from coughing onto the girls. Janna got closer, and recognised the woman. Adelina. She'd had a baby not three months before, and Janna had delivered it. Their third girl, much to the father's disappointment. They'd called her Ulla. Janna didn't want to look for it, but could well imagine the tiny grave somewhere nearby, scraped in the dirt with what faltering strength they'd had.

The next house was the same. And the next one, and the one after that. Every man, woman, and child in the village dead, laid up as though ill with a fever, black froth in their laps and around their mouths. Valle was panting now, tired and thirsty from the walk, and Janna made him lap water from her hands, poured from the leather skin she carried. It was fresh from the stream behind the forest, and the only water she trusted. It looked like an illness, but death had come too quickly to too many for it to be anything other than poison. A disease would have taken time to spread, moving from family to family; she would have been able to see it coming from the people staggering to her door in search of help. A girl Ulla's size wouldn't have survived it, but the rest of her family could have been isolated. This plague was something that had been delivered on the village.

There was a well in the middle of the village, a brick-lined pit that almost everyone drew their water from. If they had been poisoned, it was the most likely place to do it. Still, there was no reason not to be thorough. In every house, she sniffed carefully at what food there was, hoping to catch some touch of bitterness that would reveal the poison's source. There was nothing. She braved one tiny scrap that smelled suspicious, rubbing it against her arm and waiting for the patch of skin to blossom red, but there was no reaction. It had to be the water.

She expected the well to smell rank, for the dregs in the over-sized bucket to be oily and grim. Instead, it looked as it always did. The air was fresh, even when she leaned over the edge and stuck her head right in. She drew up a bucketful and poured it back, expecting the taint to reveal itself, but the water fell clear and cool back into the darkness. Hands on hips, Janna turned and looked round the village square, trying to see what she had missed. Valle was standing six feet from her, stock still, his hackles raised. He was facing the tavern.

'What is it, Valle?' The question came out a whisper, even though she'd been certain no-one in the village had survived. She hadn't seen anyone, save for the dead.

The tavern was a squat little building made of two mis-matched halves; a house that had been converted and extended into its current condition by an owner less con-cerned with how it looked so much as how much money he had left at the end of it. Janna had never been inside, but she was familiar with its trade. At the end of every harvest season, she found herself boiling her tweezers over and over as she pulled splinters from the fists, knees, and sometimes heads of the farm workers. She used to cluck at their injuries in disapproval, but the brawling was like a game to them, a way of measuring themselves against each other. They were all a thick-headed bunch, and permanent harm was rare. She made her way across the square towards it, half-crouched, taking each step slowly as though trying not to spook a deer. Valle whined at her ankles as she passed, and she shushed him with a wave. By the time she got to the door, her knees were starting to creak with the effort and for a moment all she could hear was the pounding of her own heart in her chest. Once it cleared, she could make out the sound of voices within. They were too quiet to hear distinctly, but she could hear they were male. To hear them properly, she was going to have to go inside. She lifted the latch as slowly as she could manage, felt the resistance give as it came free of the frame, and with a silent prayer to whatever God thieves worshipped, she pushed the door open.

It got halfway before it creaked. Janna froze, the voices inside fell ominously silent, and Valle barked, as if to say *I knew this was a bad idea*. Inside, a bench scraped along the floor, kicked back as someone stood. Janna didn't wait to see if they were coming to hold the door for her.

'Come on, Valle,' she said, and scrambled round the side of the building, down a tight, windowless alley that opened onto a yard at the back. It wouldn't take them long to work out where she had gone, but past the yard she could be into the tangle of houses and away, headed for the forest's edge. Once she did that, there would be no finding her.

As she came out into the yard, a man's voice called out the chase. He had come through the back door, too clever to run straight for the source of the noise. Janna caught sight of him as she sprinted across the yard, Valle ducking past her legs. He was a priest, dressed in the same shapeless grey robes and chunky iron chain that they all wore. Somewhere on the end of the chain would be a censer, reeking of agarwood and cloves; at the other, an iron-bound book of prayers. She ran past a long cart, half-laden with barrels and noted the black patches of ground where they had dripped onto the grass. Janna clapped to get Valle's attention, picked a side street, and barrelled down it with the sound of the priest's voice ringing in her ears.

Two streets later, Janna was bent almost double in pain.

For all the walking she did, she had never really needed to run before, and the sudden burst of speed had given her a stitch. Her right hand side was tight with pain; she could barely walk, let alone run. Valle barked at her and danced round her feet, urgent with worry, and she shooed him on as she staggered to the next corner. As he disappeared ahead, heavy footsteps thundered up behind her and a hand caught her by the shoulder.

'Where'd you come from, eh?' The hand tugged, pulling her round with a wince. Its owner was a tall, broad-faced man with a shapeless red lump of a nose. He looked down at her in bewilderment, as though he'd pulled her out of a bag. 'Priest said we'd got them all.'

Janna shoved at his face with her free hand, clawing at his eyes. He cried out and started back more out of shock than anything else, and she ignored the pain in her side a moment to straighten up and kick him square between the legs. The man's knees went out from under him, and Janna turned, shuffling away to keep out of his reach. As she reached the corner there was a flurry of movement, and she got her arm up just in time for the priest's censer to shatter against it. The orb exploded on contact, thin ceramic made fragile by years of burning incense, and Janna screamed into a cloud of thick-scented ash as she fell away from the impact. The priest came forward, chain in his hands, reversing it so that he brought the prayer book to bear. Standing over her, silhouetted by the sky, the priest loomed like the Giant of the Sky, the oldest God of all, the great weight of his Meteor swinging heavy from one fist. He lifted his arm, letting the chain slip through his hand and catching the book, swinging it high over his head, ready to bring it down and cave her skull in.

His inexperience saved her. He stood awkwardly, legs spread wide, and before he could finish his swing Janna kicked one of his feet out from under him. His surprised cry was like a crow's squawk, and he fell badly, pulled sideways by his own momentum. The step he took to try and correct his fall only took him closer to the wall, and he hit it head-first with a dull thud. Janna scrambled out of the way as he slid, unconscious, to the ground.

Her stitch had spread, and it made her sag over to one side. Her right arm felt numb and on fire at the same time. Janna put her good hand down and started the long climb back to her feet. A shadow fell across her.

'The fuck you think you're going?' The broad-faced man was standing again, close enough to block out the sky. Janna blinked up at him. She couldn't make out his face, but she could guess his expression. In his right hand, he held a knife, its blade keen and bright even in the shade. He leaned forward, then spasmed, throwing his hands up as Valle sank his teeth into the back of the man's knee.

Valle gave the man's leg a vicious shake, turning him, then crouched low. The dog's shoulders bunched massively for a moment, trembling with power, and he sprang for the man's throat. The man let out an odd, warbling cry, high with fear, and fell heavily against the wall. His injured leg folded underneath him, and Valle surged over his belly, aiming for his throat. The man got a hand in the way, which Valle bit and dragged at, making his scream even higher. As Valle let go and readied himself for another pounce, the man regained his senses enough to bring his knife to bear. Janna yelped, fear and surprise turning her order into nothing more than a wordless bark, and Valle sprang. The knife sank into his chest and he howled, shaking all over with sudden violence, his attack forgotten. He slumped down onto the man's chest, the breath shuddering out of him as his eyes closed. The man, his breath ragged, let out a sigh that matched it.

Janna was on her feet in an instant. All pain forgotten, she stood tall as she lifted her boot and brought the heel down as hard as she could, straight onto the shapeless lump of his nose. She kicked him again, and again, and again, fury boiling through her, refusing to dissipate. Eventually, panting from the effort, blood everywhere, she left him alone and went to Valle.

Her dog was alive, but just barely. She could feel his heart beating, how weak it was even though it seemed to echo through every part of him. His eyes were closed, but he turned his head to her, the fraction of an inch that he could manage. 'I've got you,' she whispered. 'I've got you.' Janna's arms closed around him. Her fingers tightened in his fur, and she tried to wish his wound away. The villagers were gone, and she could cope with that, but she needed him. He was all that she had. He was her world; he was everything. She felt him take one, long breath, felt him tremble with the effort of it, and then he was gone. She put her face into his fur and wept.

Night had fallen by the time the priest woke up. He'd been too heavy to carry, so Janna had dragged him back to the tavern where she had lit the lamps and stoked the fire, filling the room with a warm, welcoming glow. She had found his pack, and used one of his spare robes to make a pillow for him. He had a nasty gash on the back of his head where the prayer book had hit him, but by the time she had heaved him onto a table and got a good look at it, it was crusted over with a mat of blood and hair. There was enough rope in the yard to tie him down securely, the rope going about his ankles, waist, and chest. She tied his hands for good measure, and put a loop round his neck. If he struggled, he would risk choking himself. As she waited for him to wake, she let drops of water fall onto his dry lips, and passed a wet cloth over his brow. She could imagine how bad his headache would be, and she wanted him as clear-headed as she could get. There were questions that needed to be answered.

His eyes opened, and held her gaze as he made a quick assessment of his situation. Out of the side of her eye, Janna could see him shuffling against his bonds, testing them for weakness. She wondered if he would try to get hold of the knife under his robes, the one she'd removed some time before. She thought about telling him, but decided to leave it as a surprise.

'Let me go,' he said. He sounded like a priest. They had an odd way of speaking, as though every word they gave you was a gift you should be thankful for. Janna couldn't say for sure, but it felt as though there was a touch of desperation in the command.

'Why should I?'

'My order sent me here. If I don't go back - unharmed - they'll come looking for me.'

'They'll come looking for you? Not for the dozen barrels you brought with you?' The priest went very quiet. It was hard to tell in the firelight, but he seemed paler.

'I don't know what you're talking about.'

'There wasn't much left in them when I looked,' Janna said. 'Barely a cupful.' She held the cup out. It was a beautiful piece, a boar hunt carved in low relief round the side of it. The artist had probably never seen a hunt, but he'd had a good imagination. Most likely he was dead now. The boar's tusks curled impressively against her fingertips as she set it delicately next to the priest's head. He cringed away from it. 'So be careful, priest. I'm not someone you can lie to. Why did you come here?'

When the priest spoke, it was with surprising conviction. 'We carry the Light's deliverance. All the sinners of the world must be punished - purged - so that the chosen can start a new age. An age of purity. An age of worth.'

'Purged.'

'The Fathers had a vision. A vision of a plague that would sweep the unwanted aside.'

'And they couldn't wait for it to appear?'

'This way is quicker. We are sparing these people the pain that waits for them. That waits for you.'

Janna bristled at his words, but held her rage in check. 'And what about the chosen? Who are they?'

'The Fathers gathered them. All of the brotherhood has come together. The cloisters at Hallyard have never been so busy.'

'A golden age of murderous priests.'

'There are others among the chosen,' he said. 'Men, women, children. Whole families, even. We will guide them. We will show them a world without sin. A world that is pure.'

'A world stuffed with corpses.'

'I could speak for a thousand years and you would never understand.' He made a show, tied as he was, of looking her up and down, his face twisted in disgust. 'Impure.'

'Oh, I understand you,' Janna said. She thought about

Valle, laid out dead on top of the man he'd defended her from. Of Adelina and Ulla, a mother who would never see her child grow up. Of Burchard, stubborn to the last, dragging himself through the dirt. Of Karel, who'd tried his hardest to reach her, to save the people he loved. That they had all sinned at some point, she was sure, but not one of them had deserved to die for it. Janna swallowed, and looked at the priest with shining eyes. Hallyard was three days on horseback, but the road looped north to get round the forest. Janna had a map in her shack. If she started back now, she could set off in the morning and forage as she went. The Fathers weren't the only ones who knew how to bring down a plague. Janna lifted the cup to the priest's mouth and took hold of his nose. 'Only the chosen live, right?' He struggled, and Janna stepped on the rope to hold him still. She tipped the cup, and the thick liquid swilled into his mouth. 'Well I didn't choose you.'

# The End of the Garden

## Catherine Hill

### 10 Sleeps before the End

Jenny cried when the books disappeared. She was the only one who could read. She had tried to teach the skill to those of us with paws the right size to hold the books, but we were slow and difficult pupils. We all loved the times when we gathered on the grass around Jenny, as she sat in her red armchair and read to us. She read stories of lands beyond and other brave girls who explored them. Dorothy, Alice, Dora, we marvelled at their exploits, but each of us knew deep down that they could not be as wonderful as our Jenny.

The books lived on flat branches in a small copse of trees. When Tig the Tomcat first came upon the empty branches of the book trees he thought the books were hiding. Tig bounded over to the curvy bridge where Jenny, Mr Foon and I were watching the bright-coloured fish swimming busily back and forth.

'Jenny, Jenny, did you know that the books are hiding? I went to their trees and none of them are there.' The words tumbled eagerly from Tig's mouth. He seemed concerned, but knowing him he was also keen to be the first one to tell Jenny what had happened. Tig was rarely happier than when he was the first to know about something.

Tig led Jenny to the book trees, and I trailed behind. Jenny's face fell when she saw the empty branches, so Tig and I offered to go on a book hunt. I'm not quick at walking, but as I searched I asked everyone I saw to help. No one refused when they realised it was for Jenny, and soon almost everyone had joined in with the book hunt. The birds circled the whole Garden, and flew from tree to tree, except for Henny who couldn't fly very well. The three mice searched in all the nooks and crannies and small holes in the ground. The five rabbits searched in the bigger holes and Carmen the otter swam the stream looking for the missing books. I stuck my nose in every flowerpot and snuffled through the long grass under the slide. I even went back to my square house and checked in my three little cupboards, in case the books had snuck inside after I left. Jenny was the only one allowed on her armchair, so she searched there, pushing her arms down the sides as far as they would go. She found three buttons, an acorn, a red and blue stripy sock and a black box covered with coloured buttons that she told us was called a remote. Tig and Ferdi the fox both wanted to play with the remote, but they were too rough tugging it between them and broke it. Normally Jenny would tell them off, but she just sighed and said, 'It doesn't work here anyway.'

When everyone had finished searching we gathered around Jenny's armchair. We were tired, most of us were muddy, dirty or dusty, and no one had found any books. Jenny sat and thought for a few minutes.

'I know,' she said. 'When you're searching for lost things they're always in the last place you look. And where's the last place we would look?'

'The stream?' said Mr Foon, who had a painted, round face.

'Don't be silly. The last place we would look is where they're supposed to be. I bet if we go back to the book trees the books will be there after all.'

We all nodded and smiled, pleased that our clever Jenny had solved the mystery. Everyone followed her to the book trees, chatting and laughing as we went. When we got to the right place there was only grass. While we had been searching the trees had vanished without a trace. Jenny stared at the empty space for a moment, her mouth hanging open. Then she sat on the grass and tears rolled down her cheeks, though she didn't make a sound. We gathered close, wrapping her in our arms and wings, making a warm, soft bundle. I had to stay on the edge of the hug so that I didn't hurt anyone. We murmured comforting words to her, but I think inside we were all shaken. I know I was.

## 4 Sleeps before the End

Jenny's armchair is on a hill now. It didn't used to be. Usually it's on flat grass near the flower beds. The Time it Rained there was a tree standing nearby with long branches and wide leaves to shelter the armchair. Things move, but the armchair is the centre of the Garden.

The armchair hill was the tallest thing any of us had ever seen. It rose far higher than our heads, higher than Henny could flutter, higher than the trees. Mr Foon suggested it might be a mountain. No one agreed with him because the big hill was round and covered in grass, whereas mountains are pointy and rocky and have snow on top. The hill was wide as well as tall and it looked like the trees had slid down the sides when the hill arrived, they were clustered in clumps at the bottom. Jenny was always in her armchair when we woke up, so we knew we had to climb the hill to see her. Climbing is a lot like walking but steeper and more tiring. I was out of breath before getting to the top, and the other five who were left got there before me. When I saw Jenny in her armchair I felt happy again, even though I was tired and had gone to sleep scared and lonely.

'I saw you coming ages ago,' she said. 'The hill makes a great lookout. If we all stay here at the top I'm sure one else will get lost.'

## 9 Sleeps before the End

The birds disappeared after the books. I didn't hear them singing, though I didn't notice their absence straight away. Perhaps it was the same for everyone else. I didn't realise there was no birdsong until after I had eaten. Usually a bird or two flies down when you're eating to get a few crumbs, but none came. I looked up as I walked to see if I could see any of the birds perched in the trees or flying through the sky.

While I was looking up I nearly ran right into Fred Bear, who jumped out of my way. I explained that I hadn't seen or heard the birds all day. He looked up too and agreed that there was no sign of them. I didn't want to start another big search, not after the disastrous book hunt. I suggested that we talk to Henny and see if she knew anything about it. Henny could only flutter up to the lowest branches or the roofs of our little houses and flutter between things that were the same height and quite close together. She couldn't fly up to the top of the trees or travel across the sky, but she was still a bird with feathers, wings and a beak. After Jenny had scolded a couple of finches for making fun of Henny, and had a word with everyone about leaving others out, the other birds had been sure to involve her.

Henny's wooden house stood on short stilts and had a ramp leading up to the green front door. When Fred Bear knocked Henny poked her head out of a window and we asked her if she knew where the other birds were. She didn't, her red comb drooped, she was afraid the other birds were leaving her out again. Fred said he didn't think that was true. I said that the birds seemed to be hiding, but Henny would surely know where they had gone. She perked up a bit and we decided to treat it as a game of hide and seek. Henny fluttered up to low branches, where Fred and I couldn't reach, and called up into the leaves. We did this for every tree in the Garden, but there was never any answer. Henny started to get flustered and raced back and forth, calling and making a fuss. I regretted telling her, she got worried about things easily. After walking and fluttering around the whole Garden there was still no sight or sound of the birds and we realised that we would have to tell Jenny.

We found Jenny sitting in her armchair, with her knees drawn up to her chest and her chin resting on her folded arms. Both Henny and Fred were reluctant to tell her what we had found –or not found- and I had to step forward and deliver the news. Jenny looked confused and worried at first. I didn't like making her look like that, but when I had finished talking she thanked me for telling her. She asked me, Fred and Henny to gather everyone together by the armchair. When we returned, with small groups following each of us, the armchair was on a little mound of its own so that everyone assembled could see and hear Jenny.

'Heg has told me that the birds have gone,' Jenny announced. There was a stunned silence. The birds were always around, even if they spent most of their time above our heads. Now that their absence had been pointed out, the silence seemed bigger and emptier than before. 'I don't want any of you to worry about them,' Jenny continued. 'Birds fly south for the winter, and that's what has happened. The birds have all flown to somewhere warm and sunny where they can have lots of fun. We'll miss them, of course, but they will come back.'

There were nods at this, and some chatter as everyone dispersed. Henny stood by the armchair looking mournful, she had been left behind. Jenny knelt next to her and spoke quietly; I was sure she could make poor Henny feel better. I was glad that Jenny wasn't sad or worried, but I wondered why the birds had left. It never felt cold in the Garden, and the light was always bright, except for the Time it Rained. I also wondered why the birds hadn't said goodbye before they left.

3 Sleeps before the End

Mr Foon was gone when we woke up. He wasn't on top of the hill and we couldn't see him when we looked down the sides. He had always been a bit silly, but it seemed unlikely that he would wander away from the safest place. He might have been silly but he was also scaredy. We teased him a bit, but now that he was gone we missed him. What was scary was that his disappearance suggested that the missing people weren't leaving of their own accord.

Jenny was angry. Not angry and disappointed like when she told one of us off for teasing, or for not sharing our things. This was a different kind of anger. Her face was grim and her mouth was a thin line. When she spoke her words were hard and flat and she didn't sound like herself anymore. It made me nervous and sad at the same time.

'Someone is taking my friends,' she said. I didn't know

who she was talking to; she wasn't looking at any of us. She stared out into the distance, looking across the Garden, not focusing on anything. I tried to ask who could be taking us, but Jenny didn't seem to hear me. When she spoke again it wasn't in answer to my question.

'Being up here isn't enough. We need more protection.' Jenny leapt out of her chair and ran around the top of the hill, looking down on the Garden. 'Maybe the trees will help us.' She cupped her hands around her mouth and called down the slope. 'Hey trees! Please help us. We need you to come up the hill a bit. Come and stand guard for me. Please.'

I watched Jenny call down the hill in different directions. I never knew you could talk to trees, or that they could hear you. As far as I knew no one had ever done it before, but if Jenny was doing it then there had to be a good reason. I exchanged confused and fearful looks with Carmen, Tig and Fred, none of us knew how to react, and so we stood still and watched. If someone was behaving strangely we would ask Jenny about it, if Jenny was behaving strangely there was no one left to ask.

Later, when we were sitting and looking at the view, there was a rustling noise, like wind through leaves, except that there wasn't any wind. It was hard to tell where it was coming from. Whenever I looked in one direction the sound seemed to come from somewhere else. It was Carmen who spotted what was happening. She thought she saw a tree move. The rest of us ran round to look, but by the time we got there it had stopped. Jenny stayed in her chair. When we stopped looking at the tree Fred noticed that some of the other trees seemed to have come closer. They were standing at the bottom of the slope. We raced around and about on top of the hill, trying to catch the trees moving. Once or twice, out of the corner of my eye, I thought I saw branches twitching, but whenever I looked properly the tree would stay still and the rustling would come from somewhere else. Eventually each of us stood facing a different direction, watching the trees. The rustling died down, it was still there but faint, fading in and out. Jenny noticed what we were doing, up until then she had been staring at nothing or playing with the ends of her long plaits.

'Stop it!' Her voice was hard again, and it made me jump. 'The trees don't like you watching. Come here, all of you.' We obeyed, walking to the armchair hesitantly. Jenny told us to sit in front of her.

'I'm going to tell you a story,' she announced.

'But the books…' Tig started, before being shushed by the rest of us. We didn't want to bring up anything that would make Jenny sadder, or angrier.

'You don't need books to tell a story,' Jenny said with impatience. 'You can make stories up, using your head. That's where the stories in books come from before they're written down.'

I absorbed this new piece of information. I didn't know that stories lived in heads before they became books, there was a lot more to them than I had realised.

'Once upon a time there was a tall and lovely princess who discovered a beautiful garden, full of nice things,' Jenny began. 'There were flowers and trees and a slide and swings. There were lots of friendly people who lived in the garden and each of them had a little house of their own where they lived as cosy as could be. The princess loved the garden so much that she decided to stay and rule over all the people there. She would show them how to be good and how to do things properly. The people were so happy that the princess had come they threw a big party with lots of presents and delicious things to eat, and everyone was very happy.

'Then danger came to the garden. The people were disappearing and no one knew why. Soon there were hardly any people left and the last few came to the princess and begged for help. The princess was very angry, so she set out to stop it. She travelled all the way to the edge of the garden where she came across a terrible white monster. It was big and broad, its pointy teeth were huge and its eyes were yellow. The princess was brave and told the monster to return her people and leave her garden. The monster roared right in her face. The princess wasn't scared. The monster roared so much its throat got too dry to roar anymore. When it stopped roaring the princess drew her sword. With a powerful swing she cut the monster's head off. Then she jumped on the monster's body until it fell down dead. The princess found where the monster had hidden her missing friends and she brought them all back to the garden. Everyone was so very happy that they threw another big party to celebrate. And they all live happily ever after.'

When the story was finished it had gotten darker, I was so busy listening to Jenny I hadn't noticed the light change. The trees were standing near the top of the hill. I couldn't imagine how difficult the climb had been for them as they didn't have any legs. They stood in a tight circle with their roots in the ground, their leaves making a green crown on top of the hill. Their branches stretched above us blocking out the light. The only place that wasn't covered by tree shadows was around the armchair.

'Thank you trees,' said Jenny. 'Everyone say thank you to the trees.'

'Thank you trees,' we chorused. I supposed it was good of the trees to come, but I couldn't help thinking that it seemed very gloomy up here now. Seeing the tall trunks so close all around us felt strange. I was used to seeing lots of space, now I felt uncomfortably trapped. Jenny said it was safer, yet I didn't feel better. I looked up at Jenny and for the first time I hoped she knew what she was doing.

'The story,' Tig said hopefully to Jenny, 'is it true? Is that what's going to happen?'

Jenny looked down at him with a cross expression. 'Don't be so silly, it's only a story. Real things don't always end happily.'

## 8 Sleeps before the End

Carmen was devastated when the stream dried up. There was nowhere for her to swim anymore and she was worried about the fish, who had all disappeared with the water. The stream bed remained as a brown, rocky trench through the green of the Garden, with a dirty trickle of water still at the bottom.

After Carmen raised the alert about the stream, Jenny said that rivers and streams always run into the sea eventually. We had heard of the sea before, it was in some of the books. It was full of water and fish and was where pirates and ships lived. I had never seen the sea in the Garden, and I couldn't think of any way of getting to it. Besides the stream had always seemed perfectly happy where it was, why would it suddenly leave to go to the sea?

Jenny suggested we mount an expedition to see where the stream had gone. On her instruction we went to our homes and gathered provisions, because expeditions are hungry work. We gathered by the twisty old oak tree, which stood next to the stream that day. As a group we set off along the bank, carrying our provisions. Carmen walked slowly, despondent at the loss of her stream, the rest of us gathered around to cheer her up. Jenny offered to carry Carmen, a rare treat that normally only happened on birthdays. Sitting on Jenny's shoulders the otter towered over everyone else and became more cheerful. While we walked Jenny whistled a tune and the rest of us joined in, whistling or humming along, some less tunefully than others. Jenny, with her long legs, stayed easily at the front of the group, leading the way. We passed copses of tall trees, bushes green and bright with berries and beds of flowers in all different colours. From the back of the group I saw how peaceful the plants in the Garden were, and I felt sure that everything would be fine.

There was a place where the ground level changed and there used to be a waterfall, now there was a muddy puddle. We sat on broad, flat rocks around the edge of what used to be a little pool and spread out our provisions. I had been carrying strawberry jam sandwiches, wrapped in a spotty handkerchief I'd discovered that day. Ferdi had meat paste sandwiches and Mr Foon had peanut butter. Fred Bear had a basket of apples and Tig had some cake. We shared out the food as Jenny had taught us, before tucking in. After eating we lay in the sun, enjoying being still after all the walking. Jenny soon declared that we had rested enough and we ought to keep going. We got up, the load lighter now the provisions were gone, and kept walking in the same direction.

As we went I wondered how big the Garden was, something I had never thought about before. Things moved, but I always knew how to find the places I needed and no one ever got lost. We kept walking until we started to get tired. Everyone was walking as slowly as I normally did, and I was going even slower, when there was a cry from Carmen. The otter was perched on Jenny's shoulders with her front paws on the top of Jenny's head. At first I thought she had seen the sea, so I sped up to join the others. Looking up I realised Carmen wasn't happy, Jenny had to pull her down because she was shaking too much to keep her balance. Everyone had stopped walking and was looking at something up ahead. I went to the front of the group, the others moving aside so that I didn't brush past them. I saw what Carmen had seen, and understood why she was so upset. A little further on I saw the distinctive shape of the twisty old oak tree.

Carmen squirmed out of Jenny's arms, and ran down into the stream bed where she lay in the trickle of water. We had travelled round the whole Garden and not found the way to the sea. I remembered, as I looked at Carmen, that the sea was made of salt water, which was the same as tears. I was sure that if she had been able to Carmen would have made a whole new salty stream, but Jenny was the only one of us who knew how to cry.

## 2 Sleeps before the End

There were only three of us left, myself, Tig and Carmen. The wall of trees hadn't stopped anyone from disappearing. Tears ran down Jenny's face when she saw our diminished numbers.

'It must be something in the sky,' she said sadly, 'swooping down and stealing my friends. Maybe something like a dragon? But I'm sure we would have seen or heard a dragon.'

Jenny stood on her chair, even though standing on chairs isn't allowed. She went up on tip toes and her face went slack. She turned in a slow circle, staring at something the rest of us couldn't see. Whatever it was she didn't like it. I tried looking up, but only saw the blue dome of the sky. There were no clouds for anything to hide behind.

'This isn't fair,' Jenny said stamping her foot on the red fabric and dislodging a couple of cushions. 'This is my place, you're my friends. I don't want anything to go.'

Jenny was the decider of what was and wasn't fair. If something was unfair and she couldn't do anything about it I didn't know what hope there was.

'You need more protection,' Jenny decided. She pulled the folded blanket off the back of her armchair. 'We need to build a blanket fort. Everyone go and get sticks.'

'But there aren't any sticks up here,' said Tig, 'I think they're all on the other side of the trees.'

'Silly Tig, sticks come from trees, you can just pull them off.'

'Won't that hurt the trees though,' I said with concern. 'They came and helped us, so we shouldn't pull sticks off them, should we?'

Jenny looked down at me, her face hard again. 'The trees are happy to help us, and they'll do whatever I need them to do. So if we need sticks they'll give us sticks.'

'But…'

'Look, trees don't have feelings, so you don't need to worry.'

'Oh… OK.'

I went with Tig and Carmen to get sticks, but every time I pulled one off a tree the tree shook, as though it was scared. After the first few times I found I couldn't look directly at the tree I was harming. I tried not to imagine what it would feel like if someone pulled out my spines.

We returned to Jenny with a bundle of sticks of different sizes. Jenny found some strong white string down the side of the armchair, and showed us how to lash the sticks together. Following her instructions as best we could, we built a rectangular frame for our fort. We put it behind the armchair, Jenny threw the blanket over the top and we all huddled inside. The fort was too low for Jenny to sit comfortably, so she had to hunch over and keep her head down. With all of us in there it felt a bit crowded and cramped, but Jenny insisted it was safe.

## 7 Sleeps before the End

After I got up I went to the armchair, it looked as though others had had the same idea, though there were a few people missing. We counted each other, which took quite a long time because some of us weren't very good at counting and some missed themselves out and always came up one short. Eventually Jenny made us all stand in a line and called out our names. She called this a register, and said we all had to come and do it each morning. Then Jenny arranged us in small groups and sent us walking through the garden in different directions, to see if anyone had gotten lost. I walked with Henny and Ferdi and as we looked we realised that the slide was gone. The long grass that had grown underneath it was still there, but the slide had vanished. When we got back to the armchair to tell the others each group reported that something had gone. The swings, the roundabout, and the curvy bridge had all disappeared.

We ate together, sat in a circle. It seemed safest.

When I went back to my house to sleep I discovered that it wasn't there any more. I knew exactly where I'd left it, but it had gone and so had my cupboards and my blankets and my pillows. I ran this way and that, frantically looking for my lovely little square home. I almost ran into Tig and Fred, who were racing about looking for their houses too. Fred Bear's sleeping barrel, Henny's house on stilts, Tig's cushioned tent, all gone.

The only homes left were those that belonged to the people who lived in holes underground. The mice and rabbits still had their tunnels and burrows. Ferdi's den was still there too. We woke them with our noisy searching and they offered to share their holes with the rest of us, though the largest rabbit eyed me warily while making the offer. The mouse holes were too small for anyone else and even the rabbit warren was a bit too tight. Ferdi's den smelled strange, and anyway the soil was dirty and felt uncomfortable.

Those of us who were homeless had to sleep outside on the soft grass. I curled up in a ball on my own. My friends lay near by, huddled together in a warm, cosy mass. I felt lonely, but knew that my isolation made sense. I did not want to hurt anyone. I briefly wondered whether I should dig myself a little hole to sleep in, I could line it with leaves and it might not be so different from a bed, but it had been a long day and I was too tired.

## I Sleep before the End

I woke on my own in the blanket fort. I thought that Tig and Carmen had gone outside, or maybe I had accidentally prickled them in the night and they had left me alone. The light wasn't very bright, but then I remembered that that was because of the trees. I crawled out of the blanket fort and walked around the side of the armchair where Jenny was sitting as usual. That was the only usual thing left in this dim, shrunken world.

'Are the other two still sleeping?' Jenny asked.

'No,' I said in a small voice, 'I thought they already got up.'

Jenny looked at me with emptiness in her eyes. 'They've gone haven't they?'

I didn't answer, I couldn't answer. Jenny screwed her eyes up tight, tears spilled out and ran down her cheeks. She curled up on the chair, hiding her face from me. I couldn't bear to see her cry, and I would have cried too if I'd known how. I reached out and put a paw on her shoulder. She flinched, then turned to look at me.

'I can't stop it,' she said through her tears. 'Do you know what the rest of the Garden looks like now?'

I shook my head.

'Come up here and I'll show you.'

I had always dreamed of being allowed to sit on Jenny's armchair, I think everyone dreamed of it. It was sad that I had finally gotten the invitation under such terrible circumstances. I tried to savour the moment all the same. I reached up my front paws and gripped the top of the seat, then I pulled myself up, my legs waggling behind me. The fabric was soft under my paws and stomach, and once I'd gotten on the seat it was squashy and comfortable. I sat down and with horror felt my spines dig into the fabric. I just knew I had made holes in the chair, I felt awful and tried to sit still so Jenny wouldn't notice. Jenny wasn't paying attention. She stood on the seat, all the old rules apparently suspended now.

'Stand up and tell me what you see,' she told me. I stood, feeling my spines snag as they came out of chair. I closed my eyes, not wanting to see the damage, then realised I couldn't tell Jenny what I saw if my eyes were closed.

'I can see the leaves of the trees, they're very green,' I said, hoping this was the right answer.

Jenny made a tutting noise, full of disapproval. She towered over me and I realised she must be able to see over the tops of the trees.

'I'll have to pick you up to see properly.' Jenny bent down and reached her arms towards me. I squirmed away from her, bumping into the armrest.

'No,' I said. 'I'll prick you with my spines. I don't want to hurt you.'

'It doesn't matter,' Jenny said dully, 'I want you to see.'

She picked me up easily, she was very strong. I felt my spines brush against her skin, but she didn't make a noise. I was unused to being held off the ground and my feet kicked as they dangled in the air. She held me out in front of her, about level with her head. I was dazzled at first, a couple of days under the shadows of the trees and I could only see how bright everything beyond was. Then I realised that the brightness was the sky, which had turned white. Above the tops of the trees I'd expected to see blue above the green grass of the Garden, with the brown stream bed and the bright flowers. All I could see was white, bright, blank white in every direction. It was as though there was nothing beyond our green circle.

Jenny's arms shook as she lowered me back down and we sat side by side on the chair.

'Where is it?' I asked quietly.

'I don't know,' Jenny said, 'It's gone. I think it's my fault.'

'How could it be your fault?'

'This is my special place, if it goes that's my fault. I don't want it to happen, but I don't think I can stop it.'

I sat next to Jenny and shivered. I had never been so afraid. If I closed my eyes that terrible blankness was all I could see. Jenny put her arms around me, and I returned her hug. I didn't think of the damage my spines would do to her; I was just glad she was there.

After a while Jenny moved, she reached down between the cushion and the side of the chair. There were lots of things down there and often there was something useful. Jenny pulled sheets of white paper and a box of crayons out from the side of the chair. She looked at the paper and crayons in confusion. I noticed there were red scratches down her arm, and I felt terribly guilty.

'The chair is probably trying to help,' Jenny said. 'I don't know what I'm supposed to draw though.' Jenny carefully checked all the paper, to make sure there were no messages for her. Unable to find anything she slumped back into the chair with a sigh.

'I don't know, Heg. I think that whatever happens next is going to happen. I think its part of growing up.'

'What's growing up?'

'It's horrible. It's when you aren't the same as you used to be anymore. You get bigger, which doesn't sound so bad, but you also change and become someone else.'

'I don't want you to be someone else,' I murmured.

'I know,' Jenny said, a little kindness in her voice. 'I'm not sure I want to be someone else either, that might be why it's so difficult. But I know I don't have a choice and I think that once I grow up I won't be able to come here any more.'

'You can't leave,' I said panicked. 'I'll be all on my own.'

Jenny looked down at me sadly. 'No, you won't.'

## 6 Sleeps before the End

The underground people, the mice, the rabbits and Ferdi the fox, didn't show up for register at the armchair. After waiting for a while Jenny asked the rest of us, who had slept out in the open, to go and look for them. It wasn't long before we discovered that the ground had closed up.

There were no holes, burrows or dens to be found anywhere in the Garden. Without being able to find the entrances we couldn't tell where our missing friends might be. The ground underneath the grass was firm and flat and when I tried to dig down it was so hard that it hurt my paws and didn't take a scratch. I went to tell Jenny, and tried not to think about the others, stuck down there in the dark, desperately trying to dig their way up to the light and unable to break through. I remembered how close I'd come to digging a hole for myself and shivered.

When she heard the news Jenny had a strange look on her face. As though she was trying to listen to something far away that the rest of us couldn't hear. I had to tell her what happened twice before I was sure she had heard me.

'I'm sure they're fine,' she said dully, 'they like it underground.'

'But they're stuck down there,' said Tig. 'Won't they be scared?'

'No,' Jenny replied. 'They're perfectly safe. It's probably safer underground than it is up here. I'm sure they're having a lovely time. I expect they're all together having a party.'

'Can they breathe?' Carmen asked.

'Yes!' snapped Jenny, 'of course they can. Now everyone stop asking all these silly questions.'

## 5 Sleeps before the End

We gathered at the armchair and Jenny called out names. There were a lot of names that no one answered to. We spent the day in front of the chair, where Jenny could keep an eye on us. She suggested games for us to play, but no one was allowed to play hide and seek or any chasing games. The games that Jenny came up with were fun, and we were able to forget our problems for a short while. That was the last day that I laughed.

## 0 Sleeps before the End

When I woke up I didn't know where I was, but I had gotten used to that. At least I was somewhere soft and comfortable, with a blanket covering me. I opened my eyes and realised I was on Jenny's armchair. That made me happy for a moment. Then I looked up and saw the white sky. I remembered the horrible blankness beyond the trees. I remembered that everyone but Jenny and I had gone and suddenly I was terrified. What if I had disappeared while I slept too?

Jenny was sitting on the ground in front of the chair. The sheets of paper were spread out around her. I shuffled to the edge of the seat and peered over the side to get a better look. Jenny was leaning over, her shoulders hunched, her arm moving quickly as she drew. The papers all around her were covered in pictures.

'Jenny?'

She turned to look at me, there was a gleam in her eye, but it wasn't the happy one I was used to. She was smiling but the smile was thin as though her face was stretched too tight. I climbed down from the chair and went to look at her drawings. I recognised pictures of people and places from the Garden. Jenny was drawing what had been lost. Standing next to her I saw that her skin was lighter and there were dark marks under her eyes. I don't think she had gone to sleep. I'd never heard of anyone not sleeping when they were supposed to, but I don't think the rules applied anymore.

'I've figured it out, Heg. I know how to save everyone.' Jenny was excited.

'You do? That's wonderful,' I said. Hope sparked in my heart; I should have known Jenny would figure it out and save the Garden.

'I noticed the paper is the same colour as the sky. Then I realised that the whiteness is paper, and I have to colour it in.'

I didn't understand what she was saying, but her tone was positive so I let the hope grow in me.

'See I've drawn everyone,' she said. She pointed to different sheets of paper as she told me about each picture. 'There's

Tig in his cosy bed. Fred Bear is standing on the curvy bridge. Carmen is swimming in the stream, and I made it wider for her and put even more fish in. The birds are back too, see there they are in the sky, singing and having a wonderful time in the clouds. Also, the rabbits and mice are having a party underground, see they're all wearing party hats.'

'These are very good pictures,' I said. 'But when will everyone be saved?'

'They are saved, look how happy everyone is. No one is sad or left out and everyone is having a wonderful time.'

'But these are drawings,' I said, wondering what I'd missed.

'Yes. I think that's how it's going to work now. I can save all my friends, but it'll be different. It's all part of growing up.'

'You said growing up was horrible. You said you didn't want to do it.'

'I also said I didn't have a choice. I've thought about it and I think this is the best way. I get to keep all my friends and they'll always be happy.'

'I'm not happy,' I pointed out.

'Not yet, but you will be. I'll draw you happy.'

My stomach sank and all my spines stood on end as a prickly feeling ran over my skin. 'But I'm here, I don't want to be there.' I pointed at the paper.

'I know Heg, but it's the only way. Doesn't it look nice there?'

It did look nice, everyone was smiling and all my friends were back, and the garden was full of trees and flowers again. I examined the pictures and found my missing house, there just like it used to be.

'I can give you more rooms,' Jenny said. 'I can make sure your house is the biggest and the nicest.'

'I'll miss it here,' I insisted.

'You won't remember. I'll make it so the lovely new Garden is all you know.'

I didn't like the sound of that at all, but if Jenny was telling me it was the right thing to do then surely it must be? Perhaps I didn't understand. I looked at the pictures again. 'Where's the armchair? Where will you go?'

'I won't be in the new Garden,' Jenny said. 'I don't belong there.'

'Then I won't go either. I won't leave you.' I folded my arms.

She knelt in front of me, her face kind but serious. 'I'm afraid you don't get a choice Heg, none of us do. I am going to draw you into the new Garden, if I don't the big whiteness out there will get you. It's up to you whether you go like this, or whether you say goodbye to me properly. I need to say goodbye to someone.' Jenny's lip wobbled and her eyes were shiny with tears that hadn't fallen yet. I wish I knew how to cry. I didn't want to go, but if I had to I wanted to say goodbye.

'I'm scared.'

'I know, but I need you to be my brave hedgehog. Now give me a hug.'

My spines scratched her arms, but I didn't care. I held on to Jenny as tightly as I could. When we parted blood ran from the scratches in her skin, a darker red than the armchair. She didn't look angry or hurt and she smiled softly at me. She put me up on the chair, then sat back down on the grass and chose a brown crayon from the box.

'Goodbye Heg.'

'Goodbye Jenny.'

I felt sleepy and though I fought against it my eyes closed. The last thing I saw was Jenny.

# Part 2

*"The End is Nigh!" the man shouted.*
*"Is there still time for hot chocolate?" Riley asked.*
*The-End-is-Nigh guy blinked. "Ah, maybe, I don't*
*know."*

Jana Oliver,
*Forbidden*

# Little Daughter

## Dayna Ingram

It wasn't the being chased that bothered Liddy Vanya; she spent half her life being chased, by this guard or that, by her father or his minions, and so now it was the Queen, what difference was there? None that Liddy could readily see. No, the being chased was a nice workout—clean forest air, over-oxygenated by the old growth, maybe, but damn if it didn't burn the lungs in just the way she liked it, meaner than any bottle of rye she'd ever met; cold mud, damp enough for a decent toe-hold but too slippery for any kind of footwear (as her pursuers were surely learning the hard way); just enough light breaking through the canopy to illuminate shadows of stumps and forest debris to be avoided, branches stretched to her like aching limbs, yearning to be held. This image was enough to make her laugh, something she'd rarely done in this last decade (since her life of being chased began). No, no, the being chased wasn't bothersome in and of itself. It was the inevitability of being caught that boiled Liddy's blood.

Because where was there to run? Even as she picked her hasty way through the woods, she knew they belonged to her father, as did everything else on the island. He went hunting in them every year when the season was right; he invited Lords and Ladies from the continent to hunt in them as a party. A blood sport party. Liddy could understand the allure in that, the deep pleasure to be taken in the killing of another living thing. A thing that you had the power to save simply by resisting the urge to kill it. It was just the kind of party she would have felt honoured to be invited to, but of course she never had been. Invited, that is. Killing, she did plenty of, but never with a party.

As the darkness pressed in and the forest floor grew ever more treacherous beneath her unshod feet, Liddy decided to take a different tack. They might catch her (if not in this forest then in the next; the docks were surely fortified at this point, there was no way off the island for Liddy Vanya), but she would go down making them all wish they'd disobeyed just this one last order. They outnumbered her so an element of surprise was key. She stopped running and looked up. Climbing trees. Another thing she spent half of her life doing (the first half, from the time she could walk until she started her womanly bleeding, which came earlier for her than it did for most; what luck. Then her father wanted her indoors and no more fooling around with those other children, or with Varrick).

With familiar ease, Liddy hoisted herself atop the lowest level of branches on the closest tree. Its trunk was covered in a dark green moss that smelled like scat. She gripped the next branch above her head, dug her heel into the trunk, and pushed herself up in this manner until she was certain the darkness would hide her from all but the keenest of eyes. However brave the Royal Army could be said to be, no one had ever praised them for their eagle eyes. It would have been smarter, Liddy thought, for the Queen to send hunters after her. And perhaps she would. The night was still young.

She heard them long before they appeared beneath her. Each collective step rang through the stillness of the forest, the tolling of an unnatural bell as it clanged its way through a natural world. A wind preceded them, their breath carried on the leaves of the trees, brushing the hair along the back of Liddy's neck. She saw the spears of the footmen first, and then the coats of the riders' horses, shiny with sweat. Even in the darkness, the knights' heavy steel armour glinted as they marched, as if defying the very notion of darkness. They came in a column, two knights marching astride each other, this line broken here and there by a single rider. If they had bowmen, Liddy did not see any. She watched them march forward, directly beneath her and then away from her. It would be best to take the rear, make them double back to face her. Liddy squinted, zeroing in on a rider. The mask of his helm was raised; his entire face was exposed, as well as part of his neck. Good; the Queen had not warned them; Liddy had a chance, slim as it might be.

She let the column pass her in a languid stride, mildly hurt that the Queen thought her such an easy capture. Not one knight was running, or even jogging a little; only the horses were sweating and that was due to lugging around a three-hundred pound be-armoured knight all day. Two knights with broadswords brought up the tail end of the column, and when their backs were to her, Liddy leapt.

The first thing that broke was her ankle. She misjudged the distance and landed too far behind the column; she meant to at least pull one of them down with her, knocking the wind from him or knocking him unconscious. Unfortunately, all she caught was air, and then ground, her foot landing awkwardly on a thick root and twisting, and there went her ankle. The broadsword caught her falling, and she pulled him down atop her even as she felt her wrist snapping under his weight. He was too close to her to unsheathe his weapon, but closeness was what she needed to work her magic. She touched a finger to the knight's exposed face—the tip of his nose, to be exact—and in an instant he was still. No longer a three-hundred pound man, he became a three-hundred pound lump of solid gold in roughly the shape of a man. His golden eyes stared down at Liddy as his suddenly too-heavy body pressed her into the damp earth.

'Mistake,' Liddy said aloud, chiding herself as the air was pressed out of her.

The other knights were on her now; their gloved hands grabbed at her exposed feet as they shouted at their comrade to lift himself off her. Finally, a rider dismounted and launched himself at his comrade's inert body. The crunching of his bones as he slammed into the gold brick made Liddy smile. He moved away to recover, and a new group formed, shouting at one another and pushing and pulling at the statue atop her as Liddy herself struggled to breathe.

'No hurry, guys,' she said, or tried to say but her crushed lungs were rather uncooperative.

There was a loud clap directly beside her left ear, like that of thunder. It sent a ringing through her brain that travelled deep into the marrow of her spine. She closed her eyes against this new pain, and when she opened them again, the statue lay at her feet. She gulped in air and scrambled to get up. The forest filled with smoke—no, darker than smoke, like shadows gone gaseous. She looked around but there was no source fire. She could hear the knights somewhere behind the billowy veil but she could not tell in which direction they awaited her.

Behind her, someone cleared their throat.

Liddy spun her head. There stood a small man, hunched and wearing a rather dapper black and white suit, with tails that touched his ankles. He leaned on a wizened cane and brushed loose white hair out of his eyes.

'Damn it all,' he spoke to the air. 'I told that woman, no bangs!'

The smoke was making its way into Liddy's head, fogging up her vision and her thoughts. 'Can I help you?' she asked the dwarf.

He let the bangs fall where they may. 'Do you possess a decent pair of scissors?'

When Liddy reached for him, he batted her away with his cane. 'No touching!' The shouts of the knights in the smoke grew louder, closer. 'I think we can help each other,' he said. With the end of his cane, he tapped out a rhythm upon the earth. The roots curled back, the carpet of moss rolled up, and the mud slaked away until a door appeared. An ordinary wooden door in the middle of the forest floor. The dwarf hooked his cane around the handle and threw the door wide. A warm glow invited Liddy down a spiralling onyx staircase.

'After you,' said the dwarf.

She looked at him wearily. 'I'm having a very trying day.'

The dwarf blew at his overlong bangs and said, 'Aren't we all?' He handed her his cane and followed her limping form down the staircase, closing the door behind them.

The staircase led to a large open room heated by logs ablaze in a fireplace against the far wall. The walls were a haphazard combination of earth and stone, tree roots the width of a fist twisting through the dirt like giant worms. Here and there a shelf had been mounted to the stones, bearing jars and vials filled with a strange translucent substance encasing various figures: Liddy could make out a half-formed calf in one jar, several pairs of different eyes in another, three to six newts in vials, and a couple of bird claws. Rows of books were stacked on the floor against the right wall. A furry rug lay in front of the fire; the head of whatever animal it came from had been removed but the claws remained—a Jump Cat? In the centre of the room was a square oak table, which the dwarf motioned her toward, pulling out one of the four chairs for her. He went to the small cook stove against the left wall to retrieve a pot of tea that was whistling, its heady herbal aroma filling the room.

'Can't believe I left this on,' the dwarf muttered to himself as much as to Liddy. He puttered around in cabinets and drawers that were built into the wall, retrieving mugs and spoons and saucers. 'Fortuitous that I did. It'll be just the thing. Just the thing. You take sugar?'

Liddy hefted her injured leg onto an adjacent chair. 'How about some ice?'

The dwarf laughed through his teeth. 'You're funny. No sugar, then. Here we are.'

He shuffled over to the table, his arms laden. Liddy made no move to help unburden him. He let the tea things tumble to the table and set them right. He returned to the stove for the kettle and came back to the table. He poured equal portions of the brew and pushed a cup toward Liddy.

'Hope it didn't steep for too long,' he said, sipping at his own cup. 'I like it a little burnt, personally.'

Liddy took a tentative sip. The tea tasted familiar. She swished a larger portion around in her mouth, then gulped it down. 'Is this Vermillion Cural?'

The dwarf leaned back in his seat, pleased. 'You know it?'

'Needed it every once in a while,' Liddy said. She drank the rest down in one noisy gulp. Immediately, the skin around her injured ankle and wrist began to burn. Soon the burning would grow into a piercing pain that would be hard to ignore, as her splintered bones repaired themselves.

'I drink a cup a day,' he said. 'Doctor's orders.'

Liddy noticed the dwarf's hunch straightening out as he drank. She could almost hear his spine cracking back into place. His face flushed, some colour returning to his eyes as well, a deep, cavernous blue. She blinked away from him, and poured herself another cup.

'You're not a dwarf,' she said.

He laughed. 'When had I claimed such a thing?'

'You look like a dwarf.'

'It's these damn bangs,' he growled. 'They make me look shaggy, despite the suit. I usually cut my hair myself, but I thought today I would go on an adventure. Get my hair done in town. How would that be? Bloody impossible is how that turned out to be. There are no barbers left in the lower lands, you know. Or at least none who fit my budget. Inflation! That's another thing. Bangs and inflation. Two things I can do without.'

Pain stabbed through Liddy's wrist and ankle simultaneously, eliciting a wince and a sob. She turned her face to the fire, concentrating on the heat it emitted rather than the searing beneath her skin.

'This is strong stuff,' he said, gathering up her cup. 'You won't need a refill. It will be over soon enough, and then we can talk about payment.'

Liddy winced again, but not because of the pain. 'Payment?' She should have known; witches never gave you anything out of the kindness of their rotted hearts.

The witch dropped the dirtied dishes into a pot of water near the stove and returned to his seat. 'Payment,' he repeated. 'I believe you owe me for two services: one, I saved your life; two, I healed you up. If you'd like to make it three, I can run you a bath. Not to be insensitive, but you do have a rather rank smell about you, dear.'

The pain in her bones was already subsiding into a rhythmic throbbing. She lowered her ankle back to the floor and folded her arms atop the table. 'I suppose you'll be wanting gold.'

'The thing about you is,' he said, wagging an admonishing finger her way, 'you make a great deal of assumptions. I want a story.'

'A story?'

That was new. The last witch she'd bought Vermillion Cural from was a roving tramp who peddled his potions up and down the north-western coast, drawing most of his coin from fishermen whose spouses were tired of their stink. 'Give me Rose Oil,' they'd say. Or, 'You got anything that don't smell flowery?' That witch had sliced off his own right hand and bade her touch it. The best she could do for him was to touch his face before he bled to death; her magic didn't work on dead flesh, only living.

'My dear, yes! A story,' he said, jiggling his knees excitedly. 'You've probably already *assumed* by now that I do not get much company down here in my little hovel. In this, you would actually be correct. By choice, mind you. Once the commoners discover my witchhood they never cease to ask me for things: a potion to shut up their babies for a night, a cream for their skin conditions, a hex for this neighbour's incessant baying sheep. And love potions! Especially popular among the gentry, those boring sacs. This terrible hair cut? Traded a thimble of Randy Musk for it. At least the barber was realistic, just wanted a go-around. Who doesn't? But a story—not one of these southerly schlubs could spin me a decent yarn if they tried. But you, my dear—I have a feeling you will not even have to try so very hard.'

'Now who's making assumptions?' Liddy asked.

The witch clapped his hands, his laughter bursting through the hollow room. 'And clever too! Yes, I'm quite sure you have a grand story for me. For instance, say, how you came by your incredible gift?'

Liddy looked down at her hands, and then back up at the witch. His eyes gleamed with hunger. 'All right,' she began. 'Once upon a time—'

'Oooh!' The witch clapped his hands and stamped his feet. 'I'm sorry, I'm sorry.' He took a deep breath and collected himself. 'I just got chills. I won't interrupt again. Please, continue.'

'Once upon a time, in a land not so very far from here, in a fishing town that was once called Mooring Shore but has since been washed away by a combination of time, apathy, and grander designs, there lived a greedy man. Let us call him Brushka. Brushka was not always a greedy man, or so those who grew up with him would insist, but at the time of this little story, he was well into his thirties and had survived enough to earn, he thought, the right to be greedy. Much had been taken away from him, you see. His parents fell to the Ocean Fever when he was only a boy, and he was brought up by his grandparents, two greedy men themselves, who ruled him as much with the rod as with the hope that they might spare him from it. They died on the very day Brushka became a man, at fifteen. A house fire. Quite convenient. Brushka collected the life assurance and built his own admirably-sized homestead on the outskirts of town. Bit of a stroll to the docks, but Brushka was for it if it meant not having to smell the ocean or listen to the waves crashing every night.

'Brushka, despite his best efforts not to, ended up following his grandfather's and his father's footsteps, working the deep-sea cages. Dangerous work with the highest pay rate Mooring Shore Industries could provide, but the hours suited him and he didn't have to work with anyone else. Two dives a day, loading and unloading the catch, for one week on and then one week off. Avoid becoming fish food or drowning. No sweat. Brushka was a big man, a proud man, a confident man. His greed, as I said, would come later.

'Karan Midas moved into town when Brushka reached his twentieth year. The two became fast friends, as the saying goes. Midas was ten years Brushka's senior and very nearly gentry; he worked for the Industry in some soul-numbing numbers-crunching gig in the home office on the hill. But he liked to take long walks along the docks and watch the fishermen break their backs for their daily wage in the salty summer sun. He even accompanied Brushka on a dive once; Brushka would boast of it in the tavern for years to come, how he convinced a pencil-neck like Midas to strap on a tank and load the traps at eleven-hundred metres. Midas passed out at six hundred. Brushka carried him to shore like a hero, and Midas, gentleman that he was, seemed to not only tolerate being the brunt of Brushka's jokes, but to enjoy it.

'Midas had a sister, Vanya, who was closer to Brushka's age and was beautiful and joy-filled, and you can guess the manner of progression from there. Brushka and Vanya were married a year after meeting, Midas serving as best man, and the two spent five blissful years together. Vanya was a teacher and highly beloved; she worked hard and she loved harder, and Brushka worked even harder to feel worthy to receive such love. But nothing good lasts forever. On what should have been the happiest day of both their lives, Brushka lost the last thing he could bare to lose. In the throes of child-birth, Vanya Midas bled out. One moment here, the next gone. A child, naked and wailing, remained in her place.'

Here, Liddy was forced to stop. The catch in her voice cautioned her against continuing. She had never told anyone this story, and was mildly embarrassed to be telling it to a stranger. For his part, the witch remained silent while Liddy caught her breath. She kept her eyes toward the fire, afraid to look at the witch and glimpse his hunger. She could feel it pouring off him like waves of heat as it was. The amount of pleasure he was taking in her tale bordered on obscene. She willed herself not to think about it, and resumed her story.

'So, here was Brushka, newly widowed and burdened with the responsibility of another's life. He turned to drink to cope. Hard rye, neat. His little daughter he left to the wolves, or would have, had it not been for Karan Midas. Midas hired him a nanny, a girl of twelve when her service began. Born in the mountain village of Harsh Rock, she was of hearty stock, a muscular girl who grew into a voluptuous young woman. A woman Brushka would grow to covet. He wanted her in part because he was a man with manly desires, but mostly he wanted her because she did not want him. Her attentions, always, were for his little daughter. There was love there, and Brushka felt shunned by it. Finally, when his daughter became a woman, the day of her first bleed at eleven years, Brushka sent the nanny away. Little Daughter—for she had never been given a proper name, and was referred to only as Little Daughter by all she encountered—was henceforth expected to care for her father's every whim. Keep the house, cook the meals, tend the yard. Often, Brushka would spend his week off from the cages at the vast estate of Karan Midas, drinking together and lamenting the loss of their beloved Vanya. Not only that, but Brushka mourned the loss of a son he would never have.

'*Why not remarry?* Midas asked. *Why not try again?*

'*Who is lining up to marry a cager?* Brushka sulked.

'*A cager with land all his own*, Midas reminded. *A cager with friends in high places. How about that nanny I sent you? She possesses great childbearing hips. What's her name?*

'*Varrick?* Brushka shook his head. *I sent her away.*

'*Well*, said Midas. *Get her back.*

'Unknown to either man, Emily Varrick was already back. In point of fact, she had never truly gone. For eleven years, she had saved her wages, never needing much that her employer did not already provide her—food, shelter, a sewing kit to mend her outfits, of which she owned just three. With these meagre earnings she was able, when Brushka cast her out, to build a small hut for herself on a plot of land deeper inland, a place surrounded by a dark wood few tended to pass through. (The roads made this route less of a shortcut than an annoyance. Mooring Shore Industries had sold it to the Outland Lumber Company several years ago.) Her hut was not so very far from Brushka's homestead, and during the weeks when he would disappear to Midas's estate, Varrick would bake a pie—all manner, lemon, pork, sweetgrass, cherry, apple, bushelberry, rock toad; but never fish, Little Daughter hated fish—set it on her window sill, and wait for Little Daughter to find her.

'*You stay in this house while I'm gone*, Brushka would warn his daughter. *I want this place clean, I want my clothes laundered, and those beans picked, you hear me?*

'*Yes, father.* Half of the things on his to-do list would take her mere hours, the other half he would forget having asked her to get to in the first place.

'*You go beyond that gate, you know what will happen, don't you?*

'*The wolves will get me.*

'*The wolves will get you. Be a good girl.*

'Little Daughter learned early on that there were no Big Bad Wolves waiting for her beyond the fence. She might have invited them in if there were. Tuck them into her father's bed and wait and see what happened. But there were no wolves, only Varrick, waiting with her pies, her motherly bosom soft and ripe for hugging. Like Vanya, Emily Varrick was a teacher, but not of practical schooling. She taught Little Daughter the ways of the world. She taught Little Daughter how to be a woman. She taught Little Daughter how to expect disappointment.

'So on the day one fine spring morn when Little Daughter went to visit her friend only to find her father sitting on the stoop, silently carving a branch into a toothpick, she was able to swallow her disappointment and paste on a smile for Brushka.

'*Aren't you afraid of the wolves, Little Daughter?* he asked her. He had grown his hair out long, the dark strands masking his down-turned eyes, shaking as he whittled away at the branch.

'*There are no wolves*, she answered him.

'Brushka sprang to his feet. *I am*, he shouted. *I am the wolf.* He punctuated his claim by beating his chest with the branch. *You should fear me.*

'She did fear him, but she was brave. *Where is Emily?*

'Brushka rushed her. He wrapped her in his arms and brought his knife across the palm of her hand. She cried out, but this seemed only to draw her uncle Karan from the tree-lined shadows. He wore a crimson cloak and read out loud from a thick, leather-bound book in a language that meant nothing to Little Daughter. But his words seemed to slither inside her and then to explode. She hurt all over, and her father said into her ear, *You have brought me nothing but pain and regret. But now—now you will bring me what I deserve.*

'Little Daughter passed into darkness, and when it was light again she found she was tethered to a chair in Varrick's hut. Varrick sat across from her, also bound, her tears softly running down her neck. Midas sat cross-legged on the floor off to the side, cradling a sleeping baby. Brushka towered over them all. When he saw she was awake, he donned rough sheepskin gloves and took the baby from Midas.

'*Your gift to me*, he said, and touched the baby to Little Daughter's cheek. In an instant, it was no more than a statue. A solid statue of pure gold. Brushka roared in triumph.

'*Now do you want to hug your friend?* He spat at Little

Daughter. *Touch her, go on!* He dragged her chair closer to the crying woman and pulled her arm nearly from its socket, until the tips of her fingers brushed the lace of Varrick's blouse, and Little Daughter curled her fingers into a fist. Brushka pushed her back. *Now you will do as I say*, he told her. *You will create my fortune. You will be my daughter no longer; my daughter will be dead. You will be my—what did you call her, Midas?—my Rumpelstiltskin, weaving flesh into gold. You will live here and never leave these woods, for now you know beyond a doubt, there are wolves out there. And they will eat you alive.*

'From time to time, he brought her someone to touch. Never again a baby, but mostly the elderly or the infirm. And he asked nothing more of her until he became King. But that, as they say, is another story.'

Liddy coughed a little to indicate she had finished speaking. Her mouth was dry, as were her eyes, and the room had dimmed as the fire in the hearth slowly burned down to embers. When the witch began to clap, she brought her eyes back to him.

The once hunched and shaggy witch was now straight-backed, muscled and clean-cut, a handsome man worthy of the handsome suit he wore. He rocked back in his chair and looked at Liddy with sated eyes.

'Bravo,' he said, grinning. His perfect teeth shown bright. 'Bravo, and then some. Little Daughter.'

'I go by Liddy,' she said.

'Liddy Vanya, as I live and breathe!' The witch hooted like an owl, and got up and danced around the room, singing her name. As he danced, the fire behind him exploded into life, flames licking at his heels. 'Liddy Vanya, Liddy Vanya, Liddy Vanya! The fabled Liddy Vanya! Turns men to gold in their beds! Wins their hearts and takes their heads! Liddy Vanya!' He spun around twice more, then skipped over to Liddy and held out his hand. 'Pleasure to make your acquaintance.'

She looked at the extended appendage. He hooted with laughter again, and spun back to his seat. 'I believe you have filled me up, Liddy Vanya. Yes, my dear, I do believe I could live for a year off that story. I do have one or two questions. May I?'

'Knock yourself out.'

'What happened to Emily Varrick?'

'She became Queen.'

Laughter caught in the witch's throat. He slapped himself on the side of the head. 'Of course! Ivan Brushka, King Ivan, he is your father! And Emily Brushka née Varrick, the Evil Stepmother. You are a fable and a princess! What luck have I, stumbling across you in my own home wood! You are not even supposed to exist—and certainly no one would ever imagine you are the King's own flesh and blood—and here you are, partaking of my hospitality. This life, dear Liddy, sometimes it delivers. Sometimes it delivers spectacularly.'

'The coast is probably clear by now.' Liddy stood up. 'Think I'll be going.'

'Wait, wait, wait!' The witch pounded the table. 'Sit, sit, sit! I must hear more! There are so many gaps, so many questions. That was the Royal Army up there, was it not? Have you defied him at last? Tell me, why are you on the run?'

'I will tell you,' Liddy said. 'But I've already paid for the things you've done for me with my last story. Unless you can do something else for me, I owe you nothing.'

'How about that bath?'

Now it was Liddy's turn to laugh. She made it sound as mirthful as possible. Then she shot steel into her eyes and bore them into the witch. 'You have something I want. A talisman. Rynin.'

His eyes sparked with understanding. 'You weren't running after all. You were searching.'

Liddy shrugged. 'I multitask.'

The witch scraped a long finger across his smooth chin, thinking. 'Who told you I had this talisman?'

Liddy picked up the witch's cane and walked casually to the closest shelf of knickknacks. 'Maybe my Kingly father did,' she said, twirling the cane from fist to fist. 'Right before I drove my blade through his neck.'

She heard the witch scoff deep in his throat. 'Is that so?' He asked levelly. He didn't quite believe her, but Liddy could tell he was starting to be cautious about her.

'Yep,' she said. She hefted the cane and struck out at the

shelf of items, batting all but a stubborn unmarked tin can to the hovel's floor. The can wobbled but remained upright. Liddy swatted it with the cane and it joined the other broken items on the floor.

'Come now,' the witch said, though he made no move to get up from the table. 'As a princess, I realize you're quite used to getting what you want, but really. You're above petty vandalism, are you not?'

'Nope.' Liddy went to the next shelf of strangely coloured vials and jars. She tapped the glass of a vial of newt eyeballs, then drew back for a mighty swing.

'Wait!'

Liddy kept her stance, glanced over her shoulder at the witch.

'Very well,' he said. 'You came for Rynin, Rynin you shall have. I keep it inside the sharpfin foetus.'

Liddy dropped the cane at her feet and turned back to the shelf. The sharpfin foetus was stuffed into the largest of the glass jars, its bulbous, deformed mass floating in a dark blue liquid. She picked it up, failed to unscrew the tightly sealed lid, and bashed the glass against the lip of the shelf. The witch hissed in displeasure as the glass shattered. The sharpfin plopped to the floor, where Liddy bent to retrieve it. It felt slimy and smelled of putrescence. She felt around its serrated gills and concave, pin-sized eyeholes before locating its slit of a mouth. Bracing the thing between her thighs, she pried its jaws open, plunged her fingers into its maw, and plucked out the talisman. She let the foetus fall back to the floor.

'You could have a tad bit more respect for my things,' the witch lamented. 'Sharpfins are a rare enough find, let alone a pregnant one. Good men no doubt died procuring that foetus, and you just swat it around as if it meant no more than an insect's poop.'

'Just keep huffing and puffing, witch,' Liddy said, not looking at him. 'Does good to vent your frustrations sometimes.'

'You want to talk about frustrations! You've already witnessed the bangs debacle, but I assure you, I have many, many more.'

The witch began to elucidate his frustrations, but Liddy was no longer listening. In her hands she held the talisman of Rynin, a four inch by two inch oblong crystal that, by the fire light, shone alternately a pale pink, forlorn blue, and nearly translucent green. She expected it to have some heft, but it barely weighed half an ounce; it felt like she held a piece of paper in her hands, not the answer to all of her own (much graver) frustrations. Assuming her father had not lied to her—and on their deathbeds, Liddy found, few men did—this talisman would call forth a powerful sorcerer called Rynin. He would be able to remove her curse; for the first time in ten years, she would be able to feel the warmth and texture of another's touch.

'Thank you, witch,' she said.

The witch was deep into a tale about his manicurist's insistence on using a mandrake-based lotion as opposed to a gentler, and altogether, in the witch's opinion, less horrendously odorous aloe-based lotion, but he cut himself off mid-sentence to say, 'Excuse me?'

Liddy rolled the talisman around in her palm, mesmerized by it. 'Thank you,' she repeated. 'Thank you for this gift.'

'An item for which the customer pays can hardly be called a gift,' the witch said. 'Now, are you ready to tell your next story?'

'You know what they say about stories, don't you, witch? I'm sure you do. All stories must come to an end, eventually. I'm afraid we have arrived—'

Liddy's voice was cut off by an abrupt and snarling roar, and she looked up from the crystal to see, in the spot at the table formerly occupied by the witch, a towering black bear. The tatters of a tuxedo clung to its furry mass. It stood on its haunches and clawed the air and frothed at the mouth and made a big show of being big and scary. Then it dropped to all fours and rushed Liddy.

'Fuck,' Liddy said. She almost had time to reach the knife hidden at her shin, but the bear was witchingly fast. In a blink, it swallowed her fist—the one clutching the talisman—and chomped down, severing her hand at the wrist. The bear made a grotesque slurping noise, and Liddy watched a lump travel down the creature's throat as her hand disappeared into its stomach. Luckily, shock saved her from experiencing anything other than embarrassment at having failed so ungracefully.

Not wasting another second, Liddy unsheathed the knife with her good hand and took a swipe at the bear, but it pivoted away and made a leap toward the spiral staircase. She gripped the knife's handle in her teeth, swooped up the witch's cane, and darted after the bear. It made it to the first spiral before experiencing some difficulty maneuvering its bulk around the curve. This slowed it down enough for Liddy to hook the cane around one of its hind legs and yank the bear back down the steps. Its head slammed against the bottom step with a sickening crunch, but the bear recovered quickly and swung around to roar at Liddy. With a practiced quickness, Liddy dropped the cane, grabbed the knife from her mouth, and stabbed the pointy end into the roof of the bear's open mouth. The yowl that the thing emitted then was most decidedly human. It reared up, throwing blood across the room, and crashed back down, the impact rippling through the space like an earthquake, disrupting the stacks of books and other witchy paraphernalia along the walls, all of which fell to the floor in a tremendous cacophony.

The bear slowly and painfully transformed back into the lanky human witch. He curled in on himself and moaned, eyes squinted shut against the pain, the knife still protruding from his slobbering, bloodied mouth. Liddy ripped the blade out, knelt behind him, and plunged it through his back, aiming for the heart. She was spot on, and his spasms ceased in short order.

'Goddamn shifter,' Liddy muttered. She straightened herself and gave the witch a stern kick. 'I had a whole speech about storybook endings. I worked for like an hour on it.' Two more kicks. 'You're not even imaginative. A bear? A wolf would've at least been clever.' One final heel to the ribs. 'And you ate my fucking hand!' She pulled the knife out of his back and sheathed it.

Her hand—or rather, the lack of it—was going to be a problem. The pain hadn't kicked in yet but the blood loss was rapid and even if she was able to stop that from killing her, infection was pretty much guaranteed (when was the last time that bear brushed its teeth?). Her only hope was the Vermillion Cural. While she'd never used it to actually grow bones, she'd heard rumours this was possible. Even if not, the skin around her stump would at least seal up, infection-free. Of course, she would need to down a lot of VC for the results she wanted, and that brought with it the risk of overdosing. As the VC worked to restore the body to peak condition, it gave the heart quite a workout. Too much, and the heart would give out, or, more accurately, explode. Liddy wasn't aware of any witch's brew that could un-explode a heart.

The kettle had been knocked over in the bear quake, but Liddy righted it, fumbled around in the cabinets a bit, and got the water boiling. She held her arm to her chest, wrapping a scrap of her shirt around the end to tie the sleeve tight against the blood loss. She thought about cauterizing it herself while she waited for the tea to brew but by then the pain was coming on and she was beginning to swoon. When the kettle whistled, she wasted no time letting the brew cool, and poured the entire contents of the smouldering tea down her throat. Even as it seemed to burn a hole through her stomach, the VC worked its magic; Liddy's entire left arm was shot through with pain, doubling her over and causing her to dry heave as she struggled to hold down her vomit.

She lost consciousness for a time. When the hovel came spinning back into view, Liddy's hand had re-grown. It felt sore and numb and it was difficult to bend the wrist or flex the fingers, but it was there, brand spanking new. She wondered briefly if maybe the curse wouldn't affect this new hand, but she knew she wasn't that lucky. Her only hope still lay with Rynin. Which, as luck would have it, was now inside the witch's stomach.

Liddy crawled her way over to the witch's prone form, her entire body throbbing with the effort. She rolled him over and brought out her knife.

'A princess's work is never done,' she said, and set to it.

# Blueprint for Red Wings

## R.J. Booth

*There is a mountain that remains only in the minds of butter-flies, and the flights of Monarchs. It is marked on a voyage of four lifetimes, a journey no one Monarch makes in its entirety. Yet, for this, each one knows, instinctively, where to begin.*

More than a fortnight had gone by when the call first came up the valley. It was a fall day, long past the snap of early May and the shimmering wall of summer heat that sent us fleeing into the forest. There was no word of mouth this time, but a cadre of guards set swarming up the mountain, and a gathering the like of which we hadn't seen for a decade. Then I knew I wasn't the only one watching for Monarchs.

'I'd like to call on Farming and Emergency,' said the Speaker.

*Frozen in hibernation over the long winter, they wake slowly, in shivers that ripple over the wing-scaled canopy. Soon these multitudinous cocoons will disintegrate into a flight of millions - but for now they wait, flexing. Their muscles take time to warm, the ice to evaporate from their wings, turning them to orange lenses in the dawn light.*

'Emergency? What's he doing here? You finally found him one, huh?'

The side-show had already started by the time I had arrived – Atmos, Head of Farming (and, for us terracers, our Householder) taking his seat with the gravity of a man who'd rather be pulling potatoes on the field than teeth in a meet.

'It was felt that the situation needed a steadier hand, Atmos,' said Orville, sweeping the dust from his own spot, 'so to speak.'

'Long as they know the difference between a steady hand and one that's asleep.'

The Head of Emergency drew himself up six balding feet from his boots, and Atmos leaned on an elbow to watch him.

'Gentlemen,' said the Speaker, 'we're here for your thoughts on the issue, not to watch you trade insults.'

The two Householders looked at each other a spell, 'til Atmos cleared his throat and broke it.

'Well,' he said, rubbing his knees, 'don't know what I'm here for, 'cept to say the butterflies seem to be running late this year.'

'Butterflies? This meeting's about butterflies?' Way back in the crowd, Elias exchanged smirks with a bunch of fellow hands.

'Maybe some of you can't see why that might be a problem.' Atmos fixed him with that sharp eye of his, and the mutters faded. 'I know some of you see 'em as just this pretty thing comes round once a year, but they do pollinate a few of our more staple crops. No pollination, no plants, no food.'

'Now hold on a minute there, Atmos.' said Orville. 'It's all very well saying we've got this potentially disastrous problem, when you're not offering a solution for it.'

'Well, Orville, if you'd just let me get to it,' said Atmos, and for a moment, he clenched his hands together, one inside the other. 'Now there is an idea, comes out of China. In some places, they just sort of brushed pollen onto the blossoms, pollinated it themselves. I reckon that'd work pretty well for now.'

'There we go. We can handle that, can't we? Problem solved.'

'The immediate problem, certainly, but I'm not sure you're grasping the situation here.'

Orville rankled. 'Well, why don't you tell me what I'm not getting?'

'It's not just about the butterflies, is it? What about all the rest of them?'

'The rest of them?'

'No one thing lives here in isolation,' said Atmos. 'Those butterflies are part of a cycle every place they pass through. Here, for example, they don't just pollinate a few plants. They feed the birds. Their caterpillars, they eat the plants. S'one hell of a mess in there. So many things all tied up in knots we can't hope to untangle.'

'Surely the valley can survive the loss of a few butterflies.'

Atmos shrugged. 'Maybe it can, maybe it can't. That's not what I was getting at. These butterflies have been coming here for hundreds of thousands, if not millions of years. That path is so well-engrained in 'em, no one tells 'em where to go, they just know it. On instinct. They've made it through wars, climate change, disasters of all kinds…'

'What exactly's your point, Atmos?' said Orville.

'Problem ain't that they're not coming,' said Atmos. 'It's what's stopping them.'

*The Monarchs rise with the lengthening dawn, returning to sites marked by generations before them. Here, they mate and lay the first eggs of the year. Here, they will remain. It is the next generation, the first born of the year, who will begin the journey as it truly is.*

We all sat silent. Up across the meadow, the hum of lazy bluebottles and the last of the summer bees entwined in a discordant buzz, as crane flies danced drunkenly in the sunlight.

Orville spoke first: 'So there's something stopping the butterflies from coming?'

'Well, that I can't say for sure,' said Atmos. 'Hardly as I've been out of the valley to check now, is it? All I'm saying is those butterflies don't just stop on their own.'

'Maybe something else is coming,' said a voice to my left

'Maybe it's not safe to stay anymore,' came another.

'No, I'm not necessarily saying that…' said Atmos.

'Hang on,' said Elias. 'Why should we go? We've got it pretty good here, haven't we? Good food, good weather. Pretty nice place to raise a family, right? How is this not safe?'

'No one's saying we've got to go, Elias,' said Orville.

'And why should we? Just cos the old fool's lost a few butterflies.'

'Elias!' Orville hissed.

'There's no need for that, son,' said Atmos. 'All I'm saying is we need to be prepared, that's all.'

'Prepared for what? He can't even tell us what we're scared of!' Elias snorted. 'You know what this is? This is scaremongering, that's what. Just a sad old man scaring children with his campfire bogeymen. You should be ashamed, Atmos.'

'Elias, I think you just need to calm down,' said Orville.

'No. You know what?' Elias said. 'We're leaving.'

Elias corralled his brood in front of him, a heap of fierce winnings. I felt for him as I watched him go. Elias's roots ran deep here. Now with his ripe wife and bundle of little ones, they'd set down so far down into the valley, you couldn't rip them up without killing him.

I waited a while before I took off, quiet as I could, though few would miss me. I returned a nod from Atmos as I went – one of understanding that, sometimes, it takes a word from an old friend to talk a man down – and ignored the look from Orville as he caught what passed between us.

The sunlight, spilt across the meadow like molasses, gave way to the cool afterglow of the trees. Blinking those brilliant blue flecks from my eyes, I followed Elias's brood to the first clearing - and no further. Shapes came true from the shadows, the tree-twisted spindles. I veered off onto a path that took me further North. True, when we were kids, we'd follow each other everywhere, but that was a long time ago. He had to take his own path. Mine went towards the crown of the valley.

The Settlement had petered out this far into the forest. These cabins and nooks amongst the glades were mostly storage or safe houses. We'd all made a study of these places as kids, learning the forest had as much a will of its own as we did, and if we respected that, all would be well. There were worse things than trees out there.

Climbing up to meet the high Terraces, I tugged a suitable straw from a wild patch of grass, chewed it as I leaned on a post. Watched the sparkles from the river wend their way downstream, a daylight positive of the Milky Way on nights it stretched the valley end to end. Five hands of the Households stood like pebbles washed up along the shore. My hand had found a tight grip on the spruce next to me. I laughed at myself and patted the old thing. I'd seen Atmos do the same thing, matter of fact, as a child, a hundred times or more. Always thought the old man was a bit crazy.

The view was one of the few benefits of working that sunbald patch of mountainside. I could see them down in the hollow, still bickering like hares. Further, the dull gleam of the Monarch, the butterflies' namesake, a giant's broken tin can, thrust preternatural from the thicket, there since long before I'd been a glint in anyone's eye, yet unlike the mould-dogged shacks of the hillsides, unclaimed by roots or weeds. The forest didn't want it.

By rule, this Terrace was the furthest we were allowed on an unseen border between infrequent signposts. The points, burned into our childhoods – two paces past the last cabin on the South-West side, the crossed thicket over the East – held lines that twanged like hamstrings. Being this close felt like some guilty transgression to that part of me forever ten years old. How far had we gotten that time they caught us, mere metres over the line? For what had they hauled us in front of our respective Householders, to shame us and tan our hides? It'd felt like no distance at all. And yet, unlike all those other dumb rebellions of youth, I hadn't howled at the injustice.

See the way it was put to us, it was about us all being in it together. The Settlement couldn't do without you. You were the contribution you made, and you owed it to the group to stay alive. There could be no weak link, no frayed bind. That was understood, but that had never stilled our curiosity at what the line was for.

'I wonder if the rest of the world's like this?' I'd asked Elias one day. 'Less trees, and more rocks.'

'Don't reckon so,' Elias had said. 'Atmos says there's lots of different places. Places where it's so cold, even the ground's made of ice. Places called Deserts - they're like that sandy beach down by the Outpost, 'cept they go on forever. Places that look like here too.'

'That doesn't make sense,' I'd said. 'If it was just like here, why would they keep us out?'

'I don't know.' Elias had thought about this as he'd dug a notch into one of the tree stumps on the edge of the Terrace. 'Maybe it's all poisoned still.' He grabbed at me all of a sudden. 'Maybe you die this awful choking death.' Elias coughed his lungs out, feigned a dry retch or two and rolled about on the dirt.

'I heard it's not like that,' I said. 'I heard it's much worse…'

'Hey, we're only going to look, right?' Elias said, dusting himself off. 'It can't hurt to look.'

I reckoned he was probably right there.

We knew the mountainside well enough, knew how to pull ourselves up by this root here, that tuft there. Though the trees thinned a little by the Terrace, it wasn't until further up towards the crags that we saw spindles of woodland start to fragment and fall apart, showing our beloved, fearful forest for what it really was: A bunch of trees knotted up at their roots. As we crossed the line, we quietened, feeling that invisible twang – but if it had never been drawn, we'd have known this wasn't where we were supposed to be long before the crag gave way to empty space above us.

Elias pulled me up onto the outcrop, and we turned to look back on the valley below. We'd played at Kings by the big rocks by the Settlement. Armies fell to the swipes of our stick swords, as we argued over who would claim the tallest of those massive boulders for their own, so the biggest kingdom, and rule over all. We'd often looked up to the stub-topped peak and dreamed of how it'd be to be king of that mountain, ruling our screaming and waving hordes from the highest and boldest throne we could picture.

Yet all those mighty things seemed so much less than we'd imagined. The Households were no more than grains of sand along a trickle of sunlight, down river was lost to all but the keenest eyes. All we'd ever known seemed dizzying small and far away.

'Are you scared?' Elias said, at last.

I shook my head. 'Nope,' I said, and set my lip firm. 'You?'

'Me neither.' He coughed down a curious jerk in his voice.

We were both breathing like we'd run the valley end to end, though I could swear we'd climbed steeper than this.

'So,' I said, 'on the count of three, we turn around.'

Elias nodded. 'We count together.'

'One,'

'Two,'

'Three.'

We turned, and opened our eyes.

Beyond the grassy ledge, the ground dropped away, bare

rocks and scree became air, and we found ourselves suspended above a vast rug of green. Like the mountains, the streams and forest we had always known, yes, but more so. Beyond us lay a hundred thousand, million billion valleys just like ours, stretching away and beyond those peaks of high grey mountains. Stretching away from us and into infinity, more vast than my heart could encompass.

'It's just like ours.'

Elias's words rung with disappointment, and my joy silenced. What would I have said to the defeat on his face, to tell him I felt nothing like? I wanted to shake him, as if I could just knock the fog out of him, and make him see.

'No,' I said. 'No, it's not.'

There was a low hiss, and flickering on the edge of the trees ahead of us, like the forest unravelling. It rippled through the green rug, crawling towards the mountain with a speed that sapped that of our faltered backwards steps.

Then, butterflies. Hundreds of thousands. Through branches and trees and thickets and bushes, and over and around that haggard mountain top and beyond. In the white light, their wings caught and filtered, a flock of orange red glimpses, a million unseen perspectives of sky fluttered down into the valley behind us.

I turned to Elias. He was already climbing down.

We were found, as children often are, scant metres from that umbilical leash. We never told how far we'd gotten, but we were still taken before the householders. Still beaten for it. And when our humiliation and hurt was complete, Elias blamed me for that. Another bind snapped that seemingly no one else could see. Not even Atmos, that towering oak of childhood fear, who had attended our mock trial along with Orville, as our then prospective householders.

I still remember it. Orville, that streak of birch, had never approved of me, and to his credit, had never made a secret of that. But to see the bitterness reflected in Elias's face was worse punishment than any switch or severity the man could have levied. He would never look at me again without that veil of contempt drifting out of memory and across that face. I had been prepared for as harsh a castigation from Atmos.

Yet his manner, by contrast, had been less severe than I'd expected from a man who could force a confession with a mere glance. Oh, the thundering words were there, but to look at him? There was no fury in his eyes, not even disappointment. Atmos, he wasn't even there.

Perhaps it wouldn't have made much difference. Afterwards, Elias and I were separated into our work groups, the roles we had been expected to take up. The days of our friendship had always been numbered. We never spoke after that.

*The second and third generations mark the Summer, each one migrating further north and east, before laying the eggs of their children; who, in turn, continue the journey on. Whether each one is aware of the pattern laid down for them is impossible to know. Yet they persist, until the first signs of the Winter to come.*

I came back down the mountain by degrees, back through the thick of trees, and out into the meadow, shielding my eyes from the sinking sun and the last stragglers from the meeting. I found Atmos still sat there on one of the carved logs, and asked if I might exchange a word. He patted the bench as invitation.

'Did you find Elias?'

I shook my head.

'I figured as much. It's no secret you two don't get on so well these days,' said Atmos. 'He's got too much of his father in him these days. Maybe you both do, come to that. Come sit down, child, don't dawdle. You know,' he added, 'there was a time when we thought the two of you might…'

'Atmos, I'm not sure I want to talk for long.'

'It's not a request. Sit.'

In the light of the field, distant children turned a moment, then went on their way.

'Now, go on,' said Atmos. 'If you're in a hurry, say your piece.'

Even after so long, the man still had an awful power to unnerve me when he saw need. 'What did the House decide?' I asked.

'Oh well. The usual.' Atmos shifted his weight a little and his knee cracked. 'Much as they always do. Every one of them's got to say their piece, even if it's not their jurisdiction, but when they're all frit out of their wits, what they're saying doesn't make much sense. They're coming round to it, though. Should all work out in the end, if that's what's troubling you.'

'No.' I said. 'It's not.'

'Where have you been?'

'To the mountain.'

Atmos nodded. 'Good place to think up there. Can't say I blame you for the view. Some folks want to go up, act like they're all big news. Others get a kick out of how small they feel. Used to do it myself. 'Course, that was a good while back now, but.' He twisted a piece of grass out of the tuft beside him. 'So how far past the line did you get this time?'

I didn't answer.

'Come now. I've seen you look up that mountain, a look on your face I never see you get anywhere else. I wouldn't be doing my job if I wasn't keeping an eye on you. How far d'you get?'

'Far enough,' I said.

'Beyond the valley, then.'

'No,' I said. 'Not this time.' I cleared my throat, and I'm still not sure why, but I added, 'That was when we were kids.'

There was a moment of silence I couldn't rightly count, and when I looked up again, Atmos was staring right at me.

'So you made it up there after all. And here was me thinking they'd caught you before you'd done any damage. That'll teach me.' There was an odd spark in his eye as that grass stem whirled in his mouth.

'Well,' he said, 'the rules say I oughta punish you for this, but I think you were punished enough at the time for what the two of you did. You'll just get the lion's share of the pollination duties instead.'

I screwed up my fists on my knees. 'Atmos, I won't be painting flowers.'

'So you fancy moving to another group, eh?' he said. 'Well, I don't see any problem with that. I mean, the groups're supposed to be fixed, but if there's no objection elsewhere, then…'

'I don't want a transfer either.'

Atmos sniffed. 'Well, you know, this game's going to be a whole lot easier if you tell me what you do want.'

'I want to leave.'

'The Settlement?'

'The valley.'

We sat there for a while, Atmos and I, watching the shadows pooling in the trees.

He said, 'Where do you think you'll go?'

I shrugged. 'I don't know.'

'Might be an idea to have some kind of a plan here. Have you considered a direction? North? South?'

I had no answer for him. 'I'll know when I leave,' I said.

'Do you even know what you're looking for?'

I tried. 'I think I do.' I said, 'I've been looking for it ever since I came back down the mountain. Every time the butterflies come back. Something's been missing. Something doesn't fit, and I think I've worked out what it is.' I took a breath. 'It's me.'

Atmos shook his head slow. 'That doesn't sound right to me.'

'That's what I've got,' I said.

'Well, I just don't see it,' he said. 'You have a place here, and you do your job well. I know I'm not one for big shows of praise, but fact is, you're one of the best hands I have at my disposal. And, well, folks care about you. Can't see what's more of a fit than that.'

'I know I've got a job here. It's not… It's not the same thing.'

''It's not perfect, granted. But we all get along. About as well as you'd expect, anyways. But then, that's just about getting along with folks, isn't it? Even misfits like us have to play our part.'

'We do?'

''Course we do, child,' said Atmos, practically laughing at me. 'How else are we going to survive out here? Each of us takes a role, and we work together to get through it.'

'See that's the problem.' I said. 'Since I was born, I've had this role, one that was made for me. But, see, I didn't make it myself. Someone made it for me.'

'Well, like I said, you're free to transfer between whatever group you like…'

'That's no solution, is it?' I said as I stood. 'I can move about this valley as much as I like, but nothing's changed. I'll still be set in a role. I might as well have not moved a damned inch.'

'Well now, is that what you really think?'

'You want to know why I didn't go over that mountain?' I said, near shouted. 'Because I swore, the next time I went up there, it'd be the last. I'd be gone. I'd go see for myself what you've been keeping from me all these years. All these roles and rules. Y'all try and pretend like this is the whole damn world. Well, it's not. Not even close. That, out there, there's so much more to it…'

I was trembling at the weight of all that I'd held in for so long spilling and pouring and tumbling all out of me. Yet that question dammed it solid as a rock.

'What do you mean,' I said, 'is that what I really think?'

Atmos scratched his jaw a little. 'Well, you've been quiet so long, it's kind of been hard to tell,' he said. 'Ever since the time we caught you on the mountain. Truth be told, there was a point I feared we'd broken you. Then you always were a stubborn little dickens. Reminded me of myself at that age. I should have realised that.'

Atmos paused, rubbing his hands together. Then he dusted off his trousers and pulled himself up, his knees cracking like winter branches.

'So, you know there's more to this world than the valley. That's true, though I certainly don't think we've lied to you about that. But what do you intend to do about it?'

'Well, I'm going over the top,' I said.

'Are you now?' He said.

'I am.' I felt a mite irked all of a sudden. 'You can't stop me.'

'Certain I can't,' Atmos said. 'I think it's suicide, myself, but it's your decision.'

'Suicide?'

'Those signs aren't up there for nothing, child.'

'Then how come we made it up and back again, and we were just fine?'

'You don't know what's beyond that mountain.'

'Neither do you, from the sounds of it.'

Atmos sighed. 'No. You're right there. I don't know exactly,' he said, pulling his old hat on. 'But what I do know is this. A hundred tin cans went up in the Monarch programme, and far as I know, ours was the only one that fell back down. I could be wrong on that. Maybe there are others, but child, they'd be so far from here, the chances of ever finding them are millions to one. Now, say those signs are wrong too, say the sickness isn't so bad now. Even if you somehow manage to carve yourself a life out of the wilderness, find safe food and shelter, you'll be forever on your own.' Atmos paused. 'You've never really been alone, have you, child?'

I considered this. What he'd said was true. I'd gone off on my own sometimes, but I'd mostly been back in time for supper, and if not, there was always some abandoned safe house waiting in the forest. There'd always been someone there, but...

I felt Atmos's hand grip my arm.

'Stay,' he said. 'Pick your own patch of land. Strike out with your own group. I can talk the House round.'

There was more worry round the corner of his eyes than there was when we were kids. His hands shook slightly, slowly rubbing themselves down to the bone.

Perhaps I'd been alone a long time already.

'It'd still be someone else's dream, Atmos,' I said. Not mine.'

We shook hands, parted. He went his way, and I went to the Household cabin to pack up my things. For a moment I gave a thought to what Atmos had said about Elias, then brushed it away. But passing the fields, watching folks eating and talking, families chin-wagging, it did cross my mind, if I'd held onto something so tight I'd never let anything else in.

I climbed much the same route I'd taken a thousand times before, but this time, the air seemed clearer, the stink of earth, fresher, somehow – like, as a child, for the first time. I found myself by that same old tree on the Terrace, and turned to take in that view one last time.

I could see Atmos down by the tin can, as he turned to look up. I saw him, for the first time, not as some giant of an elder tree, but as one isolated high on the mountainside, unravelled from those spindles of forest, yet still clinging on proud. It was as if there were words unsaid in it, gestures in the flight of insects that blew into meaning, and then were gone.

*They say no one butterfly makes the whole migration, though the last generation of the year, the most northerly, does make the full journey back. Fleeing before the encroaching Winter, they will head South, across three continents, wending their way to the wintering grounds of their forebears.*

*And yet, in this ancient path, there lies a quirk. As the flights pass over Lake Superior, the Monarchs will take a sharp turn east, before they continue their southward path. This aberrant in an otherwise smooth path across the waters is all that remains of what once impeded their journey - an obstacle too vast but to go around. Some regard it as an anachronism, a curio. But this inheritance continues though the mountain has long since gone, enduring more in memory than it has in the world.*

*Finally the Monarchs reach home; the forests where their great-great Grandparents had begun their final flight all those months ago. They have never seen this place with their own eyes before, nor will the great-great grandchildren who make this same journey. Yet they know that this is the place to rest.*

'Another one gone, Atmos?' said Orville.

He 'd found the man, as he always did usual, in the Monarch, hunched over the same worn interface.

'Get the machine started,' Atmos said. 'Sample should still be fresh enough for another.'

Orville frowned and folded his arms. The Monarch was still in regular use, as expected for the younger ones just starting their own families. Yet, more than any of the other original settlers, he'd watched Atmos go through this routine every few years. Every time it was the same story.

'You care so much for these children, Atmos,' he said, 'but you always lose them in the end. You get careless about 'em.'

Orville watched Atmos flip a switch and begin tapping away at the keys with those shaky hands. His old friend's stubbornness had been such a boon in the early days, but it was now proving beyond irritating. It was becoming dangerous.

'There's too much of you in them, Atmos,' Orville tried again. 'They look up to you too much. When it comes down to it, you're too soft on 'em. Almost to the point of encouragement, in fact.'

He knew he was pushing Atmos, but no reaction came.

'Anyone'd think you pushed them.'

Still nothing. Enough was enough. Orville grabbed Atmos's shoulder and turned him. He looked his friend over, trying to find some trace of what the hell was going through the man's mind. Atmos just looked square right back at him with those grey eyes.

'You've gotta let them make their own mistakes,' he said, steadily.

'Even the fatal ones?' said Orville. 'Even the ones that mean sending them to die out there?'

Atmos stared and, for a moment, Orville thought he could see something there. A deep regret, loneliness - then, defiance, before they hardened over, and once more he couldn't see a damned thing in those stream-clear eyes.

'Especially those,' said Atmos..

# The Last Rushani

## Jonathan Ward

The gathering of the clans took place at the centre of the village, or rather where the village had once stood. The fires had raged for three full days before a storm had quelled them at last, and they had left little in their wake. Only a few charred stumps of wood emerging from the bare, ash-coated earth showed that people had ever lived here. That and the corpses: men, women and children shrivelled by the tremendous heat into blackened husks that flaked and broke apart when the wind blew strongly. Even their bones crumbled at the slightest touch.

The settlement was deep within Bask territory, but despite that the leaders of all five of the other clans had shown up. Not that they possessed much choice; the Bask were the strongest and their word was law. This time, though, coercion had not been necessary. The content of the message had been enough to bring the leaders here on their fastest horses. Now they waited, exchanging news with those from allied clans and eying their foes with suspicion. Hands were never far from weapons, but the presence of over two dozen Bask warriors ensured that an uneasy peace was maintained.

At last the leader of the Bask arrived, walking at the head of a line of his finest warriors. Unlike the leaders of some of the other clans, Dax was a warrior. In his half century of life he had ensured the supremacy of the Bask by crushing all who dared oppose him. The mace that hung from a loop on his belt had struck down more than one of the former leaders of the clans gathered there; its head permanently stained by the blood of his victims. He looked around at the assembled leaders and smiled, though there was no warmth in his expression.

'I'll get straight to the point. This was once a village of

about three hundred people. All Bask, all loyal. And all gone, in one night.'

The assembled leaders glanced nervously at each other. Lar of the Mixlan was the first to speak.

'A terrible loss, and you have the sympathies of all the Mixlan. Was it the volcano?'

At these words everyone looked west. The Wolf's Teeth Mountains could just be seen in the distance, a great plume of grey smoke rising from the largest. The volcano had been erupting for weeks now; the sun was often almost completely blotted out by a thick blanket of smoke. When it rained, which occurred less frequently now, the drops of water were contaminated by particles of grey ash. At night, a faint orange glow could sometimes be seen flickering over the mountains.

'The volcano?' Dax asked. 'No. This village was attacked.'

A few seconds passed as his words sank in, then there was a babble of voices as each of the leaders quickly tried to assure Dax that their people were not responsible. He stood motionless while they prattled on, his mouth twisted in an amused smirk that was not mirrored in his eyes.

'Enough,' he growled, and silence fell immediately. 'I know that none of you did it. Not one of you has the courage to attack us.' Some of the leaders gritted their teeth or looked away as he spoke those words, but all knew that it was the truth.

'One survived.' Dax said. 'Bring the prisoner forward!'

The warriors behind Dax moved aside and two stepped forward from the rear of the group. They held another man between them, although in truth he was barely out of his teenage years. His hair was plaited and stained in the Bask fashion, though much of it was charred and blackened. He had been disarmed, which was a serious matter for a member of that clan, and his hands and feet were bound with leather cord. The two warriors dragged him forward and jerked him to a halt just outside the circle of clan leaders. He looked up at them, or tried to. A metal collar was fastened around his neck, and from it an iron sphere hung on a rusted chain. He could not raise his head for longer than a few seconds before the weight pulled him back into a slumped position, so that the ball rested on the ground. The Bask leader stared at him for a moment before speaking again, his voice laden with contempt.

'This coward lives when all others perished. Our scouts found him two days after the village was razed, pinned to the ground by some kind of black spine that had been bent around his leg and driven deep into the earth. So deep, I am told, that it took five men to free him.' Dax snorted, obviously contemptuous of this apparent weakness. 'He did not survive due to any great feat of courage. No. He was deliberately spared so that he could pass on a message. I have decided that you all need to hear it as well.'

Dax paused, but the prisoner did not speak. He stared at the ground, seemingly unaware of what was going on. The Bask gestured, and one of his warriors immediately slammed the haft of his weapon in between the prisoner's shoulder blades, driving him to his knees and tearing a pained grunt from between tightly-pressed lips. He looked up, fury briefly showing itself in his expression before fading under the weight of the gaze of his ruler.

'The village was attacked by a firedrake.'

His words were greeted with disbelief and derision from the leaders of the five lesser clans. Lar began to laugh, but he quickly stopped as he became aware that the Bask were standing in grim-faced silence, showing no sign of scepticism.

'Surely you're not serious?' That came from Malkiss of the Black Wolves. Dax merely gazed at him for a long moment before turning away dismissively.

'Continue.'

The prisoner nodded. 'It came at night, when the full moon was at its highest. The first we knew of it was when the animals began to squeal and bellow. Then there was a great pounding noise like thunder; the beat of its wings. And after that the roar of flames. By the time all of our warriors had gathered in the open the village was already surrounded by a great ring of fire. There was no escape, no way to get our children to safety.'

He paused, and lowered his head for a moment. When he raised it again defiance burned in his eyes. 'We fought,' he spat, staring around at the Bask. 'Every one of us who could hold a blade. But the gust of its great wings deflected most of our arrows, and those that hit seemed only to irritate it. It belched great balls of flame that incinerated half a dozen at a time, while it constantly circled the village and struck down any who tried to hide or flee. It took its time. It *enjoyed* it.

'By now every building was ablaze and the creature finally landed. Those that charged it were cut down by its claws before they could even strike a blow. Some ran, but I will not speak their names. The firedrake didn't even chase them, just killed them one by one with precise bursts of white fire. In the end only I was left. It looked at me, its mouth gaping, and I could see it wanted me to charge. So I did.'

He looked round, and flinched at the clear looks of disbelief on the faces of every Bask warrior. 'I did, I swear it! The firedrake let me come within striking distance then knocked my sword from my hand. Before I could react it pinned me to the ground with one claw and stared down at me. I could feel the heat of its breath on my face; I thought it was going to kill me. But it didn't. It gave me a message to pass on. Then it took me from the village, away from the flames, and used a spine it tore from its hide to pin me in place. That is the truth; I swear it by all the gods.'

'The message.' Dax's voice was flat, his expression grim. The prisoner closed his eyes, and his lips moved briefly.

'Listen well, little thing, and take this message to those who rule your kind. The mountain breathes and I soar once again. From sea to sea this land is mine and I claim it by right of power. Submit and you shall live; resist and you shall burn. When the moon has cycled three times and waxes full once more I will return to this place to hear your decision. Choose wisely; others of my kind will one day find their freedom too, and they are not nearly as merciful as I.'

The prisoner fell silent and bowed his head once again. The clan leaders stared at each other, disbelief slowly giving way to fear. Dax took a step forward.

'So there it is. I don't believe what this prisoner has said about his supposed *courage*, but the rest of his story rings true. The firedrakes have returned, or at least one of them, and now we have to deal with it.'

'But what can we do?' Lar asked. 'Nobody has seen a firedrake in over five hundred years; most people think they are myths!'

'What do we do?' Dax snarled, and pulled his mace free from his belt. 'What do you think we do. We *fight*!' The Bask warriors behind him sent up a resounding cheer in response. The prisoner lifted his head but remained silent while the other clan leaders looked uncertain.

'I brought you here to see for yourself, so you would understand the urgency. The first full moon that the creature spoke of is already two weeks past, so our time is running out. Each of you will return to your lands and raise as many fighting men as you can, and return with them three days before the third full moon. Bring ballistae, siege catapults; any kind of siege weapon you have in fact. This firedrake thinks we are weak, but it is wrong. The clans are united and that gives us strength and purpose. Together we can defeat it. We *will* defeat it.'

The Bask cheered again, and this time the clan leaders joined in, masking their apprehension behind enthusiastic expressions. It was clear that the decision had been made. This was not a debate, it never had been. Dax spoke, and they obeyed; they had no other choice. As the cheering died away silence briefly fell, and in that moment of calm a woman's voice rang out.

'What about the blade of Haldor?'

It was one of Lar's party that had spoken. As the others parted and everyone turned their attention on her she remained still, one hand resting on the pommel of her sword, apparently unafraid. Dax gave her little more than a glance before looking away.

'Foolish girl. Haldor's blade is a myth, nothing more.'

'So were firedrakes, yet here we are.'

The Bask leader snarled. 'Lar, keep your woman quiet or I will shut her up myself.' The clan leader turned, but before he could say anything the woman drew her blade. There was a clatter as everyone around her did the same, and for a few moments everyone was frozen in place.

'What are you doing, Dana?' Lar hissed. 'Stop this madness now, before you get yourself killed!'

Dana looked at him for a moment. 'I can't do that. You see, I'm not one of your clan. Not truly.' She looked over to the Bask and raised her voice. 'I am Dana of the Rushani clan, last of my people.'

Dax froze, then slowly turned back to face her. His warriors muttered amongst themselves, several drawing their weapons and gripping them tightly.

'Impossible,' Dax spat. 'The Rushani clan are gone. I should know, I killed the last of them myself, almost twenty years ago.'

'Wrong,' the woman snapped back, and smiled sweetly as the Bask leader snarled. 'My parents fled the slaughter when I was just a baby. They knew that your thugs were chasing them so they gave me away to a passing Mixlan couple before they went to their deaths. The Rushani live on in me.'

'You are a fool, woman,' Dax replied. 'By telling me this you have signed your own death warrant.' To his surprise she smiled at this.

'Perhaps. But it seems like you have bigger problems right now; the kind that fly. And if you will not even look for Haldor's blade, I will.'

'Ha, so confident. You won't even leave here alive.'

Dana sighed theatrically. 'Very well then. I demand trial by combat!'

Everyone looked to Dax. Trial by combat was frowned upon within the five lesser clans but actively encouraged by the Bask. Their trials were brutal; injuries and even death were commonplace and no Bask was regarded as fit for rule if he had not been victorious in many such trials. Dax shook his head.

'A woman, little more than a girl? You're not even worth the effort it would take me to kill you.' He turned towards his warriors. 'Even so, a challenge has been issued. Which of you would like the honour of killing the last Rushani?'

Before he had even finished speaking one of the men had

already stepped forward. He stood almost six feet tall, and was at least twice as wide as the Rushani girl. Dax smiled and slammed his hand on to the warrior's shoulder, who took the blow without flinching.

'Good! Cal will accept your challenge, girl. Your terms?'

'When I win, I will go and find Haldor's blade. A week before the firedrake's deadline passes you will meet me here and I will hand it over.' Dax frowned, but met her gaze unflinchingly, ignoring the muttering of those around him.

'Why would you do that?' Lar asked suddenly.

'He's going to raise an army to battle this monster. He'll need the blade to defeat it,' she replied, then turned away from her erstwhile clan leader. 'Enough talk. Let's get this over with.'

Dax smiled. 'You have spirit, I'll give you that. Goodbye, girl.'

As everyone backed away to give them room to fight, Cal stepped forward and swept his sword through the air between them in a series of vicious motions. Dana raised her sword but otherwise remained where she was, her gaze fixed on him. Without warning the Bask lunged at her, bringing his sword down in a powerful slash that would have cut her apart if it had connected. Dana sidestepped sharply, moving back as the warrior twisted quickly and swept his blade out towards her. Again it hit nothing but air, and Cal let out a frustrated snarl. He recovered his footing and thrust his sword towards her belly. Once more Dana stepped aside, but as she moved she pivoted and swung her leg out, hammering her foot into the side of his left knee. Cal grunted, but didn't fall.

Now the Rushani went on the attack, unleashing a flurry of rapid strikes that Cal struggled to repel. Steel rang against steel again and again as the sheer speed of her attacks forced the Bask warrior to retreat; first one pace then another. His knee protested as he shifted his position and put more weight on his left leg, making him wince and causing his sword to waver for a moment. Dana seized her chance and stepped forward, her sword lashing out and slicing a deep cut across his chest. Cal staggered back as blood began to seep out of the wound, but with surprising speed he recovered and lunged forward again, striking out wildly with his blade.

Dana stepped forward to meet him, parrying the strike. She twisted, letting her blade slide down his until it was almost at the hilt, then she pivoted sharply, driving her sword deep into his belly before the Bask had a chance to react. Cal stiffened, an almost comical expression of bewilderment stealing over his features. The Rushani girl stepped back and wrenched her blade free; the warrior remained standing for a few seconds then slowly toppled backwards.

As he hit the ground, Dana became aware that every Bask was now watching her, each with a weapon drawn and ready to use. The clan leaders were very still; if any of them were pleased that she had won, they did not dare show it. The moment stretched out, the tension crackling in the air as she waited to see what would happen next.

'Congratulations,' Dax said, making no effort to sound even remotely sincere. 'Victory is yours.'

'So you will allow me to retrieve the blade?'

'Yes. If you want to run off on a fool's errand be my guest.'

'And you'll be here a week before the deadline?'

'I already said yes, didn't I?'

'Wait a minute,' Lar said. 'I know the legends around Haldor's blade. They say that he fell somewhere in the Blight. She can't go there alone, she'll never survive.'

'I'll be fine,' Dana snapped. 'I can do this by myself.'

Dax's eyes narrowed, then suddenly he smiled. 'I agree with him. If you really think the blade exists, then what kind of ruler would I be if I let you go alone? You can take him.' He pointed at the prisoner, who had been watching everything in silence.

Dana shook her head. 'I told you, no. I don't need any help, especially from a *Bask*.' The hatred in her voice was palpable, but the prisoner didn't seem at all affected by it.

'He's not a Bask,' Dax retorted. 'Not any more. The Bask are strong, and they stay that way by getting rid of the weak and those who would hold us back. This *worm* is a coward, and unworthy to be called a Bask warrior. He no longer has a home, or a clan. Take him.' He hefted his mace and stared at the Rushani. 'Or die here and now.'

They left quickly. The clan leader of the Mixlan had grudgingly given the prisoner a horse so that he could keep up with Dana, who already had her own steed. Some of the other Mixlan had said their goodbyes to her but the conversations were brief and awkward; nobody quite knew how to deal with the fact that she wasn't one of them any longer, that she never really had been. For her part Dana seemed just as uncertain and was visibly relieved when they finally left.

The Rushani girl headed south, spurring her horse into a gallop straight away. The prisoner followed, unable to miss the fact that whenever she looked back, she seemed irritated to see him still there. Soon the remains of the Bask village disappeared behind them, and they were alone on the grassy plains. Even here though there was a slight covering of ash, enough that clouds of it were constantly kicked up by the horses, and the grass seemed drab and unhealthy. To the west the volcano continued to belch smoke into the atmosphere; whenever he looked at it the prisoner couldn't help but imagine firedrakes swimming across rivers of magma and clambering through dark caves towards their freedom. The thought of more monsters being unleashed upon the world made him feel sick to his core; one was more than enough.

When they reached a swift-moving stream that cut across their path Dana stopped, allowing her horse to drink while she got down and stretched the aches of the journey away. The Bask came to a halt nearby and clambered down, leading his horse towards the stream. Dana watched him, her eyes narrowed, before abruptly striding towards him. Distracted by what he was doing, the prisoner looked surprised when he turned and saw her right next to him. His hand dropped instinctively to the sword at his hip; the same weapon that the late Cal had once used. Seeing her stiffen, he slowly moved his hand away and turned his palms towards her.

'Leave.'

'What?'

'You heard me. I don't need you to do this; I can find the blade alone.'

'But Dax said-'

'I don't care what Dax said, and neither should you. He forced you on me as a joke. Well, he's not here now so you can get lost. Go on.'

Dana watched the prisoner think this over, the fingers of one hand rubbing at his neck where the metal collar was chafing it. Though the other Bask had removed the metal ball hanging from it so that the man could at least stand up straight, they had not tried to remove the collar itself. Curiously, he had made no effort to take it off since then.

'No.'

'What?'

'You heard me,' the Bask repeated mockingly, and smiled as a look of fury flashed across her face. 'I'm coming with you.'

'Why? Because your *precious leader* told you to?' Dana sneered. 'Do you really think that shithead will take you back into your clan if you bring him that blade? You heard what he said about you. You're nothing but a coward to him.'

He went very still for a few moments, then took a deep breath. 'No. It's because you were right. This *is* important; too important for just one person. You need someone to watch your back.'

'No I don't!' Dana yelled, fury overtaking her. 'Especially not filthy Bask scum like you! Now leave, before I kill you myself!'

The Bask drew his sword, his eyes never leaving hers. If he was bothered by the raw hatred in her gaze, he didn't show it. 'You can try,' he hissed. 'Maybe you could kill me, maybe not. But I promise you I won't go down without hurting you badly. Going after the blade was *your* plan, clearly it matters to you. Do you really want to risk it?'

He watched her face carefully. The Rushani wanted to kill him, he knew that for a fact; could see it in the twitching of her arm muscles and the way she was standing. Her eyes flicked across his body, perhaps assessing her chances, before her gaze met his again. She snarled and turned away, thrusting her sword back into its sheath.

'We've wasted enough time here. Come on, Bask.'

'It's Brin, actually,' he said, slowly lowering his weapon. She didn't respond, grabbing her horse's reins and leading it across the stream. He quickly went after her.


It took three days of travelling before they reached the river that marked the southern edge of Bask territory. During that time they encountered nobody else; now and again cattle and sheep-herders or bands of horsemen could be seen in the distance, but not one of them came close enough for speech. Brin doubted that Dana would have had much to say in any case; anyone they met would almost certainly have been Bask, and she had nothing but contempt for that clan.

Given what had happened to her people, Brin supposed he couldn't really blame her for this attitude, but that didn't mean that he wasn't finding it increasingly tiresome. The Rushani girl only spoke to him when she absolutely had to, and even then her words were minimal. Brin had made an effort to find out more about her and build some common ground, but had been met with either cutting remarks or icy silence. After a while he gave up and sank into his own thoughts, which was far from a pleasant place to be.

She allowed him to stay though, which came as a surprise. Brin was a light sleeper, but nevertheless on their first night together he had fully expected to wake up the next day and find that she had left. Or that she would try and kill him; which was why he had kept his sword close to hand. Yet she hadn't. She appeared no happier to have him around, but seemed to have accepted the fact that he wasn't planning to go anywhere. Perhaps she had decided that she needed some help after all. Given where they were heading, that was a wise choice.

When they reached the river they dismounted and allowed the horses to drink. As well as her sword Dana also carried a bow; using it she had brought down more than one rabbit for provisions so far. She removed it from her horse's saddle and wandered away for a short distance, her eyes following the course of the river. Brin looked around as well, but there was no sign of any animal life. The air was still but cool for the time of year, perhaps due to the ash pumped into the air by the volcano; he didn't know for sure. The volcano itself was still erupting, though it seemed to be lessening in intensity, as far as he could tell by gazing at it from this distance. He looked round and saw Dana facing him, her bow almost-but-not-quite aimed in his direction. A few seconds passed, and she casually lowered the weapon.

'Bask.' That was how she referred to him. Never *Brin*, always *Bask*. With a sneer, like the word tasted foul on her tongue. 'We can ford the river upstream.'

They mounted their horses again and headed west. Almost an hour passed before they found the place that Dana had been referring to, and after they had led their horses across he approached her.

'How did you know about this ford? It's not on any maps I've ever seen.'

She looked at him for a moment and Brin started to turn away, expecting her to ignore his words as was usually the case. To his surprise she didn't.

'My adopted parents were traders. We sometimes used this ford to cross into Bask territory.'

Brin nodded, and remounted his horse. Before they started off again he decided to push his luck.

'Do they know? That you're doing this, I mean.'

The Rushani girl simply looked at him, the familiar contempt back in her eyes. Instead of answering she dug her heels into the horse's flanks and spurred it into a gallop. Brin cursed, and rode after her.


They travelled southeast for the next week; the grass of the plains giving way to monotonous flat scrubland broken only by the occasional cluster of trees. This area was close to both Bask and Mixlan territory but claimed by neither clan. The plants were unsuitable for grazing, and no mineral or coal deposits had ever been discovered. The final, most critical but usually unmentioned reason was that it was far too close to the Blight.

They stopped more frequently to hunt and gather what food they could, but there was little to be had. The few rabbits that lived out here were mangy-looking things that nevertheless could put on an impressive burst of speed when they had to. Not one of Dana's arrows even came close to hitting the mark; failures that did nothing to improve her mood. In the end all they gathered was a half-dozen handfuls of shrivelled berries and a particularly large brown rat that Brin managed to trap. Both agreed that that particular meal would be left until there was no other choice. Unfortunately that didn't mean it wouldn't still end up on the menu; eating anything that lived or grew within the Blight was not safe. Even the water could not be trusted.

As they travelled closer to the Blight sightings of animals became increasingly infrequent, then stopped altogether. From time to time Brin observed flocks of birds passing over-head; they sometimes flew south, in the same direction the two of them were heading, but always banked either east or west before they crossed into the Blight proper. It was visible now in the distance, and at first glance seemed no different to the land they had already passed through. Yet there was something about the air over it; although they could see all the way to a ridge of low hills on the horizon, the view some-times became hazy before sharpening again; as if some kind of mist was spontaneously coalescing and dissipating con-stantly. Brin found it very disquieting, and from the look on her face Dana did as well. Not that she said anything to him on the subject.

One morning they reached the edge of the Blight. Brin had not expected it to be as obvious as it turned out to be. None of the clans had bothered to build a wall or anything like that; they took the view that if you were foolish enough to want to enter that cursed land then good luck to you, and at least you wouldn't survive to have equally idiotic children. He had expected a gradual blending of the scrubland into the Blight, perhaps a different kind of vegetation slowly appear-ing, or perhaps even none at all.

Instead they found a clear border. They had travelled away from the volcano and as a result there was far less ash on the ground than there had been further to the north. Even so, there was enough to be noticeable, pools of it gathered in hollows or individual grains and lumps lying scattered on the ground. Beyond the edge of the Blight, there was none. Looking to the east and west they could see ash here and there all the way into the distance. There was not enough on the ground to form an unbroken line, but nevertheless the pattern was clear. Ash had been blown all this way by the wind, yet none of it had settled within the Blight.

Dana slowly dismounted from her horse and walked towards the border, stopping only two paces away. She glanced back at Brin for a moment before carefully raising a foot and scuffing the ground in front of her. The ash there shifted; harder pieces bounced into the Blight while the dust billowed up into the air and settled slowly to the ground again. They watched the ash for a while, half-expecting it to suddenly propel itself out of the Blight and back over the line. Nothing happened.

With the daylight fading they made camp far enough back that they could not see the ash-line. Even so, neither of them slept particularly well that night.

The next morning they entered the Blight. It only took a few minutes for Brin to begin feeling uncomfortable; and though the sensation strengthened and lessened throughout their time there, it never completely went away. There was a strange quality to the place; a *stillness*. At least, that was the best way he could think of to describe it. The wind blew rarely and then only for a short time before rapidly dying away. When they spoke their voices sounded flatter than usual, and even the thump of the horses' hooves against the ground was oddly muted. There was nothing tranquil about it; the unnatural atmosphere kept them both on edge.

They began noticing differences in the plants too. Brin had expected them to be hideous and deformed, but that wasn't the case. They just seemed… different. Leaves were twisted out of shape; strange flowers bloomed on spindly stalks, giving off odd smells that instinctively repulsed both of them. At one point the horses flatly refused to go through a large patch of yellow-grey flowers on a hillside; it took them almost an hour to find a way around. In that time Brin was unable to shake the feeling that the flowers were turning slowly, tracking them somehow. He said nothing.

Two hours before dusk on the first day they came across a rabbit. Instead of fleeing it sat back on its haunches and watched them pass, perfectly still save for its slowly-turning head. When they looked back a short while later it was hopping after them. After an hour of this Dana put an arrow through its chest and left it where it had fallen.

That night they built a large fire and sat close to it. The heat was oppressive and the light it gave off would be a beacon to anything with the wit to understand what it meant, yet neither of them cared. The idea of sitting in the darkness in this place was not one that either of them could tolerate. But for the crackling of the flames there was no sound from around them; if any animals were out they were keeping eerily quiet. Brin found himself increasingly studying Dana, who was staring into the fire with her arms wrapped around her legs. After a while he grew tired of the silence.

'So what makes you think Haldor's blade will even be in this cursed place?'

'It's an old legend,' she replied.

'Not one I've ever heard,' he said, one hand tugging at the collar around his neck.

'Not surprising. You're a Bask,' Dana retorted, though her voice was missing its usual venom when she said the name of his clan. 'It's a Rushani legend. That's why you can trust it. Rushani means *keepers of knowledge* in the old tongue.'

*For all the good it did them*, Brin thought, but knew better than to say that out loud. 'Tell me it then.'

She picked up a stick and prodded a log deeper into the fire before speaking again. 'I'll give you the short version. When the last of the firedrakes were slain or driven off by the first clan-kings, Haldor brought his blade and his men to this place. There was an even older legend about a ruin here, something more ancient than the firedrakes themselves, built atop the first of a line of hills. I don't know the detail, just that there was a power here, something that made the land different. Haldor wanted it, so he came here and within the ruin he died, along with all but two of his men. They returned to civilisation years later, told their story to the Rushani lore-keepers, and died that same night. Nobody knows why or how. They left the blade with its master.'

'And how do you know all this?'

'Reading. You might want to try it sometime. I tracked down some old Rushani books from a library that your kind had left to rot.' She looked up at him for the first time since the conversation had started. 'They were in the ruins of the capital. I had to walk through the bones of men, women and children, left where they fell after being butchered by you.'

'Not me,' Brin snapped. 'The uprising was months before I was born. Hard to wield a sword from inside the womb you know!'

'Uprising?' She laughed, the sound low and bitter. 'Is that what your clan calls it? It was a massacre. You attacked without warning, without provocation, and wiped out an entire clan, just because you could. That's not an uprising. It's mass murder.'

'I-'

'Face it, Bask. Your clan is nothing but a gang of vicious thugs that only care about fighting and killing and their so-called *honour*. But then you know that anyway. That collar round your neck proves it.'

'Enough!' For a moment they locked eyes, Dana grinning nastily at his obvious discomfort. Then a log snapped in the fire, she looked away, and the spell was broken.

Nothing else was said for the rest of that night.


On the third day they found the ruin. It stood atop the first of a line of shallow hills that curved away to the east. They couldn't be sure quite how far; the further into the distance they gazed the less certain the view became, blurring in and out of focus just as it had when they first looked into the Blight days ago.

'That has to be it,' Dana said.

'How do you know?' Brin demanded. 'We have no idea how many ruins like this are in the Blight. The blade could be in any one of them.' *If it exists at all*, he thought.

'Then we'll check them all if we have to,' Dana snarled. 'Let's take a look, shall we.'

Brin dismounted and went after her, casting a glance back at their steeds as he did so. Both had their heads bowed; their movements slow and listless. There was plenty of grass to eat but the animals would not touch it, and they had not thought to bring food for the horses.

The ruin itself was roughly rectangular, built from some kind of grey stone. It felt *old*. Parts of the walls had crumbled, though not enough to see inside, and most of the roof seemed to be missing. Dana led the way as they walked slowly around the building. She held her bow with an arrow nocked and ready; he kept his hand on the hilt of his sword. Save for the sounds they themselves were making and the occasional whinny from one of the horses, it was completely silent. The air was utterly still and felt oppressive in a way that Brin couldn't quite articulate. He hoped they wouldn't have to stay for long.

There was an entrance on the far narrow side to where they had been standing, little more than a rough hole cut into the stone and low enough that both of them had to duck their heads in order to enter. Inside twin rows of pillars dominated the room; in the past they had obviously held up the roof, but time had not been kind. Some of them had collapsed, one forming a line of rubble that cut the building into two untidy halves. Looking up through the yawning hole where the roof had once been, Brin could see thin clouds hanging motionless in the sky, as if watching them. The floor of the ruin was completely obscured by grass and other vegetation, in places it came up to waist-height. Fortunately there didn't seem to be any of the strange yellow-grey flowers that they had seen before. They slowly walked forward, but the Bask had taken no more than three steps when he felt his foot brush against something and glanced down.

A skeletal hand lay limp on the ground, fingers clenched as if it had been clawing at something just before death. It was attached to a body that was lying face down, only a few strands of hair clinging to its skull and its clothes reduced by time to little more than tattered rags.

'Found a body,' Brin called, stepping carefully over it as he scanned the vegetation carefully for signs of any other obstacles.

'They're all over the place,' Dana replied without bothering to look. 'Watch your step, Bask. I think I see a plinth at the other end of the room, there's something on it. I'm going to take a look.'

Brin followed, almost tripping more than once. Dana was right, the bodies were everywhere. Some had skeletal digits still wrapped tightly around weapons, others were unarmed. There was one thing that they had in common that Brin only noticed once he had almost reached the far side of the room; every one of them was lying facing towards the plinth, as though drawn towards it. He saw Dana pause and crouch down, and hurried to join her, hurdling a fallen pillar and landing on top of one of the skeletons with the crunch of snapping bones.

A sword lay on the plinth, its hilt bound in black leather that had started to fray under the onslaught of time. The blade itself was notched in several places and the tip had broken away; clearly a weapon that had seen frequent use. Yet time had not dulled its edge, and the letters inscribed into the steel were clearly legible, though he could not read the language they were written in. A body lay nearby, its hand stretched out towards the blade, the fingertips only a few inches from the hilt. A spear stood upright between two of the body's ribs, its tip driven deep into the ground.

'Haldor?' He asked. Dana nodded, and picked up the sword. She turned it slowly, studying it with an almost reverent expression.

'And his blade.' She looked as if she was about to say something else, but paused as a rustling sound reached their ears. They turned. Some of the vegetation was moving; at first Brin thought it was the wind but he couldn't feel a breeze. Then he realised that the movement was getting closer to the plinth. He drew his sword, noticing as he did so that other patches of vegetation were moving now.

'We should leave.'

'Agreed.'

They stepped down from the plinth and ran for the exit, both horribly aware that the pattern of moving plants was shifting, as if things invisible beneath the vegetation were slowly tracking them. Just before the doorway Brin glanced down and saw a skeletal hand no more than a metre away from him. He was certain that he saw the fingers twitch.

Brin jerked awake. He could hear the crackle of flames at his back, and for one brief but ludicrous moment he imagined that the firedrake had followed him from his dreams into the waking world. He took a few deep breaths and stared into the darkness outside the radiance cast by the fire. The stars were obscured tonight, and he found it all too easy to visualise dead things out there, dragging themselves closer and closer to the light.

As soon as they had escaped the ruin they had climbed on to their horses and headed away as quickly as possible. The horses hadn't been able to keep up that pace for long but by the time they had been forced to slow, the ruin was far behind them. Looking back, Brin had been sure he could see something moving around the building. Dana refused to talk about it. During the following nights, though, one of them had always stayed awake to keep watch.

Another half-day's ride would take them out of the Blight, and Brin could hardly wait to return to normal lands that weren't twisted and *wrong*. Even the thought of facing the firedrake again seemed preferable to spending any more time in this place.

He rolled over, and saw that Dana was watching him. As usual she held Haldor's blade, one hand wrapped around its hilt and the metal itself flat on the palm of her other hand.

'You were dreaming again, weren't you.'

Brin sat up, but didn't reply. Dana shrugged, though at what he couldn't say.

'You've had bad dreams every night, even before this place. It's because of the firedrake, isn't it?'

Brin glared at her. The urge to tell her to shut up, that it was none of her business, was almost overpowering but he forced it away. He rubbed at the collar around his neck, knowing that he was doing it but not caring.

'Yes.'

She looked down at the blade in her hands, turning it over slowly. The metal reflected the firelight and the lettering inscribed on it seemed to shimmer and ripple as she did so.

'It's true though, isn't it. What you said. That you fought the firedrake.'

Brin studied her for a moment, uncertain why Dana was asking this now when she had shown no interest in the matter before. Various responses came to mind, but he settled on the one that was the most honest.

'Eventually.'

Dana looked up, and their eyes met. To his surprise she smiled; it was fleeting, gone almost before he had the chance to recognise it, but it was definitely a smile.

'That's better than nothing.'

A few seconds passed before she looked away again, turning her gaze back to the sword. Brin wondered what to say next. He realised to his surprise that her opinion of him mattered now, that he didn't want to jeopardise that. Caring had sneaked up on him and now held a knife at his throat, daring him to say something wrong. He decided to stick to a safer topic.

'Do you really think that blade can kill a firedrake?'

'So the Rushani legends say. In the past firedrakes roamed freely across the world. Some were monsters that slaughtered at will, others kept to themselves. A few offered knowledge to those that sought it. You could summon them if you had a fire and the right ingredients.' She shrugged. 'Hard to know how much of it is true; the tales differ in the details. What they all agree on is that in the end the firedrakes were driven away or slain by men; men like Haldor wielding blades like this.'

'And you're just going to hand it over to Dax?'

Dana's expression hardened, and she turned away, reaching for something out of sight. She looked round, and tossed him the skin she kept her water in.

'Have a drink and get some sleep. I'll take the watch until dawn.'

Brin decided it was best not to press her for any more answers. He drank deeply of the water and lay back. Sleep came quickly to him, and it brought with it dreams of monsters, flames all around him, and the thunder of beating wings.

They reached the meeting place three days before the time Dana had arranged with the Bask leader, and there was nobody else to be seen. They made camp a short distance away from the remains of the village, and while Dana was busy cooking some meat for their dinner Brin went for a walk through the ruins. Much of the devastation was now obscured by ash, and it took him some time to orient himself and work out where everything had once been. He paused for a long time at the place where his home had once stood. It hadn't been anything impressive, but it had been his.

Brin had expected to feel guilt at being unable to prevent the deaths of his friends, or shame that he hadn't fought the firedrake soon enough. He felt nothing; it was as if something had reached inside him and scooped out his emotions, leaving only a hollow space behind. After a while he turned and walked back to the camp, the collar weighing heavy around his neck.

On the day of the deadline the Rushani girl's hand on his cheek woke him from his usual uneasy slumber. Brin looked up at her, and to his surprise she was smiling down at him.

'Get up, Bask,' she said, a strange edge to her voice. 'It's time.'

They stood side by side as the Bask party drew closer. Dax rode at their head, wearing close-fitting armour. It had no decoration or ornamentation except for the Bask symbol emblazoned on the right shoulder: this was a warrior's armour, made for battle not ceremony. Behind him rode over a hundred clansmen, each heavily armed. Further back were the wagons carrying the supplies for the force, and last of all came two carts pulled by teams of straining horses, each carrying a siege ballista.

The Bask force came to a halt a hundred metres from Brin and Dana. Dax rode forward alone; behind him his men were already at work setting up the ballistae and preparing defensive positions. From the corner of his eye Brin could see Dana slowly drawing Haldor's blade, and hoped that she wasn't about to do anything foolish.

Dax brought his horse to a halt, and gazed down at them for a moment. He looked at Brin, his lip curled in evident contempt, then looked at Dana, his eyes fixed on the sword in her hands. He dismounted, and walked slowly forward.

'So you found it after all, girl. I was sure that you would not. Well done.' He paused, seeing that she was looking at the men behind him. 'This is just an advance party, made up of the best warriors at my command. More will arrive soon, and when our numbers are swelled by the forces of the other clans, the beast will not stand a chance.' He held out his hand. 'Now, hand the blade over, as we agreed.'

Dana looked at him, and Brin felt a sick feeling rise inside him as he saw her shoulders stiffen and her expression harden.

'No.'

Dax growled, and one hand clamped itself around the haft of his mace. 'Don't play games with me, girl. You've done well and I was planning to let you live, but if you deny me again I'll make sure that the Rushani clan ends with your broken corpse. Now. Hand. It. Over.'

With cold certainty, Brin knew that she was going to refuse again. He took a deep breath and readied himself to draw his sword. Perhaps the two of them together could... his thought was interrupted as a cry went up from the Bask ranks; first a single voice then others raised in alarm. Dax's gaze snapped up, looking at something behind Brin, and in a single swift movement he drew his mace and held it ready to be used. Brin slowly turned.

Even though he was seeing it with his own eyes, he felt his mind rebel against the idea of something so big being able to fly with such grace. Yet it was. Every beat of its wings were like twin thunderclaps, carrying the firedrake towards them frighteningly quickly. Its four limbs were clasped against its belly as it flew, but on the end of its serpentine neck its head was tilted down towards them; the lord of the air surveying its subjects. Its brow was dominated by four great curving horns under which its glittering eyes lay in sunken sockets. It had a muzzle almost like that of a dog, albeit one scaled up to nightmarish proportions, but no canine had teeth like those in its jaws. Its mouth fell open and it roared, an orange glow seeming to flicker at the back of its throat as the deep, rumbling cry washed over them.

The Bask warriors were racing back and forth frantically. Those who had bows had arrows nocked, while those without drew their weapons and looked for cover, though there was little to be found. The ballista crews were rushing to finish readying their weapons, as Brin watched one of the Bask warriors dropped a bolt before it could be loaded and had to retrieve it under a barrage of curses from the others on his crew.

'Give me the blade. Now!' There was no fear in Dax's voice, but tension crackled in every word he spoke. Dana smiled, though there was no joy in it, and drew the sword from her belt, pointing the tip straight at the Bask leader's throat.

'If you want it, come take it.'

A shadow fell across them, and all three looked up. The firedrake was hovering almost overhead now, the air displaced by its pounding wings raising clouds of ash and loose dirt from the ground. Fighting back the urge to run, Brin drew his sword just as the creature folded its wings and dropped like a stone. When it landed the ground shuddered with enough force that Brin was almost thrown from his feet. He stepped back quickly, keeping his sword between himself and the firedrake, for all the good that would do. Dana and Dax were doing the same, their disagreement temporarily forgotten. Up close and in the bright light of day he could see that the firedrake's hide was slate-grey, with patterns of black cracks zigzagging across it that expanded and contracted as the creature moved. Clusters of dark spines sprouted from its joints and along the ridge of its back; Brin shuddered as he remembered being pinned to the ground by one of them. The firedrake swept its gaze across each of them in turn, and he quivered as its eyes fell upon him. They did not linger for long, eventually fixing themselves upon the Rushani girl and the blade she held.

'Are these the ones you spoke of?' It asked. The sound of its voice was just as Brin remembered it; deep and grinding, as if produced by great boulders being forced together somewhere deep inside it.

'He is,' Dana replied, pointing the blade towards Dax again. 'And them.' A nod of her head indicated the Bask behind them. The ballistae were set up now and Brin could hear the warriors yelling for them to get out of the way so they could get a clear shot. He was grimly amused to see that three men had started running away as fast as they could, and the weight of the collar around his neck suddenly seemed that little bit lighter.

'You treacherous bitch.' Even faced by a firedrake, Dax's expression showed no fear. His face was a mask of fury and raw hatred, his grip on the haft of his mace so tight that his knuckles were bleached white. 'You would sell out your own people to this *monster*?'

'My people are dead,' Dana snapped. 'And the only monsters are people like you.' She took a few steps back, and glanced at the firedrake. In response the creature reared up, its mouth opening wide, sucking air in like a bellows as the orange colouring at the back of its mouth intensified. Dax screamed something incoherent and flung himself forward, bringing his arm back in readiness to hammer the mace down on the creature's head. The blow never landed. The firedrake breathed out and a wave of superheated air slammed into him a split-second before he was engulfed by a spear of white-hot flame. Within seconds Dax was transformed into a towering pyre of blistering flames, the air suddenly filled by the stench of burned meat. His death-shriek was cut mercifully short as he slumped to the ground, and for what seemed like an eternity the only sound was that of the flames crackling as they hungrily consumed the body of the Bask leader.

The spell broke, and as the Bask warriors began to shout in rage and grief the firedrake leapt up into the air, its wings pounding furiously as it sought to gain height. Arrows began clattering from its hide, only a few finding a softer point, though they did not penetrate very deep. As the firedrake banked and began to spit flame towards the warriors in retaliation, Brin turned on Dana. The last Rushani stood with Haldor's blade pointed at his chest, her expression calm, as if nothing out of the ordinary was happening. He opened his mouth to speak, accusations and demands crowding into his brain and fighting to be heard. In the end he could only manage to splutter a single word.

'Why?'

'For my people,' she replied, only the slightest quaver in her voice. 'That bastard slaughtered them all; every man, woman and child. Everyone but me. All so he could take power for himself. He was a tyrant who oppressed the other clans and ruled brutally. You know that's true. Just look at what he did to you!'

Brin shook his head. 'And so in revenge you hand us all over to *another* monster? Are you insane?'

'It was easy really. As I told you, there are ways to summon a firedrake if you know how. That night in the Blight, after we found the blade, I called it. I drugged the water I gave you so that you wouldn't wake up, and I made a deal. Haldor's blade, in exchange for the death of the only one who could lead an effective resistance against it. Without Dax to force them to fight the clans will make peace, and the firedrake will rule over us instead. Maybe then things will be better.'

Brin shook his head, doing his best to ignore the sounds of slaughter as the firedrake tore through the Bask warriors. He focussed all his attention on Dana, and on the blade that wavered as she held it between them. He raised his own sword.

'I can't let you do this.'

'Listen. You may be a Bask, but I don't want to kill you.' She shrugged, and shook her head. 'Trust me; I'm just as surprised as you are.'

'You don't have a choice in the matter,' Brin said. Calmness settled over him, and he felt as if a weight had been lifted from his shoulders suddenly. He knew that even if he beat Dana, there was little chance of him being able to slay the firedrake. But he also realised that didn't matter. What did matter was that he was willing to try.

Dana nodded sharply. 'So be it. Goodbye, Brin.'

The Rushani stepped forward, her blade already spearing out towards his chest. Brin knocked the blow aside as he side-stepped, twisting as he did so and bringing his sword round into a sweep at her neck. Dana flinched back, momentarily losing her balance. Before he could capitalise on the mistake she was on the attack again, unleashing a series of vicious strikes that took all his skill to counter. As he parried one blow their blades juddered to a halt against one another and Dana let her sword slide down his, intending to pivot and gut him just as she had the Bask warrior Cal. Brin had been expecting that move, and turned suddenly, throwing her off balance as his shoulder slammed into her and sent her staggering. Before she could recover he whipped his sword round and the tip sliced across her upper arm.

Dana cried out and took a step back, and now Brin went on the attack. She still blocked every blow, but he could feel the strength in her sword arm failing as blood continued to seep out. A look of desperation blossomed in her eyes as she was forced to jump back sharply to avoid a swipe that would have sliced her belly open if it had connected. Brin continued to press her, knowing that victory was near.

His moment came when her arm wobbled as she blocked another strike. He pushed forward, forcing Haldor's blade up and out of reach as he barged into her and knocked her to the ground. He stepped to one side so that she could not sweep her legs into his and pressed the tip of his sword against her throat.

Their eyes met just as something slammed into the side of his head, lifting him from his feet and sending him hurtling through the air. His sword was jolted from his grasp as he slammed into the ground with a force that drove the breath from his body. Darkness blossomed at the edges of his vision; he tried to make himself rise but his head flared with agony and his legs would not support him. Collapsing to the ground, he sensed rather than saw Dana walk forward and stand over him. He could feel a heat so intense that it seemed as if his skin was scorching. The firedrake.

'Hello again, little thing,' it said. 'Are you to die too?'

'No.' Dana's voice. 'Not him.'

Something struck the collar around his neck; once, twice, three times. There was a muted *crack* and he felt it fall away, heard the thumps as the two halves hit the ground.

'He lives. He fought bravely.'

Darkness took him.

# The Glacier's Stone, the Mammoth's Ivory

## Alexander Danner

Martina breathed in and smiled. The air carried a lingering hint of saltiness, proof that the ocean wasn't far off. They had left the tent flap slightly unzipped the previous night to let in the breeze, trusting the sleeping bag to keep them warm. And anyway, even Alaska didn't get that cold in August, so long as you weren't too far north. She'd been awake for a half hour, enjoying the coolness of the air, the quiet of the campground, the warmth of Tolly in the sleeping bag beside her. A perfect morning.

Valdez was a small city made famous by a great disaster, but that was long in the past. There was a college, a handful of restaurants, and not much else. It was still the terminus of the oil pipeline, and it still earned its primary living in the employ of Exxon, but you'd hardly know it to look around. It was overshadowed by better things—mountains rising on three sides of the city, the ocean abutting the fourth. Most of the year, the only way in or out was by boat or propeller plane—the latter being how Martina and her small group had arrived two days prior. They'd bussed it up from Washington, through Canada to Anchorage, where they'd boarded an aircraft so tiny that you didn't even need to pass through airport security to get to it. If not for the safety ensured by their shared cause of death, it would have been terrifying.

Fortunately, such fears had been allayed some decades earlier. It had been three weeks past Martina's sixteenth birthday when her envelope arrived from The Hall of Records. The envelope was plain and yellow, printed with only her name and address, but she knew what she'd find inside: The last mystery of her life, the answer to the most terrifying of questions. She didn't even close the mailbox before she tore the envelope apart to see the document inside.

In those days, when most people learned the details of their inevitable deaths, the cause was still likely to be 'cancer' or 'automobile accident' or 'heart attack.' Unsurprising, understandable deaths. Some causes had always been a little slippery, open to interpretation, the occasional 'water' or 'poisoning.' But Martina's meant nothing. Less than nothing. 'The end,' it said on the official notification form, beneath her name and date of birth. That was all. 'Martina Gutierrez: The end.'

The end of what? A rope? A sharp stick? She had no idea what to make of it. Until she found out: Martina wasn't the first, although she was one of the first. The first of The Last.

Camille Montrand was number one, born seven weeks before Martina. Martina wasn't even number two; seventeen others came after Camille before she arrived in the world. They were in the tens of thousands by the time Tolly was born, and she was only three years younger. Child after child after child, and it became obvious. It wasn't 'the end,' they realized. It was 'The End.' Of the world. Of the human race. Of everything. No dates, no details. The 'experts' set about making predictions the old-fashioned way. The actuaries broke out their actuarial tables, looked at birth rates, and death rates, and average life expectancies. And they settled on 116 years from Camille's birth until the end of the world. We marked it on our calendars. We began to plan for it as best we could, without even knowing what it would be. Nuclear war? Environmental disaster? Tolly once said she was betting on simultaneous worldwide spontaneous human combustion. Here and then poof. Just like that.

Beside her in the tent, Tolly snuffled in her sleep, a quick burst of exhaled air tickling Martina's ear. Outside, there were sounds of movement: hushed voices, a struck match, pouring water. She'd lounged long enough. It was time to move. Martina rolled onto her side, coming face-to-face with Tolly. Or, face to hair anyway, as brown curls completely obscured Tolly's face, as they always did when she'd forgotten to tie her hair back before bed. When they had first started out on their travels, some twenty years ago now, Tolly had always kept her hair short like Martina's. It was more practical, easier to keep clean in campground facilities. Easier to wash with river water, when that was all that was available. Lately, she had let it grow out, and the curls were a surprise; Tolly hadn't had curls in her youth. Martina loved them, would pull the curls one by one, to watch them spring back. Now, though she just pushed Tolly's hair aside and kissed her forehead, softly.

'Hey, time to get up.'

Tolly opened one eye and gave Martina a brief scowl. 'The sun needs a snooze button,' she said, closing her eye again, against the invading light.

'Snoozing? I'm forty-six years old—I only have seventy years left to see all the things there are left to see. There's no time for snoozing. '

'Same seventy years as me. Same as Camille. Same as Josh and Saul, and everyone else.'

'Everyone who'll make it all the way to the end.'

Tolly opened her eyes fully. 'Half of all the babies born this year,' she said.

'What?'

'We crossed a threshold. That's what they said on the radio. Half of all babies born this year will make it all the way to The End. They'll all be exactly seventy years old.'

'Come on,' said Martina. 'I hear the boys setting up breakfast. We should get moving. We've got a glacier to climb today.' She gave Tolly a soft 'good morning' kiss, grinned, and shot out the tent flap to prepare for their trek.

'Right,' said Tolly, alone in the tent. 'The glacier.' She winced when she sat up, her muscles tight from another night sleeping on the cold, hard ground.

'The boys were Josh and Saul, twin brothers in their early thirties, more than a decade the womens' juniors. At first, Martina had been reluctant to take them on as traveling companions; they were naturally paunchy, not the most athletic looking pair. There was a lot of ground to cover in this world, and Martina intended to go everywhere, see everything.

When she suggested a biking tour of the east coast for their first joint adventure, she'd expected the prospect to scare them off, but they'd agreed readily, and turned out to be much hardier than they looked, Josh especially. The boys had kept pace admirably, and so they'd all been traveling as a unit for the past three years. Their mission was to find the special place where they would spend the final moments of history—just the right spot for watching humanity disappear.

That was why Martina and Tolly had gone out on the road. They met in a camping supply store where Tolly worked, nineteen and bored, earning her way through college. Martina was twenty-two and dead-set on hitting the road. It took weeks for her to pick out all the supplies she needed. It shouldn't have taken that long—but Tolly was there, helping her to choose each item: her sleeping bag, her propane stove, her tent. Tolly smiled whenever she saw Martina walk in the door. And somehow, by the time Martina left, Tolly was sitting right next to her in her second-hand SUV. The same one they'd abandoned in Utah two years later, taking only as much of their gear as they could carry on their backs, as they'd done ever since.

Stepping out of the tent, Martina found Saul standing over the fire pit, with a tin coffee pot heating on the grill. 'Marty, you want some coffee?' he asked, though he was already laying out mugs for each of them.

'Please. Where's Josh?'

'He went into town to pick up a new jacket. He got the fire going for us before he left, though, so coffee's just about ready.'

'What happened to his jacket?'

Saul scowled. 'He tore it trying to climb that tree this morning. He got up early, just so he could hike back to it before I woke up.'

Martina remembered exactly which tree—Josh had been eager to climb it the previous night, but the sun was already setting, and Saul had persuaded them of the importance of getting camp set up before they lost the light.

'He should have waited for us,' said Martina. 'I'd have liked to see how high he made it.'

Saul didn't look up, focused on doling out sugar into the waiting mugs. 'Well, anyway, he'll meet us there.'

Saul was just pouring the coffee when Tolly finally emerged from the tent in loose jeans and her old Purple Pie

Man t-shirt. Martina smiled; Tolly loved that shirt, but she had no idea who the Purple Pie Man was. When Martina had tried to explain, tried to tell her about Strawberry Shortcake and Raspberry Tart, and Purple Pie Man's role in their adventures, Tolly had covered her ears. 'I don't want to know!' she cried. 'You'll spoil his *mystique*!' Tolly pulled on her hoodie, leaving just the Pie Man's eyes peeking out over the zipper. She arched backwards, and then forwards again, reached for her toes. She hung there for a moment, arms drooped, slowly exhaling as she waited for the muscles of her back to begin loosening. Then she yawned and snatched a cup of coffee ahead of the others.

'I vote that our next destination should have actual beds,' she said after she'd taken her first sip.

'I know,' said Saul with a roll of his eyes. 'But good luck convincing Josh that we need to take a breather.'

'We can rest here for a couple of days if you want,' offered Martina. 'I'm sure Josh can occupy himself.'

'A couple of days,' Tolly began—she and Saul exchanged a look of…what? Exasperation? 'Yeah, great. A couple of days.'


The glacier guide office was a wooden shack. The inside was decorated with maps of the local nature spots, trails, campgrounds, and of course the glacier itself. Mixed in were posters advertising various outdoor adventures, helicopter tours, the usual things. They were a few minutes early and the office was empty, no sign of the guide they'd contracted save for a half-finished bottle of Mountain Dew on a small card table.

A little television in the back flashed the news. The camera was aimed at a hospital entrance. According to the disembodied voice of the anchor, somewhere inside that building, Camille Montrand's daughter was suckling her firstborn child.

'This is news?' asked Martina.

'Sure,' said Tolly. 'The Last are becoming grandparents. It's kind of amazing.'

As the camera panned, it picked up a group of people circling in a cordoned off area. They carried signs: <u>END your</u>

own world! one sign said. Take the EARTH: I'll be with GOD, said another.

'I don't understand what they're protesting,' said Tolly.

'Us,' said Saul. 'They think it's our fault. They want us to be the bad guys.'

'How can people be so stupid?' Martina wondered aloud.

'They're jealous,' said Saul.

'Of what?' asked Tolly. 'What do they think we have that they don't?'

'Purpose,' said Martina, without any hesitation. She picked up a remote from the desk in front of her, and switched off the television.

'The world is still full of people who'll live short lives and die badly,' said Saul. 'We aren't any help. We walk around with all our pompous names for ourselves. 'Enders.' 'The Last.''

'Bye-Bye Babies,' said Tolly. 'That's what they call themselves now. The kids, I mean.'

'But what the hell, right?' Martina cut in. 'We're humanity's final hurrah, aren't we? Is it so bad for us to want a little bit of pomp?'

Josh showed up a few minutes later, wearing a bright orange nylon jacket that swished when he swung his arms, which he did with great relish as he walked. He was accompanied by a woman the others didn't know—a young Indian woman who introduced herself as Amolika, visiting from Florida.

'Her friends wouldn't go up the glacier with her,' Josh explained, 'so I invited her along with us.'

'We take turns picking vacation spots each summer,' Amolika said, 'and this year was my turn. They're kind of mad at me.'

'That jacket looks ridiculous,' said Saul.

Josh just smiled and ignored the comment. 'I bought you a sandwich. Roast beef, horseradish, cheddar.' He tossed Saul the hoagie, wrapped in wax paper. He followed with similar packages for the others. 'Tolly, tuna salad with lettuce. And for Marty, turkey, bacon, and mayo, no tomatoes. I thought we might enjoy something fresher than trail mix and jerky.'

Tolly grinned as she stowed her sandwich. 'Josh, you really didn't have to, but I'm *so* glad you did.›

'It's my pleasure to serve,' he said, with an affected bow of his head.

The glacier guide came bouncing in through the back door, hair tied up in a ponytail, grinning, and lugging a heavy duffle bag. She gave a wave and a quick 'hey,' grabbed her soda and took a large gulp. She couldn't have been more than nineteen years old.

'God, I hate this shit,' she declared, wiping the sticky drink from her mouth. 'Why the hell do I keep buying it?' She pitched the bottle into the trash and turned to the waiting group.

'So!' she said, 'my name is Lake Winnipeg, and yes, I've forgiven my parents for that. You can call me Lake or you can call me Winnie, but don't call me Peg. We've got a short drive and a long walk ahead of us, but before the day is done, you're all gonna see the world from the top of Worthington Glacier. So: are you psyched?'

'Hell yeah!' cheered Josh, which earned him a playful shoulder bump from Amolika.

'Well, let's go then!' said Winnie. She threw a high-five at Josh, shouldered the duffle bag, and led the way out of the shack.

Martina caught Tolly's eyes—Tolly looked sceptical, but Martina was excited. 'Okay, so the guide's a little... boisterous. But, this is going to be fun, I promise.'

They climbed into the van while Winnie loaded her bag into the back. She slammed down the rear hatch, slung herself into to the driver's seat, and pulled out, grinning.

'Okay, so once we get there, it'll be about a five-hour hike to the top and back again. There are toilets at the base and nobody likes to pee on a glacier, so make sure you go before we start out. We'll take a lunch break at the top—you all remembered to pack your lunches, right?'

'She's so young, Marty,' Tolly whispered into Martina's ear.

'So what?'

'Do we really trust this little girl to take us glacier climbing?'

'Who else would do it? Old people don't lead glacier hikes, Tolly.'

'Maybe that's because old people don't belong on glaciers.'

'Good thing we're not old.'

Tolly fell quiet, and they just listened to the chatter of the group around them. Saul asked about the histories of the various landmarks Winnie pointed out to the group. Josh and Amolika took turns pointing out striking features of the landscape to each other.

Winnie pointed to a playground as they drove past. 'You see that slide over there, the tall one? I was walking around down here a couple of winters ago and caught my foot on a pipe. When I dug around it a little, I realized it was the handle bar at the very top of the slide. That's how deep the snow gets in winter.'

'If we'd decided to make a kid,' said Tolly, softly, 'she'd probably have been the same age as this girl.'

'Why are you thinking about that now?'

'When should I think about it?'

'You agreed. Tolly, you said it yourself. How could we make a kid knowing—*knowing*—that its life was going to be cut short no matter what we did?'

'Cut short…at ninety years old. Whose idea of short is that?'

They left the van in a parking lot and used the portable toilets before crossing the stony lead-up to the glacier itself. It was closer than it seemed; from a distance, it looked as if an enormous wave had broken across the mountains, only to freeze as it sloshed over the nearer side. In truth it was moving in the opposite direction, slowly receding as the years passed.

When they reached the first protruding tongues of ice, Winnie handed out equipment from the duffle bag. Each person received a set of crampons, metal frames studded with sharp metal prongs to strap to the bottoms of their shoes, giving them better purchase on the ice. Once they had all attached the crampons, they each received an ice pick as well.

'We won't be doing any real climbing today,' Winnie told them, 'but the ice does get a little steeper in places, and the pick can be a big help. When those picks are stuck in the ice, they could hold a Mack truck up by a vertical line, so don't worry about putting your weight on them. Just watch out for the ankles of the guy in front of you when you sink it in.'

Martina slipped the strap over her wrist before testing its heft. It felt good. It felt like a certainty in her hand; a single simple swing, and she could hold on to anything. They started up the slope. It took her a little while to get the hang of walking with crampons. Here at the bottom, where there were still stony patches, it was difficult. The prongs slipped off rock, and it was easy to twist an ankle. Once they reached the ice it was easier; the crampons bit in, and walking almost felt natural.

'So, are you guys Enders?' Winnie asked as they hiked. They nodded, a little uncomfortably, except for Josh who chirped 'Sure are!' as he held out a hand to Amolika, to help her up a particularly steep slope.

'Not me,' said Amolika. 'I'm a suicide.'

That brought Winnie to a halt, a moment of panic stopping her constant banter, but Amolika waved off Winnie's concern. 'Not today, though, I promise! It's not depression or anything like that. I just don't want to see The End. I don't want to be here for it. I want to know that after I die, there will still be a world here, even if only for a little while. So when it looks like we're getting close…'

'I gotcha,' Winnie said, looking much relieved.

The others were slower to find their ease again, save Josh who likely already knew. It was unusual to find a… a not-Ender within their group. There was no good name for them, for everyone else, who wouldn't be there at the final moment. All the people who still get 'diabetes' and 'brain tumour' and 'drowning' and 'house fire.' Like Tolly's little cousin, Nell, who's going to die of 'multiple strokes.' Or Martina's own baby brother, her little Roberto, whom she hadn't spoken to in years, who might have already been dead, cut short by his inevitable 'porch collapse.'

Martina had no name for them, but she had a word. She called them 'strangers.' She called them 'The people we can't let ourselves love.'

They all stuck together, The Last, The Enders, The Bye-Bye Babies. They clustered, isolated themselves with glaciers, and houseboats, and deserts. Together in the wilderness, where nothing of the temporary world could touch them. So long as they stayed with each other, and only each other, they would never have to outlive anyone they cared about, ever.

For Josh to invite one of those others in was... crass. What was he thinking?

'What about the rest of you?' asked Winnie. 'Shopping for the right place to check out from?'

'How could you tell?' asked Saul.

'I already did my shopping. That's how I ended up here. I'm from Ohio, but from when I was little, my folks used summer vacations to take me around, show me different places. And I'll tell you, this is my place. I know it. Just wait till we get to the top. You'll see.' Martina quickened her pace. She believed, as she always did, that just over this rise, just past this turn, would be the best bit yet. And she was never disappointed.

'Oh, hang on a minute, this is important,' said Winnie. She waited until the group had gathered around her before continuing. 'You see that mound of snow over there?' she said, indicating a modest pile a few feet ahead of them. 'That's the most dangerous thing up here, 'cause you have no idea what's under there. The glacier is constantly changing shape, fissures open and close every day. When the snow crusts over, it can end up sitting right on top of a huge fissure, like a pile of leaves over a pit trap. And even though the fall won't kill any of us, it would still suck to be the guy who spends seventy years paralyzed, or in a coma, or suspended in an inescapable state of living death, frozen inside a block of ice. Right? Right. So the rule is, never step on the snow. Only the ice. Everyone clear on that?'

They nodded gravely, now eyeing the mound with suspicion as they cautiously stepped around it.

Josh, bringing up the rear, paused next to the mound Winnie had indicated. A crevasse hundreds of feet deep could be lurking there, waiting to capture any passing tourist, only to close up around them on the next sunny day. Josh slowly poked one toe of his hiking boot into the mound, careful to keep all his weight firmly balanced on his other foot. At first, he only made a small divot in the mound, but he continued digging, pushing more and more of the snow aside. There was nothing underneath, just a solid floor of ice, firm and safe.

'Cut that out!' Saul yelled from further ahead. Josh rolled his eyes, but he walked carefully. The snow mounds became more frequent as they proceeded further up the glacier.

'I don't think it's possible to actually be suspended in a state of living death inside a block of ice,' said Tolly as they passed yet another potential ice trap. 'I think you'd just be dead.'

Martina smiled. 'Thank you, Mr. Wizard,' she said.

After a while, they reached a narrow crease in the ice, carved by a tiny, but quick-flowing rivulet of water. 'If you're thirsty, this is a good spot to fill your water bottles.' Winnie didn't bother with a bottle, just stooped down to dip her mouth into the stream. She invited the others to do the same. 'This water's been frozen here for thousands of years. Every time the sun comes out, the top layer of the glacier sloughs off, exposing a new layer of ice, even older than the one before it.'

Martina got down to her knees, dipping her lips right into the water, as Winnie had done. It was cold, so cold.

'Guaranteed pollution-free,' Winnie said with a smile. 'You know why?'

'Of course,' said Saul. 'Because it's been under ice since before there was a civilization to pollute it.

'That's right! No human has ever touched it.'

'Until today,' Tolly said, frowning.

Martina took another long swallow. 'Try it, Tolly. I bet we could be happy drinking nothing but this for the rest of our lives.'

'Who are you kidding? You know I could never give up coffee.' But she bent down too, cupped her hand and lifted the water to her lips.

Martina took Tolly's hand as they continued walking. It was still damp and cold from holding the water, but Martina rubbed her fingers, warming them.

'Why are there all these little holes full of water?' Saul asked, noticing the pockmarked surface of the ice.

'Reach in,' said Winnie. 'See what you find.'

Saul did, and was surprised to find a small object at the bottom of the tiny cylinder of water. 'A pebble?'

'The Glacier isn't just ice. As it moved along, it scooped up dirt and rocks and all sorts of things that got frozen inside. As the glacier recedes, they come to the surface again. But rocks absorb heat way better than ice, and once they get warm, they start melting the ice under them. That makes all these holes, each with a rock at the bottom.'

'So they'll just keep slowly falling into the ice, forever?'

'Nah, just until dark. Overnight, the water'll refreeze and the rocks'll be trapped just like they were. They won't see the sun again for years. And when they do, it'll only be for the one day, just like today.'

Saul examined the stone in his hand; it was smooth and dark, almost black. He couldn't identify it; he knew pretty much nothing about stones. But he kept it, slipping it into his pocket.

Josh gave his brother's shoulder a squeeze as he walked past.

They reached the summit after two hours of trekking. It wasn't the hardest climb any of them had ever done, but walking on ice was tiring, so they were all glad to stop for lunch. Everything else around them looked miles away; they could just make out the parking lot where they'd started, hundreds of feet below, off in the distance.

'I thought Uluru would be a fun place to consider,' said Josh between bites of his sandwich. 'Top of a huge flat rock in the middle of the outback. Get right up to the edge and watch out over the whole desert… That'd be nice. You can't get up there anymore, though. It's reserved for the aborigines.'

They all sat in a row, facing the same direction, into the wind, to keep their hair out of their faces while they ate.

'Or the lip of a volcano. In Hawaii maybe. We've been to Hawaii, but we didn't see the volcanoes. I'd like to get back there, maybe take a helicopter tour.'

'How about a boat?' said Saul. 'Just a little boat, a houseboat maybe. Out on the water, nothing around but the fish and the quiet. I could learn to use a sextant. Do any of you know how to use a sextant?' No one did. 'I've always wondered about that,' Saul ended, a little dreamily.

'I'm not going out on a boat,' said Josh. 'It's just not happening.'

'Don't tell me you get seasick,' Amolika teased, brushing a crumb of bread from his cheek.

'Something like that.'

'You guys finish your lunches,' said Winnie. 'I think I see something interesting a little way over. I'll check it out, and if it is what I think it is, I'll take you over there.'

Martina chewed a handful of trail mix, pretzels and M&M's mingling in her mouth. When Tolly leaned against her, she put her arm around Tolly's shoulder. She kissed Tolly's hair.

'I like it here,' she said. 'This could be our place.'

'It's cold, Marty.'

'It's a good cold.'

'What if it happens in winter? What if it happens when there're six feet of snow on the ground, and that's just down in town, not at the top of a mountain. We wouldn't even be able to get up here.'

'It's so beautiful.'

'If beauty was all that mattered, I'd love it as much as you do.'

Martina squeezed Tolly tighter, and they waited for the guide to return.


The feature Winnie had spotted was an ice cavern. A slow trickle of water had found an opening, and had widened it, deepened it, until the ceiling stood taller than any of the tourists here to see it. Although the opening stood like a doorway you could easily walk through, even from a distance you could see that the tunnel curved downward farther in. As the others watched, Winnie stepped slowly down the slope, right into the mouth of the cavern. With the wrist strap firmly in place, she sunk her ice pick into the wall, anchoring herself to the spot, just at the lip of the vertical drop.

'You can all come look,' she said. 'One at a time, and take it slowly. It's safe, so long as you're careful.'

Amolika was the first to step forward, once again sending the young guide wide-eyed in panic. 'Not you. I can't let you down here.'

Amolika looked heartbroken. 'But I really want to see.'

'I'm sorry. But you can't. I'd get in so much trouble, you don't even know.'

The others hesitated, reluctant to take an opportunity that had been denied to one of their group, even if they didn't really know her. 'It's okay,' Amolika said. 'She's right. It's my own fault for telling her my cause. Go, all of you. Tell me what it's like when you get back.'

Martina went first. She took her time, creeping down the slope, locking her crampons into the ice with each step. She held her pick tightly, ready to slam it into the ice if she should slip. As she approached Winnie, the girl put her free arm across Martina's belly, bracing her with surprising strength. The pit was closer than it seemed; just inside the cavern, the ground disappeared. It gaped unevenly, not cracked and angular like a fissure, but curved and organic, like the throat of a live snake, frozen in mid-undulation. A person wouldn't descend into such an opening. They would be swallowed by it.

'Isn't it awesome?' asked Winnie with a huge grin. Martina only nodded. As uneven as the walls were, she could see that every surface was slick with water. There'd be no saving your-self from a place like that. 'Have you gone down inside?' she asked.

'Sure,' the guide replied, as if it were no big deal. 'I've never rappelled one this narrow, but some of us go down into caverns all the time.'

'Worth the trip?' Tolly asked when Martina rejoined the group.

'We need to learn rappelling.'

Martina watched as Tolly took her turn to inch down the slope toward the cavern and Winnie's outstretched hand. When she reached the ledge, she stopped and stood there a long time, staring down into the depths. She could see

Tolly wiping her cheeks with her sleeve. When she returned, Martina was waiting with her arms open, Tolly still quietly crying. 'It was terrifying,' she said.

'It can't hurt you.'

'There's nothing down there, Marty. It just keeps going forever.'

'It's okay, honey. It ends, just like everything else. You just can't see it from up here.'

Josh bounced on his toes in anticipation as he watched Saul take the next turn. Saul peeked briefly over the ledge, shook his head, and started back up the slope.

'No,' he said as Josh started down toward the cavern.

'What do you mean, 'no?''

'I mean don't go down there.'

Josh just rolled his eyes as he walked past his brother. 'Of course I'm going down.' Saul reached for Josh's wrist, to hold him back, but Josh slapped his hand away, giving him a rare look of irritation. 'Saul, just stop it, okay? Seriously.' But Saul wasn't going to stop. He planted himself in front of Josh, pressed up against him, restrained him.

'Come on, Saul,' said Martina. 'Why are you hassling him?'

Josh, raised his own arms, grabbed Saul by the shoulders, and spun. Saul, with his crampons still locked into the ice as his body spun away, lost his footing, and fell onto his ass behind Josh.

'Guys, no horseplay on the glacier, alright?' Winnie shouted from below. 'You gotta be careful up here!'

Josh continued his way down the slope, but when Saul got back to his feet, he grabbed the uneaten half of his sandwich, still wrapped in wax paper, and winged it through the air at his brother. It collided with Josh's head, spraying roast beef and onions across the ice. 'Dude, come on!' Winnie shouted at him. Saul turned to Winnie now, giving up on convincing his brother. 'Don't let him near the cavern,' he shouted to her. 'You don't want him down there!'

'Saul, don't you dare!' Josh yelled, fuming.

Winnie just looked back and forth between them, not knowing what to do.

'Please, Saul,' said Josh. They locked eyes, then Josh turned, once again descending the slope.

'He *lied*,' said Saul.

Josh stopped.

'He's not an Ender,' said Saul.

Marty looked at Tolly, uncomprehending; what was Josh if not an Ender?

'He's going to fall,' Saul continued. 'His cause of death is 'falling.''

*Falling*! Martina couldn›t help an involuntary step backwards, away from Josh, away from this temporary person who had snuck into her life. Her retreat was halted by Tolly›s hand, which still held firmly to her own, while Tolly remained steadfastly in place.

Winnie snarled her disgust at this revelation. 'Jesus Christ, what the hell are you people trying to do to me?'

'It's fine,' Josh, shouted, waving his hands as if he could make his death just disappear. 'I'll be fine!'

'Asshole,' she shouted, as she yanked her pick out of the wall and started back up the ice toward Josh. She waved the pick at him as she came; 'If you come one step closer to this cavern, I swear I'll put this pick right into your ribs and drag you back down the glacier! Don›t think I won›t—I know it won›t kill you.›

Josh sagged, defeated. He turned and walked back up to the group, who just stared at him, saying nothing.

Hurt and betrayed, he glared at Saul.

'I'm sorry,' said Saul.

'How could you do that to me?'

'Because I love you, you dipshit! You think I want to spend the next seven decades alone?'

'If you want me around so badly, why are you gonna go out on a houseboat?'

'Because it's safe! For you!'

'Safe! Oh, it's safe, is it? Saul—have I ever once asked you to keep me safe?'

Winnie caught up to them, packed up her supplies in an angry huff, and called everyone to attention. 'Tour's over.

We're going back down *now*. And for God›s sake, stay on the ice and away from the snow.›

The group was silent most of the way down. Martina held Tolly's hand, her anchor in this tumbling sea of strangers. She no longer took in the landscape, watched only the ice beneath each step. The twins walked side-by-side ahead of the women, each with their hands in their pockets, their strides perfectly in synch. They had argued, and yelled, and finally trailed off to silence, the rest of the company falling silent with them. A solemn march had lasted for half an hour already when Josh finally broke it, giving his brother a playful jab with his elbow.

'You're just jealous because I look good in orange and you don't.'

Tolly laughed. She laughed! Saul didn't, but still, he smirked. Or almost, anyway. Martina wanted to yell at all of them, except Winnie who, if anything, deepened her scowl in response to Josh's renewed jocularity. How could they joke? How could they laugh at jokes? *Josh was going to die, and they were all going to watch it happen.*

'You're trying to make me laugh,' said Saul.

'I'm trying to get us off the glacier without hating each other.'

'You know I don't hate you, Josh. That's the whole point.'

'Yeah, I know. Except maybe that's *not* the point. Maybe the point is right now I hate *you* a little, Saul.›

Saul said nothing.

'You've got it wrong, you know,' Josh continued, after another few minutes of silence.

Saul sighed, as though debating whether or not to pick up the bait, before finally resigning himself to it.

'What have I got wrong?'

'The houseboat idea. It's precisely because it's safe that I know I won't be there. I'm going to die in a fall. You know I will. And that can't happen on a houseboat. So if that's where you're going, if that's what we decided… then that can only mean that I'll die before we get there. But if we choose someplace like this, someplace dangerous, where I could fall at any time… well then that really means any time. Including even right up until just minutes before The End. I could live almost as long as you will. ‹

Martina increased her pace, to stay within hearing. 'Don't,' said Tolly, but Martina only pulled her along.

'Even if that makes sense—and maybe it does—why do you have to tempt fate?'

'I don't...'

'You have to climb every tree, every pile of rocks! Volcanoes, and helicopters, and Ayer's goddamn Rock! We climb up a glacier, and that's not enough, you have to go right down to the lip of an ice cavern!'

'I know, but it's not....'

'Every ledge, every precipice, every hole in the ground, you have to walk right up and spit in its eye. What's the point of that?'

Josh hesitated. He shook his head uncertainly.

'Don't listen,' whispered Tolly into the air in front of her, not looking at Martina.

'We deserve an explanation.'

'We don't.'

'I don't know,' said Josh. 'I guess... You, and Marty, and Tolly, and even Lake Winnipeg here are all going out in such a spectacular way. The most spectacular way anyone will ever go out. And me... I'll probably trip on a curb and crack my head open in front of a Friendly's somewhere.'

'That's what you're worried about? You don't want to die at Friendly's, so you'll jump off a glacier?'

'You know what I mean.'

'I really don't.'

'He had no right to keep this from us,' Martina seethed to Tolly in the brief silence.

'But Marty,' she said—and Tolly turned to her with an expression Marty had never before seen on Tolly's face, a look of such perfect incredulity it bordered on horror—'how did you not know?'

Josh, sighed. 'No, you're right, Saul,' he said. 'You don't.'


Winnie visibly relaxed when they finally stepped off the glacier and into the parking lot, but still said nothing to them as they climbed back into the van. They reached the touring office without incident or conversation. Saul tried offering Winnie a fifty-dollar apology, but she wouldn't even acknowledge it. She unceremoniously kicked them to the curb, closed up the van, and disappeared into the office, locking the door behind her.

'My friends texted,' said Amolika to the others. 'There's a party. You're all welcome if you want to come.'

'Thank you,' said Tolly with an exhausted sigh. 'But I think I've had my fun for the day. Maybe we'll see you tomorrow.' Martina shrugged and put an arm around Tolly's waist. Tolly didn't lean into her, didn't extend a reciprocal arm. 'Give us a call if you want to get breakfast,' Tolly added.

Josh looked at Saul, his eyebrow raised. 'Not me,' said Saul. 'I'm counting myself in with the old folks. You go, though. Have fun. We'll see you in the morning.'

Josh shrugged and turned to go. They all watched together, Martina, and Tolly, and Saul.

Saul smiled when he saw Amolika take Josh's hand.

'Totem Inn?' Martina asked when it was just the three of them again. It was a tourist restaurant, attached to a hotel and decked out like a hunting lodge with the requisite flagstone fireplace and stuffed carcass décor. But the food was good and it was near their camp, so it had become their default dining when they were too hungry or tired to scout out someplace new. Tolly and Saul nodded their assent.

'I could go for some biscuits and gravy,' said Saul.

'Didn't you eat that yesterday?' Tolly asked, teasing.

'Sure did. And I'll eat it again tomorrow. There aren't many places in the north where you can get a decent southern breakfast, so I intend to take full advantage while I can. And even if I have a heart attack, it's not like it'll kill me.' There was no levity in his tone. They walked down the street.

'Hey, it's Camille,' Saul commented as they entered the restaurant. Martina started at the strangeness of running into Camille so far from the safety of her little house in Vermont, but quickly realized Saul was pointing to the television over the bar. The television crews had followed Camille's daughter home, to get the cooing grandmother's reaction. And there she was on the screen, offering the cameraman a blueberry muffin and a glass of lemonade. The whole family was there: Camille and her Last husband, and their four Enders. And the proud new mommy with her own little Bye-Bye Baby. Tolly grinned when we saw him: 'He's a sweet little thing, isn't he?'

Martina could see Camille's final day already, as she sat there in a too-firm armchair, surrounded by her children, and her newborn grandchild, and blueberry muffins, knitted blankets, and shelves of knickknacks. Her children did all the talking, gave the interviewer a tour of the house, lovingly described each piece of furniture they passed. 'I like that curio,' said Tolly, as the camera panned.

Martina turned away from the TV, to peer instead into the glass case of the souvenir kiosk in the lobby. It was mostly jewellery and figurines, supposedly all locally carved. 'Look at this pen,' she said, calling Saul and Tolly over. 'It's made of mammoth ivory.' The pen was brown and grained, almost like polished wood. It was thick, with a gold clip, the kind of pen you save for special occasions that never come.

'That's really tacky,' said Saul.

'I think it's kind of wonderful,' Martina responded. 'It's a remnant of something that lived here thousands of years ago. A mammoth. A real, literal mammoth. Part of it is still here, where any of us can touch it.'

'I can't believe you're thinking of buying such a touristy souvenir.'

'Shut up! What's your souvenir? A rock?'

'My rock didn't cost ninety bucks.'

'If you want it, get it,' Tolly broke in. 'It's pretty.'

'What would I do with it?'

'I'll buy you a notebook. You can keep a journal.'

'For what? Who's gonna read it?'

'Whoever comes next. Whatever new species evolves and comes here to sift through our remnants thousands of years from now.'

'That's right,' said Saul. 'Whatever species comes along to make keepsake pens from our fossilized bones.'

'Stop it,' said Tolly. 'You're being a jerk.'

Saul opened his mouth to retort, but didn't; he swallowed

whatever he had been about to say. 'You're right. Look, I'm going to the bathroom to wash up. By the time I get back, I'll be a nicer person again. I promise.'

Martina stared at the pen, still debating. 'He's probably right. It's a stupid thing to buy. I'd probably just lose it anyway.'

'If you don't buy it, I'm going to buy it for you,' said Tolly. 'Either way, it ends up in your pocket.'

Even as Martina began to protest, Tolly's wallet appeared in her hand, drawn like a gunfighter's revolver. Moments later, the pen was in her hand, a heavy and awkward and beautiful thing. She knew she would never use it.

A hostess appeared to show them to a table, where they each sat beside an empty chair.

'You really loved it up there,' said Tolly.

'I did. But you hated it.'

'I didn't. Really, I didn't. I'm just tired.'

'We can stop for a while. We can take a break.'

'What's a while?'

'I don't know. You tell me. How long do you need? A week? A month? We can hole up somewhere, just make camp and sit tight until you're ready to move on.'

'Oh, Marty. A month? I want a year. Or two years. Or five years. I'd like to sleep under a solid roof. I'd like to own a couch. I'd like to spend some time sitting on it.'

Martina said nothing. A couch? Where would she keep a couch? What would she do with something so big?

'It's just… I thought we'd have found our place by now. I didn't expect to still be searching after twenty years.'

'What are we supposed to do? Just stop? Stand still? We're living the last life anyone will ever live. What are we going to do with seventy years spent standing in one place? Work in an office? Take up knitting?'

'Do you remember the hotel we stayed at in Anchorage? The one night we were there. The sheets were clean. In the shower, there were those little soaps. The little bottles of shampoo.'

'Yeah, it was comfortable. But…'

'No, not that. I'm talking about the little bottles of shampoo. Someone made, those, Marty. In a factory. Someone wrote the copy for their labels. Someone filled them with shampoo, and screwed on the caps. Someone in that hotel went up and down the floors, into each room, putting a little bottle of shampoo on a little shelf in every shower. Those little things… people still do them.'

'It's absurd.'

'It makes them happy. It makes them feel like life goes on.'

'But it doesn't. Tolly, life doesn't go on.'

Tolly looked away, back to the television, and Martina couldn't help doing the same. There was Camille, still sitting in her chair, occasionally nodding or shrugging, but saying nothing. She quietly traced the pattern of her chair's upholstery with the tip of her finger.

'You've never asked me where I want to be,' said Tolly.

'Of course I have. I always ask you!'

'You always ask me about whatever place we're in at the moment. 'Is this the place, Tolly? Could we die here?''

'And you always say 'No.''

'But you've never asked me if I have my own idea. My own picture in my mind of where we are or what The End looks like for us. You've never asked.'

Martina stopped, wracked her brain, trying to think of a moment, any moment, that proved Tolly wrong. But there was nothing.

'Tell me,' she said, finally.

Tolly began:

'We wake up in a bed. An enormous bed. It's spring, and the curtain is pulled back so the sun can wake us. Gently, filtered through the azaleas that grow outside the window, softening the light. The blanket is pushed to the bottom of the bed, covering just our feet and ankles. You're awake first, but you stay there, your arm around me, waiting for me. When I finally wake up, I nestle into you, and you hold me tighter.

'I get out of bed first. I'm in the kitchen, making the coffee. It's a well-used kitchen. The stovetop is stained from all the meals we've cooked together, side-by-side, cracking the eggs, dicing the onions. But not this morning. On this morning, we just need coffee, nothing else. I pour boiling water into the carafe, stir in the grinds. You come in just as I'm setting the plunger on top.

'You're still sleepy, rubbing your eyes. Your hair is matted down on one side, standing straight out on the other. You're in your striped pyjama shorts and my old Purple Pie Man t-shirt. I'm going to give you that shirt someday. But not until after you've promised you'll never tell me who he is. Not until you've forgotten who he is yourself.

'And you're old. So old. Your hair is pure white, and you have even more wrinkles than I do. Twice as many wrinkles. I count them at night, every wrinkle another year that I've spent loving you. You walk so slowly.

'You put your arms around me and kiss me good morning. You've just brushed your teeth and you still taste like toothpaste. But so do I, so it's okay. When the coffee is ready, we each pick out our favorite mug from the cabinet. They're chipped from years of use. They've both had their handles glued back on, over and again. And we fill them up.

'We take the coffee out to the porch. We have a table out there, covered in ceramic tiles. A mosaic of all the places we've ever seen. There are so many, we can't even remember them all. Some days, we look at the table, pick out scenes, and just tell stories. Made up stories of the adventures we think we might have had, if only we were still young enough to remember.

'But today we don't tell stories. Today, you hold my hand, and you tell me you love me. And I tell you I love you too. Then we sit quietly and we sip our coffee.

'And the world ends.

'Just like that.'

Martina bit her lip. She waited. But Tolly was done.

'That's what you want for us?' she finally asked.

'It is.'

'Then we can do that. I would do that with you.'

'I know you would. But I know… I know you'd hate it.'

'Maybe I wouldn't,' Martina said. And she meant it.

But neither of them believed her.

# Demon Runner

## Dash Cooray

*For Nimal Cooray; King of the Castle, Fan of the
Artist; are you proud, Daddy Bear?*

What Suga remembered of when the British came was that
she was young enough, stupid enough, to show them how
fast she could run.

She was four or five at the time and racing the goats
through the tall grass was a joy her parents had strictly forbidden her, for the reason she found out that day.

She could not recall how many there had been save the
one woman who was not a soldier.

She had spoken to Suga's horror-struck parents, calmly
and rationally about taking her away.

Suga did not remember what exactly the woman had said,
but if she closed her eyes now she could see her mother and
father crying and fighting for Suga as she watched them pas-
sively from the arms of an British man.

She saw a soldier strike her father on the back of his head,
forcing him to the ground, when he tried to attack them with
a hoe. She looked back as they left and saw her mother writhing on the lawn outside their mud-hut home, tearing her hair
out and wailing for the old gods to save her baby.

No matter how hard she tried, Suga could not remember
their faces.

She wondered if that made her a bad daughter.

She felt Jimmy's warm hand on her shoulder, shaking her
gently.

She reached out; her eyes still closed and pushed his hand
away.

'Suga, are you awake?'

She did not answer, only turned her head away from where

she imagined him squatting, looking down at her with those blue eyes full of useless compassion.

She had made it clear to this stupid white boy that she had no time for the likes of him, but taking a hint was not Jimmy's strong point.

He was still calling her.

Suga threw a fist, claws drawn, punching a hole in the rotten log where she had tried to sleep. She felt the mushy wood sink in and a wriggling in her claws that was probably a woodlouse.

It shut him up.

When she opened her eyes, Jimmy was gone.

The prisoner in her claws turned out to be a millipede. It was dead now.

Suga pulled it free and flexed her fingers, retracting the claws.

Years since she had first got them, the claws still hurt, sitting beneath her fingernails like the soulless abomination she had become.

The plains that preceded the tiny village of Wellassa scrolled down the hillside at her feet, painted in shades of sunlight and cornflower. Suga could smell the pollen, soft and milky in the breeze.

She sat up, groaning as the pain in her calves came back.

Out of the undergrowth several quarters of a mile away, a spotted deer nosed through the vegetation. The petrichor rose from the damp earth stained with morning, leeching into Suga's nostrils as she watched, hunched against the trunk of the tree, shrouded from the deer's vision.

If she wanted to, Suga could slice her hand across the deer's flanks before it had time to swallow its mouthful of herbs. She squinted at her fingertips. She could imagine sinking her claws into the soft underbelly, tearing it open.

If she wanted to.

Suga leaned over her knees and pulled up her trouser sleeves, rubbing the ache, wishing it away.

The runners' shiny metal casing was visible in places where her flesh had not closed up. She tried to stretch her sore ankles, but with the runners still inside her feet she found it impossible.

Suga felt about on the outer sides of her knees for the levers and pushed down, drawing a rattled breath when the runners emerged from the cuts on her under-soles; half a dozen spikes protruding from a metal pedestal in each leg powered by a clockwork engine enabling the legs to move at incredible, inhuman speeds.

The pain had never gone away.

Not once, since they had first inserted the runners inside her legs more than four years ago, or maybe a thousand, Suga had lost count.

She recalled what Jimmy said about the runners.

He had said a lot, but then he made life easier for them even if he was all talk.

It was Jimmy who had built the straps for the runners, fashioning them out of his own leather belts. The straps were the casing they wore over their legs, from heel to kneecap, protecting the damaged skin from outside attacks, infections and the terror of fat, tropical mosquitoes.

Jimmy had also replaced the machinery that connected the runner to the knee, switching the pewter clockwork prongs with a smaller set made of copper. He declared it reduced the amount of toxins released. He was their official mechanic and their source of sunshine.

He suggested they embrace their new nickname one day, after Jai had come crying about the village children's catcalls.

The nickname coined by the villagers of Matale suited them well, Suga thought as she twisted her ankles around.

Clockwork-enhanced soldiers: created by the British Raj but used now as weapons against them.

They were not human anymore.

At least Suga was not. She could not be, not after the suffering and trauma she had withstood at the Factory after she was taken from her parents.

'Adoh Suga?' Rama, the oldest of the runners in Suga's pack was limping over to her from the direction of the village.

He paused to catch a breath, the uphill trek hard on his

legs when the runners were not out. His long oily hair was slicked back and down his head in very tight braids. His large forehead made him look much older than his twenty years.

'What you do to this bastard?'

His question was followed by a series of giggles.

The other children had followed Rama into the little copse.

Shreya, the only other girl had her arm wrapped around Jimmy's neck, dragging him along. She and the boys were laughing. Jimmy sported a forlorn pout and refused to look anywhere near Suga. As they drew nearer Suga could see the tear-stains.

'Why you make our baby cry?' Shreya grinned, pulling down on Jimmy, almost strangling him. 'What you do, heartless demon?'

'Yeah Suga's so mean!' piped in little Hari the miracle child.

Although he did not know why he was so special, Hari had survived the implants at a very young age when the rest of his batch had died within the first week. His grin was empty; he had lost all his baby teeth during the battle in the Matale Mountains.

Suga pulled the levers back and the runners slid into her feet.

Around her the rest of the Demon Runners were laughing at Jimmy.

Rama scratched his beard, eyeing Suga with a small smirk. 'This is why you should give up on Suga, Private Rudolf.' He told Jimmy. 'Why a Demon Runner? If you want to marry a Ceylonese girl, there are nice ones in village. Or wait till we take back Kandy from your people. Then you can have a princess or a daughter of a councillor!'

'I heard the Disawe has a beautiful daughter!' lisped Tissa. He bit on his tongue stained crimson from chewing too much beetle leaf. He was thirteen and the only one of them who knew how to read English, a fact he boasted about every day. 'He hides her in the palace because he is friends with the king!'

Rama reached out to hit him on his head. 'Fool! Where'd you pick these things up ah? The Disawe doesn't have daughters! Even yes, he can't hide them in the palace any more than you can! He's a traitor!'

Suga got up and walked away.

If Keppetipola Disawe did have a daughter she wondered, would he hide her away? Or would he insist that she fought in the rebellion alongside everyone else?

Would he spare her? Or would he not care, just as he did not care about sending seven-year-old Hari and ten-year-old Jai to the front during the previous ambushes, straight at the British muskets, not knowing when a stray bullet would end their young lives, no matter how fast they could run.

Suga had no love for the rebel leader.

After all, he had been in the British military until the latter stages of the uprising. He had switched sides so easily so who was to say he would not do so again? Run back to the white bastards the moment they offered him something shinier.

The reason Suga stuck around was for the shiny things.

When the Disawe liberated her and the others from the Factory, Suga's first instinct had been to run.

But she did not know where she could run to.

She stuck around, ready to leave at any given moment as she listened to Keppetipola Disawe welcome the little pockets of Demon Runners, inviting them to use their 'gift' to fight for the freedom of their country.

'We have liberated you,' Suga had the speech memorized. 'Now go and liberate your country!'

Suga did not join in the drunken cheers. She planned her escape that night but walked in on looters in the Factory Warden's chambers, stuffing jewellery into bags.

That was when she started.

So far, all the spoils of war collected from corpses were coins and other items of value; lockets, clocks on chains, gold, silver.

They all waited for her in a shed not too far from the banana plantation behind the village. Waited for the day she returned with whatever she could steal in Kandy.

Suga had never been there but she heard it was the richest city in the kingdom. Robert Brownrigg, the governor himself, had brought over trunks of valuables. The palace was home to the crown jewels of the Nayakar Kings and a roof that was completely encased in gold.

Once she got her hands on some of those, Suga would kiss this bloody pointless rebellion goodbye and head home to the parents whose faces she could not remember.

Maybe when they see what she brought with her they would forget that she had metal sticking out of her legs and hands, forget that she went away a child and came back a freak.

Maybe they would even forgive her.

Rumours had started spreading of how the end seemed near for the rebellion, especially since the speed with which the Disawe and his fellow councilmen had taken down the British trading routes leading to Kandy was faster than anticipated.

'My friends, we are now closer to our destiny!' The Disawe spoke to them the night before as they prepared for the taking of Wellassa. 'We are closer to freedom! Closer now, to throwing these insufferable foreigners from our beloved nation and taking it back! Taking it back for the Sinhalese,' The Sinhalese in the crowd hooted in reply, 'Taking it back for the Tamils,' The Tamil people only nodded and some attempted to raise their fists but thought better of it midway.

Suga watched with hooded eyes, sprawled on top of a gunny bag in the midst of Rama and the other children.

She wondered if it was possible for the rebels to defeat the British in this state. Though none of the Council seemed to acknowledge it, there was a deep rift growing between the rebels, one that was not present during the days Suga had first joined.

In the beginning, the rebels were less concerned with their ethnicity and more determined to gain their freedom. But lately there was a lot of friction. People whispered in corners.

Who's going to rule once we've chased the British away?

You can't trust the Muslims; did you see how they sold us all out?

Tamil leader? No, no, the Disawe should be given that post. Tamil kings? Better to be ruled by the bulls in the paddy!

If we let the Sinhalese get the upper hand we'll be subservient till kingdom come! We must act now and fast!

Suga let her gaze wander over to the Disawe bent over a roughly drawn map of the Eastern Mountains. He was listening avidly as the village Headman Marikkar was describing the landscape to Lord Duraisami.

How long would this unity last?

Who would betray them first?

Not that Suga really cared. Before the betraying began she would be well on her way out of here.

Keppetipola Disawe finished his strategy meeting and began to speak to the councillors. The rest of the rebels dispersed.

Rama stood up and taking his cue the rest of their Demon Runner pack did as well. Rama looked down at Suga and then back at the Disawe who she was watching.

'You coming Suga? Past lunch time already and I only had a coconut shell of rice before.'

Suga dismissed him with a wave.

The Disawe was nodding at something the Headman was saying. His eyes were half closed and Suga could see from the glimmer in them that the Disawe did not trust him.

What did you see in us? The day you broke into the Factory?

Are we just machines to you? As we were to the men that did this to us? What will you do once we have served our purpose? Will you give us freedom?

Or will you have us put to death?

Suga could imagine that scenario well.

British war machines, they would be called. Monsters with British hearts!

There's nothing people loved more than a good public killing.

Death did not scare Suga.

She had seen more than her share of it during her days in the Factory.

She thought back to that first inclination of freedom.

Two years, for two whole years she had been paralysed.

It shook her will even now, just to think about it.

The Factory had always smelled of death mingling jovially with the pungent aroma of formaldehyde.

It was the taste that remained in the back of her mouth after her nightmares woke her.

Suga was not 'installed' until she was in her teenage years; the surgeons had instead focused on developing her natural speed.

She remembered training daily, waking up before the rooster crowed and going to bed before sundown.

Though it was tiring Suga was happy, she supposed. Happy to be able to run, happy to gobble down any and every meal concoction the surgeons brought to her. Plates of multi-coloured fruit shipped in from all over the Orient. White rice and dhal, coconut milk and peahen soup and gotukola leaf broth.

During the surgery, the scientists had completely cut her calves, peeled them back like ripe bananas so they could taper the runners to the bone. After that the calves were sewn back and the skin on the legs shaved off to keep an eye on the healing.

The raw ache kept Suga awake all night, even though she had been shot through with coca, the sedative that knocked her cellmates to the brink of death.

Though the pain persisted, Suga healed in the expected time frame.

She was wheeled out for tests and had even run a short distance, thrilled at her heightened speed and the sense of entitlement that came with it. Entitlement, a feeling she did not know she could possess.

Suga did not remember when the paralysis hit.

Maybe she was trying not to remember.

But it came with no fair warning as she did all her rehabilitation exercises, drank all her warm milk mint and honey, peered at the clinking clockwork before she went to sleep that night only to wake up and find that her legs no longer responded to her.

Suga did not go into a panic, but calmly tried to raise herself off of the floor after she had rolled down from her hardboard bed the next morning.

She tried several times.

And then the terror hit her.

She had to be carried thrashing and screaming into the medical ward and strapped down onto a metal table with cowhide leashes. She had hammered her head against the bedrail until she bled from her nose, the viscous liquid blotting her face.

At least that was what Rama told her. The truth could have been worse. Suga had no proper memory of the details, though that fear was an impression still fresh in her heart.

After she coughed up bile and globules of blood, Suga had fallen silent.

She would remain this way for two and a half years.

For Suga, it felt like an eon; lying there, covered in bedsores she could no longer feel, her legs limp and useless, her clothes, soiled and crusted.

She shuddered at the memory.

She did not know what made her fight back after those two long years.

She had sat up in bed one night and used her aching claws to cut her bonds.

She tried to roll off to her feet but was sprawling on the cold floor instead, stunned by the fall.

She pushed back on her hands, her claws scraping silver trails, her arms shaking until she was sitting on the floor, shoved onto her knees for support.

Suga fell several times. She fell until there was a sickening crunch and her nose connected with the hard cement.

The officer on night duty found her, coated in blood, still struggling to rise. Unable to help her himself, Private Jimmy Rudolf had called Rama, who happened to live in the nearest cell.

Rama told her later that she had insisted they leave her alone, she had cried that if she did not try to stand up today she would die.

As they could not do anything to move her, Jimmy and Rama had withdrawn, watching Rama recalled, as Suga tumbled over and over again, gurgling in small breaths through her broken nose.

When it seemed like Jimmy would faint from hysterics if they watched any longer, Rama had called the wardens and Suga was drugged and tied back in bed.

The Head Warden had come to see her the next morning. Suga could try to walk using the exercise bars, she had said, if she promised to stay in bed the rest of the week.

It was her next six months at the bars that unknowingly initiated her into the group of Demon Runners that she would later call her pack. They were the youngest of the various pockets of runners in the Factory; children of slaves and minor labourers. The offspring of the lower castes.

When they learned how much Suga despised aid, they helped her by staying out of her way and being charming and cheerful and self-deprecating as Suga began to find her arms growing stronger, larger, cords of brown muscle rippling as she pulled her body up onto the metal poles, her knuckles bruised and white.


Her face was wet.

Suga drew her sleeve across her cheeks and blinked her stinging eyes at the horizon where evening approached, slowly bronzing over the landscape. There was a pair of sambhurs grazing in the plains, bigger and less wary than the deer that morning.

She watched how the buck moved parallel to the doe at all times, shielding her from possible threats.

When Suga met Jimmy, he called her 'Lalla Rukh.'

She only managed twenty steps without holding the bars and the sudden proclamation made her lose both her count and her balance.

She fell with a thump on her backside and scowled up at the pale English boy.

He had taken to watching over her, ever since she had returned to rehabilitation.

Rama claimed he was the new soldier assigned to runner guard duty in their section. Though the rest of the guards came and went, Jimmy was a permanent fixture to the delight of Shreya and Tissa who always loved a good tease and Rama, Suga suspected, though he feigned disinterest.

Jimmy walked over to her and put his hands under her armpits in order to heave her up. 'I understand now what Thomas Moore was implying by oriental women being tulip-cheeked.' He said, moving his hands down to her elbows to steady her.

He was standing close enough for Suga to see tendrils of the ocean in his blue eyes and count the dusting of freckles on his nose. She shoved him as hard as she could while maintaining her balance and that was the only time she saw him register surprise at her rebuffs.

He was there that evening as well, following her wherever she went.

He spoke to her all the time.

At first Suga ordered him away, even grazing his cheek with her claws once when she hit out at him, but found that allowing him to stay required a great deal less effort than getting him to go.

He had come down from England in the last boat. New soldier. He had been assigned to the Factory after he became the sole survivor of a Kandyan guerrilla attack on the banks of Mahaweli River. He was a lover of poetry.

Suga failed to comprehend the enchantment in a bunch of useless words strung together like a seashell necklace, conspicuous and insubstantial, but the English boy swore by Shakespeare, by Milton and by the modern Irishman Thomas Moore whose latest work about a Mughal princess was not yet famous, but very soon would be, or so Jimmy believed.

Suga never responded to Jimmy's endless tirades. Hell, she did not even understand him sometimes.

She wondered how she could be rid of his constant company but to her chagrin found he had been appointed guard to the rehabilitation chambers during her hours of therapy.

He watched over her as if she were a new-born.

She would see him flinch every time she fell and when she cried out in pain; the eyes that welled up with tears were his.

Suga did not understand how a stranger could feel for her this way. It felt too intimate. It felt wrong, dirty in some way but at the same time comforting, like a breath you were holding in suspense, released only when you knew everything would be alright. These kinds of thoughts left her edgy.

She punched him hard once for trying to help her get up.

The bruise stayed for a week, adding a bit of rosy colour to his otherwise pallid features. Yet it did not deter him one bit, though he seemed to have learned his lesson where skin ship was concerned. He did not attempt to touch her again.

Instead he told her his life story.

Jimmy was an unwanted child.

His parents had been very successful in the fishing industry until his birth.

Jimmy's father, for whom he was named, drowned when his fishing boat was hit by a storm off the coast of Dover. Witnesses claimed the waves had been over ten feet high, a sign of the wrath of Poseidon.

Within weeks one of Jimmy's brothers, the only one in the family to be accepted into a university, died in a fire.

After the tragic death of his sister, just two years his senior, strangled by her own blanket, Jimmy's family and neighbours began to believe that he was cursed and should be got rid of as soon as possible.

His mother left him and he grew up in an orphanage owned by his maternal uncle, who never ignored a chance to tell Jimmy of the misfortune he had brought down on otherwise kind and God-fearing folk who had done no wrong.

As soon as he was old enough to enlist, Jimmy was packed off to the military and shipped out to His Majesty's eastern colonies.

'It is hard, to know you have a family but find no place amongst them.' He told her one particularly hot evening, sitting a good metre away from Suga who was sprawled on a patch of sunlight, too tired to move.

Fat flies buzzed lazily overhead, fanning her streaked face with their tiny wings. She could smell the sour perspiration she knew was gathering on his flushed cheeks and shirt front. It was a scent she synchronized with solace, a scent that told you it was alright to let your guard down.

'Isn't the sun too strong?' She heard Jimmy whisper. 'Shall I block the window with something?'

She responded as usual by turning away and woke later to find him sitting across from her, shading her face with his open palms.

'Watching her struggle so hard to live, it makes me think of myself.' He told Rama once when the older Demon Runner teased the boy about the budding romance. Suga was strapping on her gear protectors nearby, secretly listening in. 'She inspires me to try to live as well!'

Suga did not know what to make of that.

For the most, Jimmy just confused her.

He made her wonder if there was more to life than just merely existing.

Sometimes, she could see hope in his shy smile and blue eyes.

Then he said things like, 'Olive skin and tulip cheeks, hair as black as raven feathers,' and she wanted to rake her claws across his face.

The Uva Rebellion reached its decisive battle in the plains of Wellassa, chilled crispy by the unforgiving October winds.

Suga did not know exactly how strong the rebels were, but Jimmy had said Keppetipola's army numbered over twenty and a thousand.

The Disawe was hell-bent on meeting the British reconnaissance in the Wellassa plains even though both Lord Duraisami and Councilman Madugalle were against it.

They said that even though having the Demon Runners gave the rebels an advantage, the British intelligence knew of it now and for sure, must have figured out a defensive counter-plan.

But the Disawe was adamant. Speed was their advantage.

Later Suga wondered about his blind faith in the Demon Runners.

Was he fascinated by their advanced mechanical ability? So fascinated he was blind to all else?

Or did he despise them so much he could not wait to sacrifice them?

As dawn approached over the blushing hillside, scouts arrived at the camp.

The Governor's reinforcements were making their way across the plain towards Kandy.

The anticipation of the kill sent shock waves surging into Suga's brain, sparking it to life.

She could feel her legs reacting to the adrenaline rush; she switched the gears in her knees, rearing to go.

Rama was checking their straps and their cowhide protectors, as he did every time they went into battle. He gave Suga a customary onceover but bent to check every lock on the two little ones.

Jimmy Rudolf hovered around them clutching an oil tin, muttering to a giggling Jai and a disapproving Tissa that he wished he could come with them.

'No one trust you!' Tissa pointed at Jimmy's face pockmarked with mosquito bites. 'You're white!'

'But he'll make a great secret weapon, no?' Jai countered. 'You should have been runner too Jimmy! Suckers won't fight you because white skin and you could kill them all!'

Rama shoved Jai forward playfully. 'Jimmy never said he was on our side,' he threw a wink in Jimmy's direction.

'But he not against us either!'

Rama nodded now smiling outright. He ruffled Hari's thatched head. 'Yes Hari, he not against us either.'

Shreya pulled a stalk from a nettle bush and looped her hair through it. 'That's why the Disawe didn't kill him no?' She tossed back her ponytail and jerked her head in Suga's direction. 'The only thing Jimmy do is romance Suga!'

Jimmy sidled up to Suga and looked her up and down. She knew he was checking her straps and she deliberately turned her legs away.

'I wish I could come with you.' He whispered from behind her, his breath ruffling strands of hair onto her cheeks.

Suga turned to throw him a dirty look.

Jimmy held her gaze for a couple of seconds and had Suga been someone else she would have been dazzled by just how blue his eyes were. How was it possible? How could eyes be the colour of the ocean?

'What can you do? Just go back to your people!'

That was the last thing she said to him.

The Runners were left at the top of the hill, hidden amongst the trees as the Disawe and his army headed down, crouched underneath the tall grass, moving towards the reinforcements, a small contingent of soldiers coming from the Port down south.

At a yell from the front, the rebels charged, taking the British by surprise.

Suga did not register much from the battle for it was now their turn.

She leapt from the underbrush and started to run. Around her the rest of the Demon Runners bolted out like arrows from their hiding places and whizzed across the plains.

Suga grimaced as the gears clanked to life in her legs, propelling her forward with rapid thrust. She let the momentum lift her in the air and attacked the first soldier that came within her vicinity with both her heels and her claws.

She felt the spikes bite into the soft flesh and warm sweet-smelling blood enveloped her fingers.

The feeling gave her an elation she savoured and had longed for since her first such battle.

She cart wheeled back onto her feet and raced across to the other end of the dirt road where several cavalrymen were making a run for it.

She let the spikes slice the tendons on a horse's leg and the animal knelt so suddenly its rider was a tangle of red gore on a tree.

Her hands and heels were soaked, the cuts and bruises and disfigurations drowned in the blood of white men.

They were winning!

Suga saw a bullet.

She did not know if it was part of her ability, something that came with the heightened speed. Though if thought about rationally, having clockwork gears in your legs should not give your eyes any power whatsoever.

The bullet sang in the air and went straight through Jai's forehead like he was made of paper.

Jai's eyes widened and diminished as a pair of weak flames would in a roaring wind and red liquid gushed from the hole in his temple.

Suga could have sworn he was smiling when he dived backwards and lay very still until the flurry of war erased him from Suga's line of sight.

A rush of shots echoed one after another when Suga realised it was coming from the cliff that faced the plains from the east.

She wondered what the Disawe would think of that.

Lord Duraisami had been right.

Suga saw a soldier aim a gun at Rama.

It was different from the usual rifles. There was a small hole the soldier held up to his eye, squinting.

The Demon Runners had not been the only advancements developed at the Factory by the British. There had been many other experiments. Most, useless, but some…

Oh? Suga thought. Precision pointers?

She spun towards Rama, her scream breaking into a million colourless pieces of agony. She cut down anything in her way, regardless of whether they were man or beast, white or brown.

Rama!

She felt something hit her on the back of her head, jarring her teeth and winking out all the light in her world.


The end of a legend was spectacular in its palpable lack of melodrama.

Suga threw the phrase around in her mind as Keppetipola Disawe's head separated from the rest of his body in one blow of an axe.

Did she have to pick now of all times to develop a poetic eye?

She watched placidly as an British soldier picked up the rolling head by the hair, holding it at arm's length so the sticky blood did not stain his boots.

The Disawe had been brave to the very end, gamely offering to tie up his hair so it did not hinder his head from being chopped off cleanly. He had asked for a prayer book and recited his gaatha; his eyes shining as if he was certain nirvana waited for him on the other side.

A lot of good it will do for you, Suga thought. The horses

will piss on your headless corpse and your gaatha would do nothing to stop them!

The worst part of the whole execution was Councilman Madugalle.

He screamed and thrashed the whole way, begging for forgiveness, offering to give up secret information about imaginary Demon Runners and non-existent rebels and long dead Yaksha witch tribes hiding out in the Matale Mountains.

It was embarrassing to watch as the former councillor grovelled at the feet of any man with white skin, tears and nasal mucus pouring down his face.

Suga wished that it was Madugalle who had died in the battlefield and not Lord Duraisami. He would have done something. He would have tried to save them.

Not that he would have been successful.

Even the Disawe seemed to have forgotten about his super soldiers.

The British officials pretended they had no idea what the runners were, or why the Crown would require oriental slave warriors enhanced by mechanical means when the Crown had brave men of unquestionable loyalty, descendants of those that had always fought for King and Country.

Abominations, the runners were called, demons, unnatural beings.

Desecrators of God's Will.

How would you know what God's Will was?

Suga argued, but only in her head.

Governor Brownrigg had come up to Kandy for the executions.

He declared that the rebels be wiped off the face of the earth and the Ceylonese people be forgiven, gracious as he was, gracious as His Majesty, their liege was, provided that they never attempt to betray their benefactors again.

He ordered the rice fields in Wellassa and other Uva villages allegedly involved, to be burnt to the ground, animals culled, the farmlands razed.

She thought about her parents.

About her pathetic dream to go back to them armed with her spoils of war.

They were probably dead anyway.

As they led Suga up to the block she searched for a glance at what remained of her pack. The grime-stained faces of Shreya and Tissa stared back at her but Suga's eyes blurred over and she could not make them out properly.

She did not want to see them now, only remember them as they had been.

Wails of despair drew her gaze elsewhere, on to the pinched pink face of Jimmy Rudolf, sobbing like a brand new babe on his baptism day.

He had shouted out for the innocence of the runners. He had confessed to spending time with them, confessed to knowing of their origins. Proposed to take the governor and anyone willing to the Factory. To where it all began.

'They should not be blamed for their fate,' he cried. 'Spare them!'

He was being held back by two of his comrades now, cringing and begging in a voice that had long lost its ability to form coherent words.

The soldier leading her kicked her hard on her clockwork knees, forcing a grunt out of her as she fell to the ground.

Before they laid her head on the block she locked eyes with Jimmy. Silver gemstone tears cascaded from his ocean eyes; raw from crying they were almost bleeding.

His mouth moved, chapped ruddy lips forming three words.

Suga smiled.

# A Sailor Girl Goes Ashore

## Margrét Helgadóttir

The mere thought of the many buildings and streets crammed with humans had always made Nora hurry past the Svalbard Islands as if there were a snapping monster at her heels. Even now, as she stood on deck marvelling at the sight of the sky-scrapers glittering in the sun, it was a struggle not to turn the ship around. Her every pore screamed to her: 'Get out of here! Save yourself! We'll fix this another way.' Her knuckles whitened as she gripped the helm, holding her course straight towards the city that covered every inch of the land in front of her.

The wooden ship objected with loud creaks as the heavy wind strained its sails to the limits, pushing it forwards through the waves. A rather petite vessel; it was the smallest she'd sailed. It was old and worn, too. Nora looked up at the yellowed sails fondly. It was a miracle that they'd lasted this long, cooperating with the buffeting winds without rest for many seasons now. And Nora and the ship had been through some strong gales together. Excellent craftsmanship, Nora thought and, as she often did, pondered the ship's origins: who'd made it and what waters it'd sailed before she stole it.

She'd been certain that the ship wouldn't last long on the high seas, and that she'd soon have to find a replacement, but she'd been pleasantly surprised. Her ship might not cover vast distances in as short a time as the bigger, heavier sailing-ships she was used to, but Nora could turn Naureen around or change direction quickly. She could swiftly put dis-tance between her and the ships she plundered. Sometimes, it seemed as if the ship responded to her thoughts, as if there was a weird invisible bond between the two of them. 'Naureen. Us sailor gals must stick together,' she sometimes said aloud, as if the ship could hear her. Nora always talked to her ship. Clearly a sign she'd been on the sea for too long, she mused.

Naureen. Nora didn't know who'd named the ship or what the name meant, but she thought it strangely fitting. It graced the bow of the ship, painted in beautiful calligraphy. Nora saw it whenever she was aboard another vessel, rummaging for furs or bones of extinct animals she could sell, or food. The sight of her ship always made her heart flutter with happiness. There was a time when Nora would steal the ships she plundered, if she liked them and was in the mood for a change. But not after she stole Naureen. Well, not stole, she corrected herself. When she'd come across the tiny ship, she'd found the salt-rimed corpse of the hollow-cheeked owner sprawled face down on the deck. He'd probably starved to death. His body had not been the first one Nora'd found drifting at sea, nor the last. Her gut feeling told her she'd stumble over several more in the future.

The dark skyscrapers towered over her now. Nora tilted her head back, trying to see their tops. The buildings seemed endless, stretching up into the sky, the cold sun glinting and sparkling in their thousands of windows. Nora imagined people standing behind them, examining her, judging her. Shuddering, she furled the sails and set course towards a huge sign: "Guest Docking." The city's docks stretched along the coast in both directions, bristling with a multitude of piers. She manoeuvred the ship into place at the pier under the sign.

Two tankers loomed in the distance, surrounded by a jungle of sheds and cranes. The massive ships looked ancient, almost prehistoric. They must have been anchored there for a very long time, Nora reflected.

Seeing no mastheads, she frowned. She'd imagined there would be thousands of sailing-ships, considering how many people must live here. But the harbour seemed strangely empty and abandoned.

Nora had learned to trust her instincts after all the years at sea, and they screamed at her now. Something wasn't right. She wobbled around on her sea legs, mooring the ship to the huge bolts jutting out from the pier, all the while casting nervous glances at the piers, the tankers and the high buildings. Hesitating, she stood for a long time on the berth, clutching the last rope in her hands. She wanted nothing more than to leave. Then she looked down at Naureen and sighed. During the many dark seasons, small rifts had of course appeared in the ship's sails now and then, and she'd quickly mended them. But the huge hole that had appeared in the main sail during the last storm was too big for her to repair out at sea. So she'd stitched the edges of the hole roughly together and set course for the nearest shore.

'It'll be all right, Naureen. I'll repair you as fast as I can and then we can leave this place. I promise,' she declared with a firm nod.

Someone giggled. Nora froze, then leaped aboard her ship and crouched down, examining the pier above her. There! Something was moving behind a stack of wooden barrels. Hurrying into the cabin, Nora grabbed her rifle from its hook and ran back onto the deck, her heart roaring in her ears.

'Come out so I can see you,' she shouted. Nothing happened. Whoever was behind the barrels was silent.

'Come out,' she shouted again. 'I would be delighted to meet you.'

Nora sniggered nervously on the inside. She'd learned that it was better to be extra polite when she met other people, no matter how frightened she was. That way even the most scary-looking men would think she was harmless. Around her neck hung her proof; a killer whale tooth, torn from the neck of a scarred pirate captain after she'd killed him. Nora still remembered his confused eyes when he realized that the rum she'd served him and his men was poisoned. She didn't regret killing them. *Actually*, she thought, *I did the sea a favour. Bloody pirates! Worst people out at sea. Killing, raping, plundering…and then they destroy the ships so no one else can use them.*

Nora would never kill people just to rob them. She only stole from people already dead or long gone. Actually, she'd turned into quite a hermit and tried as hard as she could to avoid others, unless she needed to trade or swap furs for food. She'd rather run than stay and fight, though she knew she could fight if necessary. The killer whale tooth might bring her a decent outcome if she traded it, rare as it was. It looked ancient, so it had to be from a real whale. But she wouldn't trade it. She kept it as a reminder not to trust other people. Or that's what Nora told herself. The truth was that she'd kept the tooth to remember not to become a cold-blooded pirate herself. It'd been easy to kill those men. Far too easy.

'Come out,' she shouted again.

There! At last. A head, obscured under a hood, popped up behind the barrels. Nora couldn't tell if it was a man or a woman.

'I have food,' Nora offered.

The person emerged from the barrels and, moving closer to the edge of the pier, stared down at Nora from the depths of the hood.

'Y-you have food?' a tiny voice asked.

'Yes,' Nora answered. 'Not much, but you can have some of it.' She held her rifle ready behind her back.

The other person pulled down the hood, revealing a small face, large eyes, long black hair. A girl, Nora decided and relaxed. The girl looked haggard, but didn't appear to pose any immediate threat.

'That's very kind,' the girl said. 'But I don't have anything to give you for it.'

'Maybe you can help me out in return?' Nora said. 'I need to repair my sails.'

The girl pondered this for a moment, then smiled broadly, her grimy face suddenly beautiful. 'I can help you.'

Nora jumped up on the pier and reached her hand towards the smaller girl, who flinched but then shook hands with her.

'I'm Nora.'

'Aida.'

The girl quickly stuffed her hand back into the outer pocket of her parka. Nora studied her. Up close she could see how the skin lay tight over the girl's high cheek bones, how the long tousled curls were caked with dirt, how the golden-brown eyes flickered, as if not daring to look up at Nora. Everyone Nora met nowadays had a plagued and hunted look in their eyes, but it was unnerving to see such old eyes in this young face. She'd seen things, this one.

Aida's parka, stained with dark spots, looked too thin for the cold weather. The clothes Nora glimpsed underneath the parka didn't look any better. Nora frowned. The girl looked and smelled like she hadn't seen a bath or food for a very long time. Nora grimaced. 'You never know who you'll meet,' her mother used to say when she was a girl. 'It might be the man of your dreams. It might be a president.' Her mother's exhortations had stuck with her. Even though she rarely met people out at sea, she always tried to keep herself clean and presentable, spending time every morning combing and braiding her long hair. Her mother would have been proud.

Nora shook her head to clear her thoughts. Aida stood silent, staring down at the ground, swallowing visibly.

'You look like you need food,' Nora said at last. 'We'll eat, then you'll help me find a sailmaker.'

Aida looked up at her. 'I don't know of any sailmaker, but I know where you can find new sails, and I can help you put it up.' She sounded so eager.

Nora scrutinized the other girl's face. Aida seemed sincere.

'All right. Sounds like we have a deal. But if you betray me, I'll kill you. You understand?'

Aida paled, but nodded.


'Where is everyone, Aida?' Nora asked. The girls sat on Naureen's deck. Aida had hopped down to the deck in one smooth motion, as if she'd done it hundreds of times before. They'd eaten a decent meal, Nora thought; a can of cold broth, some bread and a bottle of filtered sea water. She'd stopped Aida from wolfing the food down too fast, afraid the girl would become sick.

The sun was high in the sky now. Nora wanted to be back at sea before the evening and the darkness arrived. She didn't like the silent city. Why had no one come, besides Aida? Nora knew men. They should have been here already, lurking around the pier, attracted to the new arrival and promises of furs, food, booze, women, things she didn't want to think about. But there were no men in sight. The harbour looked abandoned.

Aida lay on the deck now, staring up at the blue sky, looking tired but content. She fell silent at Nora's words.

'Why are there no people here?' Nora repeated.

Silence. Then Aida gave her a long, searching look.

'They're dead,' she said at last.

'Dead?'

'They're all dead.'

Nora cringed at the pain she saw in Aida's eyes. But she couldn't believe what the girl was saying. Aida must have spotted the scepticism in her face, because she sat up and looked at Nora intently.

'We had a plague. We don't know where it came from or when it started. There were so many new refugees arriving every day. So many died shortly after they came, exhausted from travelling over the seas, I guess. Starving.' Aida paused, as if searching for words. 'Then local people started getting sick, people who'd lived here for years. The hospitals were so crowded. The doctors didn't know what disease it was, what caused it. They didn't have any medicines for it.'

Nora noted the calm distance in the girl's voice and studied her, curious. Aida's behaviour and the way she phrased her words whispered of a finer background and years poring over books. *Where does she come from*, Nora thought, *this stranger who speaks like she's older than me, but looks like she's barely into her teens? She's standing in Death's court, yet she acts so calm.*

'It went so quickly,' Aida continued, interrupting Nora's pondering. 'You died a couple of days after you were affected. We think it was airborne. Dad forbade us to go outside the flat. He was so afraid we'd get infected.'

'Your dad?' Nora asked with a sinking feeling. 'You had family?' Then she chastised herself. Of course Aida had a family. She was so young.

Aida didn't seem to notice. 'Yes, my dad and my brother, Zaki. We came here when I was a child.' She stared out at the sea. 'Dad had a small ship, just like this one. It was called Naureen too, after Mum. But someone stole it.' Images of a salt-rimed corpse popped into Nora's mind. She'd rolled him out into the cold sea water.

'It went so quickly,' Aida said. 'So many people died. Whole buildings emptied. Schools closed. People panicked, plundering stores for food, rioting in the streets, killing each other. The authorities were helpless. The smoke from the crematorium hung above the city all the time.'

Nora listened, feeling cold inside. 'Is that why there are no ships here?' she asked. 'People ran?'

'Yes. Many escaped by sea, probably going to North East Land or Edge Island, or maybe even south to Bear Island. I hope they made it. Others went by foot, hoping to reach other cities or the mines, I think. Dad said we had to get out of here. He said we'd die if we stayed. He talked about a land west of here, where we could make a new life. Said it was once called The Green Land. Said there were several massive vaults filled with seeds there, so we could grow our own food if we wanted to. He wanted to buy a new sailing-ship, to get us out of here. But the days went by and nothing happened.

'My brother disappeared one morning. My dad thought he'd tried to escape on foot. I don't know why Zaki abandoned us.' Tears started to run down Aida's cheek. She brushed them away. 'Dad knocked on my door late one night, said he didn't want to come in; he thought he'd become sick. That I'd find a bag with some furs I could sell, some food and clothes, outside my door. He said he loved me dearly, but I had to get out of there, use the furs to buy a berth on a sailing-ship. Escape. He said I had to leave him. I cried and cried, but he told me to obey him. S-so, I did.'

Aida bowed her head. Her long black curls covered her face.

'I'm sorry,' she said between sobs. 'I-I can't seem to stop crying.'

'It's all right,' Nora murmured and patted the girl's shoulder, feeling awkward.

The dark skyscrapers towered over them. Nora craned her neck, looking up at them. She wondered how many people had survived the plague, if any. Her gut feeling told her that it was not a good idea to examine this city too closely, or to stay anchored in the harbour too long. She looked at Aida. She couldn't fathom what the girl had been through. It was easy to imagine what'd happened. The girl probably wasn't used to taking care of herself and must have been easy prey for thieves and others who meant no good. She must have hidden down here at the harbour for a long time. Whatever food she'd brought with her probably hadn't lasted long. Maybe the girl had searched the nearby houses for food. She mused that it had likely been a while since the girl had last been inside the city. It was a miracle that she was still alive.

Aida had stopped crying. Once in a while, a loud sniffle escaped.

'The sails,' Nora asked, 'are they far away?'


The streets were deep in dirt and rubble. Glass crunched under their boots. Here and there, corpses stared at them with blank eyes. The bodies were weirdly intact, mummified, as was often the case in this cold climate. Nora tried to ignore them, having seen plenty of dead people out at sea, but she noticed that Aida walked closer and closer to her.

They'd walked several street lengths when Nora discovered someone or something was following them. She glanced sideways at Aida, but it seemed the girl hadn't noticed it yet. In the broken glass shards that still hung, defying gravity, in the large shop windows they passed, Nora could see their reflections: two lone figures in a vast street. She might have laughed at the differences between the two girls if she hadn't felt so numb with panic.

Aida picked her way carefully, paying close attention to where she put her feet. She'd pulled her hood up again, concealing her head. Like Nora, she'd also covered the lower part of her face with a scarf. Only her golden brown eyes were visible. Nora noticed Aida casting curious glances at her now and then.

A sensation of rising and falling washed through Nora's body, as if she was still on her ship. But she refused to let her sea legs or her fear of the foreign city and the tall deserted buildings overcome her. She strode down the middle of the empty street with long steps, straight shoulders, long blonde braid swinging from side to side, rifle hanging loosely on her shoulders, and her fur coat open at the front, flapping in the wind. Occasionally she stopped to wait for Aida to catch up.

There! She spotted it again. A shadow. The first time she noticed it, she'd thought it was the sun playing tricks, glinting in all the glass. But now she saw it move. Heart thudding, she pulled the rifle from her shoulder and murmured to Aida: 'We're being followed. Hide behind that tram carriage.' She pointed further up the street. 'I'll catch up.'

But the girl shook her head. 'No, I want to stay with you.'

Nora heard the stubbornness and noted the fierce eyes. Maybe she'd underestimated the girl. She sighed. 'Okay, but stay behind me, and run if I tell you to.' Aida didn't answer. She just stepped behind Nora, who sighed again, but soon forgot about the girl. Turning, she saw the shadow moving behind a pile of rubble and heard weird scratching sounds. She pointed the rifle and shouted: 'Show yourself!'

Nothing happened.

'Look!' Aida cried out and leapt forward. It happened too quickly; the girl was several metres down the street before Nora could react.

'Stop, you idiot!' she yelled and chased after the girl, cursing.

But Aida didn't stop until she reached the pile, crouched down and held out her arms towards the shifting shadow. Nora couldn't believe it. Had the girl gone mad? She ran, rifle lifted, heart thundering in her ears, thinking she'd be too late.

But when she reached Aida, she lowered her rifle, eyes wide. In front of the girl stood a four-legged creature. An animal. *A dog*, Nora thought. She'd seen pictures. It was ragged and extremely malnourished, its ribs like a washboard under the dirty, tousled fur. And yet, she thought, it's a beautiful animal. The fur was black and white, the tail thick and bushy, and the eyes clear ice blue. Someone had done a fine job creating this animal. She wondered if it'd been hatched in a laboratory in this city or if it'd arrived with the refugees.

'Be careful,' she warned. 'We don't know where it comes from or if it likes humans.'

Craning her neck, Aida looked up at her. 'Of course she's friendly. Can't you see that she's wagging her tail?' She rolled her eyes.

As if the dog understood what they'd said, it bounced into Aida's arms, leaning into her with a heavy sigh, making Aida's hood slide down, and put its head on her shoulder. Aida stroked its back, and the animal shuddered from head to tail. Nora studied them.

'She?'

'Yes, it's a girl. Amazing, huh? They usually only make male dogs, since they're for the most part used as guard dogs. Guess people think males are more aggressive. This girl is special. Bet she was someone's pet.'

Aida lifted the dog's head and looked into its eyes. Nora's heart jumped at the sight of the sharp teeth so close to the girl's face.

'You're special, aren't you?' crooned Aida. The dog lifted its head and let out a loud complaining howl. Aida laughed and hugged it. The dog licked her face.

'You seem familiar with dogs.'

'We used to have one when I was a child. It was before we sailed here.' Aida looked down at her hands. 'It was Mum's idea. She thought we needed some extra protection.' She fell silent, but kept on patting the dog's head. Nora took a careful step towards them and stretched out a hand. The dog sniffed it, then growled. When Nora snatched her hand back, Aida laughed. 'She probably thinks you smell strange. You know, the sea smell and all. Let her get used to you.'

Nora looked around, fearing the dog's howling would bring attention, but the street was still empty. The shadows were growing longer, though. 'We better get going. The night is coming.'

Aida nodded and got up reluctantly. 'It's not far,' she said, pulling her hood on again. Nora put her rifle back on her shoulder.

They hadn't taken many steps when Nora noticed the dog trotting after them. She stopped. 'It's following us'

'Yes, Tarik likes us,' Aida said and, seeing Nora's furrowed forehead, added: 'She'll be useful. I promise.'

'Tarik?'

'I thought she looked like a Tarik, a star. You like it?'

Studying the girl and looking down at the dog, Nora sighed heavily and started walking again. Aida and the black and white dog trailed behind.

The door was unlocked. Aida's eyes were barely visible in the dark corridor. They'd climbed to the eighth floor. Nora had counted as they crept up the many stairs, obscured in darkness. The air was musty with the smell of old things. Nora tightened the scarf around her nose and mouth, and cocked her head, listening, suddenly sure she'd heard distant noises. But all she heard was the unnerving silence. Probably her imagination, she thought.

'Are you sure you want to do this?' she asked as she took her rifle from her shoulder.

'Yes,' Aida whispered, her voice shaking.

They entered the flat, Nora with her rifle at the ready, Aida close behind. The dog trotted before them, sniffing. Stopping now and then, it looked up at Aida with a searching glance. Large windows covered one wall entirely. The sun reflected in from the windows across the street, casting long shadows across the living room. The flat was small and sparsely furnished. Dust covered everything. Nora saw a couple of books on a shelf, a black vase, a yellowed poster on the wall, an embroidered cushion on the couch. But there were few personal items. Aida and her family hadn't brought much from overseas.

They looked into all the rooms, but the flat was empty. Aida let out a sigh. Nora wondered if it was because she was relieved or disappointed. Maybe both. She watched the girl run around the flat with the dog close behind, opening cupboards and drawers in a frenzy. Aida packed a couple of rucksacks with clothes, a blanket, the cushion, a little box. Nora wondered what was inside. It was obvious that Aida had no plans to return here.

The kitchen cupboards were of course empty. Nora had seen the foot prints in the dust. Somebody had been here, probably looking for food, not long ago. We'd better hurry, she thought, and grabbed the books from the shelf, handing them to Aida. 'Here.' The girl looked at her, but didn't say anything, just put the books in the bag. Then she ran into one of the bedrooms and returned with a large bundle. The sails. Nora sighed in relief.

'Why did you have sails here?' she asked.

'My dad got them just before he became ill. He planned for us to escape by sea. I know he talked with our neighbours about buying their ship. They were old and didn't want to leave the city. Dad said the ship needed some repair, but that it would do. He even got these.' Aida showed her a couple of paper rolls. Maps. 'I think they are maps of the land in the west.'

Nora glanced out of the windows. The sun was lingering low on the horizon. 'Did he have any weapons?'

Aida thought for a minute, then nodded and ran into one of the bedrooms. Nora heard a loud screech that sounded like heavy furniture being dragged across the floor. Aida came back with a rifle and boxes of bullets. And torches! Nora was starting to like Aida's father. He'd been practical and fore-sighted, this man.

Tarik whined softly. It sat in the door way, staring out into the dark corridor, its ears cocked forward.

'We have to go,' Nora said, grabbing one of the rucksacks, the rifles and the packet of sails. Aida took the other rucksack and lit one of the torches, but Nora shook her head. 'I don't want to attract any attention.' Aida stared at her, wide-eyed, but switched it off without objections.


It would have been wise to stay in the flat overnight, Nora thought later, but she just couldn't bear the building or the dead, looming silence in the city anymore, or the not know-ing what lurked in the dark corners. She desperately longed for fresh sea air and strong winds against her face.

It'd been difficult to move through the streets in daylight. Now, with no light except for the stars above, it was extremely hard to move at all. They walked slowly, their feet searching for safe places to step. The extra weight of the sails and other things they'd gathered at the flat felt like sacks of rocks on their backs. Nora had more than once been on the edge of throwing it all down and leaving it behind. But the thought of Aida stopped her. These were her precious things, Nora chastised herself. All she had left from her family. Everything she owned.

Aida walked behind her, her hand on the dog's back. She

didn't speak, and she was wheezing. Then Nora heard a long deep sigh, as if the girl was fighting to calm herself and steady her breathing. Aida was clearly exhausted, but didn't complain. A huge respect for the girl kept growing. Nora could identify with her; being alone, trying to survive. They didn't feel like strangers to each other anymore. Aida was the first person Nora'd spent this much time with in the many years since she'd decided that the seas were her home. She wondered where Aida would go, if she'd find her brother, if she'd make it to the land in the west.

The only sounds were their breathing, the dog's panting and the crunching glass underfoot. Nora fought to keep the panic rippling through her body from erupting. She found having Aida and the dog with her oddly comforting. Several times, she thought she heard other footsteps and stopped to listen. But like before, all she heard was the overwhelming silence.

Finally she heard the waves against the pier and smelled the sea air. Even though they were in the sunny season now, and the nights were shorter, it was still dark. She was anxious to locate Naureen. She knew it was a risk, but she reached for Aida's rucksack and pulled out one of the torches.

'I need to find Naureen,' she murmured, scanning the harbour. The single light beamed through the night.

'There!' Aida cried and grabbed Nora's sleeve.

When Nora saw the mast, she thought she might burst into tears of relief. She almost dropped the light in her haste to switch it off. The two girls hurried towards Naureen, the dog close on their heels.

They threw the rucksacks and the package of new sails down on the deck and Aida sprang down. The dog hesitated, but then jumped after the girl. Nora hurried around the pier to loosen the ropes that moored the ship. She knew it'd probably be wiser to wait for daybreak, but her panic was close to the surface now. All she wanted was to be back on the sea, where she felt safe.

Something shuffled behind her. The dog barked madly. Alarmed, Nora spun around. A gaunt man burst out of the dark, running towards her with wide and bloodshot eyes.

Instinctively, Nora hit him in the head with her rifle. He wavered a little, then attacked her, his hands reaching for her throat, madness shining in his eyes. She kneed him in the groin. He grunted, but his hands still clutched her throat. She hit him in the head and kicked his knee, but still he held her in his strong grip, strangling her slowly. His stinking breath nauseated her.

Then, when Nora thought she couldn't take it anymore, that she was going to pass out, he suddenly let her go. She fell to the ground gasping for air, the world spinning around her. As if through a fog, she heard awful noises and the man screaming. Then a shot resounded through the night.

'Are you all right?'

It was Aida. She crouched next to Nora on the pier. The dog put its head between the girls. It seemed to scrutinize her. Blood dripped from its mouth. Nora sat up slowly. Her body felt bruised, but she was still in one piece.

'Yes, I'm all right,' she answered, her voice hoarse. She struggled to speak. 'What happened?'

'We killed him,' Aida answered. She seemed unaffected, but Nora heard the tremble in her voice.

Emerging over the horizon, the sun stretched long arms of light towards them. The man lay in a pool of blood a couple of metres away, the scarlet gash in his throat gaping towards her in the meagre light. Nora shuddered at the sight. She stood, leaning momentarily on the girl's shoulder. Aida and Tarik jumped down onto Naureen's deck. Aida held on to the pier while Nora loosened the last rope. Then Nora sprang down, falling as she landed. She cried out in pain.

Staring up at the dead skyscrapers, she said: 'Can you sail, girl?'

'Yes.'

'Consider yourself hired. Now get us out of here.'

'Aye, Captain!'

Aida pushed them away from the pier and had the sails up quickly. They flapped before they caught the wind. Nora lay on deck, exhausted, as Aida seated herself behind the helm. She seemed at home there. Her long black hair danced in the wind. Nora thought she heard the girl humming some odd, jolly tune. The haggard dog looked comfortable on the ship too. It lay down next to Nora on the deck and leaned its head on her stomach.

Naureen ploughed her way through the waves. Nora watched the skyscrapers disappear on the horizon, their thousands of traitorous windows glittering in the sun. She listened to Aida's distant humming, almost lost in the roar of the wind, a strangely comforting duet. The girl was stronger than Nora'd thought. *She's even stronger than me,* Nora reflected. *She could have run away, but she stayed and helped me. I'd be dead if it wasn't for this girl. And the dog.*

As if it had heard her thoughts, the dog lifted its head to look at her with its ice blue eyes. The blood around its mouth had almost dried, but Nora could see red drops glistening in the black and white fur. For a moment, she considered pushing the dog's bloodstained head away. Instead she lifted her sore arms and patted its head. The pains stung through her body. The dog sighed heavily and closed its eyes.

Nora fingered her bruised neck, searching for the killer whale tooth. She startled. It was gone! It must have been torn off during the struggle with the man on the pier. Her heart thudded faster, the panic welling inside. What would remind her now to stay unchanged, to keep her integrity in this cold world?

'Which way, Captain?' Aida shouted.

Nora looked over at the calm black-haired girl with her wide-legged stance behind the helm. Nora relaxed. *Strange,* she thought, *but I really don't mind their company. Maybe I can get used to sailing with Aida and the dog.... It feels like they've always been here.*

Next to her on the deck, she saw the package containing the new sails and the maps. They spoke of a new adventure; a new world. The land in the west; maybe it was time to stop the restless drifting at sea without cause or meaning. Her new goal.

'Go west,' she answered.

Aida grinned broadly. 'Aye, Captain!'

Nora watched her turn the big helm, then adjust the sails.

Confident. A sailor. *Don't worry*, she told herself. *You don't need the whale tooth. The girl will remind you that not all strangers are foes.*

Friends. Nora tasted the foreign word. *We'll have to stop at some point to repair the sails, but it's not a problem anymore. I can do this out at sea now that Aida is here to help me. I bet we could accomplish just about anything, if we just stay together.*

'Naureen,' she murmured, on the brink of the merciful darkness of sleep. 'Us sailor gals must stick together.'

# Rolling in the Deep

## Cat Connor

Everyone needs a vacation, everyone, even SSA Ellie Conway. If the universe could just accept that life would be so much easier.

'Fourteen days of Saturday?' I asked leaning on the car door. No phone. No internet. No badge. No gun. Fourteen days of Saturday. And unreachable by normal means. It appealed.

His voice was clear over the cell phone I held to my ear, 'Something like that. You up for it?'

'I've got four weeks off, so yeah, I'm up for it.'

Four weeks off sounded better than being *stood down* for four weeks. On the plus side I still got to keep my badge and I was being paid. I'd skated a thin line and survived with nothing more than some enforced vacation time and a slap on the wrist from the Director.

'When do you want to leave?'

'Tonight,' I replied. 'I want to leave tonight.'

'Just you?'

He sounded hopeful? Maybe he thought I'd bring Delta. Nope. We're not joined at the hip despite what it looks like.

'Yes just me.'

'Want me to go ahead and book the tickets?'

'Yep, I'll meet you at your place later this afternoon.'

'We running today?'

'Absolutely.'

'Then I'll come to you.'

'Okay.'

'See you soon.'

I hung up and pocketed my phone. Kurt walked toward me carrying two coffees in take-out cups. The winter sun bounced off the edge of his sunglasses. I lifted mine from the top of my head and pushed them on.

'All good?' Kurt asked handing me a cup of coffee.

'Yep,' I replied, taking the lid off the cup. Steam rushed out, fogging my glasses. It took a moment for the steam to clear. 'Who's driving?'

'Me,' Kurt said. 'Scoot.'

I walked around the car and slid into the passenger seat.

'We're done, yeah?'

'Yes,' Kurt said checking the mirrors. 'We're done. How long are you off for?'

'A month.'

He glanced at me. 'Going away?'

I smiled. 'Yeah, I am.'

'You going to make this hard?' he asked pulling out into the traffic.

I sighed. 'I'm lucky I still have a job…' I wasn't feeling chatty.

'We all are,' he replied. 'We pushed Assistant Director Owen to the very edge.' Kurt glanced at me. 'And my question stands, are you going to make *this* hard?'

'I'm going to a place by the sea with a friend.'

Not a lie. It is by the sea, just not a sea in this hemisphere. I smiled thinking about how far we were going. It was the sea at the end of the world.

I caught his interested glance and ignored it.

'Virginia Beach, Norfolk, Chesapeake Bay?'

'No, it's in the south.'

It doesn't get much more southern and yet still remain warm enough for me to enjoy it. I'm not a penguin. I felt the smile on my lips. Not a penguin but sometimes Mitch referred to me as Penguin and I liked it. I couldn't remember a time in my life where anyone had given me a nickname. New. Nice.

'Gulf of Mexico?'

'More southern than that,' I said and drained my coffee.

'Cotopaxi is not by the beach,' Kurt mumbled.

'I never said Ecuador,' I replied. 'And how did you hear about Cotopaxi?'

'Iain Campbell mentioned you, him, and Mike Davenport were talking about climbing Cotopaxi in January.'

Snow drifts were piled by the roadside, melting in the winter sun. It was definitely January. I wasn't in a mountain climbing mood.

'They're going without me,' I said. I felt like walking on a beach not struggling for oxygen at the top of a cold mountain, as much fun as that would be, it's not what I wanted or who I wanted to be with. 'I'm going away, Kurt. I'm out of cell range and will have no internet for two weeks. Then I'll be back and I'll tell you all about it.' Maybe.

He pulled up my drive way. The gates opened and then closed before the car got to the house.

'Be safe Conway,' Kurt said as I opened the car door. 'Hope the mystery man is worthy.'

'He is,' I replied. 'See you in a couple of weeks. Keep Delta ticking?'

'We'll be waiting.'

I shut the door. Kurt waited for me to go inside before he drove off. I walked into the empty house. It felt cold, I knew it wasn't cold, the heating was always on, but empty houses feel cold. They lack life. At the living room door I spoke. 'Computer, listen. Bon Jovi.'

Seconds later the opening bars of the first track on the latest Bon Jovi album filled the emptiness. The cat jumped off a chair by the window and stretched. He ambled over and purred around my legs.

'Come on, I'll feed you, then you're off to Aidan's for two weeks.' Shrek was used to being bundled off to Aidan's. It happened so often I wondered why I bothered bringing him back home again. Pretty sure the cat liked Aidan better than he liked me.

By the time I'd fed the cat and packed. Mitch had arrived.

He looked good and I was feeling playful. I steadied the smile on my face, then swallowed it and replaced it with disappointment and took a breath.

'Bad news…'

'What?'

He leaned his hip against the kitchen counter.

'Work, I've got to go away,' I said with the steadiest voice I could muster.

'You serious?'

'Yeah.'

'But we…'

'I know, it sucks,' I replied. 'Sometimes shit happens. I don't like it much either.'

Mitch sighed. I smiled.

'For how long?' he asked, a hint of resignation in his voice. I knew it wouldn't last long. He bounced back faster and harder than anyone I'd ever met. I was pretty sure that was a large part of his charm. Upbeat optimism. Solution orientated. He was infectious.

'Dunno. A few days, a week, longer maybe…'

'Who am I going to run with if you're gone a week or longer?'

Already I heard his smile returning. I looked up and saw the sparkle in his eyes.

'You're good,' he said with a grin. 'And evil.'

'I thought I was good. Occasionally a little evil.'

He leaned over the counter and kissed my cheek.

Sweet. Affectionate.

He was driving me crazy and judging by the twinkle in his eyes, he knew it.

'Fire… you're playing with it,' I cautioned.

His smiled widened. 'Buddy, pal, best friend…'

All words I'd heard before.

'Having fun?'

The smile on his face said it all. Fun, he was having it in spades.

'Take it slow…,' he said.

'Yeah, yeah. Pretty sure we both agreed…'

'Friends remember?'

'And again…'

I wanted to reach across, wrap my hands around his lapels, pull him over the counter and have my evil way with him, right there on the kitchen floor.

'El, you're hopeless.'

'Me?'

'If you drag me over the counter there's no going back.'

'Yeah, well.' I stopped. Confused. 'How'd you know?'

'The look in your eye and the way you bit your lip.'

Deflect.

'Time for a run?'

'Good idea.'

I leaned over the counter and looked at what Mitch was wearing. Jeans. Really? Sliding back I straightened up before temptation got the best of me. Or Mitch did.

'You got your gear?'

'Yep,' he replied bending and lifting up a bag from the floor.

'Let's get changed then.' Not quite trusting myself to walk past him without touching I added, 'Go on. Guest bedroom okay with you?'

Mitch looked over his shoulder and smiled. 'That'll do me.'

'Top of the stairs on the right,' I said and followed Mitch down the hallway and up the stairs.

He pointed to an open door on the right. 'Here?'

'Yes,' I said and waited until he entered the room before I hurried to my room. I changed into academy sweats and running shoes. My gun and holster sat on the dresser next to my badge and phone. Tempting. I left them where they were. Running not working. At the door I changed my mind and went back. I scooped everything into my gym bag with my water bottle and towel. I wasn't on vacation yet.

Mitch waited at the bottom of the stairs. Water bottle and car keys in his hand.

'Ready?' I asked.

'Always.'

I didn't doubt that for a second. As he opened the front door his car keys jangled. I dropped my bag on the floor in the back of his car and climbed into the front passenger seat. My door closed. Mitch smiled through the window as he walked around the hood and opened his door.

We ran at Rock Creek Cemetery. Running every path that wound through the undulating cemetery and avoiding the creepy circle of crypts.

Two hours later we were back at my place.

'Airport by six,' Mitch said. 'I've got everything with me. Mind if I use your shower?'

I froze. Mind if I join you was sitting there on the tip of my tongue. I nodded. Not safe to speak.

He laughed at me. He wasn't laughing with me.

My phone buzzed like a bumble bee trapped in a paper bag. I freed it from my gym bag. The image on the screen caused an eye brow to rise.

Mike Davenport, the famous actor brother of Delta's Lee Davenport.

I read his text. *'Morning wifey, how are you?'*

Funny man.

I replied: *'Great. How are you? Still enjoying being the tragic widower?'*

*'Beating them off with a stick. Smiley face.'*

As I knew he would.

*'And you wanted?'*

*'Come away with me.'*

Vacation invitations in all directions. I'd never been so popular.

*'Thanks for the offer but I have plans.'*

*'You don't know when I'm going.'*

*'It's January. Ecuador.'*

*'Smiley face. Be more fun with you.'*

*'Rules. Remember? We can't be seen together.'*

He replied with a sad face. *'Take care Ellie.'*

When I looked up Mitch was standing at the top of the stairs.

'All right?'

'Yeah.' I waved my phone in the air. 'Lee's brother trying to get me to climb Cotopaxi with him.'

'Do you want to?' He walked down the stairs and stopped two above me.

'No, I want to go to New Zealand with you.'

'As long as you're sure.' A smile filled his voice. It was infectious like him.

Seventeen hours of flight time was followed by another twenty minutes in a Cessna and an hour and change in a rental car. Mitch was surprisingly comfortable driving on the wrong side of the road. Me, not so much. The trip was fun. My cell went several times before reception dropped off. I smiled as I turned it off for the first time in my memory.

Goodbye world. I'm out.

The winding road afforded glimpses of the sea through the bush at irregular intervals. Promise of relaxation drifted on the tide.

'We're here,' Mitch said turning down a steep driveway and parking in front of a garage.

'Nice,' I replied, opening my door. Escaping the confines of the car felt good. I stretched. Standing on solid ground felt a little weird. Everything felt like it was still moving. Jetlag.

'You okay?' Mitch looked at me over the roof of the car.

I smiled. 'Yep.' I stretched again, easing the knots out of my muscles. I wasn't designed to keep still for extended periods of time. 'Where exactly is here?' I followed Mitch to the right of the garage to a staircase. At the bottom of the stairs I saw a house.

'This is where I come to fish.'

'It's a long way to come for a few fish,' I muttered.

He ran down the stairs, then another smaller set of stairs and unlocked the door. Mitch opened the door wide and said, 'Welcome to paradise.' He ushered me into a foyer. Stairs rose in front of me, another stair case descended to the right. The ascending stairs led to a mezzanine floor. French doors were visible from where I stood. I guessed there was a balcony up there.

I followed Mitch down the stairs; he opened a door at the bottom that led to the vast living area.

The house was a far cry from a fishing cabin. I wandered to the left and stood in front of large windows. The driveway came down the left of the garage and the house, curved around the front and then carried on down to the sea.

Noises behind me caught my attention. Mitch in the kitchen, making coffee. I walked across the room, through the dining area and to the kitchen.

'Fishing?'

Mitch smiled. 'Yes.'

'You come all the way out here to *this* house and go fishing?' Incredulousness crept into my voice. I watched him as he moved about in the kitchen. 'So who lives here when you're not around?'

'What makes you think someone lives here?'

'There's no dust.' I walked around the kitchen table and opened the fridge. 'The fridge is full.' I picked up a bottle of milk and checked the date. 'The food is fresh.'

He laughed.

'The couple who live next door take care of this place.'

'Uh huh. And?'

'No and, they take care of the house when I'm not here.'

'Mind if I have a look around?'

'Go for it, I'll yell when the coffee is ready and bring our bags down.'

'Want a hand?'

'No, you go explore.'

I opened the door to the stairs again and decided to start with the room at the end of the hall. I walked past another stairwell. So many stairs. The room at the end was a master bedroom, walk-in-wardrobe, en-suite bathroom. Nice.

At the top of a much darker stair case I paused. I could feel cold rising from below but couldn't see anything. I followed the stairs to a landing. There was nothing on the landing, round the corner more stairs. At the bottom of those stairs the cold grew. A tiled floor, glass doors, on the right a solid door on the left another solid door. The door on the right had a key in it. I turned to the left and opened the other door. A wine cellar. Racks of wine bottles lay covered in dust. No one had been in there for a while.

The other door beckoned. I turned the key and swung the door open. Another garage. A double garage. There was a boat on a trailer on the far side. The side nearest me was empty. No car. Tools. Fishing rods. Life-jackets. Nothing remarkable just functional.

Mitch's voice rang out. 'Coffee!'

I closed the door on the tidy garage and climbed back up the stairs. A loud crash of breaking glass echoed below me. I turned trying to determine where the noise came from. Garage? Cellar?

Cellars don't have windows but they are full of glass.

Garage.

Mitch's voice rang out from above. 'All right down there?'

'Yeah, not sure what that was,' I yelled back.

'I'm coming.'

My right hand sought the grip of the Glock that was always on my hip and came up empty. I looked down. Nope no gun. No holster. Unarmed. Not good. I took a deep breath.

New Zealand not Virginia.

How bad could a crashing noise really be?

I heard Mitch running down the stairs. He slowed for the last few steps then stopped beside me.

'Garage,' I said.

Mitch turned the key in the lock and swung the door wide. Light streamed from the window on the other side of the garage. It wasn't broken. Everything looked the same as it had except for a pile of boxes. They'd toppled over. Broken glass spilled from an over turned box onto the garage floor.

'Think we found the source,' Mitch said.

'Why did it fall?'

I wasn't convinced. I scoured the garage looking for a reason. Another noise. Tapping. Mitch heard it too. He stopped and turned around. My heart pounded. There was something or someone in the garage.

I crouched down, peering across the floor I saw feet way over by the boat trailer.

'A bird?' I said pointing to the trailer.

Mitch pressed a button on the wall. The garage door slowly began to lift. We watched as a large brown bird strutted out of the garage and down the driveway. It was as big as a chicken but with much longer legs and a long pointy beak. Kinda like a taller bigger kiwi just going by the kiwi I'd seen at the zoo in Washington, D.C.

'What the hell was that?' I asked.

'A Weka,' Mitch replied. 'They're inquisitive. He must've got trapped in here.'

'Guess I got him all excited when I opened the door earlier?'

'Yeah, he probably thought you were going to let him out.'

Mystery solved. I smiled. 'He was kinda cute.'

Mitch closed the garage door. We locked the interior door and headed back upstairs for coffee.

Half way through my coffee I put my cup down and looked at Mitch.

'Problem?' he asked.

'How'd the Weka get in the garage?'

'I don't know,' he said setting his cup down. 'Neighbours probably opened the door for something …'

That seemed reasonable.

'So, the beach?'

'Definitely the beach. You want to finish exploring the house first?'

'I think so,' I replied. 'You could show me to my room?'

He bit his bottom lip. 'I could.'

'Did you get our bags?'

'Yes.'

I didn't see them anywhere.

'Mine is?'

'In your room.'

'Thank you.'

Maybe I should go find out where my room was by myself. I mentally ticked areas of the house off a list. What was left? Up. My gaze shifted from the coffee on the table to the window as I tried to determine time of day. Afternoon. But what day?

'Mitch?'

'Tuesday about three-thirty in the afternoon.'

This time I didn't question how he knew what I was thinking. Where Mitch was concerned just-go-with-it seemed to be the best philosophy.

A yawn escaped unchecked. Mitch smiled. 'Tired?'

'Little bit.'

'Been a long two days.'

Been a long life.

Another yawn crept out.

'Why don't you go have a nap?' Mitch said. 'Your room

is upstairs on the right. You'll find everything you need in there.'

Everything? I doubt that.

'I think I will. What are you going to do?'

'Think I'll sleep too.'

I stood up, placed my cup in the sink and found my room.

I rolled over, light peeked through a gap in the curtains. Life sang outside. Beautiful songs I'd never heard before.

I was beginning to see what Mitch travelled all the way out here for and why he referred to Marlborough Sounds as paradise. The clock on the dresser said five-thirty. I'd slept for two hours and felt fantastic. With no place I needed to be I rolled onto my back and attempted more sleep. Half an hour of tossing and turning later I lay still and stared at the smoke alarm on the ceiling. Counting seconds between flashes of the tiny red LED that said the alarm was operational.

Counting to occupy my mind.

It failed. My brain was already thinking about Mitch. Was he asleep? I could go make coffee. He might be awake by now? Could I go make coffee? What if he wasn't up? Take him a cup and wake him up? Risky.

The internal debate raged until I heard a door open and close. He was up. I hit the shower, cleaned my teeth, dressed in fresh clothes, and casually walked down the stairs. I paused at the bottom. Left or right?

Mitch's bedroom? No. The living area. I turned right. When I opened the door I could smell the coffee. Mitch looked over from the kitchen.

'Morning, sleepyhead.'

Puzzled I joined him in the kitchen.

'Morning?'

'Yes.'

'I woke at five-thirty in the morning? That's a little more than two hours sleep.'

Mitch grinned at me. 'You slept like the dead.'

No wonder I felt so good.

'You know this how?'

'I checked on you a few times,' he replied. 'Breakfast. Coffee. Then we'll go for a walk.'

'All planned then?' I laughed as he poured cereal into a bowl and pointed to a chair at the table. I sat down.

'Breakfast,' he said, setting the bowl in front of me.

'Thanks.'

Breakfast carried on, amicable, chatty, fun. All the things I associated with Mitch.

'Beach?' Mitch asked taking keys from the counter near the back door.

'Awesome.'

We left the house via the back door. I didn't want to go back down the internal stairs to the door at the bottom. Something about the cold air down there made my skin crawl. We passed the garage and carried on down the steep driveway. At the bottom was an upside down dingy. We carried on following the driveway to the left. Climbing over driftwood. We stood on the gritty sand. I breathed. Deep breaths. Across the sound a bush clad mountain rose from the still water.

Paradise.

Mitch walked up the beach. I watched him pick his way around rocks. The tide was out.

'You coming?' he called.

'Yeah,' I replied. Just enjoying the view. Seemed best to keep that to myself.

I caught up with him.

A familiar smell wafted on the light breeze. Once you've smelled a decomp you never forget it. Dead fish maybe? Hopeful. I knew it wasn't fish. My stomach churned as I scanned the tree line and the beach. I saw the cause lodged by a tree at the edge of the beach.

'Mitch…' I moved toward the trees. The smell grew stronger and completely over-shadowed the clean sea air. Bile rose. By the time I reached the tree I knew I was right. A body. I struggled not to retch as I saw maggots writhing and wriggling as they fed on the person's face.

I spun around as Mitch came up behind me.

'Don't, you don't want to see this,' I cautioned. 'Does your cell work?'

He nodded. I could tell by the look on his face that he'd glimpsed the body.

'On my beach?' he mumbled, dragging his cell phone from his jeans pocket.

'We're going to need police.'

He made the emergency call.

I crouched by the body and began a visual examination. Female. Slim build. Light brown shoulder-length wavy hair. Obvious facial wounds. I looked at her hands, no abrasions that I could see. She was wearing a diamond engagement ring. I moved around her, stepping with care. The back of her hair was matted with blood and sand. The body didn't appear waterlogged. Maybe she hadn't been in the water or if she had she wasn't in it long? She was wearing jeans, sneakers, and a fitted tee-shirt. Her clothes appeared dry. I patted my own pockets expecting to find latex gloves.

Nothing.

Damn.

Vacation.

'Hey, Mitch, you don't happen to have a first aid kit down here anywhere?' Ever optimistic. First Aid kits usually contain latex gloves. I didn't want to contaminate the body by searching for ID without gloves on.

'Isn't it a bit late?'

'Not for her. I need some latex gloves.' I had another thought. 'Can I use your phone, please?'

Mitch half-smiled. 'Sure.' He threw it to me. A thoughtful look crossed his face. 'Actually, yeah, there's a first aid kit under the dingy. I'll be back.' He took off at a run.

While he was gone I photographed the body and surroundings with his phone. There was a two foot long broken branch a few feet behind her that interested me. Hair and blood stuck to it, I only noticed because I got close, the blood splatter and hair strands looked like they were mostly under the branch and divided by a break. I looked from the wood to the body. Did she fall and smash her head on the branch? Hopeful but not likely. The way the branch lay, it had been thrown or dropped. Could be a murder weapon. I took a series of photos of the branch and the body.

Mitch appeared next to me with latex gloves.

'Thanks.' I swapped the phone for gloves and pulled them on. I had to search the woman's pockets and clothing for anything that would tell us who she was. I don't like unidentified bodies. I like to know who I'm dealing with. She was wearing a backpack. I could clearly see the straps over her shoulder.

'Supposed to be a vacation,' I mumbled and then gave the woman my undivided attention. I rolled her toward me. Maggots fell to the sand. I supported her with one hand and inspected the back of her head. Looked to me like she'd been hit with force. Bits of bark were lodged in a large wound, there weren't maggots in that wound, yet. I tried to free the backpack with the other. It was quite a struggle. Dead people are heavy. Dead weight is a truism.

I tossed the pack out of the way once it was free and lowered the body back down.

Moving away from the smell I sat on the sand and opened the bag. It was a day pack. Snacks. Change of clothes. Suntan lotion. Tissues. A phone. I set the phone aside. A wallet. A passport. As soon as I pulled it out I knew it was American. My heart sank a notch or two as I opened the passport and recognised the woman on the beach.

'Nancy Medina,' I whispered.

'El?'

'Mitch, she's American. Her name is Nancy Medina and she's twenty-three years old.' I set the passport aside and checked her wallet. Cash. Credit cards. Travel card. A university identity card. Not a robbery then. 'College ID, she attends Caltech.'

I put everything back in her wallet. 'Can you photograph the pack and contents, please?' I asked Mitch.

He took his phone back out of his pocket and did as I asked.

I pulled the gloves off, balled them up and dropped them on the sand.

'Okay, done,' Mitch said. 'You okay?'

Until he asked I hadn't realised I was frowning. 'Yeah, just, you know, supposed to be on vacation.' I shot him a smile.

'What do we do now?' Mitch asked sitting next to me in the sand. 'I'm presuming our day just got screwed?'

'Pretty much,' I replied. 'I'm going to use your phone and call a friend, then we'll know.'

Mitch passed me his phone. I called home. Well, not home exactly but Iain Campbell's cell phone. I needed to talk to someone in the State Department.

'Hey, It's Ellie Conway,' I said as he answered. 'I got a *messy* problem.'

'Thought you were on vacation?' he replied. 'I'm off tomorrow, good timing on your problem.'

'I am on vacation.' I remembered the conversation with Mike. 'You climbing?'

'Yes, heading down to Ecuador tomorrow. Now about this problem …'

'I'm in New Zealand.' I'm at the end of the world and still shit happens. 'Just found the body of an American woman on a beach. What now?'

'Seriously? What is it with you?'

'I dunno,' I said with a hefty sigh. 'What now?'

'I'll contact the embassy, we'll send FBI. You want to work this or walk away?'

I looked at Mitch. I wanted to walk away but I wasn't sure I could. I could *try* walking away.

'Send agents. We called local police. I'll hand over to them and FBI can pick the case up when they get here.'

'Address?' I gave the address and Mitch's phone number, just in case. 'Enjoy your vacation.'

'Yeah, you too.'

I hung up and this time gave the phone back to Mitch.

'Do we have to be here by… Nancy?'

'Yes. But not this close. We could move back down there,' I pointed back down the beach to the jetty. 'Should also have a quick look for other victims or the person who did this.'

Mitch touched my arm. 'It wasn't an accident?'

'I don't think so.'

He breathed in sharply. 'She couldn't have fallen or died of an illness?'

'Maybe, but I don't think so. I think, someone hit her

across the back of the head with a branch. And hit her hard enough to snap the branch. I also think the person turned her onto her back. She fell forward, hence the scrapes and wounds on her face. She didn't put her hands up to save herself. Either it was a fatal blow or she was unconscious and died later. Whoever did it, then rolled her onto her back.'

'Why?'

'Check she was dead? Looking for something? I don't know. If we find whoever did it, we'll ask,' I said with a smile. 'Shall we?' I pointed to the jetty. 'Close enough that I can watch this area, but far enough that Nancy isn't our only focus.'

Mitch nodded. He stood up and brushed sand off his jeans. I followed suit.

I sent Mitch ahead of me, then turned back and had a quick look around the area, just in case there was another body or someone lurking. Nothing. No footprints, no sign anyone else had been in the area.

Catching up to Mitch I asked, 'How many properties can access this stretch of beach?' I could see rocks and unfriendly coast line to the east and west. Estimating about a quarter of a mile of accessible beach frontage from the land. The sea was a different matter.

'Four, I think, yeah, four.'

'Don't suppose you know if any of your neighbours rent their houses out or run bed and breakfast accommodation?'

'Sorry, no.'

'When was the last high tide?'

We sat on the jetty. I could see how high the tide rose by the line of driftwood and marks in the sand. Didn't look as though it went up as far as Nancy's body, but maybe far enough to wipe footprints from the sand. Hers weren't there.

Thinking aloud. 'She could've come off a boat with the Unsub.'

'Unsub?'

'Sorry. Unknown Subject.'

Mitch smiled, nodded, and checked a tide timetable on his phone.

'Twelve twenty-eight this morning. Next high tide will be twelve-forty this afternoon.'

'So if they came ashore from a boat it was before the high tide or during…'

'No footprints,' Mitch said, nodding.

'How long before police get out here?'

'Nearest cop is Havelock, forty-five minutes away, give or take.' Mitch checked the time on his phone. 'Should be here soon.'

He bumped my shoulder with his.

'Want something?' I asked nudging him back.

'What will happen when police get here?'

'We'll give statements. I will hand over the crime scene and we'll get on with our vacation.'

'Can you walk away?'

'Yes.' Wow, that was definite. I was just a little impressed by how sure I was. That was new territory. Life with Mitch in it had a different focus? 'Yes I can walk away. Our State Department will have contacted local police and let them know that it's my scene until hand over – and who I am. And that FBI agents are on the way from Wellington to *assist* in the investigation.'

Mitch said nothing. He smiled but he said nothing. We sat, our legs dangling over the water, and waited.

I was conscious that the body was degrading as the minutes ticked by and become an hour in the hot sun. Eventually I heard gravel crunching under foot and two police officers emerged from the end of the driveway.

We stood up and waved. They acknowledge us and waited as we clambered back over rocks to greet them.

'SSA Ellie Conway,' I said offering my hand.

'Senior Constable Simon Curnow,' the first officer said shaking my hand.

The second nodded and shook my hand next. 'Constable Jack Barron.'

'This is Mitch Iverson —that was his driveway you came down.'

They shook Mitch's hand.

'The body is over there,' Mitch said pointing down the beach past the trees. 'If you don't mind I'll wait here.'

They nodded.

I led the way.

'The body is an American citizen, have you been briefed?'

'Yes ma'am,' Curnow said. 'FBI are expected to take charge sometime today.'

'If you can take it from here… I'm on vacation,' I said.

'Go right ahead, agent. Just as soon as you've given me a complete statement.' He pulled his notebook from his pocket.

The other officer followed suit and went back to Mitch. Made sense.

Ten minutes later I was signing the statement in his notebook and ready to leave.

Back at the house I asked Mitch if I could use the computer in the living room and uploaded the photos from his camera.

I scanned through them quickly, then paused on one, and scrolled back to the previous two. All three photos showed more bush than the others.

'Mitch!'

He appeared next to me. 'Yep?'

'Look at this picture, what do you see?' I zoomed in on an area in the bush, the foliage was thick but there was something else there.

'A hand?'

'Yeah, that's what I thought,' I replied.

'There was or possibly is someone else down there?' Mitch did not look pleased. 'Dead or alive?'

'Alive maybe? We have to warn those cops.' I emailed the photos to Caine and asked that he forward them to whoever had the case in Wellington then looked at Mitch. 'Don't suppose you have a rifle?'

He nodded. 'For rabbits.'

'Can you get it please?'

He disappeared then returned empty handed. 'It's gone.'

'What?'

'The gun safe is empty.'

Not good.

'Ammunition?'

'Two boxes, last I checked. They're gone.'

'Where were they stored?'

'Gun safe is in the bottom garage. Ammunition in a cabinet in the garage up top.'

'Someone knew? Doesn't sound random?'

'Must've, nothing else is moved or gone.'

Potentially there was an armed Unsub on the property and I wasn't.

Vacation?

I should just give up all notions of ever having a vacation. Yeah I was going to make it all about me. I thought for a few minutes. I had to go warn the police officers, that was a given, what about Mitch?

'Okay, we're going down to the beach. We cannot leave those officers alone knowing someone was in the bush and that a gun is missing.' And I didn't want to leave Mitch alone either.

He nodded.

We locked the house, just in case it made a difference to the Unsub and hurried down the steep stony driveway. Near the bottom I announced my presence. Sneaking up on police wasn't smart.

Mitch's hand sought mine. 'Stay together,' he whispered.

Okay by me.

One of the officers met us by the driftwood pile. I spoke to him quietly, telling him about the photos, showing him the pictures on Mitch's phone and then about the missing rifle.

'Not good news,' he said. 'I'll call it in.'

He walked toward the jetty, far enough away from the bush clad area near the body that no one could over hear him.

Minutes passed.

He beckoned for us to join him. Walking toward him I saw him talk into the radio on his shoulder. 'Jack is coming over to join us,' he said. 'FBI have landed at Woodbourne airport and are on the way out here. I've asked for AOS support.'

'AOS?' I asked.

'Armed Offenders Squad… our SWAT.'

I nodded. 'There is no real cover down here. If that person is still in the bush and our Unsub, potentially they're armed.'

The cop looked around. 'The boat shed?'

'It'll have to do, we'll sit it out over there.'

I heard movement. The three of us looked up at the same time. Constable Jack Baron was walking toward us. Two shadows fell on the ground. He stepped sideways just enough for us to see a woman behind him and a rifle barrel.

'Ellie?' Mitch whispered.

'I see her,' I replied. 'This isn't ideal.'

'No kidding,' Mitch whispered. 'Now what?'

'Well, it's tricky but not impossible.'

I leaned toward Curnow. 'That a Glock 17 on your hip and is there a round in the chamber?'

'Yes to both questions.'

'How good are you with that?'

'Proficient,' he replied.

Yeah but I'm probably better. It's how it is.

'Ever fired at a person?'

'No.'

'Give it to me.'

He started to shake his head. The woman called out. Kiwi accent. 'I'll shoot him if you don't let me leave.'

I whispered to Curnow, 'Would she expect you to be armed?'

'No.'

'Give me the gun.'

Mitch moved in front of me. Curnow reluctantly handed me the Glock. I shoved it in the back of my jeans. Then stepped away from Mitch and Curnow. I smiled at Jack, using my left-hand I tapped my head and pointed to the ground then held two fingers up. Hoping like hell he'd understand. I needed him to drop and cover on two. I still held two fingers up. Jack watched my hand.

'No one is stopping you,' Curnow told the woman. 'Let my constable walk over here and you go on up the driveway. We'll stay here.'

I didn't want to speak and give away my nationality.

'I'm taking him with me,' she said. She was calm. Calm is good, less chance of accidental gunfire.

Even so, I couldn't let her take Jack up the driveway.

'You don't need Jack, let him stay here,' Curnow said.

I reached behind me and grasped the grip of the Glock. As I pulled the gun free of my waistband I closed my fist. Jack dropped. I fired as soon as he moved. My bullet hit her in the shoulder. My preference was head but this wasn't my country.

No second chances.

The woman's face registered surprise for a moment, the rifle fell from her hands as she sank to the ground. Jack scrambled to his feet, taking the rifle with him and ran over to us.

'Okay?' I asked him, my eyes focused on the woman, the gun now aimed at her head.

'Yes,' Jack replied. He didn't sound it.

'Curnow, you got cuffs? Now would be a good time to use them,' I said. 'Just don't cross in front of me, go around.'

He did. He cuffed the woman, inspected her wound, and called for an ambulance. I lowered the gun and handed it to Jack. Mitch grabbed the first aid kit and gave it to Curnow. He dressed the wound.

A conversation ensued between me and the woman.

Her name was Rachel Bridgeman; she was a New Zealander and studying at Caltech.

'All right Rachel, let's talk, shall we?'

She shook her head. Then changed her mind. Wise.

'You shot me.'

'That was unfortunate. You are ruining my vacation. Tell me what happened here.'

'She was my best friend,' Rachel said, making an attempt at sorrow. I wasn't buying.

'Usually people don't shoot their best friends. Waiting for an explanation here,' I rocked on my heels. 'And getting bored. You don't want that to happen.'

'He asked her to marry him!'

'Who asked her?'

'My ex-boyfriend,' she said. 'This hurts.'

'Yeah. It does hurt when you get shot. Moving on. Paramedics will be here eventually.' The police officers watched as I continued. 'Why was Nancy Medina here?'

'We were holidaying together.'

A horrible feeling swam up my spine and entered my brain. It sloshed about, whipping itself into a frenzy before falling off my tongue as words.

'Your ex-boyfriend is here isn't he?'

Her eyes widened.

I glanced at the senior officer. 'Do we have another victim?' he asked.

A sick little smirk tweaked the edges of Rachel's mouth. She didn't say anything.

'How did you get the gun, Rachel?'

'My parents look after Mitch's holiday home for him. I know where everything is.'

Nice.

'Where are your parents?'

I hoped the killing spree had stopped with the boyfriend and best friend.

All the colour ran out of her face. She wavered. Her body swayed. I reached down and pinched her arm.

'Ouch,' she squawked.

'Focus. You don't get to pass out before I'm done talking with you,' I said with a growl. 'Where are your parents?'

'Nelson. They won't be home for a few days.'

'I'm sure they'll be thrilled when police find them and tell them what their delightful daughter has done.'

A tear slipped down her face. Must've been hard to force one out. She didn't look at all remorseful.

'I told Nancy not to date him!'

'You can sit here and bleed while Constable Barron watches you. Senior Constable Curnow and I are going to search the property. What'd you say your ex's name was?'

'I didn't. You can't leave me here,' she whispered.

'Yeah I can. Who are we looking for?'

'Jerry Ryan,' she replied.

It took us fifteen minutes to locate the body of the fiancé in the potting shed by Mitch's garage. It was cooler in the potting shed, his body smelled less, and thankfully there was less bug activity. Single gunshot wound to the head.

Rachel provided us with a time line of events. She killed the fiancé first. Nancy tried to run away, that's how she ended up on the beach.

The double murders took place about eight hours before Mitch and I arrived in the Sounds. Rachel said she saw us arrive. We didn't leave the house until morning and she followed to see what would happen next. Really? What did she think would happen?

Guess she didn't expect to get shot. Pretty sure no one expects to be shot at the end of the world.

She stopped talking when my FBI back up arrived.

Mitch and I finished writing additional statements for both the FBI and police, an hour after everyone arrived we grabbed our bags and drove away, intent on a vacation no matter what.

# Sophie And The Gate To Hell

## Carol Borden

A month ago a bladder full of water formed on my kitchen ceiling, slit itself open neatly and emptied a thick stream of musky, brownish water on the shelves below. It was disturbing, but it was, in fact, more disturbing to watch my landlord Rick hack the remaining pouch open with a screwdriver and then peel a sheet of rubbery, almost fleshy paint off the ceiling.

Rick pushed an old iron basin with chipped white enamel on top of the shelf to catch any water that the ceiling might not have peed out. He stood on a spider web covered ladder and poked at the exposed layers of old paint, older paint, water-damaged plaster and the ceiling's original wood.

'Well, Sophie, I'm not sure where this leak is coming from,' he said. 'Maybe the toilet. The toilet's right above?'

'Yeah. That's the toilet, that's under the sink and that's under the bathtub.' I pointed to where the bladder had been, over the stove and generally over my head.

'Probably the toilet. Could be the shower, though. We had trouble with the shower drain. You can see some of the older repairs.' Rick stared at the ruined patch of ceiling with the desperation of a man who really did not want to be bothered with doing anything at all. He decided the first thing to do in any home repair was to assign blame.

'Any problems with the toilet backing up?'

'No, but the shower drain backs up sometimes.'

'Have you used a plunger on the toilet?'

'No. The pipes in this house are too old to use a plunger on.'

'So you haven't used a plunger on the toilet?'

'No.'

He adjusted his back brace. It was medical supply,

perforated, white plastic. He wore it over his t-shirt and sweatpants. 'This leak, walk me through it.'

'I heard water running in the kitchen. I went to look and it was like a faucet pouring down from the ceiling. I ran upstairs to make sure I hadn't left the bathroom tap on and called you. Then I cleared the dishes off the shelves while I waited for you to get here. It happened maybe twenty minutes ago.'

'You hadn't just flushed the toilet?'

'No. I saw the leak. I made sure the bathroom tap wasn't running. I called you.'

'You didn't notice any ballooning last night?'

'I would've noticed. It was a pretty significant… ballooning.'

'And you haven't had any trouble with the toilet?'

'No.'

'Well, I don't know what you want me to do.' Rick climbed back down the ladder. 'I guess I'll call the plumber. I don't know if they can get here today. Give me a call around five o'clock, let me know if there's any more water coming through and I'll let you know about the plumber.'

Rick gave me a look. 'Given your vertical challenges, I'll leave you the ladder in case you need to get up there.'

'Okay.' I said, knowing I would not be getting up there.

'Talk to you later this afternoon, Sophie.' And he left.

I started loading the dishes from the shelves into the dishwasher. Of course, the most contaminated were my nice, handmade ceramic cups and mugs; the ones I put on a shelf. One of the upsides of this house was that it has a dishwasher. I'd lived in city apartments for so long that having a dishwasher was like a dream. The dishwasher and the front porch were the main reasons I stayed in the house.

I was taking out a second load of dishes when Rick knocked at the door. 'Sorry to disturb you, Sophie. The plumber wants to know if you've noticed any drainage problems.'

'The shower drain backs up once in a while.'

'But nothing with the toilet?'

'No.'

'And you haven't used a plunger on the toilet?'

'No.'

'There wouldn't be anything wrong if you used a plunger. I'm just trying to get a handle on the situation.'

'No, I haven't used a plunger on the toilet. The pipes are too old to use a plunger with. I haven't had any trouble with the toilet.'

'Well, give me a call at five p.m. and let me know what the status is.'

'Alright.' I locked the door after Rick

I called Rick at five o'clock and told him there'd been a little dripping.

'Nothing more?'

'Just dripping.'

'I don't want to ask you not to use the bathroom, but maybe you could just take it easy. You know, not take really long showers. Don't flush a lot. Give me a call if there's any change—even if it doesn't seem significant.'

'I will.'

'The plumber will be there between nine and ten on Monday morning. I called the plumber I use for my own home. He's very cost-effective.'

'I'll be here.'

I stood with my phone in my hand and stared at the red stain where all the water had poured out of the kitchen ceiling. It had an air of moist malignancy.

By Saturday, the red stain seemed a little bigger. A swarm of houseflies came up from the basement through the furnace intake vent. They were big and very black, with none of the iridescence of houseflies. The flies were so slow and stupid that I felt bad about killing them, so I caught them one by one and took them outside. It seemed wrong to be able to catch houseflies as easily as fireflies. The swarm grew overnight, but there was no more water coming from the ceiling, so I didn't call the landlord.

On Sunday afternoon, I sat on my porch, drank some lemonade and read *To The Devil A Daughter*. Mostly I stared at my book and thought about how nice it was to get away from the ceiling, the flies and Rick. Just thinking that thought seemed to summon him.

'Hi, Sophie, I thought I'd touch base and see if there's been any more water from the ceiling?' I looked up from my book and there was Rick, standing on the lawn.

'No leaking, but there are a lot of flies coming up from the basement.'

'But no water?'

'No.'

'And you have been taking it easy? Haven't been taking really long showers? Haven't been flushing anything down the toilet?'

I shook my head.

'Gee, I really think it is the toilet, but we won't know till the plumber comes.' He looked at the house, hands on his hips. 'Well, I just wanted to touch base. The plumber will be here tomorrow morning between nine and ten.'

The plumber arrived close to ten o'clock, but Rick was closer to nine. They called to say he was on his way. They said he'd be here in ten minutes and that was fifteen minutes ago,' he said standing beneath the growing stain. Rick could not stop fidgeting, like he felt every minute he waited burrowing under his skin.

'You know, this house was first built in the eighteen-hundreds, this whole kitchen section was added when the plumbing was installed in the nineteen-twenties. The laundry room used to be the entryway and stairs to the upstairs. I love old houses, but they are always trouble. I had an old house in California, in Santa Rosa. It had a beautiful Mexican tile counter. Of course, I had trouble with the plumbing there, too. The end of the kitchen faucet broke off. Water sprayed all over. The plumbers told me they'd have to rip up the tile because the faucet and basin were all built in to the counter. It would have cost a fortune, so I went to the junk yard and found a faucet head, plonked it on and ta-da, it worked. Just goes to show you.'

'You never know.'

The plumber's van pulled into the driveway. It was dark blue with a logo of acid green tentacles bursting through a circle with a No slash through them. "Mike's Plumbing, Heating & Drain Cleaning." Rick hurried over to the front door. Mike the plumber had a blond crew-cut and his work wear looked a little more cop or commando than I expected. Black cargo pants and something that looked kind of like body armour. It was both reassuring and alarming as Rick led him upstairs, 'It's probably the toilet. We've had some trouble in the past. It could be the shower drain, but I'm pretty sure it's the toilet.'

Plumbing involves a lot of banging, pounding and vacuuming—way more than I had ever imagined. I tried to get some work done, but it was hard to concentrate. Instead, I flipped through online articles looking for information on big, slow, dumb flies and ever-growing red stains. As I read, Mike the plumber passed by me. 'We'll have you fixed up soon,' he said on his way out the door.

Rick filled me in. 'So it looks like it was the toilet after all. The bolts holding it together and to the floor have corroded through and the toilet's seal was broken. It might've been years in the making. Strange how everything poured out at once.'

Mike the plumber came back in carrying a crucible with tongs. His aura of professional competence was so strong that I wouldn't be surprised if he had poured his own bolts in the van. Rick scooted after him.

There was more pounding and vacuuming and then I heard them coming down the stairs. Mike the plumber was saying, 'Next time, call me sooner. It's a simple matter of upkeep. You do the job right and it'll last you for years.'

The plumber readjusted his shop-vac under his arm on the way to the door. 'Hey, let me get that for you…' I said.

'No, no, when you're one you're a one-man crew you get used to opening and closing doors for yourself.'

'Thanks for fixing the toilet.'

'No problem. I just try to do the kind of job I'd want someone to do for me.'

I went up to look to see the remains of the smashing, pounding and vacuuming, but the toilet—and the bathroom—were pristine. He had actually removed some mineral/rust deposits around the toilet that I was having trouble scrubbing off the floor.

Back downstairs, I saw Rick in the driveway, standing next to the van trying to talk with the plumber. Mike was scowling and did not look up. He just kept filling out his invoice. Even after he got his copy, Rick kept trying to talk to the plumber. I felt kind of bad for Rick, until he came back inside.

'So.' He said. 'Lutz will be coming by to patch the ceiling. It's going to take a few days, so I'd like it if he could come by early tomorrow and make a few passes at it. About nine thirty?'

Lutz arrived after nine thirty. In fact, Lutz and Rick showed up while I was eating lunch. They often show up when I'm eating, like they've sworn an oath to prevent me eating lunch. While Lutz set himself up in the kitchen, Rick went to check the water heater in the basement. I never go down there. It's all spiders and spider webs. There's an old coal bin and pipes that come into and go out of the house for seemingly no reason. I heard some banging from below while Lutz climbed up the ladder and began to scrape paint, plaster and effluvia off the ceiling.

Rick contracts out all his home repair work to Lutz, despite the fact that Rick doesn't consider Lutz a very conscientious worker. Rick is impatient and patronizing with Lutz, though I wouldn't be surprised to discover Lutz has a secret doctorate in astrophysics, geology or entomology. For his part, Lutz is six feet two, easily fifty years old and sad all the way through. Whenever he works inside my house, Lutz talks to me, usually a long monologue about science fiction or politics. This time, as he smeared spackle onto the original wood of the ceiling, he told me that the characters he identifies with always end up dead. 'You know Piggy in *Lord of the Flies*? That's me. I'm Piggy. And when I see a character who's like Piggy, I think, 'There's me!' Then, when he dies, I think, 'Dammit, there went my character.'

I don't think Lutz has the chance to talk to many people. Every time he's in my house, I think, 'What can it hurt to talk with this sad guy for a little while?' But after a while it does hurt, especially when he compares himself to Piggy in *Lord of the Flies*.

As he talked, Lutz tried to cover the red stain. The spackle he laid over it turned a crusty, mucus yellow.

'Rick wants it perfect, but I don't see how it can be perfect.' He climbed down the ladder. 'That's all I can do today.'

'So when are you coming back?'

'Tomorrow at ten-thirty good?' Lutz scraped the edge of his palette knife on the lip of the "Brite White Vinyl Spackle" can. The spackle's plasticky smell wafted around the kitchen.

'Sure. See you, Lutz.'

But despite all his work, the red stain seemed bigger, blooming against the white spackle.

The damage on the ceiling still wept almost imperceptibly the next day. Lutz climbed up, felt the sealant with his bare hand and sighed. 'Still wet.' Some of the spackle flaked off under his hand.

I looked up from my lunch. 'I think it's not dried out from the leak.'

'You know, you might have a point,' he said.

We stood and looked at the ceiling for a minute. The red bled through the white and yellow.

'It probably shouldn't do that,' I said.

'I don't know. I'm a NIMS-certified machinist. I work with metal. I tell Rick that, but he doesn't listen to me. Which reminds me, he wants me to go down and check something in the basement real quick.'

'Okay.' I stared at my cold pizza. It stared at me.

I heard him talking and then swearing below and some kind of metallic booming. It seemed like I had a situation.

Lutz clomped back up the stairs. 'Well, I'm going to have to come back.'

'Do you know when? I have work.'

Lutz shrugged hopelessly and left. I went and reheated the

pizza in the microwave. One of the big, slow flies floated overhead. The red stain said I shouldn't let Lutz cover it. The fly agreed. Stupid fly.

I definitely had a situation. I didn't look in the basement. Looking in the basement has not gotten anyone anywhere good in these kinds of situations.


Unholy forces were at work and they were impeding my life. I was exhausted. I was getting a cold sore and there was a painful lump under my chin that I hoped was a swollen lymph node. The spackle was not drying. For the next week there was no sign of Lutz or Rick. Rick wouldn't answer his phone. He wouldn't answer emails, not even when I wrote to him about the stain's whisperings or the scurrying in the walls.

I found the source of the scurryings standing frozen in mid-scurry at the entrance to the bathroom. It was an adolescent fox squirrel. The squirrel ran into my office and knocked everything off my desk before disappearing, leaving a trail of smoke behind. Thankfully, there was no fire. The next afternoon, during lunch, I heard a thump upstairs. When I went to investigate, the squirrel skittered out of my bedroom and ran back into my office. I called the Humane Society to come over and catch it.

'Humane Society Emergency Desk, this is Amir. How can I help you?'

'Hi, Amir. I have a squirrel in my house.'

'Where is it now?'

'I have it confined in my office. I think it's smoking in there…'

'Smoking?'

'Yeah. It smells like cigarillos.'

'Those cigarettes that look like cigars?'

'Yeah, the flavored kind. Maybe cherry.'

'Anything else?'

'Well, yeah, there's something whispering in the kitchen.'

'Something?'

'Definitely some thing. It's not right, not right at all.'

'Can I get your name?'

'Sophie.'

'Okay, Sophie. We'll send Hannah over to help you out as soon as we can. We're catching up on a backlog today. I have your number, so I'll give you a call to let you know what time to expect her. It'll probably be this evening.'

'Thanks.'

'Have a great afternoon.'

'You too.'


Four hours later, Hannah and I locked ourselves in my office. The whole room was a blue haze of smoke, but there were no ashes or stubbed out cigarillo butts in sight.

'So is your landlord refunding you a month's rent for this?'

'I doubt it, but I'm definitely taking your visit out of the rent.'

Hannah had a net on a long aluminum pole, a pair of leather gloves that covered her arms to her elbows and a beige plastic cat carrier. The carrier was covered in strips of masking tape with symbols on them in permanent marker. Some of them looked recent and to have been written in a hurry. They were smeared and there were still some smudges on Hannah's hands.

Hannah stuck the end of her net behind my bookcase and the squirrel chittered. She went around the other side and poked at the squirrel from there. The squirrel came shooting out. It looked like a regular squirrel. It even acted like a regular squirrel as it jumped onto my desk, up into the blinds, bounced off Hannah and raced back behind the bookshelf. It made the same full figure eight over and over until we somehow interrupted its rhythm, and it jumped out the open window, giggling.

'Well,' Hannah said.

'Yeah,' I said.

'Let's take a look at the things in your kitchen.'

She followed me past the bathroom and down the stairs to the kitchen. We stood in the doorway and looked at the bloodshot eyes blinking through the red stain. It whispered in our minds to join it, to cross over.

'They're more active at night.'

'They?'

255

'There's another one. It's different, though. It has its glands on the outside. It's gross.'

'Yeah, this is not something I'm trained to deal with.'

'Any advice?'

Hannah leaned on her net. 'My advice? Screw your landlord—go to the bulk store and get yourself a lot of rosemary, red peppercorn, and salt.'

'They don't like it?'

'Not at all.'

'Okay, thanks. So, seventy-five dollars for helping with the squirrel?'

'I really don't feel right about taking your money when the squirrel evicted itself.'

I handed her seventy-five dollars in cash. 'Enjoy my landlord's money.'

Hannah smiled.


It was increasingly obvious to me that my toilet was some kind of portal to another world that had been sealed until recently, maybe even a Hell Gate, though much damper than I would've expected a Hell Gate to be. Ever expanding red stains, whispering eyes, smoking squirrels and really slow stupid flies are not normal, even for old houses. Most obvious of all was the fact that Rick did not want anything to do with any of this. And, honestly, I wasn't sure that I wanted Rick or Lutz to have anything to do with it. The chances of their unleashing incomprehensible, devouring evil on the world seemed pretty high.

So I decided to be proactive. I dumped out my bottles of sea salt, rosemary and a few red peppercorns from my spice rack and ground them up with my stone mortar and pestle. It didn't go far, just a tablespoon or so. I'd been making pizza a lot lately.

As I was pouring the whole mixture into a small plastic container, Rick finally texted me saying that Lutz would come by on Monday to finish priming the ceiling and check out the scurrying sounds. 'The whispering sounds are probably just the house settling,' he added.

Lutz did not show up on Monday. He did not show up on Tuesday. He showed up on Wednesday, climbed up the ladder and started sanding and sanding. He didn't even wear a mask. His whole face went buff from the dust. Bits of red started peeking through the ceiling again. His hands were red and abraded, but he was smiling more.

'You know, I think I might've left my tape measure in the basement when I was here last. You mind if I go down and take a look?'

'Go ahead.'

There was a thump, then another, and then swearing in the basement. The can of spackle that Lutz kept calling "primer" was sitting on the counter. It smelled different. It was muskier. It reminded me of the smell of the water that had come through the ceiling. I knew it wasn't primer, but I started to wonder if it was not spackle either. I stirred my red peppercorn, rosemary and salt mix into it. Maybe Lutz would notice. Maybe he wouldn't.

'Found it!' Lutz held up his tape measure. 'Keep losing this thing in the most gosh-darn places. Now, what was I doing?'

'I thought you were going to prime the ceiling today?'

Lutz grabbed the can. 'Oh, yes, I'm priming it today.'

His palette knife scraped on plaster and made an awful sound, like a shriek. It felt like the sound scraped my vertebrae. 'Ever hear of botflies?' he asked, smiling even more.

'I'm trying to make my lunch, Lutz. Parasites aren't conducive to lunch.'

'My father was a parasitologist for the UN. Once, I found a rat with a botfly stuck in it and I pulled the botfly out. I was so proud; I took it to my father. He shook his head and said, 'Too late, the botfly's already laid eggs in it.''

He laid in more spackle while I leaned on the counter over my sandwich and salad. Was Lutz being abnormally or normally creepy?

'The other day, I was driving and I saw a bird flapping around on the street, so I stopped my car to pick it up. When I got closer, I realized that it didn't look right. There was something wrong with its wings. They were complete wings, but they didn't look complete. I put it in a box to take to the

Humane Society. I didn't want to look in the box, because, you know, so many animals you rescue don't make it. But I finally looked in the box and you know what?'

He turned to look at me, so I answered. 'What?'

'The bird coughed up a live cricket.'

Lutz slathered more spackle onto the ceiling. I slid my lunch into the trash. Bye-bye, sandwich and salad.

'All done,' he said, climbing down the ladder. 'You know that show? What's the name of it? Oh, gosh, I can't remember. Anyway, they have really good blood. I think they used chocolate for the blood. It looked really good. Most film blood is, you know, translucent.'

He collected his tools and his can of spackle in a plastic bucket.

'A lot of film blood is corn syrup and dye.'

'But why wouldn't they use chocolate? It looks so good. It looks real.'

'Chocolate is more expensive than corn syrup.'

He stared at me. I looked at the white flecks covering the lenses of his vintage Seventies aviator glasses. 'I hadn't thought of that.'

He started out the door and then stopped. 'You know what would be really cheap? Going to a slaughter house.'

'I don't think actors sign up for the risk of blood-borne illness.'

'I guess not. Well, see you.' Lutz nodded nervously and carried his bucket out the door.

The stain thought I should climb the ladder and see if I was in the hell hole and the other side is the real world. It seemed like it might be a good idea.

Instead, I sat on my porch, which the things in the kitchen hated because of The Accursed Sun and The Joyousness of the Fireflies.

Rick called me. 'Hi, Sophie. Did Lutz fill the hole where vermin come through?'

'He spackled the hell out of the ceiling, if that's what you're asking.'

'Any more water from the ceiling?'

'No more water, but there were a lot of flies and there's… things…in the kitchen.'

'But no more trouble with the toilet?'

'No, but there are things in the kitchen—weird, wrong things.'

'You could get traps for those.'

'I don't think so.'


'Pineal! Pineal! Pineal!' the thing gibbered at me, waggling its gland in my face. All its glands were out, flapping around, but it liked to extend its pineal gland out the farthest. I considered calling Rick. Assuming he answered his phone, he would just stand and gawp or send over Lutz to stand and gawp. Pineal Guy seemed out of the Humane Society's line, too.

'Knock it off. I'm trying to do my laundry.'

I was kind of getting used to the things in the kitchen. Pineal Guy was frisky, though, and it was getting tiresome. Apparently, using a combination of rituals reconstructed from movies, books from the library's reference collection and Heavy Metal, he managed to open up a portal to the Hell World when Rick had rented out the house. That's what Pineal Guy told me, one word at a time, screamed three times each. And  he shared way more than I was interested in knowing. I only knew his story because he talked to me every time I went into the kitchen, tried to pass through the kitchen to the washer and dryer or took the garbage out the back door. Whoever had put in the plumbing in the house had lined it all up along the same vertical plane from the bathroom upstairs down to the kitchen and laundry room and to the water heater and pipes in the basement. The Hell Portal was centrally located.

'Don't make me get the floor sweeper.' I said.

Pineal Guy faded back into the red stain with a whimper. The sweeper is great—it can be broken down into three sections handy for whacking waggly glands.  Pineal Guy also seemed to believe that the sweeper was made of silver and that 'The touch of silver burns!' I suspect the burning is just the charge on the disposable static pads.

Meanwhile, the Cloud of Inflamed Eyes still tried to lure me through the portal, but it didn't whisper from the stain anymore. It manifested just below, where my shelves had been, and dripped ectoplasm on the floor, slippery, visible only in the dark ectoplasm. When I first slipped and fell, I freaked out. Ectoplasm is disgusting. But it actually cleans up easily. It rolls up neatly like a fruit snack and has the weak tackiness of post-it note adhesive. I wasn't reckless, though, I wore gloves when handling it.

'How do you know you are not trapped in the Hell World now and only believe yourself in your own? Enter the portal and escape this horror.' Cloud-of-Inflamed-Eyes said in a voice like the agony of a thousand people who had gotten cayenne right in the eye.

'I'm pretty sure you wouldn't tell me to climb into that portal if it were going to be any good for me.'

'Can you be certain, Fated One?' the eyes said. 'Resist no longer. You are the Inheritor of the Gate. Take up the plunger, unseal it, defeat the trials and claim wonders as your own!'

'If I wanted to do that, I'd be a property owner. What is a landlord for, if not to go into hell portals and complete trials for tenants?'

Rick would make Lutz do the trials, though. Or, Lutz would decide he could no longer resist the call of the Hell World and shuffle inside. And if Lutz did, sadly, no one would ever know how he saved the world. I would probably be eating lunch and reading the news, comedically oblivious to whatever horrors he battled right above me.

Cloud-of-Inflamed-Eyes interrupted my thoughts. 'You do not have title to the House of the Toilet Gate?'

'No, I'm a tenant.'

Cloud-of-Inflamed-Eyes began an unholy screaming, sounding as if at least a thousand more poor souls had gotten cayenne in their eyes. From the wall behind the stove, I heard an angry chittering and there was the sickly sweet smell of cherry cigarillo smoke all around. Pineal Guy began to shout, 'No! No! No!'

'Okay, I've had it with you guys.' I told them. Twenty

minutes later, I walked into to the dollar store. I picked up a couple of spray bottles, nicer ones with multiple settings and a thicker stream, and bags of ground red pepper, sea salt and rosemary from the bulk foods section.

'Do you guys have any glitter?' I asked the cashier.

'If we have any left, it will be over in aisle three.' She pointed back toward the door.

'Thanks.'

There were a couple tubes of red and gold glitter and one tube of silver. I was set.

With the entities watching, I poured out the sea salt, rosemary and red peppercorns and ground them up with the mortar and pestle.

Hell Squirrel was sitting on the edge of the stove and smoking openly, cigarette in a cheap plastic holder held daintily in one paw.

'You best put that out, squirrel.' I added the glitter, then divided the mixture between the bottles and filled them with water.

'Cigarillo! Cigarillo! Cigarillo!' shouted Pineal Guy.

'If you guys don't settle down, I will spritz you. Hell Squirrel, put the damn cigarette out.'

Hell Squirrel looked right at me with blank, black eyes, took a pointed drag and blew a smoke ring. Spritz. Hell Squirrel's fur smoked where it had been sprayed, but the cigarillo was still burning.

'Put it out. Outside on the patio. No fires.'

Hell Squirrel pushed open the back door, stubbed its cigarillo out on the back porch. The squirrel kept the white plastic holder.

Cloud-of-Inflamed-Eyes started screaming, 'We are Legion! Our endless armies will destroy you, Fool! You who could have reigned from the Throne of Hell will now suffer Our Wrath!'

Pineal Guy emphasized this speech rather than offer any input of his own. 'Legion! Legion! Legion!' he shouted, his pineal gland wildly waving. 'Fool! Fool! Fool!'

'Suffer! Suffer! Suffer!'

'I told you to settle down.' I sprayed each entity once. That startled them into silence. 'There are no Legions. You three are it—Red Eye, Pineal Guy and Hell Squirrel.'

Cloud-of-Inflamed-Eyes blinked a multitude of eyes. Pineal Guy's glands drooped. Hell Squirrel chewed on the cigarette holder.

'The way I see it, something big in your Hell World tried break into my world through the toilet. The seal that kept you guys out was so corroded and weak that the whatever it was did some damage. The plumber resealed it. Hiring that plumber was probably the only competent thing Rick has ever done. Anyway, you guys are the only ones who made it through. The ceiling is spackled, the stain is covered and you are cut off. The best you can do is hassle me and maybe try to convince Lutz that he is doomed.'

Pineal Guy started shrieking, 'Doomed!' but only got one repetition out before I sprayed.

'These spray bottles are just a start. I can get a power washer. I have credit.'

Pineal Guy was carefully stroking his singed pineal gland. One of Red Eye's inflamed eyes was singed black. I had picked up both spray bottles, realizing that I was outnumbered.

'You've got moxie, kiddo. I like that.' We all turned to look at Hell Squirrel. 'Let's make a deal,' the squirrel said.

I lowered my spray bottle, just a little. 'As long as nobody's waggling their pineal gland in my face, dripping ectoplasm in the crisper drawer, or pooping in the skillet and I can use the laundry room and the kitchen, I'm okay.' Clearly negotiating needs is crucial in housemate relationships.

We came to an arrangement. Pineal Guy and Cloud-of-Inflamed-Eyes could stay in the kitchen and the basement, if they could reach it. Hell Squirrel could stay wherever it had been staying, as long as it didn't wreck the wiring. The first and second floors were mine and they'd stay the hell out of the bathroom and the fridge. They would not try to help whatever might be trapped in the water heater and I would not spray them, much, or destroy them with a power washer filled with red pepper, salt, rosemary and silver glitter water.

The flies stopped emerging from the furnace intake vent. Whoever was pooping little pellets in my iron skillet stopped.

I was pretty sure it had been the Hell Squirrel, but I really couldn't say for sure. I wouldn't put it past Pineal Guy. There was no more smoke inside the house, but Hell Squirrel always looked a little guilty, like it had just stubbed out a cigarette. I set a litter box for Red Eye's ectoplasm below the patched up portal.

The day after we made our deal, Rick and Lutz knocked on the back door. It was early and the Hell Entities weren't manifest yet. Lutz headed down to look at the hot water heater again. Rick said, 'I need to turn off the water. The bill is way more than it should be this month. There's gotta be a leak on the other property somewhere.'

'You don't need to turn off the water here?'

'No, no, for some reason the water for the place behind your house runs through your house, too.'

Rick wore his improvised back brace. It is white, quilted and a little too small. His brace reminded me of diapers or sanitary napkins. While waiting for Lutz, he examined the sealed Hell Portal. 'Well, you can't match the colour perfectly. And the paint on the wall is a lot older.'

Lutz lumbered up to Rick and said, 'The water heater's meter is spinning around like gangbusters now. When the water was on, it was barely even moving.'

'Anyway,' Rick said, turning away from Lutz, 'I have the plumber here digging up the street and he needs to get in to turn the water on and off.'

'Can you guys just let yourselves in and out?'

'You'll have to leave it unlocked. I'm not sure if I have the key.'

I sighed and unlocked the deadbolt on the back door. 'Just remember to lock it behind you when you're done. I have work to catch up on.'

'We won't bother you. You'll barely know we're here.' But I heard clomping in through the kitchen and down the basement steps most of the morning. They slammed the door a final time just before noon, getting the deadbolt latch to catch. I heard nothing from Pineal Guy or Red-Eye. Hell Squirrel sat in a tree watching almost like a normal squirrel except for the tiny nicotine patch on its haunch. Rick was hovering around the equipment tearing up the street. The hole in the cement was smoking with hot tar.

I went back inside to my office, where I am currently ignoring pounding on the back door. There is a blue jay angrily screaming. I can only assume that Rick or Lutz can no longer resist the urge to tear out the spackle and return home through the Hell Portal in my kitchen ceiling. I'm not going to answer.

The end of the world isn't my problem anymore.

'Nosiree,' agrees Hell Squirrel.

# Part 3

*"…So when the last and dreadful hour*
*This crumbling pageant shall devour,*
*The trumpet shall be heard on high,*
*The dead shall live, the living die,*
*And Music shall untune the sky"*

John Dryden,
*The Major Works*

# All Things Fall

## Chloë Yates

There is a cottage that sits at the end of the world. On one side stands a thick forest that stretches for a hundred leagues or more. On the other lies a garden, rich with vegetables, and a lake with water fresher than any mountain spring. Beyond that, there is the end. Sheer cliffs slash down into the blackness of Below, bringing the world to a halt. The fecundity of the garden and the purity of the lake's waters belie the irrevocable nothingness so close at hand. They call it an ocean, the sea that rings the world, but that is to keep the nightmares at bay.

The white horse grazes quietly beside the lake as the lush green woodland behind her darkens with the dying of the light. As the day passes into night, the horse changes too. Soft white hair turns to pale skin, muscled hindquarters to long slim legs, the hard hooves to soles used to going barefoot. The change is not conditional upon the close of the day. It is merely her habit to run through the surrounding woodland at twilight, stopping to take a long drink from her lake before returning to the prison of her human form.

The man waiting in the shadows knows this.

He has been watching her for days.

The woman, sky clad with only hair the colour of winter snow to cover her, moves gracefully through the tall grass. Her keen ears and eyes keep a check on her surroundings, but no one ever comes to her grove and perhaps she has become a little complacent. He watches her, his mouth dry, the heat he feels low down something he hadn't felt for a long time before he first saw her, before he heard her song. He can hear it now; her soft tones drift across the water towards him, caressing his ears, his heart. He has lived a long time and has travelled through many lands, but he has never heard anything quite so beautiful.

Alas, he knows it for what it is. A siren's song.

And yet it calls to him. *She* calls to him. He waits.

Her skin itches, it always does. The bath is running; it's not the lake but it will do. Besides, what else is there? She wraps the silk robe around her, cinching it in at the waist. She is impatient to feel the water on her skin, it would be heaven to slip into the lake beneath the rays of the crisp white moon, but she cannot take the chance. Night is lit by fire and fire is her enemy.

As it so often does, the window that looks out onto the lake catches her attention and she wanders over to it, sighing at the sight of the moon-bathed waters below. A flicker at the corner of her vision surprises her and she turns towards it, straining to see past the gloom into the dark forest beyond. There is nothing there. She has had a feeling that something is coming for days now. She tries to tell herself that it is nothing but the anxiety of this constant waiting, but her voice is less sure with every telling. The forest has settled back into stillness. She waits for a few minutes, senses strained, but there is nothing more.

With a sigh, she takes one last look at the lake before turning away from the window. Another long night awaits.

They come in the night. Red haired foxes that glow in the cold fire of the moon. They devour the crops and damage the small levee that channels the water from the lake into the cottage's supply so that the gardens are flooded. Years of work are ruined in a matter of moments. The man watches on. There is no satisfaction in overseeing such a thing, waste is always unappealing, but needs must and he needs a way in. He watches his charges frolic in the moonlight, envying them their freedom even as he pities their frailty.

All things fall.

The morning light is harsh as the breeze whips sharply around the side of the building.

The last building at the end of the world.

Nyx flinches at the unusual brightness of the day as she steps out onto the porch. It is usually marred by the endless darkness beyond the cliffs; only her skill and what lies at the bottom of the lake keep the garden growing. The light at the end of the world is not the stuff of summer days, but it is far brighter than that which the rest of the world has begun to labour under. She is sent a bird once every turn of the moon. The news is never good and yet receiving it maintains her hope. The most recent bird is overdue. It is ominous; the sense of impending doom haunting her cannot be written off for much longer because she knows the truth of it.

It is coming to an end.

She takes comfort in the smallholding that sustains her. The practicality of everyday work, the feel of the earth beneath her hands, and the faint sunlight on her back all serve to make her appreciate the moment. What will come will come. Despite what her mother told her, she has never believed that her task will be indefinite; she has always known the frailty of the hope that she carries.

All things fall.

It is only when she steps down onto the path in front of the cottage, as her bare feet slip in the watery mud that should not be there, that she sees what has been done. The garden is a mess, her work ruined. Hitching her skirt, she slips and slides as she runs to check her crops. What isn't gone is half eaten. The shock of it makes her skin tighten against her bones, her eyes smart with tears she refuses to shed. What could have done this, what could have... her ears prick at the sound of what can only be a footstep. It cannot be. She has not seen another living soul for so long that it must either have been her imagination or whatever lives in the forest playing tricks on her.

No. Another step breaks a twig under foot.

Quick as a flash, Nyx grabs a pole that was once in the embrace of runner beans and hurries back to the porch, sliding quietly along the side of the cottage. It is coming from the other side of the building. Someone is going to walk around the corner and she will...

Stare.

She will stare – is staring – at him. She can't seem to do anything else.

A man. Broad and tall, stronger than any she has ever seen before, with thick black hair that hangs wildly down to his shoulder blades and eyes that are so bright they glow amber even in the glare of the unnaturally harsh morning light. Like fire waiting to ignite. He should have a beard, is all she can think as he takes a step onto the porch towards her.

Neither says anything. He does not come any closer and Nyx doesn't back away. Something about him is… inevitable.

No.

Finally the alarm she should immediately have felt at this intruder rings out sharply in her mind, and Nyx whips the pole up, holding it like a bat, ready to strike.

'Who are you?' Her voice sounds strange to her ears. She hasn't spoken, only sung, for the longest time. She watches as the man blinks, hiding those eyes for a moment, and her alarm becomes sharper. 'I said, who are you? And what did you do to my garden?'

'My name is… Sam.' She knows a lie when she hears one, but Nyx motions for him to continue. 'I didn't do this to your garden; it was like this when I got here. I need shelter, I swear that's all.'

'And you thought you'd find it here? Nobody comes here, least of all for safe harbour. Keep on walking through the trees and you'll find a hut about twenty leagues from here. I don't know if anyone lives there now, but at least it will offer you the shelter you seek.'

'Twenty leagues? That's so far. Please, I can see you need help, that your garden is flooded, your crops ruined. I would gladly sleep in your shed, if you'd only give me a little water and a blanket, in return for helping you.' His voice is deep, all velvet and chocolate, designed to tempt the weak, to get him what he wants, but she is not weak. She has a purpose. She hasn't so much as contemplated letting him inside, letting him touch her, wondered about the feel of his mouth on her skin… Enough. He must go.

'You'll have no more mattress than the dirt floor in there.' The words come of their own volition, surprising her as much as they do him. His eyes flare and something inside her answers. She turns away before she can run to him. 'I'll fetch you some water and that blanket, then I will show you where I keep my tools.'

'Thank you.' That voice, it is so familiar to her. She can't place it but it has settled upon her with the certainty of something more than acquaintance. It is right.

She must be out of her mind. She knows a trap when she sees one, but damned if she can send him on his way. This is his destination. She feels it. Stepping into the house, she quickly pulls the front door closed behind her and locks it. She thinks about sliding the bolt across too, but is it to keep him out or to keep her in?

He waits on the porch, determinedly not thinking about having her so achingly close to him. He has wished for it for too many days, dreamed of it during the endless nights, but still he had not been ready. It was her scent that bewitched him, he tells himself, the scent of fresh woman and open pasture, enough to drive someone who has lived like a monk for so long to distraction. He knows the lie for what it is. The soft paleness of her flesh is a sharp contrast to his rougher, darker skin. He aches to feel the balm of her beneath his callused hands, to have his burning fever assuaged by her cool lushness. He is going to scare her away if he does not keep himself in check.

They work together in the gardens all day. It is back breaking work and yet each of them toil as though their lives depend upon it. Nyx tries not to stare as Sam removes his shirt; the sight of the hard corded muscles of his torso glistening with sweat almost enough to bring her to her knees. She digs on in a frenzy of purpose, determined not to succumb.

Sam tries not to notice when Nyx splashes water on her face to cool down, the resulting rivulets trickling down her neck onto her chest, dampening her pale blouse, making it see-through. The baseness of his desire shocks him even now and he ploughs on with vigour. By the time the light begins to darken, they are both exhausted but neither wants to stop. What is certain to come next is too much of a temptation. They shouldn't.

'Would you like a bath?' The words are out of her mouth before she can stop them. 'To clean up, I mean. After all, you have worked so hard and it's only fair, it would be nice for you to…'

'Yes, thank you.' His simple answer cuts through her babble and she is grateful.

She leads him into the cottage and up the stairs, the scent of his sweat slicked body almost more than her senses can stand. Opening the door to the bathroom for him, she fights the urge to throw herself at him, to beg him for whatever he wants to give her. Steeling herself, she does no such thing. He squeezes past her in the small confines of the cottage's landing and he can smell the fresh air on her hair. It makes him wonder what her skin tastes like, if it tastes like sunshine and rain. His desire for her heats in his veins, making his eyes glow brightly in the darkening light, his breath comes quicker, his chest tighter than he has ever felt it.

He cannot – will not – fight it any longer.

Nyx turns from him before she is swept away, but he reaches out for her, takes her by the wrist and swings her around to face him. Nyx gasps, but as Sam pulls her to him and his mouth comes down on hers, she welcomes him. His hands on her skin are like fire, the heat echoing through her veins, licking across her skin as his tongue slips between her lips and makes her want, makes her take, everything he offers.

All things fall.


Their days pass in isolated bliss. It is as though they are the only two lovers in the world. Neither one had expected to find the other and now they are together it is as though it has always been this way. This is meant to be.

The bird still does not come and, despite the happiness that has swollen her heart to near bursting, Nyx cannot shake her anxiety. If anything it is worse. The world around them seems alarmingly bright sometimes, the wind sharper, crueller, and yet the salve of his lips against hers, the scent of him on her skin, his strength bearing down onto her softness all serve to make her forget for a while.

Nyx wakes in the night, wrapped in Sam's arms. She is not sure what has woken her, does not want to leave the warmth of their bed and his embrace yet she is drawn to the window. Slipping out from under his arms, careful not to wake him, she crosses the room to look out at the lake. That is what has woken her.

The light.

It glows from the bottom of the water, a warm orange radiance that frightens her. She knows perfectly well what it is. Her heart aches, even as she knows it could never really have been stopped. Tears gather in the corner of her eyes and spill down her cheeks, splashing onto the windowsill where her hands grip the wood in agony.

'Nyx?' His voice, that deep seductive voice, is heavy with sleep and concern. She wants to go to him but she holds herself back. This time there can be no indulgence.

'Go back to sleep.'

'Come back to bed. We can…' The orange light is suddenly stronger; it illuminates the room now, reminding Nyx of fire. Her enemy. She looks over her shoulder at Sam and her heart stops. She did not want to see it before but now it is so clear she wants to scream at her own flagrant stupidity.

His eyes are aflame.

He is fire.

Hissing, she backs away from him, edging slowly towards the door as though he's a wild animal bent on her destruction. She almost laughs at that. That is exactly what he will be soon enough. Not taking her eyes from him, she edges towards the door.

'Nyx, please, I'm sorry. I should have told you.'

'No.'

'Please, I…'

'I know!' She shouts the words, her wilful blindness angering her too late. Sam tries to rise from the bed, but she calls the change upon her before he can reach her. The tidal wave of transformation rips violently through her body in a push that affects every cell, from her heels to her head, in an incessant fizz of activity. Sam can only watch for the short moments it takes. As the white horse pushes back with its muscled legs, Nyx's face disappears in a flourish of long shaggy muzzle. Only her eyes remain. He wants to beg her to stop this, to plead with her to just listen to him, to do all the things it is in his very nature not to do.

'Please Nyx, no…' But his words are too late. Fired by the change, she charges for the window, leaping through the glass with no regard for sharp edges, landing on the ground below with a heavy thud but, keeping her hooves beneath her, Nyx thunders on towards the lake. As she lets her legs fly, her hair streams out behind her, catching the moonlight. He watches her for a moment from the broken window, torn between what must be and what he desires. He has come a long way for what he seeks but now he has found it, he finds he wants something else far more.

He wants her.

He cannot have her.

All things fall.

With a roar of anguish borne of a frustration that has existed as long as there have been lovers, Sam feels his own change begin. His muscles pulse with growth, his bones throb, and his head pounds. His body, so large but graceful as a human, swells relentlessly, his cells splitting and reforming over and over in a fury of expansion. His weight becomes intolerable for the small cottage and his legs burst through the floor of the bedroom, thrusting down into the living room below. He screams in agony as his arms smash through the walls of the bedroom, as his back tries to push up through his skull, the unrelenting growth a torment that burns him, stretches him from the inside out, outside in. He bursts through the roof and the tiny cottage pulses in a final stab of resistance before it explodes, sending splinters of wood and brick shooting across the grove.

Nyx looks back at the sound and stops. Terror grips her at the sight of the giant Sam has become. Who he always was.

Surt.

Ruler of the land of fire.

He has come for what is his. For what must be done.

All things fall.

Defiance rages through her and she ploughs on, heading for the lake.

'Nyx!' The giant's bellow makes the earth tremble. The very roots of the trees shake in fear at the sound. Waves form upon the surface of the lake, disturbing the peaceful moonshine, making it more dangerous to leap into, but leap she does, ignoring his demands, ignoring the tremors upon the land. There is nothing left to lose. She must try.

As she leaps, Nyx changes again, soft white hair and foam flying from her mouth changing to pale skin and red lips once more. She arches over the water, reaching out as far as she can, wanting only to make headway, to evade the giant. He could crush her so easily, level the area and destroy the lake, but he needs her to bring him what lies at its bottom and she will fight to protect it.

The cold rush of the water thrills her as she breaks the surface, plunging into its depths with a cry of joy. It is a balm to her muddled senses, to her righteous fury, and as she swims, her body undulating along with the water, caressing it, she feels more hope than she has felt for a long time. It fuels her, pushes her on, makes her faster. The light is the key. It hurts her eyes but she heads for it, its pulsing frenzy a beacon. The water swirls around her as the giant steps closer, washing her further than she wants to go, surging up her nose, stopping her breath. She has to fight to the surface. She is not a fish; her lungs need air. As she breaks through the water, she sees the world around her has turned to fire. The giant's anger has been turned loose on the woodlands and the land beyond, his scorching fury impossible to contain. He stands over her lake, staring down into its depths desperate to catch sight of her. Of course he does. She is the one who must hand him the sword. She must give it to him of her own free will.

She will never do it.

Taking a deep breath, she ducks back under the churning waters, kicking hard to go deeper, to get to the bottom. She does not know what she will do but she knows she must reach it first. One of the giant's hands plunges into the water, trawling along the bed of the lake to find either her or the sword. He makes the water wild, it froths and eddies against her, and she has to fight the demented current he has created.

As she gets closer, the sword gets brighter, its fiery orange glow all but blinding her. All she can see is fire, but she carries on, feeling her way towards the prize. She reaches out with her hand, willing the sword into its grasp. For long moments, her long legs kick harder and harder, her oxygen gets lower and lower, panic settles in her gut and grows. Despair mocks her but desperation stretches her… and finally she feels the hilt of the sword against her palm. Quickly, she curls her fingers around it, gripping it tightly. It is hers. Relief soothes her overworked muscles and she allows herself the luxury of floating to the surface.

It may be the last indulgence she ever knows.

As her body is carried upwards, the water tossing her gently in its embrace, her mind works frantically. She has no idea what she is going to do, what she intends. As she breaks through the water once more, she is disoriented but one gasp of air quickly rights her. She looks up into the face of the giant. It has the same face as the man, Sam. It grips her heart like a vice. For a moment, they simply stare at each other.

The eye of the storm.

'I'm sorry.' The giant's rumble is the saddest sound Nyx has ever heard. She closes her eyes against the tears that threaten. She tells herself that this is not the time for her to pity her enemy but, when she opens her eyes to look at him once more, her throat thickens with those unshed tears. It had only been for a brief moment in time, a speck in the grand scheme they are trapped in, but she loved the man that wore that face. She wants to touch him again, to feel his rough skin beneath her smooth fingertips, his darkness to her light. She remembers the way they had laid together, the way he had made her understand her human form. Frustration and regret almost steal her breath away.

'I love you.' She doesn't realise she has spoken the words aloud until the light in the giant's eye dims and one huge tear gathers in its corner. It does not fall, but slides slowly down his cheek, petering out as it nears his chin. The lid closes slowly over the eye Nyx stares into and a great sigh almost blows her out of the water. The trees shake and the ground trembles, but nothing falls.

The giant slowly straightens up and takes a step back from the lake. Treading water, Nyx watches as he begins to contract. The process is quicker, but no less painful. She can see the strain the change takes on him, the veins in his muscular forearms and the side of his strong neck popping and con-vulsing with every beat of his surely overtaxed heart. He is Surt, he is Jotnar and he is the bringer of All-Fire. His fate will be to destroy the land of men and her soul aches with the inevitability of it, she must do something but…

The stories her grandmother told her come to her in a rush as she faces the giant. Her mother's dictums, to hide the sword, to protect it and keep it from the Fire Bringer, the scourge of man and gods, ring pointlessly next to the other memories she all but cast aside under her mother's tutelage. She sees the truth of them. She is the girl at the end of the world, but this will not be the end of all things. The world has run itself out; it has been brought to the point of irrev-ocable destruction. It must be cleansed, but it must also be reborn. What does love matter in the face of that? What is love if not that?

With the sword slung over her shoulder, Nyx kicks out for the shore. Despite her tired limbs, she swims quickly, reach-ing land as Surt's form finally reverts back to Sam's. He is not Sam, she reminds herself. He is Surt. He will set fire to the land, the realms will battle and the world will be destroyed. Yet, that is not the end of the stories her grandmother taught her. Two will hide within the world tree's branches. They will emerge after the fighting is done and theirs will be the charge of repopulating the world. It is a cycle. It is not for her to stand in its way.

She throws the sword at Surt's feet. She will not kneel before him and offer it to him. However great the necessity of allowing the world to turn, she cannot stomach the thought of the violence to come. She is complicit but she will not condone it.

Surt stares at the sword at his feet. Finally, his beloved sword. Lost so long ago to thieving Nixie hands. Their inten-tions were good, he can see that, has always seen it, but they were misguided. It must be done.

All things fall.

# A Pilgrimage for Saint Salima

## Alex Helm

*If you were given the ultimate weapon, would you use it? When all you have ever known in your life is violence and terror, death and destruction, would you take the chance to stop it and save the world, no matter what the consequences? This then is my testimonial. I had that chance and I made my choice. Now the world is ravaged yet I am revered as a hero. How can that be?*

The monk frowned as he read the introduction to the memoir. Although the ancient yellowed papers were stained with dust and dirt, the printed type had survived the centuries and was still legible. It was not the condition of the journal that concerned him however. The writer had bound the pages in a plastic sheath, ensuring its survival against the elements, if not the wilful destruction of curious hands and eyes. The type was in the long-disused Arabic script, but he had expected that and had studied for a decade to learn the language. The text ran right to left, but again that had been anticipated. It was the words, the words that bothered him. They weren't what he was expecting. He reached out a withered arm, its dark skin bleached and mottled, and its flesh flaking and rotting, and turned the page.

*I suppose I should start at the beginning. What is this, some Charles Dickens story?* It sounds so silly, doesn't it? I was born. It seems so unimportant now, but if this is to be a record for the ages, then so be it. Fine! I was born. I was named Salima Fayed Al-Jahid and I was born in Baghdad at the height of war. Maybe you, my reader know the sorry history of Iraq in the early years of the new millennium already. Maybe you don't, so here it is in brief.

In the late twentieth century, the part of the world known as the Middle East was ruled mainly by authoritarian dictators propped up by the wealth of oil. My country, Iraq, was no exception and our own tyrant was considered to be the worst of the worst. In the early years of the twenty-first century, a madman orchestrated the worst terrorist atrocity in history, attacking the United States in a convoluted but tragically successful fashion. The US and their allies responded in kind, dispatching hundreds of thousands of soldiers to find the perpetrator and his allies including our own insane dictator.

At first we were happy. Yet, what replaced him was arguably worse. Our country descended into anarchy and sectarian violence. Our government was weak and ineffective against the power of the militants. Guns ruled the streets. Bombs and violence were our norm.

Can you imagine growing up in that kind of environment? Where just going to school each day involved running a gauntlet of snipers, fanatics and street bombs? Every day that I returned home in one piece was a day that my family gave thanks.

Even though this was the only life I had ever known, I knew it wasn't normal for everyone. I had books depicting both happier times in my own country and across the rest of the world. Television and the internet showed other nations where the only concern for most was being able to get to work on time. Getting there alive was something taken for granted. I would exclaim to my father and siblings that it wasn't fair. Why did we have to live this way when others didn't? What kind of God would allow this?

By luck, fate or the gaze of God, I survived to adolescence. I dreamed of going to university, of making a difference. With my friend Faiza, we planned our revolution in which we would sweep Iraq clear of the guns and the bombs through the power of education and tolerance. We would rule our country, Faiza and I. We would bring peace and good governance and the world would be a better place. Between our vivid plans for the future, we played games and enjoyed our favourite music, a British pop band called One Direction.

Whatever the environment we had grown up in, we were just typical teenage girls.

Everything changed when Faiza was killed in a street bombing. She had only boarded a bus to pick up some medicine for her sickly grandmother. Someone had planted a bomb underneath the bus and it exploded, killing nearly fifty people and injuring a hundred more. She was just sixteen, as was I.

The monk's hand trembled as he turned the next page. That the journal had been written personally by Saint Salima was no longer in doubt. Her words resonated with the power that the young woman had become famed for. She had stood at the end of the world and battled the darkness so that life could continue. She had banished the demons and she would be forevermore remembered for it. That her life began in personal tragedy came as no surprise to him. Why then did he have such a sense of foreboding? What could these dusty pages reveal about the honoured saint whose words he had sacrificed his life and health to find?

I screamed and I howled and I denied God. No higher power worth my love would have taken my Faiza away like this. My faith shattered, I threw away my headscarf and cut my hair. I pledged that no longer would I live by the words of holy men. My life was my own, and I would find a way to stop this madness. I would make Baghdad safe once more, just like in old times. I just didn't know how.

That Faiza's sick grandmother should show up on our doorstep a week or so later was surprising at the time, but not entirely unexpected. She said she had been wracked by guilt for sending Faiza out that day. Of course, I tried to be polite and reassure her that it wasn't her fault – that chance and fate were fickle and that she shouldn't take the blame for the evil of the militants. Nonetheless, she pressed a package into my hands, before shuffling off, mumbling and praying. It wasn't until later that I learned the old woman had died shortly after the bombing. Whoever or whatever had delivered this gift had been false.

I retreated to the safety of my room to open the package, wondering what Faiza had granted me after her death. I expected to find books – our love of learning what was had brought us together as friends after all. And so I was surprised to discover that the gift contained a musty old lamp – the ancient kind shaped like a jug which could be filled with oil and lit at the spout. Despite the pain and misery of my bereavement, I laughed. I realised it was exactly what Faiza would have sent me to remind me of our dreams. She had given me a magical lamp with a genie inside to grant my wishes; something to remind me of what we wanted to achieve.

I smiled and I sobbed. I held that lamp tightly, and I remembered my friend. I rubbed the lamp with my fingers, just like Aladdin, wishing that that the genie could be real and that it would pop out to grant my wishes.

I am sure that you can imagine my surprise when that is exactly what actually happened!

Of course, the legend of the djinn was a fundamental part of Arabic and Iraqi culture. They were spirits mentioned throughout the Qur'an and other Islamic texts that could assume human or animal form, bringing power and gifts. Many people I knew believed in them, as did I until my faith had been destroyed by Faiza's death. Even so, believing in something spiritual was very different to having it suddenly pop up in front of you.

This particular djinn had taken the form of an Arab woman. Her upper half was naked and perfect in every way with long dark hair hanging over her breasts. Yet a pair of curved horns rose above her head, while her lower body consisted only of hazy smoke.

I am ashamed to say I yelped in surprise. However, I challenge you, dear reader, not to have done the same.

'Shhh…' said the djinn. Her voice was soft and calming, and I suddenly felt nothing but peace at her presence. She drifted closer and put her arm around my shoulders. It was gentle and comforting. 'Salima, you are my child; my poor precious child.'

'Who are you?' I asked, my voice broken with tears and pain.

'I've come to help you,' she said. 'I've come to make your dreams come true.'

'I abandoned my faith,' I replied sorrowfully. 'Why come to me?' Deep down at the back of my mind, I wondered how this could be happening. Why was this happening? Yet I didn't challenge it. The djinn had me completely under her spell.

'You may have turned from God, but God hasn't turned from you,' she said, her voice still singing sweetly in my ears. 'A loss you have suffered; a sister stolen by evil. I know, and I understand your pain, child.'

She held me then. She held me tightly as I was wracked by sobs. I cried for Faiza, I cried for myself and I cried for this crazy evil world that I had grown up in.

'It's alright, Salima,' she whispered to me as I cried. 'You are allowed to cry.' Never before had I been with such a comforting presence.

'I just want it to stop,' I said and my words choked with tears. 'The bombs, the shootings. I just want it all to go away.'

'We can make that happen,' she replied softly, holding me tightly.

'The evil men that commit these acts – they should pay for what they have done.'

'Yes, Salima. They should.'

'The world – it should be cleansed. Started anew.'

'It can happen, child.'

'Make it stop,' I begged her, choking in my sorrow. 'Make this evil go away.'

'This is what you want?'

I nodded and rested my head against her shoulder. 'This is what I want.'


The monk put the journal down and stood, wincing in pain from arthritic and weakened limbs. He stared through the ruined window, looking at the devastated landscape beyond.

So this is where it had begun. He had seen the ancient maps and he knew he was standing on land that had once been the troubled nation of Iraq, homeland of Saint Salima. Was the journal true? Had his beloved Saint been responsible for the devastation that had befallen the world? That the journal had been written by Salima herself? He already believed that beyond doubt.

He looked across at the dusty ruined buildings. The ravages of time had made it impossible to distinguish between the devastation caused by the demons and the ruination caused by humanity's attempts to fight back. Only pockets of the planet remained habitable within an irradiated wasteland. He had left that safety to embark on his pilgrimage, and he had always known that he would never return. The holy birthplace of Saint Salima would be his grave – the hostile environment had seen to that well.

He slowly settled down once again and continued reading. His pilgrimage would not be in vain, not matter what the revelations.


I suppose I should speak more on the matter of djinn. In the western nations, they became the genie, a fantasy spirit capable of granting your deepest desires. Here in the Arabian world though, our djinn are a religious concept, perhaps more similar to the angels and demons of Christian myth. Indeed, in the Qur'an, djinni are said to be one of the three sapient creations of God, alongside humans and angels. They are spirits beyond mortal comprehension, capable of great good and benevolence or terrible malevolence. Just like humans, really.

In time, I realised that the creature who had found me willing was no djinn whatsoever. Masquerading as one, it had preyed upon my sorrow and anguish, using my dreams for its own terrible purpose. This was no holy spirit, nothing the Prophet had ever envisaged. It was something far more inscrutable and unknowable, something from a dimension far from our own that had seen our weakness and used me as its conduit. To my shame, I did not realise this until it was too late. To you that are judging me, I offer a challenge – would it have been any different if you had been in my place?

Suffice to say, at that point, the appearance of the djinn restored my faith in God. Meeting a holy spirit face to face just had to have that effect. I once again donned my headscarf and began to say my prayers. In the meantime, the djinn began to grant my wish.

I don't know what I expected to happen. It felt like I was in a dream. Perhaps my sorrow at the death of Faiza had claimed me as well and I was merely a spirit drifting through a distant reality where djinni would appear and grant your wildest dreams. I suspect I was merely under the creature's spell, dulled and witless, eager to accept whatever it would give me. Later on I would wonder if I had fallen for the classical genie trick of not defining my wish. I wanted the violence of Iraq to go away but I hadn't specified how. In time I grew to realise that it wouldn't have mattered. I may have been the trigger for what happened next, but I was not the cause.

What can only be described as portals opened across Baghdad. Great gateways they were, doorways to another dimension that shimmered like quicksilver. For two days they just remained there. Nothing came out. Nothing happened at all. Of course, people investigated. It was just minutes before someone tried to put his hand through one of the portals, only to scream and withdraw a second later. His hand was gone, quite literally bitten away by something that left ragged teeth marks on the bloody stump.

That didn't deter someone else from walking through the portal. A militant who was armed to the teeth, bowed and prayed towards Mecca to cheers of the crowd before stepping through the shimmering doorway. He was never seen again. None of the brave, reckless or insane souls who followed him came back.

In a way, my wish had already come true. The violence did stop as the entire city came to investigate this strange phenomenon. The news quickly spread across the rest of the world, and the city was soon packed with journalists of all nations reporting back on the mysterious portals of Baghdad. Prominent clerics representing all aspects of the Islamic faith soon arrived to hold prayer sessions. The city's mosques were packed to the brim as people praised the next coming of the Prophet. It wasn't long before the other major religions of the world got in on the act as well and soon Christians, Jews, Hindus, Sikhs and more were praising their gods for this sign from the heavens.

New portals began to appear in other locations across Iraq. They mainly showed up in the cities and major population centres, but a few emerged in rural and desert regions as well. Aside from the priests and clerics, nobody could offer an explanation. Scientists arrived and tried to conduct experiments, but all were baffled. Samples were impossible – the quicksilver surface of the portals revealed nothing to the sensors and devices applied to them. Theories were created and discussed across the world, both rational and irrational. As well as the priests and clerics, all the crazies had been drawn out to offer their opinion. Aliens were discussed alongside angels. Detailed theories about dark matter and alternate universes competed for attention with crop circles, cube worlds and the return of Elvis. The only thing the disparate theorists could agree on was that without knowing what lay on the other side, it was impossible to tell what the truth could be. That just inspired more fanatics to throw themselves through the portals, but still none ever came back.

There was consternation of course. Some demanded a military presence, claiming that the portals obviously presented a threat. The issue was discussed at the highest levels of the United Nations, and there was talk of a peace-keeping force being sent, but it was caught up in legal wrangling and societal objection. In the end, the only military presence around the portals was a token showing by the security forces, and they were more interested in keeping the peace amidst the volatile crowd of opposing fanatics.

During this time I remained in my dream state. I remember drifting around the city, watching the chaos unfold with a quiet sort of detachment. No one stopped or questioned me. Nobody cared about Salima Fayed Al-Jahid, a sixteen year old Iraqi girl in a black headscarf. When I returned home, it was into the embrace of my djinn.

'What is happening?' I asked her.

She just hugged me. 'Hush, Salima. You'll see when all is ready.'

'Why did you choose me? There must be thousands of bereaved people in this city alone. Why me?'

'Why not you?' she said gently. 'Perhaps you are not the only one. Perhaps you are simply the first who made the right wish.'

Deep down I knew that should have worried me, but I was too far under the djinn's spell to challenge it.

It was around a week later that two things happened more or less at the same time. The first was the appearance of a portal outside Iraq. It turned up in Rome, close to the entrance to the Vatican City. However, the flurry of activity by both Catholic and non-Catholic Europeans alike was soon overshadowed by the news of something emerging from the first portal back in Baghdad.

My djinn had warned me that the time had come. She advised me to go and see but to keep my distance. I took her at her word and picked an elevated spot on the ledge of a holy building. I felt safe enough and I watched with interest to see what would happen.

The opening of the portal was foreshadowed by a change in its flickering surface. It darkened and turned red, the colour of blood. Then the first creature emerged.

I don't know who it was who started to call these things demons. I'm guessing the name just came around because in a way they bore some resemblance to demonic monsters – not so much the creatures from religious lore as those from movies and video games.

The beast was massive and its bulky skin was mottled red and black. Bloody spikes and chains protruded from its flesh and it wore some kind of armour forged from otherworldly obsidian metal that glistened strangely in the sunlight. Its head hung low, pressed down under the weight of the huge curled horns upon its giant skull. It raised its infernal axe into the air and bellowed a war cry that shattered windows and eardrums alike. Behind it, more creatures started to pour out of the portal. These were smaller ones, some shaped like dogs with drooling fangs like serrated knives. Others were more like goblins, small and chittering, and clutching spiked mauls and axes. These smaller ones swarmed around the feet of the giant creature like vermin at a feast.

I honestly didn't know what I was expecting, but I would never have imagined this. It was if the gates of some hell had opened, disgorging its denizens into our world. As I watched, the giant bellowed another battle cry and the army of demons charged into the crowd of shocked and terrified spectators. The security forces were taken complete by surprise and barely managed to get a shot off before they were destroyed by this visceral force. I screamed as limbs were ripped away, blood fountained into the air and death walked the land. I cried as a pool of blood spread out across the square, pouring into the gutters and staining the pale Baghdad brickwork deep red.

I don't remember climbing down from my ledge, but I do remember running for home. I ran as if my life depended on it, and most likely it did. I burst into the house – nobody was home, but I am ashamed to say that the fate of my family was not the first thing on my mind at that time. I needed answers and explanations and there was only one being on the planet that could provide them.

I charged into my room, coughing and choking from the fear and the exertion rolled into one. My room looked safe and normal. My One Direction poster remained on the wall. My books and DVDs remained lined up along the shelves. The djinn was nowhere to be seen, but the ancient lamp sat on my dressing table. I picked it up and shook it violently. 'Come out, damn you, come out!'

With a puff of smoke that was woefully inadequate for the purpose, the djinn appeared in front of me. It looked much the same as it had before, but I sensed something had changed, or perhaps I was now merely seeing it for what it truly was. Its face seemed cruel rather than beautiful, and the horns on its head looked worrying like those I had seen on the giant demon.

'Salima, my child. What is wrong?' It spoke with a predatory grin. Its lips were turned upwards in an expression of smugness and it tried to sound comforting. I wasn't going to be fooled by its lies this time though.

'What did you do?' I yelled. 'What have you done?'

It tipped its head and gazed at me petulantly. 'Only what you asked, my dear Salima.'

'People are dying!' I cried. 'They're being ripped apart by those… those things!'

'You wanted the evil men gone, did you not?'

I hesitated, gulping back a sob. A stab of pain struck me right in the stomach, causing me to gasp and hunch over in agony, but no demon was responsible. I didn't know it yet, but this was the first time I realised that somehow I was to blame for this massacre. It wouldn't be the last. 'I… I just wanted the violence to stop!'

'And it will… when there are no people left,' she replied.

'No!' I screamed. 'Make it stop!'

'It's too late for that, Salima. Come, join my embrace. You'll be safe, I can promise you that.'

The djinn seemed to grow before my eyes, its beautiful pale skin burning with fire and turning red before my eyes. I backed away as it seemed to fill and consume the room, all the while staring at me with those wide cruel eyes. I slammed the door shut and ran down the stairs. The house still seemed normal – silent but safe, unaware of the monstrosity it contained. I hurried over to the closet, reached up to the very top shelf, and I picked up my father's gun.

In a city and nation where violence was the norm, my family was not unusual for having a gun. My father kept it within reach, just in case armed men invaded the house, or someone tried to threaten us or kidnap us. Such events were not unknown or even infrequent in this city. The gun was an assault rifle, one of large numbers of similar ones that had been left behind by the American forces many years earlier. I couldn't say any more about it than that – I knew little of gun makes and models. All I knew was how to fire it – Father had ensured that the entire family knew how to handle the gun. I picked up a couple of magazines and slid one into the well, whilst dropping the other into my coat pocket. Suitably armed, I headed back up the stairs and into my room.

The demon was still there, and I felt a sense of satisfaction at seeing its look of surprise at my return.

'Salima,' it said, for once sounding hesitant. 'You came back? What is that you hold? A weapon?' It laughed at me, its cackles withering and depreciating. 'For millennia, your race has tried to fight back,' it continued. 'With sticks and swords and cannon – nothing can hurt us.'

'Oh yeah?' I said. 'I bet you haven't encountered one of these before!' I squeezed the trigger and unleashed a storm of bullets. Despite the training I had received from my father, I was still surprised by the recoil. My One Direction poster was shredded instantly, as were my photos of my family and Faiza, and the pink paper on the walls. I didn't care though. I forced the gun back towards the demon and my eyes widened in both horror and glee as the creature disintegrated before my eyes. Blood and gore flew as limbs were blown off it, and its cackles turned to a scream of death. The sound of the gunfire in the small room was truly deafening.

After just two or three seconds, the gun sounds turned to clicks as the magazine ran empty. I just stood there, still holding the trigger down, and stared at the space where the demon had been. All that was left of it was a battered corpse that before my eyes turned to red goo which seeped across the floor in a growing puddle. I stepped back before it could reach my feet. My ears were buzzing loudly from the noise.

I stared down at the gun in my hands. 'Well, shit,' I said, and I left the room.

The monk paused again as he processed what he had just read. The origin of the demonic invasion of Earth had remained a mystery throughout history. The involvement of Saint Salima in creating the apocalypse was a revelation – it was a certainly that he was the only person alive who now knew. He sat back on the dusty floor and clasped his hands together as he considered all he had studied of history.

The arrival of the demons had taken the world by surprise, although Christians, Jews and Muslims alike would all point to chapters in their respective holy books that supposedly foreshadowed the coming apocalypse. It had happened before, the priests had said later. In ancient times, the demons had come, harbingers of God's wrath, and they had destroyed humanity again and again. These were the warnings laid down by the seers, prophets and disciples. This was the price of man's ignorance and blindness to God's grace.

Saint Salima's journal had confirmed one thing though. This may not have been the first time the demons had invaded Earth. However, this time, Mankind was indeed somewhat better armed to fight back…

'You can shoot them!' I yelled. 'They are vulnerable to guns, and bullets and… just kill them!'

I was running through the streets of Baghdad, shouting my revelation to anyone who would listen. I must have looked like one of the crazed terrorists I so loathed, running and shooting and waving my assault rifle around like a violent madwoman.

Some people seemed to have figured it out for themselves. I could hear gunfire echoing through the streets from multiple directions. One of the hellhounds dashed out of an alleyway, charging towards me with a snarl, and I snappily turned and fired a burst of shots towards its head. Enough hit the target for the creature to yelp and sink to the ground, dissipating into the same type of red goo as the djinn.

'Yes!' I cheered instinctively. I turned to see a handful of terrified people watching me. 'We can fight!' I said, my eyes wide and gleaming from the adrenaline rush. 'Get your guns!'

'Who are you?' they asked me.

'Salima! Go!'

To my amazement, one of them seemed to listen to me. A man, no a boy, he was perhaps a year or two older than I. He grinned and ducked into the house behind me, emerging a moment later with a pistol.

'I'm Kamil,' he said as he started to follow me.

'Do you know how to shoot that thing?' I asked him.

'A bit. And I've played video games!'

I actually laughed. This whole situation felt like a video game, apart from the fact that people were actually dying. Together, we ran through the narrow alleys, picking off any loose demons. The streets were in chaos, and we could gauge from the panic what had been happening. All the portals across Iraq were now opening, and the demon army was pouring forth into our world. What's more, portals had started popping up across the whole planet, causing consternation in the United States, Russia, China and beyond.

We peppered a chitterling with bullets and destroyed three more hellhounds as we moved onwards. We didn't know where we were going – we simply moved with the flow. Everywhere we went, there were bodies, ripped and torn apart as if by ravaging beasts. Men, women and children had all perished. Islamists and secularists, militants and civilians; the demons didn't care about Iraq's sectarian divisions. Baghdad was a city where death was a common sight, but never before had there been anything like this.

'God must be angry with us,' said Kamil as we walked through a street that was silent apart from the sickly trickle of blood.

'No,' I said. 'Whatever these things are, they did not come from God.'

'There, look!' said Kamil as he pointed down a side alley. 'One of the big ones.'

We looked at each other, and nodded.

'For Allah,' said Kamil.

'For humanity,' I replied.

We circled through the network of alleyways that made up this part of the city. The demon warlord appeared to be lost and had started to smash through buildings, perhaps in frustration at being trapped, or simply in a search for blood. As we approached, we could hear gunshots.

'Pistol,' whispered Kamil.

'An ally then,' I said. I gestured for him to head down one alley while I went down another. I think this manoeuvre was called a pincer movement, at least if Hollywood was anything to go by. We timed it carefully and I took cover behind a trash can. The demon didn't seem to notice me – it was too distracted with whoever was already shooting at it.

I counted down and then opened fire with my rifle. I was much more used to the recoil now and aimed low. The first burst of bullets destroyed the merchant stall next to the demon before I managed to veer the gun over onto the target and fire another burst.

To my dismay, this one didn't die as quickly as the djinn or the hellhounds and chitterlings that we had faced so far. It roared in anger and turned to face me, ignoring the pistols. I could see Kamil attacking it from one side, and the stranger, a bearded man in desert-camouflage body armour, shooting from the other.

The warlord smashed away the trash can with its massive claw, leaving me completely exposed. I threw myself backwards and kept shooting.

I've seen enough movies and read enough books to have heard of the concept of time standing still when your life is in danger. It felt to me that this is exactly what now happened. I probably screamed – I honestly can't remember. The demon raised its huge clawed fist, ready to smash it down upon my prone form. I raised my rifle and squeezed the trigger as hard as I could manage. Another burst of fire peppered the demon, causing it to jerk violently as the bullets penetrated its flesh and pinged against its armour. Yet still that mighty fist continued to slam downwards.

I pointed my rifle higher at its face. Its mouth was gaping wide, drool dripping down from its fangs. I fired straight into its dark maw. This time it really staggered back from the impact. I think I must have screamed again, sensing victory was near… and then my rifle magazine ran empty.

'Shit!'

Yet still I could hear gunshots even though my rifle was only clicking. I realised that Kamil and the new guy were still shooting the demon. While it had been distracted with me, they had got right up behind it. With a roar, the demon swung around to face them, sensing I was no longer a threat.

'I guess you don't know about reloading either, huh?' I muttered as I slammed a new clip home. I opened fire at point blank range and blasted it into red goo that splashed all over me.

'Salima!' yelled Kamil as I dizzily sank back to the ground.

I was shaking so much I thought I was about to tear myself apart.

'Well, shit,' I said again as he embraced me.

I became aware of the other man watching us with a frown. 'Good shooting,' he said to me.

'Thanks, I think…'

His name was Hussein. Although he didn't say as much, I suspected he was a militant of some description, maybe even a terrorist. Perhaps he had been responsible for the bombing that had killed my friend Faiza and set this whole thing in motion. I didn't like him. I don't think he liked me. However, he seemed content to follow me.

I had ripped my headscarf away and used it to mop up the goo from my face and arms. I felt glad for my short hair – it couldn't fall into my eyes and block my view.

My motley squad moved onwards through the streets, and it soon began to pick up more members. Most were men, but there were some boys and a few women and girls. They were of all ages and backgrounds, most native to Baghdad, but some were not. One was even a woman journalist from America who had come here to report on the portals. She was now recording my leadership as a video on her mobile phone. All were united in their desire to fight back. All seemed willing to follow me. I didn't understand why.

'You're the only person in the city, or perhaps even the world, that seems to have a plan and be seen taking a lead,' said Kamil.

'What about the security forces or the police? The Government? Shouldn't they be doing something?'

'Running for their lives, I expect,' said a man named Tariq. He was the oldest member of my little army and also the most cynical.

'Tariq is probably right,' said Kamil. 'We're it. We're the saviours of the world, or at least Baghdad.'

'I think it will take a lot more than the few of us to save Baghdad.'

The city was in ruins. Smoke poured from fires across the city. The gutters ran red with blood. Demons ran amok, killing anyone they could find. We shot a lot of them, but more continued to pour through the portals.

'We need more ammo,' I said. I had managed to scrounge some more magazines for my rifle off people with similar guns, but as a group we were all running low now.

'I know where to get some. More guns too. Bigger ones,' said Hussein. The militant had remained mostly quiet during our expedition, much to my relief. As he spoke though, everyone fell quiet and watched me. I had expressed my concerns about him to Kamil earlier, but I guess anyone could sense the tension.

For a moment I just didn't know what to say. I really didn't want to know about the stockpiles of Hussein and his friends. I really didn't want to touch equipment that was stained with the blood of innocents. Should I have asked him where his stuff came from, why it was there?

'Fine, let's go,' was all I said in the end.

Kamil gave me a reassuring nod.

'I guess war really does change everything,' I said wearily, and we headed onwards.


The monk adjusted his position. His weak bones ached and every so often he had to shift his limbs to avoid straining them. The stale air was making him cough and his breathing was ragged. Judging by the subtle shift in the gloom under the dust cloud that encircled the earth, night was beginning to fall. He retrieved a torch from the pockets of his tatty faded robe and continued to read.


That's how I found myself perched on the balcony of one of the taller minarets in Baghdad with a shoulder-fired missile launcher. Kamil was there to assist me, and our exploits were being broadcast by Theresa, as the American journalist was called, who had now been joined by two colleagues named David and Kieran, bringing with them a proper camera and boom microphone. I gather they were broadcasting our adventure live across the world. Last week, the thought of being on international television would have thrilled me.

Right now, I was more focused on the task of firing rockets at demons.

Of the muezzin whose minaret we were using as our mobile rocket platform there was no sign. In all likelihood he was dead. By this point in time, the demon army packed the city and aside from the couple of hundred people in my force who had survived so far, there were few living people to be seen. I had a horrid feeling that the vast majority of the city's population was dead, and the rest had probably fled.

From our vantage point, I could see the blood-red demons swarming through the streets, running into the pockets of resistance of my army. Unsurprisingly, the most effective group seemed to be Hussein and his militant friends who were deploying their illicitly-held arsenal to the maximum. There was perhaps some irony to be had in seeing them fight alongside members of the security forces that just a week ago they had been waging a brutal terrorist war against. Now was just not the time for remarking on this social shift though.

'There,' said Kamil, pointing between the buildings to one of the city squares. 'Three warlords, all grouped up.'

It was us who had named the demon types. Some we had encountered and named earlier, like the warlords, which were the huge monsters who appeared to be the leaders. Meanwhile, as well as the chitterlings and hellhounds already encountered, we had now identified shockers – human-sized demons that were lightly armoured and bearing jagged swords who appeared to be the foot troops, warlocks – tall spindly creatures with tentacles that appeared to attack from range by spitting acid, and bulls – squat heavy-built beasts that charged down their enemies at high speed and impaled them on the huge thick horns, or simply trampled them into the ground.

I looked to where Kamil was pointing and nodded. 'Loaded?'

'Ready to fire.'

'Locking on target… Three, two, one…' I squeezed the trigger. With a pop and a puff of smoke, the cylinder jerked and ejected a small missile, which sped straight for the congregation of warlords. There was an explosion a few seconds later and smoke, flames and demon goo filled the square.

'Good shot!' cheered Kamil.

I smiled and glanced at Theresa who was babbling in English into the microphone. I only knew the basics of the language, but I recognised my name being spoken and could guess that she was reporting on our activities. She was interrupted by her mobile phone ringing, and fiddled with it urgently trying to make it stop without breaking the flow of her speech.

I stared over the railing across the city and shook my head. All the streets were swarming with demons, and more were pouring through the portals. I could see a few pockets where my army were fighting back, but the effect we were having was minimal. What's more, from what I had managed to pick up from the Americans, portals were now popping up across the whole world.

'We may be winning the battles, but we are not winning the war…' I said forlornly.

Kamil put his hand on my shoulder. 'We can't give -'

'Salima!' The interruption came from Theresa, who spoke in patchy Arabic. 'Leave the city we must!' I turned to her to see her face screwed up into a look of utter terror. Her phone was at her ear and she was switching between speaking urgently into it and talking to me.

'What? Why? What's happening?' I asked, trying to keep my language simple for her benefit.

'There is bomb coming. Big bomb!' She frowned, not knowing the Arabic word, so she settled for the English one. It was a word that was instantly recognisable, even with my basic understanding of the language. 'Nuclear!'

There wasn't much I could say to that. 'Well, shit!'

'We have a van,' said David in English. He was a handsome young African-American man wearing a Star Wars t-shirt. 'Let's go.'

'Wait, what about the others?' I said. 'We can't just leave them.' They didn't seem to understand me, so I tried in English. 'The others!'

David and Theresa looked at each other. 'Phone?' said

David. He used his fingers to mime a phone. I shook my head. I had one but it had been lost hours ago, and I had no idea if the others had them. 'No phones.'

Kamil tapped my arm. 'I don't think Allah will mind…' he said, pointing to the minaret's microphone and speaker system that was normally reserved for the muezzin to proclaim the holy call to prayer.

A minute later, my voice was echoing across the city, broadcast at full volume. 'Evacuate!' I called out to anyone who could hear me. 'They are going to nuke the city! A real nuclear bomb! You must leave!' I am sure the demons could hear me, but given their experience so far, I doubted they knew what a 'nuke' was.

I repeated the message three times then added '*Allahu Akbar*' for good measure. God is greatest.

'We must go!' said Theresa urgently in English. Kamil nodded and tugged at my sleeve again. 'Come on!'

David's van turned out to be an airport rental vehicle. It wasn't in the greatest of condition, but it did start up after a worrying number of engine turns. David and Theresa sat up front. I, Kamil and Kieran the sound man piled into the back along with our rocket launcher and remaining missiles. We also still had our guns and ammo.

David hit the accelerator and the van lurched off down the road, heading out of the city. Kamil peered through the small window in the van door. 'They're following us,' he yelped. 'They have bulls!'

We'd seen the heavy charging demons in action. Their speed was phenomenal and they could easily catch us. 'Open the door!' I said, gesturing to Kieran to help me with the missile launcher. There were two rockets left.

Kamil leaned forward and pulled the lever to open the rear doors. As soon as they were released, they slammed wide open, caught in the draft of the moving vehicle. I caught a glimpse of half a dozen bull demons closing in on us rapidly.

'Shit!' I fiddled with the rocket launcher, trying to mount it over my shoulder and aim correctly, something that wasn't as easy in a moving van which juddered over every pothole and crater on the Baghdad roads.

'Come on Salima…' said Kamil, who grabbed one of the assault rifles and sprayed the approaching demons with bullets. The bulls were well armoured though and the hail of fire just bounced off them.

'Trying!' I yelped. The launcher bumped up and down on my shoulder and I lost my aim once again. Kieran seemed to sense my distress and tried to hold it steady for me.

'I guess we have about ten seconds!' warned Kamil. 'Nine. Eight. Oh merciful God, they are getting close. Six. Five…'

I could see them through the aiming reticule window on the shoulder-firing missile launcher. I waited until the gaping maws of the charging demons filled the view screen and then I pulled the trigger. Once again I felt the cylinder jerk as it spewed out a rocket, which hurtled straight into the oncoming demons and detonated with an explosion that blasted us backwards into the interior of the van.

'Did I get them?' I asked from flat on my back, my head ringing painfully from where it had smashed against the van bulwark.

'Yeah, you got them, Salima,' said Kamil, peering through the open doors at the huge puddle of goo. 'You got them.'

A few minutes later, the van hurtled out through the outer limits of Baghdad, heading into the desert. We left the doors open – trying to close them while the vehicle was moving too quickly was just needlessly dangerous. And so it was from the distance of many miles that we could watch the city's final moments.

A streak hurtled down from high altitude, leaving a stream of vapour in its wake. It disappeared into the cityscape of domes, minarets and high-rise buildings, and for a moment all was quiet. We flattened ourselves onto the floor of the van and buried our heads in our arms. There was a blinding flash that left spots in my vision despite them being closed and covered, and a few seconds later a deep rumble like thunder that roared and roared and didn't stop.

When I looked up I could see the city enshrouded in dust, the distinctive mushroom cloud rising above. Baghdad had survived centuries of bitter bloody conflict – the crusades of distant past, the tyranny of recent history, the war, the terrorism. However, it could not survive this.

There would be time to mourn for the dead – my family and friends, my neighbours, the millions of residents I never knew, even the militants. Was it entirely my fault? I fear I'll never know. What I do know is that I can fight back. Can I still save the world? Or will the planet follow in the footsteps of Baghdad?


Much to the monk's most profound dismay, the journal seemed to end there. What was left appeared to be more of a postscript, although still in Saint Salima's impeccable Arabic typing. He shifted position again, ignoring the painful creaking in his legs and continued to the very end.


The nuclear bomb on Baghdad was the first in humanity's war against the demonic invasion, but it was not the last. Over the course of the next ten years or so, the world's entire stockpile of nuclear weapons was deployed against countless targets across the world. The consequences were terrible. Life had been pretty much eradicated across much of the planet. Only a few areas remain untouched – parts of Africa, Canada and China seem to have escaped the worst of it.

It is estimated that around ninety-five percent of living beings on the planet died, many at the hands of the demons themselves, others caught up in mankind's attempts to fight back. Still more died in droves at what came next. The animal kingdom suffered even worse.

Perhaps the most deadly consequence is the one the world will have to live with for the next few hundred years at least – the worst predictions of a full scale nuclear war come true. A dust cloud, hundreds of miles thick now blankets the planet's atmosphere, blocking the light of the sun completely. Planet Earth now exists in perpetual cold and darkness. Only modern technologies kept life sustainable until a better solution emerged from the most unlikely of places.

However, we won. The demons attacked in billions, but they were not prepared for the level of firepower that humanity was now able to fight back with. It eventually became clear to us that while the demons were numerous, they were still ultimately limited in number. A turning point eventually came after countless nukes had been dropped, napalm had been deployed, rockets and missiles fired. The flow of demons from the portals began to slow to a trickle and then stopped altogether.

I was at the forefront during the whole period. It turned out that Theresa's footage of me leading my force against the demons in Baghdad had been transmitted across the entire world. Right from the start, I was seen as the expert in demon warfare, the general who would lead the forces of humanity to victory. I was summoned to meetings with political and military leaders from across the globe. These old men and a few women hung on to every word I said, me – just a teenage girl from Baghdad.

To date I have no idea whether the advice and leadership I provided helped, or if I was simply an inspirational figure to rally behind. I don't think it really matters though. The outcome was as good as it could get. The demons were gone, destroyed now and forever more. Expeditions sent through the remaining standing portals returned intact and unharmed, stating that while the demon realm bubbled with fire and lava, there was not a single demon left to be found. Already scientists are collaborating to find a way to harvest that energy to power our world left without sunlight.

The priests and scholars of all faiths are up in arms. For millennia they have been warning of the forthcoming apocalypse. They never expected that the humans would actually win. Nothing in the holy texts predicted that outcome. In this post-apocalyptic period, I suspect the old religions will fade way to be replaced by something new.

I have returned to what's left of Baghdad. I stand now in the place where it all began, and I leave this memoir for a future age. What will the world be like in ten years? A hundred? A thousand? Will I be remembered, or will I be forgotten? I do not know.

In all this time, I have never told anyone that it was I who called forth the demons. This guilt I carry is a burden for me alone. Yet, it too should not be forgotten. To you, who are reading this – now you know. What will you do with this information, I wonder?

Walk in the light of God, dear reader. *Allahu Akbar*.

Salima Fayed Al-Jahid – General of Humanity's Forces against the Demonic Hordes.

With Salima's signature, the memoir came to an end, and the monk sat back in contemplation. He pulled himself to his feet, groaning at the explosion of pain as he did so. He turned and stared across the tattered remains of the ancient room.

'Your secret stays with me, my saint,' he spoke in the modern tongue, his voice raspy with sickness. 'You were not to blame. The djinn itself said as much.'

There was no response to his mutterings but a faint breeze stirred the dust.

'You were not forgotten. You have been remembered as the saviour of the world. It is with your grace and leadership that civilisation exists at all.'

He turned to leave, to wander back into the wilderness to die.

'I take your burden, Saint Salima. I take your guilt, relieving you of it. That is my new pilgrimage. This I promise.'

He headed towards the remains of the doorframe and his foot knocked against something that rolled into the corner with a clatter, whipping up more of the dust. It was a lamp, one of the truly ancient types that was made of copper and shaped like a jug.

As the monk left the room, a wispy plume of smoke puffed out of the lamp's spout, almost as if a genie were to pop out. The vapour mixed with the dust and was gone.

# Only So Far

## A. Rodenberger

*This was when
the world was burning…*

First came the mighty multi-hued oaks that grew overnight. The scattered shard of stained-glass window had turned to drip in the bake of over-violet sun, melting and melding into the thirsting, bony-fingered roots of struggling saplings. The liquefied remains of Christs and Marys and saints and sinners all pooled up on dying fields, becoming one and the same, swirled into each other above loamy topsoil, a vision of pooled vertigo.

Amaranthine red, carmine pink, the deep blue of midnight's silence, emerald, mint, ochre, and onyx filled the brittle bark veins that snaked up weak limbs held out as if asking for rain that hadn't come in months.

Soon after, the fragile limbs fell to earth and spilled their *coloursapblood* like secrets across cracked pavement and brown grass. Rotting fruit remained hanging, calcified and petrified, split open upon striking ground. Each broken piece contained abalone swirl, each section a stone whirlwind of shine and gleam. The pericarp, the septum, the loculus pulp all glimmer and shine in the overbearing daylight. Incredible, inedible. A feast for eyes, but not belly.

The oceans receded slowly at first, relieving themselves of dying fish on sandy beaches at low tide. Lakes dried up, withered like aged skin, left carcasses of once moaning frogs and the silent shells of tortoise. Yellow heat had touched the world with sickness, had parched its skin and kept on, burning out the retinas of the few who'd tired of dying slow and ached for natural wither. The freedom in death was stronger than the prison of living.

*This was when*
*the red fire of the east coast*
*danced a cross-continental Lambada*
*with the yellowed smoke of the west coast…*

Televisions sang lullabies of black static and white noise. No reports, no warnings, no sirens, just the hum of soft harp through speakers set up hastily on street corners and meeting places, on street lamps and roving garbage trucks. The pluck of harp strings was quiet in the beginning – soft, soothing – but had come to scratch like nails along the metal of our ears.

The harp sounded, another block destroyed.

The harp sounded, another hundred people missing.

The harp sounded, but only after the explosions.

The harp sounded, and sounded, and sounded…

Until it became a thing to drown out, to ignore. No longer a symbol of calm, the harp came to be its own angel of death, waging war on senses and gonging long into the night like a death knell on repeat.

We could hear it reverberate through our teeth and in our dreams as we wept over oceans we could see, but could not reach. The ringing caused waves to swell and strike beaches cluttered with cans and plastic, sloughed skin and dying birds, eyeless heads of fish and kelp the colour of melt. Each ring of strings sent us into convulsions, made our insides shake, liquefied our cellular structures.

Sunsets ceased to be, never came, never left. Perpetual bright on every horizon; dull red to the west, gaseous yellow to the east. We wondered if we were the orange middle of everything. We wondered if everyone else heard harps before dying too. We wondered if, once planted in the earth, we would still hear them long after death. Would our ears cake up with dirt and earthworm and maggot and rot and harp?

Strangers came from both sides, holed up in empty houses, made homes of hollow, nests of leftovers, wanting to live in our orange. The orange was getting smaller, crushed in from outside. Strangers slept atop us, piled up in rooms one on top of one on top of another like human bunk-beds. Soon no one could sleep through the always *harpsong*.

*This was when*
*the screams of Boston*
*sounded like the screams of Atlanta*
*sounded like the screams of Houston*
*sounded like the screams of Seattle*
*and everyone burned the same...*

Twelve hours, fourteen hours, seventeen hours a day; the sun kept constant vigil over the earth's browning surface. Ground split, cracked, dried up like skin set to be leathered.

The thirsty sucked final drops from spigots and wells, lay beneath open taps with dried and wishing mouths open, sucked dry every bottle at every gas station and grocery store before they ever had time to store them up in bunkers. The hot came too fast and within a week had allowed only a single hour of moonlight every day. For twenty-three hours, the world baked without reprieve. No way to turn off the oven, no way to keep cool.

Basements became as hot as lawns, but there was warm shade. Whole families curled up in dark corners, like vampires hiding from the yellowed-world. They slept fitfully, sweating together against the walls that seemed to bow inward from the heat, the home in slickery melt around them. Brother smelled like sister smelled like father smelled like mother, their tears becoming sweat, their sweat becoming sticky.

The metal of the family car crinkled, smooshed, pancaked into a goopy driveway mess of paint, rust, and rubber. Oil snaked out from the puddle and into the street, a black slither that stunk up the neighbourhood and fouled the air with putrefaction. This was the new pollution, the earth was all heat-melt.

The house sank. Soil crawled through brittle foundation, buried some alive, still curled up in their corners hiding from the daylight. Earthworms slinked across cobwebbed basements in search of moisture, found none, dried up like twigs along windowsills and doorways.

*This was when*
*skin boiled, flaked, and flew into the skies*
*mixed with the ash and sparse rain*
*that never seemed to be enough...*

If left out in the sun too long, a person's skin sloughed off, fell to the ground, lay puddled up and stinking in the lawn like old deli meat. There was no burn, only melt and puddle. Like a pile of human there in the grass, folded in upon itself and melting together as if under heat lamps.

Rain showed its wet face again. Brief and taunting, a quick minute of downpour surprised us over and over again. We sat in darkened doorways, staring up at skies that promised only ash snowfall. We emaciated, dry, stick figures stood in silence, mouths upturned, drinking past the ash that collected on lips and tongues, stuck to lips like lovers' kisses we no longer wanted. The ash was briny, bitter to the taste, a sour death upon the palate. It was the taste of neighbours, their children, the taste of strangers sun-baked and withered and picked up by uncaring gusts of wind and dust and carried up into what atmosphere remained.

We could taste their religion and their fear.

We could taste their passion and their dreams.

We could taste their silence and their screams.

We tasted air and death, waited for the sky to open up and fill our bellies with drink, soak our faces and bodies in wet. Green clouds turned brown, swirled menacing but still the sun penetrated. And still we stood in doorways and watched our arms and legs drift off in pieces of tallow skin, never to be seen again until landing on another's tongue across the city.

Would that they could taste my religion and my fear.

Would that they could taste my passion, my dreams.

Would that they could taste my silence since I refuse to scream.

> *This was when*
> *the Sun's settings and risings*
> *were at their most vibrant,*
> *but no one had the time to stop and watch;*
> *they feared being gobbled up*
> *by its clumsy, earthly protégés…*

Some learned to speak the language of fire, spoke in tongues of flame, tasted heat and ate in hellish burn. Their voices were ash and soot, their eyes betraying *hyperviolence*, their fingers twitching and in need of heat. Nimble with wires and timers, hands flew across containers and tape and bits of nail and screw, ball bearings and hurt compacted into hand-sized packages. Some learned to harness anger and madness in the time of anger and madness.

The silence before the booms made tension, crackled up spines, up into craniums, tickled nervous systems in awkward ways. Little spurts of voltage climbing up backs and muscle. The sound of nothing echoed off long-empty basketball courts and cul-de-sacs, vacant apartment buildings and businesses already half-blown to char. The air was fat with possibility; death hung like fog across neighbourhoods.

Uncle got caught in the beginning. No one could tell amongst all the rubble, but he stepped wrong on a trashcan lid, became supernova there in the middle of the street. He became starlight, orange and white, smoke and flame, alpha and omega all in an instant. We never knew who left that one for him to find, but it didn't matter. Soon, everyone was a firebug. Everyone had a missing limb, a missing friend or relative, a missing pet; all blown skyward and scattered across a dying city, little clouds of flesh and red. We were all part-phantom.

Mother became martyr. Weary of hiding, we strapped flame to her body, hid it beneath fabric finery, robes, a t-shirt from my childhood. She called out to them, they came, surrounded her, smelled her as victim as she feigned fear. They circled, grinned. Saliva dripped from snarling lips, blackened fingers reached out to grab her.

She did not scream. She did not flinch. In the moment before loudest silence, they saw the fire in her eye, turned to run, felt the ground shake beneath them as she unleashed her own Prometheus valentine upon them. The streets are quieter now. The city naps longer and so do we.

*This was when*
*everyone's lips cracked,*
*when sleeping in a full bathtub*
*seemed logical…*

When the constellations reappeared, they were askew. None were recognizable anymore though no one could remember their original positions. We just knew. Ursa major was a cluster of gleam, Cassandra shined black - obsidian. Libra leaned heavy to one side, Taurus became a mewling calf.

We drank soured milk, thirsted for the clump, became ravenous for *greenmoldbread*. Pus dripped from sores at the corners of our mouths and rot replaced enamel. The skin hung from our bones, oozed and peeled and left in heavy footprints behind us. We were walking dead, too weak to run from the fire that was surely on its way to consume us. We could see its phosphorescent glow beyond the mountains on either side.

Our ribs were song-less xylophones, our fingers frail tools corroding, breaking down into slender maim. We never felt the blood dribble out and off the fingertips. Never felt our hands go numb from loss. Our lungs sang in whistles and breathlessness. When the fire came, we could only stand and watch.

The porcelain protected. Too slow to get out of the way, we turned our makeshift houses into battlements; metal sheeting around the sides, slathered in creams and frozen. We hid in bathtubs, their slickery white an armour against the laughing, dancing flames that rose up over mountain ranges and sprinted across *deadgrassfields*, hungry just to burn.

Thin and frail, we all fit in the tub together, me and son and daughter. Like sardines, staring up through holes in the roof at cloudless sky. The fire ate around us, over us, singed bits of hair and parts of diseased skin. I wondered why the moon smiled down at us. I wondered when we last smiled. The fire passed, turned brown fields to black, left in smoking ruin. Still the moon smiled.

> *This was when*
> *everyone ran*
> *towards the middle of the country,*
> *clamoured over mountains and*
> *fought over soon-to-be dry rivers…*

I awoke from a dead dream, full of nothing white and soft ringing. Hands reached out to me from the ether, tugged, pulled, pushed, waved off. They laid their hands on, cupped my face and twirled my hair, ran fingers over my eyes and touched grey matter through the crevices. The voice of rotting angels made love to my ears, filled me with cold and want, pimpled the skin on my arms, whispered that it wasn't my time, that I was time, that time was all I had left. It was the most touch I had felt since... ever. I wanted to stay. I wanted to remain in someone else's cold grasp.

I awoke in a field, a bed of burned grass beneath me, stiff stems of char my pillow. Ashen scars covered exposed skin like I was sacrifice. The sun's corona bled through the black clouds above, burned its image against my eyelids, kept shining when eyes closed. I saw the earth in circles, each object magnified by this new corona-sight. Everything was rounded, shaped, curved into itself over and over again, never breaking the rim. The oily clouds above parted, spilled red light onto the surface, covered us all in hot, broiled the ground. Some died of heat-stroke. Others wished they had.

I awoke sheathed in metal, hot from the sun and smoke clamouring towards the mountainside. The ranges were visible; snow-capped pyramids in the distance. I wondered if I could remember ever seeing snow. It was so white. I could only remember red and yellow, orange, black, grey, dust, char. White was a nothing colour, snow was a nothing thing. I could see it, so I could touch it and if I could touch it, then I could taste it. The metal got heavy and I moved again, plodded towards the mountains.

I awoke in melt, snow dripping down my scarred skin. I had packed myself away in ice, hoped to avoid the mob racing to the top of the screaming mountain. I had covered myself in snow-crystal, waited, watched through the magnification and replication of molecules, like spider's eyes, as their heavy feet thudded over me like thunder. I was thirsty, drank from the walls of my hiding place, remembered the names of my children as the fluid coated my throat, wept at how things had become and drank those tears as well.

I awoke in a bombed-out shed. A concrete structure bathed in graffiti and old lives I could smell as if they were standing right beneath my nose. Rubble coated the floor, dust and mud covered the shattered windows that remained. In the moment, I felt new and clean. No one else had found it yet and I claimed it as mine. Snow-chill wafted through crevices, crept up legs, tickled hair and skin, reminded me of its constancy. They had not come yet, but someone would come across my place (*my* place!) at some point. Would that I could fight to keep it. Would that I could fight to stand any longer. Would that someone would simply end me and let me pass on.

> *This was when*
> *an untouched field of wheat*
> *was a danger instead of a way to feed…*

We awoke in drown, lungs full of flood. Restless, placental. We floated in the home, watched our life swim by and sink below us. Fractured picture frames, unpaid bills, the family pet, good china, building blocks, a dimly lit lamp still plugged into the rotting wall, glowing beneath the surface. The brick house eroded from the inside, the insulation tearing like dead tissue.

Our bodies filled, bloated, dead whitened. Fingers plumped like sausage, broke wedding rings. Shirts stretched, tore, ripped with the sound of soft breath and broken lovers' hearts. On the wall: the childrens' heights, marked in pencil and pen, slowly being erased. I screamed at the vanish, inhaled more water, forgot the names of my children.

The wall clock cracked under pressure. The big hand between twelve and one, the little hand hung limp in the current, swinging between five and seven. We could hear the chimes faintly through the water, fighting tide and flow.

Water filled my orifices; clogged my nose, my ears, found ways past my eyes and filled my skull. I could feel me bubble up from inside, liquid fill rising. I heard the waves crash against the arterial walls inside me, collapsing against blood-lines and pumping organs. Water mixed with blood mixed with water mixed with blood.

The phone floated by. I put it to my ear, heard sea-sirens on the other end scream-whispering as if a universe away.

> *You have our deepest sympathies.*
> *Our condolences.*
> *You have such a lovely home.*
> *The picture is heartbreaking.*
> *Your clock is broken.*
> *You are drowning.*

The water kept me, floated me, bumped me into the ceiling and the chandelier and other furniture. I let the phone sink to the floor, watched its hypnotic drowning, a spiralling downward. My wife was sending the children up the chimney, motioned for me to join. I wouldn't fit and she knew it. Our eyes locked, our fishy lips locked, held each other until the bloat made that impossible and soon she was gone. I floated there in the quiet roar, watched our things float and sink, move and sway, before sitting in the chair still by the fireplace. I waited for the return I knew wasn't coming.

My skin began to prune, spoil, suck in on itself.

I waited.

> *This was when*
> *the roads clogged with automobiles*
> *full of gasoline, dormant and laying like a wet wick*
> *across the world*
> *ready to be lit by*
> *the fires on either end…*

The sign is portal, remnant history, memory leavings. Sun-faded red and black paint, the words indecipherable now. But we know the gist, we know the slant. The signs are nothing marks, near-prehistoric scribbles made by ancestors recently dead, paid for by ancestors recently dead, followed by ancestors recently dead.

Chunks of concrete where the road used to be. Chunks of buildings where our cities used to be. Chunks of bite where our skin used to be. The world halved, cleaved in two, the pieces falling into smoke and ruin. Char-rusted cars became playgrounds as we make-believed our way from the flood of flame behind us, crawled and jumped on exoskeletons made of Chrysler and Ford, Volkswagen and Audi, Honda and Fiat. What was left almost made us laugh in its obviousness; the world was here on the road, dead or dying. No country had escaped the burn; we all burned the same.

> *This was when*
> *the explosions, like firecrackers,*
> *started in Santa Barbara and Miami*
> *and didn't sleep until*
> *the last car had been*
> *kissed with flame in Topeka weeks later...*

Crushed by the waiting. No news came from anywhere, silence from the television, the radio. Papers had been hoarded, turned into a million wicks, gave us inky snow. Words curled in the air like frost breath:

> *Another fi*
> *highway shut-do*
> *ies on the brin*
> *no answers fr*
> *engulfe*
> *nic ensu*
> *e missi*
> *mass graves*

Someone had set the earth in revolt, tilted its axis askew, found the chip in its shoulder and dug fingers deep inside the undulating wound and kept digging until they finally scraped its heart. I hope they burned themselves in the process, lost hands to magma rising, core melt, lost self within the shifting plates because our hearts are made of dust now.

Dried out, crumbled, held in place by the fear that

cocoons us. No one touches anymore. We hug for protection, not for affection. Held hands means helping someone run from the noise. Kisses are meant for the dead and the dying. Tradition, decorum, history… these mean nothing now.

Everywhere looks the same. Ash coats the air depressing grey. Our clouds are anaemic, in need of sun and fresh air.

The world is arid and the sky thirsts the way we do.

*This is when*
*we could see*
*flaming highways*
*from the heavens…*

A postcard, still (unbelievably) stuck to a kitchen wall: *"Be glad you weren't here."*

*This was when*
*hiding out in open fields*
*made of burn and fallout*
*was our best solution…*

A rabbit stared at us from its one remaining eye, as if to blame us for the one that dangled low from socket. Optic nerves kept it in hang, coated in blood-dried maroon and crust. No movement from his furred face or ears; whiskers limp and twitchless, one foot mangled from some other nameless terror. He hid beneath the porch, became family, eulogized with us but broke none of the bread we left out as apology.

It was the first animal we'd seen in forever. Pets had disappeared or died in waves; cats and dogs became vanish, song-less birds flew far out of eyesight, we were lucky to hear crickets over the destruction. Rivers and lakes were coated in dead fish, rot-float, glimmerless scales and scum. We took to eating root and plant, nut and berry where they hadn't mutated into things inedible. Our mouths tasted like earth, gaps in teeth filled with topsoil, blackened at the gums, ached for something juicy.

Our lips wetted over the rabbit. We hungered for a single

leg of deer or frog. A sparrow would be feast in this moment, red breasted and roasted over ruby fire. Old meat in the pantry, spoiled and brown-rotted, but we ate it anyway. Got sick on ourselves, sat around in wallow and filth. Felt the sick inside us, gnawing away at our insides and withering our bones to brittle.

I wondered if there would be future generations to excavate our bones and what they would think when they dug us up, great holes blown out of our skulls, our cheeks, our femurs and ribs. What will they think when our brittle bones dig up black instead of off-white? What will they think when they see whole families buried together, bones clung together as if to shield from blast? What kind of history will they put together from the stories that our bones tell them? Will they even care?

The rabbit moved from beneath the porch. We all gave chase.

> *This was when*
> *we understood real fear*
> *and ran away together…*

They had warped. Neighbours had become fun-house mirrored versions of themselves, morphed into flat-faced reflections with no mouths and no noses. Their rheumy eyes stared out from skin web-cracked like divorce china or newly split earth. A small army stood at the foot of the porch, itself warped and cracked from rumblings deep beneath the foundation.

The stars fell to whisper. The neighbours breathed as one, rapid wheezy whistles, and stared. It was no use for us to hide behind tattered drapes; they smelled us inside, aware that we were whole and unmarred. They could smell our completeness, could hear our blood running quick beneath bruised and yellowed skin, pumped through better veins and aortas and arteries. Our living was loud, our lives were grate against whatever they had become.

Daughter clung to teddy behind the couch, crouched as if waiting for explosion. Son stood, shaking with eyes closed, on the other side of the window. Mother had passed already, falling into sickness before trying to claw her way through the walls in search of death's chariot.

The divots of her nails left tracks along the wall, the only physical proof of her travels, maps of her descent into the virus. Bits of blood still splattered the once beige walls. Bits of hair and nail, tears and dust, remained along the floorboards.

Son stopped shaking. Daughter whimpered. Son looked out the window, sighed and gripped the rebar tight, white-knuckled around the rusted brown. Strength blazed somewhere deep behind his pupils; something inside him had caught fire and burned hot. We waited for them to come... and then they did.

# Somebody to Play With

## G. Clark Hellery

'Will you play with me?' Sarah's porcelain white hand gently nudged the flesh of the young boy. The boy looked back at her inquisitive face but he didn't move. She nudged him again then pulled back her hand in disgust: it was covered in a clear slime which smelled faintly rancid. Sarah wiped her hand on her bright red pinny as she looked into the blood-shot eyes of the boy. 'Will you play with me?' she repeated. He didn't reply.

Sarah looked around her. There were lots of people laying on the ground. She frowned. Was this some form of Sleeping Lions, the game where you have to lie perfectly still or you were out? Sarah pouted. Well that wasn't very nice of every-body, to play a game and not invite her to play as well. She looked more closely at the little boy on the floor, and the woman laying next to him whom Sarah assumed was his mother. They were both very good at Sleeping Lions she thought, but what a strange place to play, right here in the middle of the supermarket.

Sarah spun slowly on her kitten heels, looking at all the other people playing Sleeping Lions. Then she spun again, a little bit faster and giggled as her dark blue skirt billowed out around her. She continued spinning until she got dizzy and had to grab on to the cold metal shelves for support. She staggered away from the boy and his mother, still laughing to herself.

Sarah closed her eyes and steadied herself before slowly peeling open one eye to check if the room was still spinning. It was, so holding onto the shelves she carefully tip-toed to the end of the aisle, keeping her eyes closed the whole time. The next time she opened her eyes she was in the chilled foods section. She wrinkled her nose at the mixed smells of mouldy cheeses and slices of dead flesh, their wrappers split open. The chill air descended from the open freezer doors like a mist. Sarah could just make out the outlines of other people playing Sleeping Lions but they didn't seem to be covered in the same slime as the people Sarah had seen before. Sarah started to approach an old woman but stopped suddenly. She cocked her head to one side thoughtfully. She was about to ask the old woman to play but something in her expression stopped her: she looked like she was in pain. A lot of pain really, with her eyes open wide and her mouth set in a silent scream. Sarah decided to leave the chilled food section.

Sarah hurried passed the canned goods aisle, then the preserves and hot drinks, her small heels clip-clipping as she went. She paused as an idea struck her, then looked around self-consciously. No one was looking. Well that wasn't quite right, everybody was *looking* with their eyes wide, but nobody was *watching*. She tapped her toe against the dirty linoleum. Tap. Tap tap. Tap. A smile slowly spread across Sarah's face as she tapped out a rhythm then as her confidence grew she threw her hands in the air as she danced up and down the aisle, past the now green bread and weevil-infested flour.

Phew! She finally stopped dancing, exhausted but her heel caught on the bottom of her dress and she found herself falling. She tried to catch herself against the shelving, tearing the sleeve of her dress but landed heavily. She lay on the floor for a moment, too stunned to move. Finally she put her hands under her body and tried to lift herself. She fell heavily, her face smacking the floor with a loud crack. Rolling over she put her hands in front of her face. Her right wrist hung limp and flaccid but she couldn't feel any pain. Sarah groaned as she rolled onto her side and used her left wrist to help her stagger to her feet. She held her broken wrist close to her body and looked up at the signage high above the shelves. Her eyes raked back and forth until she saw the aisle she needed. She hurried, jumping over the people playing Sleeping Lions until she got to the healthcare aisle. Perusing the shelves she finally found a bandage. Tearing open the package she tried unsuccessfully to wrap the bandage around her broken wrist. She flopped down on the floor, her skirt floating around her like a small pool. Sarah focussed. She clasped the end of the bandage between her thumb and forefinger and carefully started to wind it around and around, pulling her wrist back into place. Gritting her teeth Sarah braced her hand against her thigh and taking a deep breath pushed hard, hearing a loud crack. Tying the bandage she gently flexed her hand. Her cool white fingers wiggled but she could hear a grinding noise which was worrying. She hoped she wouldn't lose her hand, she was quite attached to it. Before all this, there were people who would be able to fix her but now, Sarah looked at all the Sleeping Lions and sighed. But now... Her thoughts trailed off.

Giving herself a mental shake, Sarah stood up and brushed the dust and grime off her dress. She looked around, trying to decide what to do next. Surely there would be somebody in the supermarket who was not playing Sleeping Lions and would play with her. She hoped they would like tea parties, perhaps a picnic, or they could go exploring. She had already explored much of the supermarket but there was so much more to see. If Sarah made a friend, they could even venture *outside*. Sarah never went outside without a friend, somebody to hold her hand and help keep her safe.

Sarah walked through the aisles. She paused frequently to ask the various people if they wanted to play with her rather than continuing to play Sleeping Lions but none accepted her offer and just stared at her with blank eyes. Feeling rather dejected, Sarah found a mirror in the furniture section and studied her reflection. Large, bright blue eyes with long black eyelashes stared back at her, her face set with a little rosebud smile. Dark tresses curled around her face before bobbing like a bottle on the sea of her shoulders. She ignored her bandaged wrist and looked at the rest of her features. Her dress hung just above her knees with the red pinny adding a flash of colour and there were chubby white legs peeking out from underneath ending in her red shoes. How could anybody not want to play with her? She was adorable! Sarah frowned and pursed her lips. They were all meanies, that's what they were. All these people laying around, ignoring her, not wanting to play. Sleeping Lions was fun but not *that* much fun. Not as fun as pretend tea or hide and seek. Deciding the best place to find a play mate would be the toy aisle, Sarah moved in that direction.

There was a strange feeling in her stomach. She couldn't explain it but knew there was something inside her, something which was not part of her fabric. She thoughtfully poked her soft stomach and felt something move, something very tiny, twisting in her fibres. Sarah thought briefly about going back to the medicine aisle. She knew about germs and dirt. There was a lot of dirt in the supermarket. Sarah hoped she hadn't picked up some germs. Having germs stopped you having friends until you were fully clean. Perhaps that was why nobody wanted to play with her, because of her germs.

Shaking off her concerns, Sarah decided to look at the toys in the toy aisle, that always made her feel better. Rounding the corner she saw there were a lot of people playing Sleeping Lions, mostly children. They all looked like they were going to win as none of them moved at all, not even their eyelids. Sarah looked up at the shelves of toys. There were so many to play with, she didn't know where to start. She didn't like the frozen faces of the plastic toys, they weren't real friends at all. Sarah frowned at the stuffed creatures; there was something about their squidgy bodies which unsettled her and she moved swiftly on. Finally she found what she was looking for, the board games. She studied the titles closely before selecting a game. She stretched up to drag it off of the shelf but couldn't reach it. Putting her hands on her hips she looked around for something to stand on. She was about to wander over to the household items aisle in search of a ladder when the face of one of the girls caught her eye.

She squinted and moved closer to the girl on the floor, studying her face closely. Yes, she was sure of it. She knew this little girl. In fact they had played together. A flash of a memory, a tea party in a sunlit garden with tiny tea cups and a rose painted tea pot. Sarah thought hard and tried to remember the little girl's name. They had been friends for such a long time, Sarah even living with the girl for a time. They would snuggle under the covers and whisper secrets late into the night. Sarah had believed they would be friends forever but then the little girl was gone and Sarah had never seen her again. Sarah had gone to live with another little girl after that, but hadn't shared her secrets as she had with the girl who now lay at her feet. So why couldn't she remember her name? Frustrated she kicked out at the little girl, her small foot making contact with the girl's slimy face but barely making an impact on the drooping flesh. She absently flicked out her foot to get rid of the slime from her shoe.

Her desire to play a game left her and she crossed her arms angrily across her chest before dropping down onto the floor. Her lower lip quivered. No tears erupted from her eyes but Sarah's chest heaved in dry sobs.

Sarah thought she would cry forever but a sound stopped the sobs. Her head turned, trying to confirm where the noise was coming from until she had pinpointed its origin. She jumped to her feet, feeling suddenly rejuvenated and hurried in the direction of the noise. Peeking around the tinned fruit Sarah could see the front entrance. There were people there! Real people, not like all the meanies she had encountered in the supermarket who were so busy playing Sleeping Lions they didn't want to play with her.

Sarah watched them as they prised open the doors. It looked like a family with a mother, a father, a teenage boy and a little girl. A little girl! A smile pulled at the corner of Sarah's mouth. A little girl, somebody she could play with. A new friend. Sarah thought frantically about how best to approach the family. She noticed the weapons they all had strapped around their bodies; the cricket bat across the teen's back and the string of long knives strapped around the mother's waist. Even the little girl was carrying a golf club. No, she couldn't just walk up to them, they might attack her and she didn't want that. They all wore face masks like she had seen one time on a television show about hospitals. Perhaps they didn't want to smell the mouldy cheese either.

The doors flew open with a ping and the family was inside. Excitement flooded Sarah as she watched them.

'Fantastic, it looks like this place hasn't been hit by other scavengers. Jackpot!' exclaimed the father.

The mother looked around cautiously. 'We need to be quick,' she said. 'Grab as much tinned food as you can.

There's plenty of storage in the van, but not too many puddings,' she looked sternly at the children. 'Off you go. I'm going to collect more cleaning supplies. Everything needs to be sterilised before we pack it. Your dad will get the bottled water. Don't touch anything else, we don't know what's contaminated. Understood?'

The boy rolled his eyes, 'You say the same thing every place we go, mum. We know, we know. Touch nothing, grab the tinned stuff, get out quick. Got it.'

'We know you know,' smiled the father as he hugged the little girl close to his side, 'It's just since this virus, we need to be really careful and it looks like there's a lot of victims around here so let's be extra quick shall we? Long drive ahead before we get to the medical camp. I heard that there's a lot of survivors there. Just think, all those other children to play with. Won't that be fun, Ellie?' The little girl nodded solemnly up at her father. 'Go on then, off you go. We'll meet back here in ten minutes, decontaminate the tins and be on our way.' The father gave his daughter a gentle nudge. She looked at him once more then ran off after her brother, her oversized back pack bouncing against her legs.

'Wait for me,' Ellie called.

'Hurry up,' he snapped.

'Can we look in the toy aisle?' Ellie begged.

Her brother sighed dramatically. 'No, you heard what the folks said, we have to be out of here in five minutes. Anyway, there'll be lots of toys at the camp. Come on,' he urged.

The little girl lagged behind. She wanted a new toy. Her favourite teddy bear had been left at the house when they had left. The virus had struck so quickly, there hadn't been time to pack much and sadly Ted was still stuck on her bed. She missed her old friend who she had slept next to every night since she was very little. At first she had begged her parents to turn the van around and go back to collect Ted, but they had refused, claimed it wasn't safe and that Ted was now dirty and unsafe. As if her friend, who she had spent so many hours playing with, was unsafe or would do anything to harm her. The little girl rolled her eyes; her parents were so paranoid. Something caught her eye. It was a little doll in a bright blue dress with a red pinny. The girl knelt down and reached out for the doll, but quickly pulled her hand back. It might be dirty. It might have *germs*. The little girl studied the doll again, her white porcelain face with big blue eyes and a small rosy mouth. She frowned when she saw the bandage around one wrist and reached out again, her fingers caressing the dark curls which framed the dolls face.

'Where are you?' shouted her brother.

Ellie's head snapped up as she looked to see where the rest of her family were. Her mum was already back by the door, disinfecting the numerous bottles of water her father was stacking by the door but she couldn't see her brother, he might find her at any second. After a moment's hesitation Ellie looked back and snatched up the doll, stuffing her into her rucksack. The doll wasn't as cuddly as Ted but she knew they would be firm friends, someone with whom she could share all her secrets and hide under the covers. Carefully zipping the bag she climbed to her feet.

'Coming,' she called, running back to her family.

# The Beast Within

## Christian D'Amico

Clamping his hand reflexively over his stomach, Jonathan frowned as a deep growl came from somewhere within him.

'Be quiet', hissed Selena, pressing herself into the shadows of the alleyway as she scanned the main road, eyes wide, alert to movement. In her hand sat a torch, turned off.

'I'm sorry sis,' Jonathan apologised. 'We've not eaten in three days. I can't control it.'

Selena paused from her vigil and turned towards her brother, her features softening as she did so. 'I know, I'm sorry. We will find something to eat soon, I promise. Your big sister would be pretty awful if she didn't take care of you, right?' She ruffled his hair, smiling softly as she did so.

Jonathan smiled back meekly. 'I guess. I don't blame you though sis. This isn't exactly… normal.'

He fiddled with the edge of his dirt-covered shirt. It was torn and falling apart. His trousers weren't faring much better, and his shoes were covered in so much grime that they looked like a brand new pair of black trainers.

They hadn't had a proper night's sleep in days, and basic things like food and hygiene had gone out the window since…

Selena wondered what she must look like to Jonathan.

With a sigh, she slid the torch into her belt and drew her younger brother in for a hug. 'We'll be fine. Just got to get to the spaceport, OK? Get off this hell-hole and we can find some food, yeah?'

Jonathan nodded silently as she hugged him. Selena felt it against her chest.

'We'll be fine,' she repeated. Another low grumble sounded, and Selena smiled slowly.

'You have to control your tummy for a bit though. Can you do that for me?'

Jonathan lifted his head, looking straight into Selena's eyes. 'That wasn't my stomach.'

Selena froze, eyes suddenly wide, looking over the top of Jonathan's head. The growl came again, this time much closer, and behind her.

In horrible slow-motion, like something out of a pre-colonisation horror-film, Selena let go of her brother and turned to face the noise. It was dark, and whilst the sound was crystal clear, the view was not. What *was* clear were the stark, bright red eyes peering out from the gloom in front of her.

The red slits of light bobbed in the dark. A tiny glint just below it gave a hint of teeth; many and sharp. It was unnatural.

The eyes exuded malice. Worse still, they exuded intelligence. The creature was enjoying the moment. Baring yet more teeth, it moved forward silently.

Selena couldn't break eye contact with it. Those eyes; there was something there. Something… primal. As she watched, Selena noticed the creature shift slightly, looking past her, to Jonathan. It wanted *him*.

*The smaller of the two is shaking. The fear cascades off him in waves; it's invigorating, making me stronger. The female doesn't interest me. Only* him*. We are connected, he and I; I must have him.*

'Run.'

Jonathan looked confused. He had been staring at the creature, right into its deep crimson eyes, mesmerised by something, as if the creature was connecting with him. This whispered word had been unexpected. 'What?'

'*Run!*'

This time it came through louder, and took on a recognisable, female tone. Selena was stepping backwards into him, sliding her arms up and out either side to make herself bigger and block line of sight from the monster to Jonathan. A veil lifted as he broke eye contact with the creature, like stepping out of fog into a clear summer's day. His reaction was instantaneous.

Grabbing Selena's arm, Jonathan spun on his heel and bolted down the alley. His grip slipped on Selena's sleeve, but she had turned to follow and was right on his heels. The pair of them pounded down the narrow back-street, not daring to look for fear of what they might see. As it was, they would have seen nothing. The creature had disappeared.

A scream made Jonathan slow down as he approached the end of the path. It led out onto the main market location for the town, but he barely had time to look at the source of the noise before Selena barrelled past, grabbing his arm frantically and pulling him out on to the road with her.

She turned right and carried on running. Jonathan craned his neck around to make out the disturbance. He caught flickers of movement on the side of a building; what looked like a rag-doll seemed to be pulled up and over the top of the roof tiles by… the darkness? Jonathan struggled to understand, and stopped trying shortly after as he concentrated on not tripping over his own feet as his sister pulled him down the market road.

Other screams echoed as they ran. Each time, Jonathan could barely see the scene taking place. People were being attacked by… things. He couldn't make anything out other than shadows and darkness, and each time they were strong enough to lift and remove the person involved from the scene of the event. Nothing was left behind; it was as if it had never happened in the first place.

'Where are we going?' asked Jonathan as another scream sounded behind him, this time more distant. Jonathan wondered if it was the same person or not.

'We're heading for the spaceport,' replied Selena, her ragged breathing causing the sentence to come out in stops and starts. She turned her head for a moment to reassure her little brother. 'Come on. Keep up.'

Jonathan looked up at Selena, but was distracted a moment later as what looked like another person came hurtling out of another side alley and collided painfully with his big sister.

Selena and the newcomer hit the road hard, drawing yelps of pain from both parties.

Jonathan lost his balance, turning almost three hundred and sixty degrees before falling onto his knees. Selena's torch rolled up and nudged gently against his left leg. He looked down groggily at it, slowly realising whose it was. He picked it up and turned it on. Pain shot through his legs as he stood up. He turned to face his sister and the stranger.

The stranger collected himself and continued running without a second thought. Selena looked up, trying to get her bearings, and saw Jonathan.

'Jon, drop, right now!'

He had learnt these past few days to trust his sister's judgement, and was rewarded with a face full of road and a sudden gust of wind that passed over him. It was bone-cold, and he shivered involuntarily.

Jonathan lifted his head and caught a glimpse of a black mass landing in front of him. It must have been going at great speed, as it turned its head to look at him but was unable to change its path of direction. Instead, the creature's head snapped back round to face Selena.

Selena picked herself up from the floor. 'Jonath-'

The monster slammed into her with the force of a truck. Selena disappeared into the darkness.

Silence.

There was nothing. Not even a scream. Jonathan dared not move, not even blink or take his eyes away from the gloom in front of him. Slowly, he lifted his sister's torch and pointed it at where Selena had been. He flicked the switch.

A weak beam of light jumped from the device, and illuminated the few metres in front of him. He waited, making no sound for fear of what might happen. After a full minute, he chanced it.

'Sis?'

Before he had finished whispering the word, Selena hit the floor, landing halfway in the pool of light. Jonathan could only make out her body up to the waist as she lay in a collection of slowly expanding gore.

Jonathan moved forward gingerly, repeating his last question through strained tears, a quiver in his voice.

'Sis?'

Selena lifted her head with a start, suddenly alert. Blood was streaming down the right side of her head and Jonathan could see claw marks on her neck and through the torn clothing on her arms and torso.

'It's not me it wants. It's y-'

With a scream, Selena was dragged backwards into the dark. All that remained were red tracks where her fingernails had caught and split on the hard surface.

'Selena!' screamed Jonathan in desperation. The response wasn't what he expected. A pair of red eyes appeared in the darkness, accompanied by a low, guttural snarl. A heartbeat later, he was running.

As he ran, Jonathan could see other people fighting for existence. They were failing.

To his left, a man tried to bar a door in vain against a creature as it smashed through the thin metal frame. Further down, a woman rocked back and forth on her knees, eyes wide, as a monster bared its claws for the killing blow. To the right, a group had teamed up in a desperate, almost comical attempt at a last stand. The shadow-monsters moved with such swiftness that, even as Jonathan watched, the group was isolated and split apart, before the creatures quickly finished them off.

Jonathan continued running. He ran until the sweat was so heavy it felt like another layer of skin. He ran until his muscles screamed at him to stop, and then ignored them. He ran until his veins pumped battery acid instead of blood. And then he stopped.

It took a moment for Jonathan to realise where he was. It was an open expanse, walled off by a curved enclosure that had become overgrown with moss and vines. At the half-way point behind him stood an open gate, swinging ever so slightly on its hinges, but making no sound.

*Did I pass through the gate? I don't even remember how I got here.*

Jonathan considered the situation for a moment, before he finally realised where he was standing.

He lifted his foot and gingerly moved over the soft loam. This was a graveyard. As he stepped on to firmer ground, he looked up and saw the church. It was lit!

For the first time in ages, Jonathan felt a glimmer of hope, and found the energy to run for the door. As he ascended the steps, he slowed down as he thought he heard noises inside. His heart skipped a beat as he considered the monster might already have been waiting, but then dismissed the idea as there was obvious light coming from inside.

Placing his right hand against the door, Jonathan leaned his weight into it and pushed slowly. The door gave way with the smallest of creaks, receiving a frown in return from the boy. He continued pushing until there was enough room to slide in.

Jonathan allowed his eyes to become accustomed to the wan light of the church as he gently closed the door behind him. The noise he could hear outside was louder here; there was definitely someone, or *something*, inside. It wasn't a growl, however, which sparked the tiniest thought of relief in Jonathan's mind.

Crouching to keep hidden, Jonathan moved between the pews slowly and quietly. The church smelled of damp. The benches played host to a sporadic sprouting of plant-life from various nooks and crannies.

The room was as vast as it was tall. Giant striated colonnades held aloft a vaulted ceiling covered in murals of angels and demons as they fought over humanity.

Stained-glass windows adorned either side of the building. They played with the light coming from the many candles decorating the altar, as if enjoying the moment in spite of everything going on. Jonathan managed a weak smile at the irony of the place, before movement in his peripheral vision caught his eye. Something was at the altar.

Straining to keep low and silent as he approached the dais, Jonathan moved to the end of the pew he was using as cover and craned his head around to the right to get a view of the altar from the far left of the church.

The shrine was covered in candles, the light dancing and flickering across every surface. A torn, stained red cloth covered the top of the centrepiece, providing stark contrast to the marble grey of the table. This was standing on a wooden floor that looked sturdy and immovable: Oak most likely.

Huddled under the overhang of the cloth was what Jonathan could only make out as a black shadow, slowly moving back and forth. Jonathan was reminded of a rocking-horse, and let out a laugh at how absurd his thought process was in the situation. He instinctively clamped a hand over his mouth as the sound left him, but it was too late. The shadow stopped rocking, before uncurling and turning towards the source of the noise. It had heard him!

Jonathan ducked back from his viewpoint at the end of the pew and mentally cursed himself. He gripped his sister's torch with both hands, wringing it like some maddened serial killer holding a victim's neck.

*thunk*

It was coming! This wasn't good. Jonathan had nowhere to run.

*thunk*

No growls this time. The shadow simply walked slowly towards the location of the noise, padding across the wooden dais in meaningful steps.

*thunk*

Jonathan decided if this was his time, he would go down fighting. No running. He was tired of running. He shifted his weight to his back foot, ready to spring forward and take the fight to the creature. The torch was held tightly in his left hand, drawn back and ready to swing at whatever he could connect with.

*thunk*

At this distance, Jonathan could hear the monster breathing. Short, shallow breaths gave credence to Jonathan's mind's-eye, and he imagined a giant dog-like creature standing on its rear legs, claws bared and ready to rend its victim's flesh from bone. The timbre of the creature's footsteps changed as it dropped down from the wooden dais onto the stone floor.

*clack*

It was on the other side of the pew! Jonathan could stand it no longer, and rose from behind the bench, screaming for all his might and swinging the torch like a maul. He connected with the right side of the creature's head, receiving a yelp of pain as reward, as he pushed forward to knock it off balance. The creature reacted in shock, retreating backwards and tumbling over the edge of the raised floor to land on its rump. Jonathan stifled a victory cry, surging over the pew to lay into the mass of clothing and dirt that co-

Realisation hit him like a freight train.

*Clothing? Dirt? This isn't a creature. It's a person! A human being!*

Jonathan froze with sheer horror at what he had done. The bundle of dirty rags on the dais lay there unmoving. Jonathan dropped to the person's side, grabbing their shoulder and shaking them violently.

'I'm sorry. Please get up! I didn't mean it. I thought you were one of them!'

There was no response. Jonathan considered he may have killed the - now apparent - man.

'Please, sir. Please get up.' Jonathan's voice took on a begging edge as his desperation turned to guilt. This was never meant to happen. Jonathan just wanted to be a little boy, growing up with his big sister to look after him and play with. He didn't want any of this.

Tears streamed down the child's face as he leaned his head back and looked up at the stained glass window on the far side of the room. It showed a daemon impaling an angel as it charged through the air towards the creature. Jonathan couldn't help feeling he was the leering, red devil in the image.

A hand shot up and grabbed the guilt-wracked boy by the shoulder. The grip was strong, made stronger by the man's apparent lack of realisation that he wasn't being attacked by a monster. He shoved Jonathan forcefully backwards, sending the child slamming into the front row of benches with a bone-jarring crunch. Jonathan fell to the floor, tears now streaming from his eyes not from guilt or fear, but from the pain.

'Stop, please stop! I didn't mean it. I thought you were one of them!' said Jonathan as he repeated his earlier line.

The man halted, taking in his surroundings and realising his attacker was nothing more than a boy. He lowered his fist, which had been swinging for Jonathan's head just a moment before.

'Who are you?' he asked as the anger and fear bled out of him. 'What are you doing here?'

'I saw the light outside. I was just looking for somewhere to hide,' replied Jonathan.

The man said nothing, continuing to eye the boy with borderline suspicion. Sensing a chance to explain, Jonathan carried on.

'My name's Jonathan. I lost my sister outside and I'm not really too sure where I am or what I'm going to do. I came in here to get away from...'

Jonathan's explanation trailed off as he thought about his sister and what had happened; what they had been through. The man said nothing, but placed a hand softly on the boy's shoulder. Jonathan looked up.

'Jonathan. My name is Gabriel; Gabe for short.'

Jonathan smiled, his tears making him look almost clown-like they cut their way through the grime on his face.

'Nice to meet y-'

The sound of the church door swinging open suddenly made both of them turn. It had started raining hard outside, and in the flash of lightning that streaked past, the pair of them saw the silhouette of another survivor.

'They're coming, they're coming, they're coming, they're coming...'

He wouldn't stop saying it, and he pivoted on the spot to grab the door edge, bringing it around forcefully to slam against the frame.

'No don't!' roared Gabriel, but it was too late. The door slammed into the frame with huge force, sending out a blast wave of air through the church. The candles spluttered and waned, straining to stay lit in the wake of the elemental assault like some strange parody between the survivors and the monsters. Like many of the survivors, the candles lost. Heavily.

'You idiot!' screamed Gabe. 'You've signed our death warrants you fool!'

The stranger slumped down with his back against the door. His legs gave way just before his backside hit the floor and they splayed out in front of him like a rag-doll. He was exhausted, and a look of relief flooded his face as he sat down for what must have been the first time in hours, possibly days. The look vanished as he noticed Gabriel striding down the centre of the room towards him.

'You have no idea what you've done,' roared Gabe as he purposefully marched towards the newcomer.

As he arrived in front of the stranger, Gabriel took hold of the man by the clothing around his shoulders and hefted him up onto his feet. The man looked like he had been dragged through a hawthorn bush backwards, and had scratches and claw marks all over him. Blood was running freely from wounds on the side of his head, and for a moment he looked like an odd mirror to the head wound on Gabe's own head.

'The-they were be-behind me. I had no ch-choice,' stammered the man, his tone a mix of apology and justification. 'I don't w-want to die.'

'You may end up doing that anyway at this rate,' retorted Gabriel, who threw the man back down against the door, placing him in almost the same position as he had been previously. Exasperated, he turned back to Jonathan, who had been watching the whole thing in fear.

'There are lighters behind the altar boy,' said Gabe. When Jonathan didn't move he added 'Quickly!'

The boy started and ran to the dais. Finding the lighters, he began to strike them to get a flame going. The flint ends refused to light, and he struck faster and faster trying to make a spark. Just as he was about to give up, a spark caught and the lighter burst into a healthy flame.

'I've done it, I've do-'

Jonathan was cut off as the church door splintered inwards. Two massive black arms punched their way through the thick wood. The stranger screamed and cowered inwards, drawing himself into a foetal position as sheer terror engulfed him. The arms extended past the man, before unfurling to show massive claws that shone in the dull light from the remaining few candles.

With a howl, the creature behind the door turned its arms inwards and clamped onto the stranger. The man screamed again, this time in pain as the claws dug into his flesh, sharp enough to cut to the bone. A moment later, the door creaked as the creature strained against the giant wooden aperture. With a screech of tearing hinges, the doors came away from the frame and the stranger was dragged out into the pouring rain.

His screaming continued, and Jonathan was certain he could hear something tearing. He wasn't sure what, but Gabriel looked away, well aware of what tearing flesh sounded like. The screaming stopped after a few moments. The creature had gone.

Jonathan stepped from the raised platform and ran for the candles dotted around the room. He managed to reach the first stack and light a couple before the stained glass window above him burst in, showering him with coloured, razor-sharp shrapnel. He dropped the lighter and lifted his arms to defend himself from the deadly rain. A shadow flew through the gaping hole where the window had been a moment before and landed hard in the middle of the room.

'Go boy. Run,' shouted Gabriel as he turned to face the creature.

The monster was oblivious to the boy, staring directly at Gabe as the man advanced to needlessly put himself in between the creature and the boy.

*It's not here for just anyone. It's like each monster has a particular target.*

Jonathan's mind raced with the realisation of what he was seeing and what he had seen before. This wasn't just mindless slaughter by a race of creatures. This was something else. He considered other facts. No two of the creatures appeared to be the same. It was as if each monster was tailored to the person they were hunting. He considered the monster he had been chased by these last few days: red eyes; multiple rows of giant teeth; long snout; shaggy mane; muscular enough to smash through anything. Pretty much his ultimate nightm-

*That's it!*

The answer struck Jonathan like a lightning bolt. These creatures were each person's worst nightmare. They were being made manifest somehow, and they were hunting the person who created them.

A roar of pain shook him from his reverie, and Jonathan could make out Gabriel grappling with the creature. The man had taken a candle-stand and was using it like a spear against the creature. Jonathan watched the fight, and saw the look of fear on Gabriel's face. There was fear, but there was also acceptance. There was bravery to face that fear.

At that moment, Jonathan noticed the window above the ensuing scrimmage. It was the window depicting the devil and the angel from earlier. Jonathan considered how the moment had changed in terms of who held the spear, and at that very moment an ear-splitting roar emanated around the room. Jonathan looked down again, and saw that Gabriel had managed to skewer the creature through its right leg with the candle-stand. Gabriel turned to look at the boy, as if sensing a spectator.

'What are you waiting for?' he shouted, straining to make his voice heard over the rain, thunder and the roar of the creature in front of him. 'Go, I will keep this one occupied.'

Jonathan wanted to tell him; to explain that *this one* wouldn't go for him anyway. It was Gabriel's nightmare, not his. He wanted to say it all, but he couldn't. He didn't want to break Gabriel's illusion of bravery. Instead, he ran.

As he reached the door, a blood-curdling scream reverberated around the church, followed by that sound of tearing again. Jonathan put his hand against the now-mangled door frame and turned with reluctance to see what had happened.

Nothing remained. Literally nothing. No bodies; no creature; no blood. Nothing. It was as if Gabriel and the monster had never existed. The only evidence of any struggle was a few broken pews and the candle-stand Gabe had been using to defend himself. Jonathan spun on his heel and sprinted out into the night.

Crossing the church yard, he took care not to trip on the headstones scattered haphazardly throughout the graveyard. The vast majority had fallen over, been dislodged or even in some cases, ended up metres from their original location. Jonathan's thoughts turned to those in the graves. He didn't want to join them. His pace picked up.

Leaving the graveyard behind, Jonathan stepped out onto the road and turned left, running away from the building and away from where he had come from. Head down against the wind and rain, he concentrated on running, barely able to see what was ahead of him as he went. He followed the road, winding through the city like some steam-train, passing other survivors as they struggled with their own nightmares. The screams became nothing more than background noise; just another sound in the endless turmoil of sensory input that assailed Jonathan.

A sharp pain flared through Jonathan's forehead as he collided with something. He was flung backwards, his arms and legs sprawling for purchase but finding none. He landed hard on his back, the tough road beneath doing nothing to cushion the impact. He let out a pained yell, and scrambled backwards across the tarmac trying to get away from the looming shadow in front of him. It stepped forwards to follow him and he panicked, turning over on all fours to clamber and begin sprinting once again. His monster had found him.

As he rose to full height, Jonathan felt something strong and solid clamp onto his left shoulder, and he screamed as terror flooded his system. This was it. He closed his eyes.

'Jonathan?' said a voice, a hint of scepticism apparent in the tone.

Jonathan opened his eyes slowly. Were his ears lying to him? Was this some trick of the mind? Perhaps the creature had figured out to use a voice to lure him in. He decided it was worth the risk.

With agonising slowness, Jonathan turned in place to face

his assailant. The hand dropped from his shoulder as he did so. He looked up into the face of the shadow and saw…

'Selena?' Jonathan's voice broke even as he spoke the word. Fresh tears instantly filled his eyes.

The shadow stepped forward, raising an arm as it did so. Jonathan stepped forward, smiling as he did so.

'Sis, I-'

'Down. Now,' hissed the shadow as it sped up.

A glint of light from the arm gave truth to the fallacy. It was a weapon, some kind of metal bar.

Selena stepped past Jonathan, pushing him down with her right arm as she swung the rebar out and across her in a horizontal arc, screaming as she did so.

The resounding crunch told Jonathan that something had been behind him, and he turned as his sister slammed into the monster with all the fury of a sibling protecting her family. He had never seen her so filled with physicality. His older sister had always been the stronger one, but that was an emotional strength, born from the need to take charge. This was very different.

Selena brought the bar up, bringing her free arm up with it and gripping it double-handed like a sledgehammer. She swung it around the back of her head and down onto the creature, aiming for where she thought the head might be. A howl of pain rewarded her, so she gritted her teeth and swung again.

And again.

And again.

Each time the howls became more desperate; more strangled.

The howls stopped.

All she could hear was breathing. Her breathing. Ragged, bubbling, like something had been popped or opened. She looked down.

The monster was dead, but it hadn't gone without a fight.

As the adrenaline faded, she felt a weariness hit her like a mag-freight slamming into her.

She looked at her clothing and saw red. A lot of red.

Bringing her hands to her stomach, it was plainly obvious

that the creature's claws had left their mark. She wouldn't last long.

Long enough.

Selena stood up, dropping the bar as she did so. With a weary sigh, she turned to her brother.

'It's me, Jonathan,' she said with a tired smile.

It was Selena, but not as Jonathan remembered her. Gone was the confident, smiling big sister he looked up to. In its place he found a broken, dishevelled girl who had gone through hell and back. Her clothes were cut to shreds, hanging almost by threads on her skinny frame. Her hair was knotted and torn, and her face and body were covered in scratches, cuts, bruises, blood and dirt. In places, Jonathan swore he could make out glistening white in the cuts. Was that bone? A ligament maybe?

'Sis!' shouted Jonathan in glee. His eyes lit up and he launched forward into Selena's arms.

She winced as he buried himself in her, hugging with all his might. She was hurt, but to her little brother she had to be the rock he had always known her as. She bore the pain as he held her, smiling as she felt him against her again. It was worth it, she thought. The pain was always worth family.

'I'm glad you're back,' said Jonathan as he stepped back again. 'I missed you.'

'I missed you too,' said Selena, her voice trembling.

They stood in silence for a moment, glad to be in each other's company again.

'I've figured out what's going on,' said Jonathan. 'These monsters, they're our worst nightmares.'

'You can say that again,' sighed Selena with a slight smile to her brother.

'No you don't understand. They're literally our nightmares. What we consider to be the worst monster in our mind becomes real. It's what hunts us. It's why each monster looks different and only attacks one person. There's never anything left after. It's like they're taking people away to some place.'

'Hell?'

'Maybe,' Jonathan considered. 'Or Purgatory?'

Selena looked at her brother, shifting her weight as she

placed a hand on her hip. 'You're smarter than you look, you know that?'

Jonathan smiled. 'I know.'

The conversation was cut short by the noise of shuffling behind them. Jonathan immediately flicked up the torch from his belt and turned it on, shining it at the darkest patches of shadow. Something retreated. Another movement to the right caught his attention. Their nightmares had found them.

Jonathan frantically tried to use the torch to keep both creatures at bay. Selena slowly backed herself towards the nearest building, pulling Jonathan by the shoulder as she did so. They needed to get away and find the spaceport.

The torch flickered. A look of concern crossed Jonathan's face and he froze momentarily.

'Jonathan?' asked Selena.

'It's nothing,' he replied, examining the torch. A crack ran the length of the shaft, ending on the lens in a spider-web effect. Jonathan hit it with the base of his hand a couple of times. The light stopped flickering and held steady, much to his relief.

A moment later, it went out.

'Selena,' whispered Jonathan as terror crept into him.

'I know, li'l bro. I know,' she replied stoically. 'We're together, at the end. I love you.'

'I love you too, sis,' said Jonathan, and he turned to hug his big sister.

Selena squeezed him tight, placing her chin on top of his head. Tears were rolling down her face.

'Close your eyes,' she said as she stroked the back of his head. 'Think of mum and dad.'

As they embraced each other in the dark, the nightmares moved in.

# In the Absence

## J. M. Perkins

Melissa laced her fingers around the cup of coffee, drawing in heat through the Styrofoam. 'God,' she thought, 'I hope they don't take coffee away next.' They'd already taken away so much. Her thoughts drifted, turned to the incomplete art school applications sitting in their folder at home. Even before all this, it had been stupid of her to think she could be an illustrator and it had only become more pointless now. She vowed to finally throw the things away and just get on with her muddling through the rest of her life, or what was left of it anyway. She sipped at the coffee.

The squeal of tires and jolt of a crash startled her. She glanced outside; one of the black sports cars had crashed into a monochrome truck. 'They' had removed the traffic lights last week, and there had been a lot more accidents ever since. Of course, as far as she could tell, no one else noticed the absence. Just like they hadn't noticed that there was no more RC cola, or cars in colours other than black, or pork chops or any of the hundred other bits of her life that had been stripped away in the past year.

Melissa got up from her seat, splashing a trinkle of dollar coins onto the table to pay for her drink. At least they'd taken away credit cards, that was one thing she didn't have to miss.

She walked down the street, marvelling at all the small ways the ambient city noise had changed. She didn't know for sure if there were actually a 'They' doing all this, but it helped her get through the day to think that way. Because if this was some sort of grand social experiment, then there might be an end. There might be a point.

Other options she had considered: this was some kind of weird mutation of generalized entropy or that she had gone insane. Both much less pleasant.

Melissa walked down the sidewalk towards her job, wondering if it would still exist next week.

Near Fifth and Broadway she absently bent down to put some change in a homeless man's cup. With so many of the jobs disappearing, the one thing that seemed to be growing was the homeless population. How could they not know what had happened?

The man mumbled his thanks, resumed his conversation with his feet.

'You know what I miss? Hotdog carts.'

Melissa stopped, turned to stare at the bum. The man quirked an eyebrow. Recognizing something in her face, he managed a small, sad smile.

'Oh, you remember too huh?'

Melissa nodded.

The homeless man leaned back against the filthy concrete façade of the ancient bank building. 'Buy me a cup of coffee?'

'So, when did you start noticing?' Thomas, the man's name was Thomas, asked. As he talked, he poured grocery store 'Gold Star' brand whiskey into his cup, his hand shaking. The rest of the diner seemed to be staring at them, Thomas had the identifiable odour of sweat rolled and rerolled into clothing worn once too often and Melissa had no doubt that at the office her boss would be freaking out.

Honestly, she didn't give a shit.

'About four and a half months ago, March 24$^{th}$ to be exact,' She said.

Thomas nodded, gulping down his coffee.

'Yeah that's the same for all of us. I just ask to see if the answer ever varies.'

'Us,' Melissa said, 'You mean there are more... more people who remember?'

Thomas waved over the waitress to refill his cup. The woman scowled at him as she poured the steaming liquid, chewing a mouth full of gum. She sashayed off without a word and only when the chomping faded into the generic background murmurs of the coffee shop did Thomas continue.

'Were. There were more of us: the twins, Roy and Karen, plus Jody and Terrance and Frank. The support group we called ourselves, heh. Lot of good we did each other. There were probably more of them, of us out there; but I've never met anyone else. Except for you.' He lifted his mug in toast, splashed in another two shots to dilute the blackness.

'What happened to them?'

'Hmm well let's see. I know that Karen and Terrance are at a psychiatric institution. 'Easiest way to get meds' they'd told me before they'd publically freaked and gotten diagnosed as paranoid schizophrenics. Roy's in prison, still don't know what happened there but one day something was gone and at some point in the remade past it meant that he'd killed someone. He wrote me a letter, back when I still had a house, in crayon. Said he's doing ok, that he's actually having an easier time inside. Less day to day uncertainty I guess. Fewer things to miss. I dunno what happened to Jody: she either left or disappeared or died. And then Frank killed himself.'

Finishing his second cup, Thomas glanced back towards the waitress. He looked back towards his mug, shrugged, and poured the last of his fifth into it.

'We all got our ways of coping…' he said as he put the bottle back into his pocket. Silence claimed their booth and they sat across from one another, not making eye contact.

Desperate to change the subject, Melissa said, 'So you said you had a house? Did your job disappear?'

Thomas chuckled. 'Yeah, I used to be somewhat well to do. Remember Mozart?'

She hadn't thought about Mozart in weeks, hadn't remembered the trill of his compositions in her ear. Maybe she would have forgotten altogether if Thomas hadn't broached the subject, how long would that have taken her?

'Yeah,' she said.

'Well, back before he disappeared, I was considered one of the preeminent Mozart scholars. I was tenured, had a couple books in print. I was set.'

'But then one day I woke up and Mozart had disappeared. Less importantly, my life and my comfort had disappeared with him. That morning, I'd woken up on the street wearing what you see today. When I called my Mom about it, she hadn't really wanted to talk. Seems she'd given up on me years ago. She was convinced I was on something, but somehow

I talked her into telling me the story of my life; the life I couldn't remember. Seems I just never stuck with anything, I'd just sorta drifted. Developed a taste for booze, done the rehab shuffle a couple times until everyone I knew just kinda gave up on me. That's their version anyway. As for me, I remember hearing Die Zauberflote for the first time, how it changed everything for me. But there's no more of that. Now, there never was and there never will be.'

Melissa reached out, put her hand on Thomas'. He looked like he was about to cry, instead he shook his head and wiped a dribble of snot coming from his nose.

'Aww but you don't want to hear about me. So Melissa tell me, what do you miss?'

They talked for hours that first day and every day afterwards. Melissa told her boss that she had been sick. Every week more was gone, but it was somehow bearable now that she had someone to talk with. A month passed and they discussed everything: the Frisbees that Melissa had loved, Dashiell Hammett books that they'd both been aware of primarily through the movie adaptations, yellow painted corvettes and the smell of green beans. But there was more besides.

Every morning they'd mention whatever had gone missing that day. Some days though, they couldn't figure out what was gone and these were the worst. Oftentimes, they'd discover the absence later – by accident. Melissa would walk into a store to buy Thomas a bottle of whiskey and notice that Heath Bars, or Bubble Yum or linoleum floors could no longer be found. Sometimes though, the absence was something neither could put their finger on: the air would smell different or the day would be unseasonably warm.

Some days the absences were more abstract: birdsong or impressionism or Jungian psychology.

Some days they argued.

'Are you really telling me you think some mysterious 'they' is doing this to the world? That's utterly ridiculous.' Thomas said. Every day he seemed more sober, his mannerisms drifted closer to the professor he'd once been. Even if he never did quite lose his smell. At least the other denizens of the diner had stopped staring at them when they came in for their daily 'talks.'

'Well what do you think this is Mr. Academic?' Melissa said, relishing her indignation.

'Ahem,' He said, clearing his throat, 'I believe that the hyper abundance of emotionally charged existential aspects hit a critical mass, an event horizon of concern. Now, all the 'stuff' people used to care about is simply being sucked away as though into a star collapsing into a black hole.'

Melissa blinked, looked up from her sketch pad.

'That's the stupidest thing I've heard today.'

'True, but it makes way more sense than that there are some kind of 'conspiracy' of them.' He said, humour in his eyes.

Melissa's smile pushed through her attempts to suppress it. She sipped her coffee.

'Obviously, the simplest explanation is that we're crazy.'

'Obviously.'

They chuckled together.

'So, are you finally going to come over, take a shower, shave your face and let me buy you some clean clothes?'

Thomas inclined his head. 'Thanks but no thanks, the street suits me just fine.' He said, adding at a lower volume, 'Besides, why get used to anything...' He always said something to that effect. His obstinacy frustrated her, made her sad.

Noting this, Thomas tried to change the subject. 'So what are you sketching today?'

She looked down at her paper, saw the rough outline of an MP3 player. She'd doodled just about every time they talked and she'd stopped being strictly conscious of what she was doing.

'My old music player, some kind of cheap iPod knock off. I always thought I would replace it eventually, but the damn thing would just never break.'

'Oh God, I remember having ten thousand songs in my pocket. Putting it on shuffle was a leap into unknown darkness.'

This was more than enough to guide the conversation back towards music, his favourite subject.

And that's how things were. They were happy together, mostly. Until the weather changed.

Melissa woke, her teeth chattering like they were a plastic novelty toy that didn't exist anymore. A thick blanket of snow covered the ground. It was sometime in mid-July, and it hadn't snowed in the city in decades. Something big, something essential had left the world, and even as she shivered she was looking forward to discussing with Thomas what it might be. Something about cloud formation she guessed.

She pulled on pants and a heavy jacket she found in her updated closet, walked out into the street. Cars had disappeared last week and Melissa enjoyed being a pedestrian in a way that she never ever had before.

Melissa found Thomas at his usual spot near Fletcher and sixth. Prodding him with her foot, she said 'Come on sleepy head, wake up. Let's go get some coffee in you.'

He didn't respond. She stooped, assuming he had passed out in a drunken stupor again. 'Come on sleepy.' She shook him, and his head lolled back and forth.

'Thomas?' She said, reaching to feel a pulse she already knew wouldn't be there. She started to scream 'Help! Someone call an ambulance!' Before she remembered that there was no such thing as ambulances anymore, and nobody else would know what a call was.

The passersby streamed down the walkway as she knelt in the snow and cried. There was more than one homeless person who had died the night before, and the city workers with their sanitation pigs would be out shortly to deal with the bodies.

Melissa couldn't watch that, so she walked away. Without meaning to, she found herself on the bridge.

Melissa stared out over the churning waters, sail boats bouncing in the chill winds that blew in from the south. Some small part of her mind reminded her to apply Chap Stick, but such a thing didn't exist. Watching the bay, Melissa didn't know what she felt. She reached into her pockets, pulled out what she had.

A cluster of papers clumped in her fist: what amounted to a state ID since plastic had gone away late last year. She released her grasp, and the paper drifted out into the water. Then she grabbed and threw a handful of bits, all the money she had on her, to crash into the waves below. She tossed her address book next, and finally all she had left was her notebook.

Melissa stared at the little black volume. The breeze rustled it open to a random page, and she had to grab at the thing to keep it from drifting out into the bay. On either side of her thumb were two doodles: one of superman and the other a pair of sunglasses.

She looked at the pictures for a long time. Finally, she closed the book and placed it back in her pocket. She took a long time walking back to her house thinking about what she'd do next.

Melissa began to paint. She recreated what she remembered as best she could, working in the diner or out on the street. Everyone who saw her work was amazed by the impossible things she imagined: things she called airplanes and submarines, rosemary and cell phones, comic books and desk lamps.

Sometimes, she would meet someone else who remembered; someone who would cry, or scream or try to hug her. Melissa did her best to be kind--at first--but things were going missing so fast now she never knew which of her new acquaintances would wake up dead.

She learned to keep to herself and keep to her work.

When there were no more acrylics, she took to spray painting huge murals on the sides of the office towers and thatch-roofed huts. When the spray paint disappeared, she took to sketching with pen and pencil on napkins, leaving heaps on the floor of the diner to be swept up by the long suffering janitor. No one ever asked her to stop because—she suspected—at some level they all remembered.

Finally, 'They' took the pencils, the napkins and the diners. Melissa took to walking to the beach and drawing with her finger in the drifts of gray snow and gray ash.

She drew and drew and drew…

Until there was nothing left.

# "ZomPoc in Nashville"

## Scribe Unknown

*Editor's note: This ripped lyric sheet was found in the rubble after the late 20th century zombie apocalypse, apparently the work of a budding country star whose name has been lost to the ravages of time. Archivists worked to reconstruct the lyric sheet, but were only able to rescue [a brief portion of audio](#) from the 20th century magnetic tape medium. The ms. dates from a time when "country music" enjoyed a brief period of nostalgic popularity alongside the so-called "bluegrass" and "folk" revivals. Attempts to identify the writer have suggested an association with the Memphis locale, but linguistic experts suggest a more northern origin for the artist.*

> ~ Dr. K. A. Laity,
> *A Compendium of Pre-Apocalyptic Popular Culture*

# Zompoc in Nashville

*Chorus:*

When the zombies have taken old Nashville
The living might envy the dead
The world's gone to hell in a handbasket
Since I shot my man in the head.
Me and my man moved to Nashville
With visions of fame in our hearts;
We were singing our way into stardom
When the zom-poc ripped our dreams apart.

*Chorus*

The first wave of zombies were there in the crowd—
We thought they were singing along;
But when they chomped down on a fan's waving arm,
We knew something was terribly wrong.

*Chorus*

So I smashed one in the face with my Fender bass,
Doc clocked one with her autoharp;
My man, poor Dan, with a dulcimer in hand
Got a chunk bitten out of his arm

*Chorus*

When Browning wrote Barrett "Grow old with me"
The undead were not on his mind;
Now I love my man river deep, mountain high—
But I won't shack up with zombie-kind.

*Chorus*

*Repeat chorus and fade*

# Sleep Sweet Children

## Nathan Lunt

*Throw caution to the wind, my children,*
*Dance as well you like,*
*For by this time tomorrow we may all be entomb in Ice,*
*Sing your little hearts out, children,*
*Sweep your cares away,*
*For by this time tomorrow we may all be Ash and Flames,*
*Dream the biggest dreams, my child,*
*Wish for all you're worth,*
*For by this time tomorrow we may be swallowed by the Earth,*
*Give thanks for all you have, dear child,*
*With every grateful breath,*
*For by this time tomorrow*
*There may be no more tomorrow left.*

# Contributors

**Andrew Reid** is a writer obsessed with the fantastic and the adventurous. When the end comes, he will be bitterly disappointed that he never invested in a walled commune while the going was good. Born in Scotland, he lives in Yorkshire, far closer to cities than apocalypse safety regulations would advise. You can find him on Twitter as @mygoditsraining, where he shares tips on purifying water and recipes for the modern-day scavenger.

**Christian D'Amico** is a science fiction, horror and genre fiction writer based in Surrey, England. Any similarities between his county and any dystopian futures are entirely coincidental. When he isn't writing he spends his time involved with street dance, reading, gaming and in the gym, both as a fitness enthusiast in his own right and as a personal trainer. Recently Christian has agreed on an on-going series of short stories and novels with his publisher, Fox Spirit, encompassing a world 9 years in the making, titled "The Unity Wars". www.chrisdamico.co.uk

**Dash Cooray** is a juvenile copywriter who secretly creates fantastic worlds in a filthy upstairs den in her parents' farm in the chill and mist flavoured mountains of Kandy, Sri Lanka. She was born with an uncanny obsession for stories as all writers are and when she is not writing, she is engrossed in her other obsession – music. She tweets obsessively about her obsessions at the handle @dashdidntdoit and blogs sporadically at dashcooray.wordpress.com. *Demon Runner,* combining fantasy with uniquely Sri Lankan history; is her first published short story. Twitter: @dashdidntdoit.

**Dayna Ingram** writes about girls who inhabit various worlds. This one time, during the apocalypse, she fought alongside Michelle Rodriguez to quell the zombie scourge, and then wrote a memoir about it. Unfortunately, both her publisher and her therapist deemed this event "just a dream," so she was forced to publish her account as fiction (EAT YOUR HEART OUT [BrazenHead/Lethe Press]). She's currently working on expanding "Little Daughter" into a full-length novel. When not making up stories, Dayna enjoys making her mini-pig wear dapper sweater-vests, making her co-workers listen to her tales of epic failure at getting her pig to wear sweater-vests, and making out with pirates. Some day, she hopes to have Joss Whedon's babies, but, like, not in a gross way. Visit her at <u>thedingram.com</u>.

**James Dorr**'s latest book, The Tears of Isis (Perpetual Motion Machine Publishing), is a 2013 Bram Stoker Award® nominee for Superior Achievement in a Fiction Collection. This joins his two prose collections from Dark Regions Press, Strange Mistresses: Tales of Wonder and Romance and Darker Loves: Tales of Mystery and Regret, and the all-poetry Vamps (A Retrospective) from Sam's Dot/White Cat. An active member of SFWA and HWA with nearly four hundred individual appearances from Alfred Hitchcock's Mystery Magazine to Xenophilia, Dorr invites readers to visit his site at http://jamesdorrwriter.wordpress.com.

**James Oswald** is the author of a series of crime novels featuring Edinburgh-based Detective Inspector Tony McLean, the first of which, Natural Causes, was the pick of the 2013 Richard and Judy Book Club Summer Reads. He was also short-listed for the National Book Awards New Author Award in 2013. His epic fantasy series, The Ballad of Sir Benfro, will be published by Penguin, starting in late 2014 with Dreamwalker. When not tied to his writing desk, James runs a 350 acre livestock farm in North East Fife, where he raises pedigree Highland Cattle and New Zealand Romney Sheep. You can find him at <u>jamesoswald.co.uk</u> or as @SirBenfro on Twitter.

**J. M. Perkins** writes Science Fiction, Action Horror, and whatever else will pay the bills. He spent the first 14 years of his life preparing to flee to the wilds of Canada to escape the forces of the Antichrist. Since then, he's graduated from UCSD, worked at a candy factory, and performed a variety of unsanctioned sociological experiments. He's had over a dozen of his short stories sold, published, printed and adapted. In 2012 he used a successful Kickstarter Campaign to publish his first novel CHEMO: How I Learned to Kill. He co-hosts the podcast 'John vs Patrick.' J.M. Perkins lives in San Diego with his roller derby playing photographer wife and his dog. You can find out more at J.M. Perkins' website www. strugglingwordguy.com

**Jonathan Ward** is a science-fiction, horror and fantasy writer hailing from the sprawling urban metropolis of Bedford. He has wanted to be an author since the age of eight, though it's questionable whether his writing talents have improved since then. When not writing he can be found reading a good book, out exploring new places, or in the pub being sarcastic to his closest friends. Jonathan's Author Central page containing links to all of his published work: www.amazon.co.uk/ JonathanWard/e/B002BLQ8HA/ref=ntt_dp_epwbk_0

**Margrét Helgadóttir** is a Norwegian-Icelandic writer who started to submit fiction in English for publication in 2012. She lives in Oslo, Norway, and is highly influenced by Nordic culture, climate and personality in her writing. Her stories have so far appeared in several magazines and she's got stories in the 2013/2014 print anthologies *Girl at the End of the World, Impossible Spaces, Fox & Fae*, and Fox Pockets volume 1, 2, 3 and 5. Her short story in this anthology, "A Sailor Girl Goes Ashore," is also to be found in her debut book, *The Stars Seem So Far Away*, which is out late 2014. Find out more about Margrét on her site: http://margrethelgadottir. wordpress.com or on Twitter where she's @MaHelgad

Academic, creative director, writer and Final Girl, **Tracy**

**Fahey** has battled the apocalypse on many fronts, using her wits, pluck and an inordinate amount of information gleaned from horror movies. Her short story in this collection, Coming Back, is dedicated to fellow foot- soldiers from the front line, Tara and Scott, with thanks. Tracy runs a fine art department and an art collective, Gothicise (www. gothicise.weebly.com). Previous short stories have been published in the Impossible Spaces anthology (2013) and in the forthcoming Hauntings anthology (2014), both published by Hic Dragones Press. Her research and creative writing alike are continually fascinated by aspects of the unheimlich, from doppelgangers to haunted houses to the inevitable return of the repressed. In her spare time she relaxes by writing a PhD.

**Adam "Bucho" Rodenberger** is a 34 year old writer from Kansas City living in San Francisco. He holds dual Bachelor's degrees in Philosophy & Creative Writing and completed his MFA in Writing at the University of San Francisco in 2011. He has been (or will be) published in Alors, Et Tois?, Agua Magazine, Offbeatpulp, Up The Staircase, The Gloom Cupboard, BrainBox Magazine, Cause & Effect Magazine, the Santa Clara Review, Crack the Spine, Penduline Press, Bluestem Magazine, Aphelion, Glint Literary Journal, Lunch Ticket, Eunoia Review, Serving House Journal, and Phoebe. He blogs at http://triphoprisy.blogspot.com.

**Cat Connor** lives in Upper Hutt, New Zealand. She is the author of The_byte series published by Rebel ePublishers, USA. An FBI thriller series about the life of SSA Ellie Conway.

Her short stories have appeared in anthologies, ezines, and journals in the UK and USA.

A coffee addict and a lover of red wine. Recently described as irresistible, infectious, and addictive. Cat believes music is essential. She knows where to hide the body and where you hid the body and more importantly where the stocks of anti-virals, antibiotics, and weapons are kept. There will be survivors.

**Dr K. A. Laity** is an English professor, specialising in medieval language and literature with a specialisation in apocalypse studies. Her examination of late 20th century artefacts of the Zombie Conflagration has uncovered evidence of a widespread international conspiracy between conservative political parties, but she has been unable to follow up on the suggested connections since her appointment to the lucrative post as Head of Research at the Royal Institute of Filthy Lucre (formerly the London Business School). All posts relating to these discoveries have now been scrubbed from www.kalaity.com

**R. B. Harkess** scuttles around the abandoned wasteland north of London, avoiding the search and detain sweeps of the Angel militia as he scribbles the warning notes and hides them in the info-caches that are the only way to share information between the Free as they claw out an existence in the Dark Times. All his notes are signed www.rbharkess.com, though nobody can remember what it means.

Leaving the rotting carcass of her alien pod far behind her, **Chloë Yates** defied her xenomorphic Queen and took to the open road, refusing to be held down by "the man". Mixing metaphors and confusing pop culture, she has trailed a blaze of defiance in the post-apocalyptic landscape of both Slough and Grenoble (neither of which she's been to). Catch her in Chalmun's Cantina at weekends, where she plays her harp made from the skin of mutant managerial staff – but don't accept a drink from her; she was once a pupil of the renowned Catherine Deshayes. She writes accounts of her prophetic dreams and expects another Apocalypse tout de suite… She's available for most things of a writerly persuasion. Bring your own gloves. www.chloeyates.com

The Ancient Wise Ones told of a woman who would chronicle the end of the old time and the beginning of the new one in the life domes and robot-monitored underground bunkers. **Carol Borden** is that woman. Living in the heart of apocalypse, she dons her enemies' skins, still dripping with gore, and takes up her brush to paint upon the walls of a crumbling parking structure a sorrowful story based on true enough events, "Sophie and the Gate to Hell." You may read some of her other stories in Fox Spirit Books' Weird Noir and Noir Carnival, her articles on comics and Godzilla at The Cultural Gutter, and see her other doings at her personal website: www.monstrousindustry.wordpress.com/

**R.J. Booth** lives in the shadow of sandstone, on the edge of a valley of trees. There she runs, writes about metal for magazines, sings of the dead in Cathedrals, photographs music makers and drunks for their own purposes… and tells tales, such as this one. Her ancestors were sheep thieves and sailors. Her descendants will sing under orange skies. Follow her at @ruthmidget on twitter, or at www.ruthbooth.com.

**G. Clark Hellery** thinks a lot about the end of the world: while Buffy & the Scoobies saved the world (a lot), does she have enough Apocalypse Girl training to survive? Geraldine has written about running in heels from zombies, killer fae, murderous grad students, rampaging dragons and things that go bump in the night which has hopefully given her a rounded view of survival (or rather, how to die in blood-curdling ways). A country girl at heart, Geraldine's collection of short stories and poems, set in the 'Weird Wild' woods will be published by Fox Spirit Books in 2014. She lives with her ever present evac bag by her side along with an aged computer, a manic puppy and a very patient husband.

**Catherine Hill** grew up in Worcestershire, England. She spent much of her childhood with her head in a book and played games in which her toys escaped from a variety of unexpected catastrophes. She now lives in Birmingham with her husband. While blogging with the Girls Guide to Surviving the Apocalypse collective she discovered that she has a lot of ideas about how to end the world. She may have published a post on the internet about how AIs can successfully wipe out the human race. She is certainly not responsible for our inevitable doom.

I'm afraid **James Bennett** did not survive the apocalypse. His clone did, however, and is writing this now. If anyone is out there, in the dead and derelict cities, in the black and barren hills, you might want to take a break from killing zombies for a minute and read one of his stories. http://jamesbennett72. blogspot.co.uk/ Twitter: @I_James_Bennett

**Alexander Danner** has contributed science fiction stories to Machine of Death and Bound Off. He also writes comics, which can be found at TwentySevenLetters.com and TwoForNo.net. Alexander teaches online courses in writing comics at Emerson College, and his second textbook, Comics: A Global History, 1968 — Present (with Dan Mazur) was published in summer, 2014 from Thames & Hudson. He is also president of The Writers' Room of Boston, a non-profit organization dedicated to providing safe, affordable workspace to writers in the greater Boston area.

**Alex Helm** has always had an interest in the fantastical, the futuristic and the bizarre and has frequently been accused of having her head in the clouds. A keen live action roleplayer, historical re-enactor and cosplayer, Alex likes nothing more than spending a weekend dressed up in heavy armour and running around outdoors taking part in battles and pretending to be someone far more interesting (and with more interesting problems). She currently lives in Paris, France with her two feline overlords, and works for a video game company.

**Foxspirit.co.uk**

'After nourishment, shelter and companionship, stories are the thing we need most in the world.' Phillip Pullman

Skulk: *noun* – a pack or group of foxes

Fox Spirit believes that day to day life lacks a few things, primarily the fantastic, the magical, the mischievous and even a touch of the horrific. We aim to rectify that by bringing you stories and gorgeous cover art and illustrations from foxy folk who believe as we do that we could all use a little more wonder in our lives.

Here at the Fox Den we believe in storytelling first and foremost, so we mash genres, bend tropes and set fire to rule books merrily as we seek out tall tales that excite and delight us and send them out into the world to find new readers.

With a mixture of established and new writers producing novels, short stories, flash fiction and poetry via ebook and print we recommend letting a little Fox Spirit into your life.

 @foxspiritbooks

 https://www.facebook.com/foxspiritbooks

 adele@foxspirit.co.uk